Series: TBD
Title: *Malice House*
Author: Megan Shepherd
Imprint: Hyperion Avenue
In-store date: October 4, 2022
Hardcover ISBN: 978-1-368-08928-9
Hardcover Price: US $26.99 / CAN $33.99
E-book ISBN: 978-1-368-09039-1
Trim size: 6" x 9"
Page count: 384
Ages: Adult

We are pleased to send this book for review.
Please send two copies of any review or mention to:

Disney Publishing Worldwide
Attn: Adult Publicity Department
77 West 66th Street, 3rd Floor
New York, NY 10023
dpw.publicity@disney.com

MALICE HOUSE

Nominations due: September, 1, 2022

Nominate for the October Indie Next List –
Due: 8/1/22

MALICE HOUSE

A Novel By

MEGAN SHEPHERD

HYPERION
AVENUE
LOS ANGELES   NEW YORK

First Edition, October 2022
10 9 8 7 6 5 4 3 2 1
FAC-020093-22231
Printed in the United States of America

This book is set in Baskerville and News Gothic.
Designed by Amy King
Illustrations © Shutterstock.com

Library of Congress Cataloging-in-Publication Data 2022935438
ISBN 978-1-368-08928-9
Reinforced binding

Visit hyperionavenuebooks.com

TO JESSE

CHAPTER ONE

One step away from our world lies another: a land of violent fantasies, of sharp-toothed delights. . . .

—From the Introduction to
Bedtime Stories for Monsters

❖

I NEVER MEANT to find the manuscript, but maybe it meant to find me.

I'd arrived in Lundie Bay five hours later than planned, after a delayed flight and a stop at the Seattle-Tacoma airport bar, much to the chagrin of Dahlia Whitney, who stood beside me in the overgrown gravel drive, frowning up at the peeling paint of Malice House.

"So you're an artist," she said reproachfully.

I looked down at the canvas bag flopped open at my feet, bleeding out brushes and tubes of paint.

"Watercolor and ink," I said, rubbing at a black ink stain on my thumb. "I do children's book illustrations mostly."

She folded her arms and didn't ask to see my work. Her chin jutted toward the house with a grunt. "Well, let's get started."

How long had it been since I'd last seen Malice House? Three spindly stories that rose from the sea cliff unsteadily as though even after a hundred years they might not withstand one more. The smell of the nearby ocean mixed with overstuffed memories of a house bursting at the joints with books: books lining the shelves, stacked in the hallways, boxed up in the attic. The first time I came, I had set up an easel along the cliff and tried to sketch the house. But it had defied two dimensions. No matter how I worked on the perspective and planes, every drawing felt wrong. There was something so interdimensional about Malice House that without the smell of the pines, the taste of the sea spray, the ever-changing shadows on the rooftop, it was merely scratches on paper.

I thought of the last time I'd visited my father before his death, dragged there by my own guilt that it was only the two of us, and that he hadn't been such a bad father that I was allowed to be such a bad daughter. Dad's mind was already slipping. Dementia was an efficient beast. Eating holes in a once-sharp mind. It had been late summer, two years ago, and we'd taken the long walk into town down along the bluffs and sat at a coffee shop on the pier, where he'd calmly told me about the demon living inside the house's walls. It was a pale crustacean the size of a small person with garden-shear-like claws. At night, he said, he heard it slithering beneath the main bedroom floorboards.

"It's Haven, right? You should stay in the guest room, Haven." Dahlia climbed the porch steps with no little difficulty, muttering about stiff joints, and unlocked the front door. The musty smell of old books and damp wood enveloped us. Moving to stand in the open doorway, I swept my eyes over the entry hall and spruce-beam archway that led to the library; rooms that felt unfamiliar even though I'd been in them countless times. Dad had been gone for six months—enough time for a coating of dust to have settled over the tables and lamps.

Dahlia unceremoniously tossed me the ring of house keys.

I narrowly caught them, stumbling forward as though waking from a dream.

"I thought I'd take the primary bedroom," I said. "For the view."

She made that deep-throat grunt again. "Suit yourself."

Dahlia Whitney hadn't liked my father, and the feeling had been mutual. Somehow the two of them had rattled around the old house together for years despite his paranoia that she was trying to kill him and her determination that he should accept Christ. If he had to have a caregiver, he protested, why couldn't it be someone who didn't resemble a lumpfish in an apron? For her part, Dahlia Whitney did her duties, cashed my father's checks, and only had one condition of employment: she would never sleep a single night under Malice House's roof.

I let out a long breath as I took in all the work ahead of me. After my father's death, I'd hired a Seattle cleaning company to drive the two hours north to Lundie Bay and do the initial purge: strip the bedsheets, donate his clothes to charity, rid the house of anything perishable, wash and put away the small army of coffee cups he left on every surface. Since then, though, the house had remained untouched. Every shelf burst not only with books but yellowing paperwork, mugs the cleaners had overlooked, a half dozen long-dead houseplants. If they sought resurrection at my hand, they were out of luck.

An end table in the sitting room held a battered old typewriter and several picture frames that had been turned facedown as though to protect them from dust. Curious, I stood the frames up one by one. The first held a picture of Dad accepting a literary prize—they'd all blended together after a while. There was my parents' wedding photo from their elopement, the same one I had framed back in New York. The last one was a photograph of a small group of people holding teapots in mock seriousness—I only recognized my father and the bookstore owner in town, whose name I couldn't recall.

None of the photographs were of me. Grumpy, but not altogether surprised, I turned the frames facedown again.

"Electricity and water are still on." Dahlia switched on a lamp. "And the landline. There's a phone in the kitchen and another in the upstairs hallway. The utility company cuts off service whenever a deed transfers hands, but since no one's taken up residence since your father died, they let the account sit."

"What about internet?"

She grunted. "Your father never had it. You'll have to sign up with Comtek. There's an office down on Boardwalk Street."

I mentally added signing up for internet to my to-do list. My old phone was useless now since it was on Baker's plan. I'd picked up a cheap pay-as-you-go phone in La Guardia, but it was talk and text only. In the meantime, one of the coffee shops in town would have Wi-Fi. Lundie Bay may have had a reputation as a sleepy seaside village, but being only two hours from Seattle, it drew the kind of tech investor second-homers who required constant connectivity even on vacation.

I followed Dahlia Whitney on a shuffling tour of the house as she pointed out a vent in need of repair, a box of long unanswered mail, which burner on the stovetop worked and which didn't, how to jiggle the back door open when it got stuck. We wandered past my father's bar cart in the library—Scotch decanters long empty, resting next to the engraved copper Pulitzer Prize medal; the surprisingly small kitchen; the overly formal, never-used living room; the creaky stairs to the bedrooms on the second floor; the sleeping porch off the primary bedroom with the sea view and molding wicker furniture. I'd have to do something with all of it. The musty rugs. The drawers full of old files. The towels and linens. And the books, books, books; they watched from every corner of every room like vigilant gargoyles.

I was exhausted by the time I opened the door to the attic and tugged on the single light's cord. The bulb blinked to life lazily. "I guess we should check out the attic."

Dahlia Whitney gave another grunt, this one definitive. "I'm not going up there."

I hesitated. I'd been in the attic enough times to know that my father, a closeted hoarder, had squirreled away countless boxes and stacks of who-knows-what up there.

"I don't know what to do with everything," I argued. "What needs to be shipped back to his publishers, what can be thrown away . . ."

She shrugged tensely.

Wasn't this why I'd hired her? To show me what needed to be done?

"Mrs. Whitney—"

"Nope."

From where I stood at the base of the stairs, a sudden coldness bit at my neck, coming from the direction of the attic. My ink-stained fingers grazed the uneven wall, patched over time and time again, and I shivered. The smell of dirt wafted down from up there. Freshly turned dirt.

As I was about to climb, Dahlia let out a small exclamation.

When I turned, she was staring into my father's bedroom. I was on the verge of asking her what was wrong when I joined her and saw broken glass on the bedroom rug.

"Well, that's just great," I groaned. How much would a broken window cost to fix? I grabbed a tissue from the bedside table and knelt to collect the broken shards. "Can you tell what broke it?" I asked over my shoulder as she hovered in the doorway. "Maybe a branch?"

I glanced outside. Beyond the window was the front lawn. There weren't any trees on that side of the house.

Dahlia was quiet for a few moments, her jaw working. She pulled out her phone and checked the time as though anxious to be on her way. "Teenagers, probably. Pranksters."

But there wasn't a rock or brick to support her theory. With her silence beginning to make me nervous, I tugged on the decorative iron bar framing the broken pane. "Good thing Dad took security seriously."

It hadn't been more than a year after he'd moved into Malice House that the first stalker showed up on his porch. Dad had written a literary horror in 2000 called *Other/None Other*. His creepiest fan mail came from readers of that book—letters accompanied by gruesome art or that were written *to* the story's murderer, as though the letter's author couldn't separate fiction from reality. My father was unlisted in the phone book, but that hadn't stopped weirdos from knocking on the door every couple of years, wanting an autograph or attention—the worst incident being the time an aspiring writer broke in at gunpoint and made my dad listen to him read his bad poetry. After that, Dad installed a security fence around the property, added extra locks on the doors, and paid a small fortune for custom windows with narrow iron panes to prevent entry. No cameras, though. He didn't like the idea of anyone, even a security company, watching.

Wind slithered through the broken pane, making me shiver.

"Can't keep out what's already in," Dahlia muttered.

My eyebrows rose. Dahlia Whitney was the type of woman to wear a silver cross necklace and proudly display a bumper sticker for a megachurch on her Kia.

"You don't believe this place is haunted, do you? I thought that was just my dad."

Her head snapped to me. "Don't be stupid." But the wavering in her watery eyes didn't match her sharp tone. The wind whistled, and she kneaded her hands together and slid a glare back in the direction of the hallway. "Of course I don't believe in ghosts. Neither did Amory, until his mind started to go. He got it in his head there were spirits here. Used to leave toast out to appease them. Under the bed, tucked in dresser drawers . . ." She scoffed. "It only drew the mice."

I shifted the tissue full of broken glass from one hand to another. "He, um, mentioned a demon living in the walls."

She pressed her lips together a few times. "I'm aware. Said he heard it under the bed. He kept a golf club by his pillow. Just in case."

This time we both looked fixedly at the bed.

"What I'm saying is," she said while wrapping her sweater more tightly around her torso, "*I'd* take the guest room."

After Dahlia left—begrudgingly accepting my excuse that I was out of cash and would have to send her a check for keeping tabs on the house since my dad died—I dragged my suitcase up the stairs and unpacked a few things into the primary bedroom closet. I wasn't the type to be deterred by moldy toast and phantom drafts. Besides, the screened-in sleeping porch off that bedroom would make a great studio so long as I could keep the rain out. Regardless, before I headed back downstairs, I found myself pausing by the bed and, after a second's debate, bending down to peek underneath.

No demons.

Just dust and an empty china plate the cleaners had missed.

I straightened, chastising myself. I had greater worries than an old man's ghosts. Before I'd left the airport, I'd checked my bank account. After the rental car fees and the two airport drinks, the account had sunk to high two-figures territory. Not enough to pay Dahlia for the upkeep she'd done over the last few months. Certainly not enough to set up an internet account. Or buy much more than a frozen pizza, really.

Running from my past life, from my marriage, wasn't cheap.

The whole world assumed that Amory Marbury's estate was worth millions, and it would have been if he hadn't made a series of bad investments in the last years of his life. The courts had ruled that the copyrights to his extant works and all royalties those works earned go to pay off his creditors in perpetuity. All that was left to inherit after settling debts and draining bank accounts had been the house. Tomorrow, I'd set up my painting supplies on the porch when I could judge where the best light fell, but even if I completed and sold an illustration tomorrow, it would take months to get paid. And thus far my art business had brought in exactly, well, zero dollars, so I'd found other ways to pay the bills in the interim.

On the drive up, I'd swung by a pawn shop in a strip mall just north of Seattle and bought a five-dollar used VHS player. Now, I pulled a bootlegged VHS cassette out of my bag and went downstairs to connect the player to my father's bulky old television set in the living room. When

Rob, screen name SlasherDasher, had first offered me the gig, he'd promised to pay under the table and, more importantly, pay promptly. He hadn't let me down yet. And a three-hundred-dollar transfer to my account tomorrow was worth staying up for all night tonight.

I riffled through my father's old Scotch bottles until I found one with a few fingers left.

Though the handwritten label on the cassette read *Anderson Anniversary Vacation—1991*, it actually contained an underground slasher film about a family who managed the off-season maintenance at a summer camp. I took notes on my laptop while sipping from Dad's crystal decanter. There was an interesting twist halfway through about the daughter and the drained lake. My eyes were bleary from watching the cheap VHS player's wavy images, and when I reached for the bottle again, I found it empty. With a sigh, I paused the movie, untangled myself from the sofa, and poked around the kitchen for more booze, finding nothing. The cleaning crew from Seattle had probably absconded with most of what had been left out.

The light, I noticed, was still on in the attic stairwell.

I frowned up at the flickering bulb. A recluse who collected expensive Scotch would likely have an emergency supply stashed away somewhere, right?

The stairs creaked as I made my way up. Inside the cramped space, a sloping roof hid all manner of boxes, old furniture, insect-eaten stacks of clothes. On the other side of the single attic window, a moth hurled itself at the glass. Barefoot, I stepped over creaking boards that I didn't trust not to wield loose nails and made my way past towering stacks of old manuscript copies, piles of research books, lesser-known awards my father hadn't deemed worthy enough to display downstairs with the Pulitzer, and boxes of promotional tidbits his publisher had sent him over the years, mostly bookmarks and posters and custom bookplates for his signature.

After the funeral, his petite editor with a white streak of hair and tortoiseshell glasses had cornered me at the reception. "You'll go through his office, of course," she'd said with a wave of wineglass in hand. "He was such a complicated man. A writer's office is like their soul. He wouldn't want anyone but you to glimpse within it."

Without thinking I'd answered, "I guess his soul was composed of promotional coasters for *Exit, Nebraska*."

The editor had blinked from behind her glasses and gone to talk to the other publishing professionals around the buffet table.

Complicated didn't begin to describe my father.

Now I picked my way through the attic's maze of shadows. In one box, I found newspaper articles about my father that perhaps he'd meant to put in a scrapbook but never got around to. In another were too-small clothes he'd stored up here when he'd gained weight, ever hopeful of fitting back into them. I reached for another, smaller box and paused at the earthy scent. An odor I'd noticed earlier but that had faded amid the other musty attic smells.

To my surprise, it *was* a box of dirt. Not packaged soil from a plant nursery, but hard clumps of soil, some still clinging to dried grass, as though my father had dug it right out of the garden and boxed it up.

Okay, Dad . . .

Pushing the box away, I dusted off my hands and spotted a promising-looking wooden crate below the window. It was filled with packing straw, the kind of crate that came nailed shut and probably had required a crowbar to open it. I dug around in the crate until my fingers glided over a bottle. *Jackpot.* Inside were dozens of bottles of Scotch, their labels printed in a language I couldn't immediately place, which I assumed meant they were either very good or very bad. Knowing my father, I suspected the former.

As I grabbed two bottles and turned back toward the stairs, I saw the pages.

They were yellow and curled, tucked into a desk drawer that had warped from years of humidity. Though the drawer had a lock, a portion of its bottom had rotted away, revealing the sheets.

My father had his quirks, but it seemed odd to lock away papers in his own home when he was the sole resident. Was he worried about Dahlia snooping?

Curious, I set down the Scotch. Jiggling the drawer confirmed it was locked, but I grabbed a brick-like copy of *Bodies of Water*, my father's second book, and knelt down to batter the drawer bottom's desiccated particle board until the rest of it broke off. Chunks of wood rained down along with wafting yellowing pages like curled autumn leaves. If there had once been a string or rubber band to bind them, it had long ago rotted away.

I inspected the first few pages in the poor light of the single bulb. They were small, about five by seven inches, with a rough edge as though ripped from a notebook. The writing on them was undeniably my father's, which was strange, since he usually typed everything on a battered old typewriter like the one downstairs. In my childhood memories, however, he wrote by hand and had only moved to typewriters later in life. When his editor had sent him a computer sometime in the late nineties, urging him to join the modern world, he'd smashed the thing in front of reporters and fired the editor, then moved to a new publishing house that offered him twice as much for his advances. Judging by these curled, handwritten pages, he must have written them decades ago.

My eyes scanned over random lines about grotesque mermaids and horned beasts, and it became clear that the unnumbered pages had shifted out of order when they'd fallen. I tucked my feet underneath me and settled in to put them in order, hunting until I came to what looked to be a rumpled title page.

He'd written the title in small, unassuming letters: *Bedtime Stories for Monsters*. Below the title was a table of contents:

"Beasts of Sun"

"Extremities"

"The Decaylings"

"Sweet Cream"

"Kaleidoscope"

"Sundown Coming"

"Everyone's Favorite Uncle"

"Late Fees"

There was no date, no author credit to Amory Marbury or anyone else for that matter, which struck me as odd. Frowning, I flipped over the paper as though maybe an explanation had been scribbled on the back. But it was bare.

Doubt crept into my mind. Maybe this *wasn't* one of my father's old projects. It didn't match the tone of his hefty literary tomes like *Bodies of Water*, novels about suicidal businessmen and the dissolution of marriage and the quiet desperation of swing state politicians. None of his other works had even a whiff of the paranormal. Besides, why would he keep a manuscript secret? I'd never known him to be shy about discussing works in progress.

Still, there was no doubt that it was his handwriting.

I settled in to read the first page, and my sense of confusion grew with each line. It was, as the title suggested, a book about monsters. Literal monsters. The introduction read like a macabre fairy tale. *One step away from our world lies another: a land of violent fantasies, of sharp-toothed delights. . . .* I flipped through the unordered pages, trying to get the gist of the story. From what I could gather, it was set in a twisted world reminiscent of the 1950s mixed with the most depraved fantasies of the Brothers Grimm. Each of the eight stories centered on a different character. One was a witch who sold dubious potions at a Night Market, another a kestrel that could take on a human form, another a traveling salesman with an uncanny way with words.

What had inspired such characters? Neither my father's imagination nor his habits had never struck me as morbid: He collected Scotch, not, say, some serial killer's demented prison artwork. The only time I could recall him mentioning anything macabre was when he'd described our distant relatives, deriding them as criminals and occultists and murderous dentists.

I tried to order the pages the best I could and ended up with a semblance of a complete manuscript. At around fifty small pages, the manuscript was far shorter than my father's other works, yet there was something familiar about the writing style, especially compared to his early efforts, when he'd experimented with magical realism and extended metaphor before settling into contemporary realism for the bulk of his career. Those early stories hadn't gotten much attention, though they were among my personal favorites.

Headlights shone through the window, throwing unwelcome bursts of light in my face, and I grimaced. The neighbor's house, higher on the cliff, was mostly hidden behind trees during the day but fully revealed itself at night when the lights were on.

I blinked, disoriented. What time was it? My phone was downstairs next to the empty Scotch bottle.

Shit—the movie. If I didn't write the summary, I wouldn't get paid.

But a summer camp killer was the last thing on my mind now. Rubbing the dust from my eyes, I gathered the manuscript pages in the basket of my arms and grabbed the neck of one of the Scotch bottles. I paused when I saw the headlights outside, still burning. When my father had bought Malice House, it must have been the only home for miles, buried in the steep seaside forests, built when the only lifestyle it could possibly suit was that of a recluse. But in the past few decades, Lundie Bay had gained a reputation as a seaside getaway for the outrageously rich, and now the road to my father's house was dotted with mansions each more modern than the next, built from local Washington timber and steel beams salvaged from old fishing yards. The neighboring house had been constructed a few years ago (my father had been livid to have people so close), a multi-million-dollar steel box overlooking the ocean.

I watched as the distant headlights shone on a figure—a man—lugging armfuls of something from his car trunk to the side yard. After another minute or so, the headlights were switched off, and I almost turned away until I saw a small flash of light in the darkness. The man had lit a match, and with a sputter of fuel, a bonfire erupted.

I stared at the blaze, hidden by the neighbor's tree line to everyone but me. What kind of person, I wondered, was awake at three a.m. on a weekday, alone, sneaking around their own house?

Then I realized with an unwelcome shiver that, apparently, *I* was.

CHAPTER TWO

The last watery gleam of sunlight had died out fifty-nine hours ago; one more until the sun rose again. In this last scrap of long night, a man in black moved through a forest whose trees grew in perfectly geometric rows. In the dark, one couldn't tell his hair was silver, though there was no mistaking the blood. It stained his right hand from fingertips to elbow like a leather glove. Shiny drops fell on stones and wormy logs and lapped up the moonlight—a grisly breadcrumb trail.

—From "Beasts of Sun" in
Bedtime Stories for Monsters

I SPENT THE night with the pages of *Bedtime Stories for Monsters* fanned out on my bed, piecing them together like an archeologist, uncovering layer after layer of my father. I made an alarmingly large dent in the bottle of Scotch in my excitement to solve the puzzle of this manuscript. I found myself reaching into my canvas bag for a paintbrush as I read, craving the sensation of running my thumb over the bristles. I often thought best with a paintbrush or pencil in hand—an artist to the core.

Soon, I had the manuscript more or less in order. I settled back with the same tingle of anticipation that I always got when poised to crack open a new book. As I sipped my drink, I read in fascination about a monster that hid under the bed, waiting to pinch bare feet off with crab-like claws, not unlike the demon my father believed lived in the house walls.

The stories were loosely stitched together, all taking place in a demonic world called, interestingly, Malice. Taken from the name of my father's house, of course, even though it had already been named Malice when my father bought it eleven years ago—a corruption of the previous owner's name: Miss Alice. M'Alice. Which—if the towns-people were to be believed—fit mean old Alice Halliday perfectly well.

There were no real plotlines to the stories, though one charac-ter named the Harbinger did appear in several different stories on a search for some ultimate monster. My mind spun with a thousand questions. When had my father written this? During his brief affair with cocaine in the nineties? No, that didn't seem right—as bizarre as the stories were, they were too well-structured to be some sort of coked-up ramble. Had he been testing out a new style under a pen name? His editors would have balked at a collection of macabre fairy tales compared to his award-winning literary works. Or were these stories he'd heard from those disreputable distant relatives in Lisbon and Helsinki and Joshua Tree?

By the time daylight filtered through the bedroom windows, I had finished reading the last page but was no closer to understanding why my father would have written such stories, and more curiously, hidden them away for decades under lock and key. But my hands were trem-bling with excitement. They might not have been the type of stories my father's editors would hold in high esteem, but I adored them. They were *my* kind of stories. Stories of madness. Of monsters. Of magic. My skin was prickling—this lost manuscript was a buried gem.

It wasn't until later in the day, eating a crumpled granola bar I'd found in my purse in a poor excuse for lunch, that it occurred to me that the manuscript could also be a financial opportunity. I almost choked as the realization hit me: An undiscovered Marbury manuscript could be worth hundreds of thousands of dollars. My father's creditors owned the copyrights to his six previously published works, but this one wasn't named in the settlement. They had no claim over it. Granted, *Bedtime Stories for Monsters* was no usual Marbury work, but with the right cover and marketing campaign, anything with my father's name would race up the bestseller list.

Excited now, I started to think through the idea. The problem was how to get the manuscript into the right hands. Over the years I'd met my fair share of my father's publishing contacts, but I hadn't gotten on well with them; whenever I'd told any of them I wanted to illustrate children's books, they'd avoided me, afraid I'd pester them for a contract. And, to be honest, I hadn't left the best impression when I'd gotten drunk at his funeral and told most of them exactly where they could shelve their condolences.

Then I remembered the framed photograph next to the old typewriter, one of the ones turned facedown. I went to the library and took a second look at the portrait of the small group. Besides my father, the only person I recognized was the owner of Lundie Bay Books. Catherine Tyson? Tisdale? *Tybee*—that was it. Catherine Tybee. We'd met a few times at his book signings in town. She and her husband had been in a book club my father started in an effort to bring more culture to Lundie Bay. She'd struck me as a fawning older woman beaming in the presence of the revered Amory Marbury, but she was sharp and professional and, most importantly, hadn't been at the funeral to witness me making a fool out of myself. As I remembered, her husband—probably the white-bearded man in the photograph with his arm around her—had been a big-shot editor in New York before retiring.

A bookseller and her editor husband would certainly have publishing connections, or at least know which direction to point me in.

I considered the idea over the next few days while I attempted to rearrange the house and make it feel less like I was living in a dead man's shadow. Eventually, I decided it was worth getting in touch with the Tybees, which meant making myself look presentable.

I tugged on clean pants while I considered my hair. It didn't like the Pacific Northwest's perpetual damp. And tossing and turning in my sleep had left my hair unattractively curly. My flat iron was back in Baker's apartment along with nearly everything else to my name. When I'd left, all I'd grabbed were my art supplies, laptop, and a few clothes—just the essentials until I could get myself back on my feet.

I pulled my hair into a low ponytail, brushed my teeth of the lingering film of alcohol, and grabbed the manuscript and my laptop. I was nearly out the door when a voice in my head whispered a warning.

I looked down at the small notebook pages that held *Bedtime Stories for Monsters*.

Lundie Bay wasn't only famous as a getaway destination for tech investors. My father had left a permanent mark here, as much a tourist draw as the nearby Mayfelt Islands. There were people out there obsessed enough with his works to break in at gunpoint. What would they do if they knew about an undiscovered manuscript?

An old tin of Werther's caramels sat on the entry table. My father must have been the only one in the world who still sucked on them, picking up the habit when he gave up smoking. I folded the manuscript pages in half, threw out the ancient, half-melted candy, and hid the story inside.

Outside, the sun was mottled behind clouds—normal weather for the area. Either that or steady rain. I smelled the sea mixed with pines as I opened the rental car door. Pulling out the gate, I hit the remote-controlled button to close it behind me and caught a glimpse of the neighbor's driveway, thought again of the car pulling up so late at night, the tangerine flare of a lit match, then the blaze.

What had my neighbor been burning?

From here I couldn't see the lower level of the house, only the steel point of the roof. But I caught the name as I drove by the mailbox.

Kahn.

When my father had first visited Lundie Bay, it was a quiet fishing village, nothing more than a cluster of wooden shops at the base of the cliff and a boardwalk leading to the docks. But the tourist industry had discovered it, and B and Bs started to pop up, and the humble fish-and-chip place was raved about by a celebrity chef. For the next two decades, the village grew in popularity with the tech boom down in Seattle, until cliffside mansions were going up left and right, and town itself was filled with a small brewery, an art gallery famous for its resident cat, restaurants that charged exorbitant prices for pub food, and a handful of cafés clustered along the boardwalk.

On such a dreary day as today, town was deserted. A cluster of people huddled near the dockmaster's station, planning a gloomy excursion to the Mayfelt Islands. From what I could remember, the bookstore was two or three blocks back from the water. I turned the corner and spotted it. Just as I remembered, it was housed in a neoclassical revival–inspired building that had once been a bank, its columns softened now with a quirky blue-and-green awning and chalkboard placard out front that read:

READ FICTION . . . BECAUSE REAL LIFE IS TERRIFYING.

I started to push open the door, only to stop and stare at a sign taped to the glass below the OPEN sign.

BODIES OF WATER CAFÉ NOW OPEN!

"Well, fuck," I muttered.

Bodies of Water was the book that had blown my father's career wide open, the winner of the International Booker Prize. He'd flown to London to accept the award, and I, being eleven, had stayed with my aunt Rose, working on my science fair project. He'd called to say he'd met a woman and would be gone for another month of travel, which turned into six.

It didn't seem I was going to be spared my father's ghost anywhere, not even when it came to coffee.

Regardless, as far as bookstores went—and I'd been dragged around to many—Lundie Bay Books was undeniably adorable. They'd embraced the former-bank theme and still had the same counter with its teller stalls. Wide tables displayed staff favorites and seasonal picks. Book-themed candles and word art and socks with literary quotes were mixed in with the latest bestsellers. An Irish instrumental ballad played on the speaker system, evoking stormy seas and greener pastures. A few patrons milled around the new releases. The only thing that had changed since the last time I'd been there was the addition of the café. They'd knocked down the shared wall of the neighboring store, a yarn shop once upon a time, and expanded into the newly open space with lattes and teas and baked goods. Several aging hipsters leaned over laptops at the café tables. Lining its walls were black-and-white images of my father, most of them autographed—I'd never known him to turn down an autograph—along with framed posters of his book covers and copies of articles from the *New York Times* and the *Atlantic* about the famously reclusive author of Lundie Bay.

I suppressed a shudder and went to the main bookstore counter, where a guy in a flannel shirt and black-rimmed glasses blinked up at me. His nametag read ORION and declared his favorite book to be *Steppenwolf.*

"Is Catherine Tybee in?" I asked.

Orion was about to answer, but I had already been spotted.

"*Haven!*" Catherine emerged from the back shelves with hands outstretched as though we were old friends, though we'd only met a handful of times. She waved dismissively to the cashier. "Orion, it's fine, I'll handle this."

She was a well-put-together older woman, wrapped in a watercolor-inspired shawl, with her salt-and-pepper hair pulled back in a perfectly imperfect twist. She threw her arms around me and drew me into a hug that felt too personal. I was eager to slither away.

"I didn't know you were in town!" she admonished. Her voice rose precariously as though my appearance had rattled her little kingdom. She was the epicenter of all things literary in Lundie Bay, and she didn't seem to appreciate that I hadn't announced my arrival the moment I'd come.

The espresso machine started screaming in the bookstore café area, and I waited for it to quiet.

I forced a smile. "Hi, Mrs. Tybee."

"*Catherine*, please."

My smile stretched. "Yeah, I got into town a few days ago. I came back to take care of the house. I was able to get the deed changed over to my name. I might fix it up. Or sell it as is. I'm not sure yet."

"Oh, you'll have lots of interest in *that* house. There aren't many historic structures left here. I even tried to get your father to sell it to me before he started to get sick. . . ." She paused, thinking better of bringing up grim memories. "I know an excellent Realtor, if you don't have one—"

"You were in a book club with my father, right?" I interrupted. "You and your husband?"

"*Book club?*" A muscle jumped in her jaw. "Oh. Yes, of course. You mean the Ink Drinkers. It was a *literary salon*, Haven. Not a book club."

I didn't really see the difference, but I could tell I'd said the wrong thing.

She pressed her lips together tightly and then said suddenly, "Coffee? On the house."

"Oh. Okay." I was in no position to turn down free drinks.

She motioned to an empty café table by the windows. We slid into chairs, and she twisted toward the barista.

"Kylie? A cappuccino for me and . . ." She looked to me questioningly.

"Latte," I said. "Large. Double shot. Whipped cream."

If Catherine was paying, I wasn't going to go with my usual black drip.

The barista, somewhere in her early twenties, tattoos running along her light brown forearms and curly hair held off her face with a few braids, grabbed two mugs and set the espresso machine to scream again.

Catherine Tybee arranged her shawl around her shoulders. "*Le buveurs d'encre*. The Ink Drinkers. It was about ideas, about radical thought. Your father brought us together. Lundie Bay is better known for its fish and chips than its educated population, you know, and Amory wanted to create a place for deep thought. At first it was just the three of us: your father, myself, and my husband. Jonathan headed an imprint at Random House for twenty years, you know. He and your father knew a lot of the same authors, the same editors. Later we invited a librarian from Bainbridge University to join us. We used to have the most animated discussions up there at Malice House."

There was something wistful yet sharp in her eyes, like the leaves of a bearded iris.

"Coffee!" the barista called. She appeared by our table with two steaming mugs in hand and an infectious smile. This close, I saw that the tattoos on her forearms were quotes. I scanned them quickly, relieved that none were from my father's books.

"Thank you, Kylie," Catherine said.

As soon as we were alone, I lowered my voice and said, "That's why I wanted to talk to you. I'm looking for connections in the publishing world. As a bookseller, I thought you might have some contacts, or that your husband still has colleagues in the business. You see—" The espresso machine thumped and clicked loudly as the barista started making another latte. I waited until she finished, then continued, "I found a manuscript that I believe my father wrote. I've never heard of it before. I think it's never been published."

Catherine Tybee's face was impossible to read. I could only imagine what must be going through her mind. Surprise, of course, and undoubtedly excitement about this discovery. But she, like me, must have intuited how sensational this news would be if it got out, because she scooted closer and tented her hands beneath her chin.

"What kind of a manuscript?" she asked carefully.

"Well, it's strange. I won't lie. It's sort of a grown-up collection of dark fairy tales. It's titled *Bedtime Stories for Monsters*."

She was quiet for a long time. An uncomfortable tingle ran up the back of my neck. I tapped my foot anxiously. The photographs of my father on the wall, larger than life, stared at me from beyond the grave.

"I'm glad you came to me," she said at last, pressing her palms on the table as though to keep them from shaking. "This is something my husband . . . my *ex-husband*—he bought a house in Bellingham after the divorce—will want to know about right away. We'll have to have it authenticated, but if it truly is an unpublished Marbury, our discovery could be one of the most significant literary finds of the decade." She paused, then added pointedly, "And lucrative."

I smiled, relieved and hopeful that the Tybees' connections would come through for me before my bank account dipped too low.

Catherine took a sip of her coffee—her hands were shaking. She set her mug back down a little too hard and, after dabbing up the spilled coffee with a paper napkin, cleared her throat. "I'd advise that we keep this between us for now, Haven. We wouldn't want word getting out before we know exactly what we have."

I almost told her about the Werther's tin where I'd hidden the manuscript, but I didn't like the way she kept slipping first-person plural pronouns into her speech. What *we* have. *Our* discovery.

I nodded tightly. "I agree."

She stood up in a graceful swoop and adjusted her shawl. "I'll call Jonathan right away and ask him to discreetly speak to some of his former colleagues. Can I have your number? I'll let you know what he says. I expect he'll want to drive over immediately. Bellingham's just thirty minutes away."

I thanked her and gave her my number. I must have sat at the table after she'd left longer than I'd realized, staring into my empty mug, because in another moment the barista was suddenly by my side.

"Everything okay?" she asked.

I nearly jumped. "Oh. Yes. It was Kylie, right? Do you give free refills?"

She pressed a finger to her lips with a mischievous smile. "Only when my boss isn't looking. And Catherine's occupied over in New Releases." She went to the counter and made me another latte. As she brought it over, I thought I saw her glance at the main bookstore counter, where Orion was pricing pencil cases, then back to me. "You're Haven Marbury?"

I shifted my gaze to Dad's face plastered on the wall behind her. "Are you a Marbury fan?"

The girl's nose wrinkled. "I tried reading *Feast of Flowers*. Not really my thing."

I relaxed. There was nothing worse than being caught in conversation with a Marbury fan. "To be honest, it's not really my thing, either."

She chuckled. "You aren't a writer like your father?"

I shook my head. "Illustrator. Well—aspiring illustrator. I haven't found the right project yet."

She glanced in Catherine Tybee's direction again and then slid into the chair opposite me.

"Listen," she breathed out in a rush. "I hope you don't mind, but I overheard a little of what you and Catherine were talking about. Between us, you could make a lot more money if you sold that manuscript yourself. I have a side business auctioning literary memorabilia online, and I've been looking into crypto. I wouldn't touch it personally, but there's a lot of suckers out there. We could maybe get *millions* for an undiscovered Marbury book if we mint it as an NFT. Online buyers are where the real money is now, not in old-school publishing."

She must have read the apprehension on my face because she raised her hands defensively and said, "Just think about it, okay? Don't worry, I'll keep the information to myself. Even if you don't want to sell the manuscript, let me know if you find anything else valuable in Malice House. Special editions of your father's books, or pens your father wrote with, or—man—one of his typewriters. That would be worth a fortune. I'll sell anything you find and give you two-thirds of the profit."

I wondered if Catherine knew of her barista's side job. I toyed with my ceramic mug, trying not to look desperate at the mention of money, all too aware that my bank account was anemic and that even if I sold *Bedtime Stories for Monsters*, the money wouldn't clear for months.

"I'll . . . have a look," I said noncommittally. "He bequeathed his personal library and most of his first editions and journals to Bainbridge University. They came up and got it all shortly after his death. That's probably where all the valuable stuff went. But I'll see what I can find." Outside, a light rain was beginning to fall. I pushed to my feet to beat the coming storm.

"Great. Let me know." Her face fell into a frown. "And hey, be careful up there. In Malice House."

I paused, thinking of ghosts, of boxes filled with dirt, of Dahlia's refusal to spend the night at the place. "Why?"

Kylie's eyebrows pinched together. She motioned in the vague direction of the end of town—of the cliffs where Malice House perched. "People have spotted bears in the forest up there. Last summer, one mauled a couple people."

"I'll keep an eye on the woods," I said.

Kylie nodded. "Do that." She stood, too, picking up my empty mug. "And hey, from an aspiring author to an aspiring illustrator . . . good luck with your art. Keep looking for that right project. You just need the right inspiration."

As she returned to the counter, she added over her shoulder, "You never know what surprises might turn up on your doorstep around here."

CHAPTER THREE

The bed had been passed down from Elin's grandmother to her mother and now to her, and the sagging mattress proved the legacy. The ancient springs groaned whenever she rolled over, rusty from decades of children peeing themselves or spilling midnight cups of water. Her parents were arguing in the next room with the record player cranked up as loud as it would go. Some warbling cowboy singer that her mother loved. It was stiflingly hot. Her room stank of something briny.

She threw back the covers, sweating.

"Lord," she muttered. "That smell."

—From "Extremities" in
Bedtime Stories for Monsters

I STOPPED ON the way home to buy wine and groceries with my dwindling funds, then swung by the post office. In my hurry to leave New York, I'd had all my mail forwarded to Malice House's address, not realizing what a colossal mistake that had been. The postal worker laughed darkly when I said my name, only to return with fifteen white plastic crates full of fan mail. Clearly, neither Dahlia Whitney nor anyone else had picked up my father's mail in a long time.

I didn't want to face the unanswered letters. Each one like a ghost, someone on the other side, a stranger, reaching out to a dead man. Maybe I could forward them to his publisher and let some poor intern respond. Or burn them—who would know? As I drove the winding road home, they itched at me, each of those letters. Fans who confused my father's books with my father himself. Thought they adored the man when really, they didn't know him at all. He was much more than his books. *Never meet your heroes*, wasn't that the adage? If they knew the real Amory Marbury, would they still write fan mail? He was no saint, though he hadn't been a monster, either. Maybe that was the whole problem. He was just a man. In the end, there was nothing extraordinary about him at all.

I ended up lugging the fan mail to the garage, where I could banish the letters from sight if not from mind, and carried my groceries into the house. The television was still on in the living room, paused on a frame of the summer camp lake, drained for the winter with bloody boot prints tracking through the mud. I looked guiltily at the groceries on the dining room table. If I wanted to continue to eat, I should finish the movie and write the summary so I'd get paid. I certainly wouldn't get any money from Baker. About two months ago, I'd quietly gotten in touch with a divorce lawyer acquaintance to see about my options, only to learn—and this had been news to me—*we'd never actually been married.* Our paperwork hadn't been correctly filed. Never mind the wedding in Beaufort, the three-carat diamond ring, the three years sleeping in the same bed as husband and wife.

So, I'd been trapped. Unable to leave without a means to support myself. *Everything* had been Baker's. The apartment. The furniture. The trust fund set up by his grandfather, a famous French explorer who had a whole National Geographic rip-off TV channel named after him.

Cursing, I pulled out my new phone and created a contact entry for Baker. The last time I'd seen him, our living room had been left with my favorite mug smashed to pieces, a sharp-edged paint scraper on the floor, broken glass, blood soaking into the carpet.

Now I texted his number before I lost the nerve.

This is Haven. New number. If you want to talk, I'm here.

I dropped the phone onto the sofa as though it was a chunk of rotten flesh and turned away. *I* had nothing to say. But I had no idea who might end up eventually reading those texts—lawyers, the police. I needed a record of playing nice.

I ran a hand down the still-tender bruises on my left shoulder, hidden by my sleeve. The debit card linked to Baker's bank account had bought me the plane ticket to Seattle, two months of a cheap rental car lease, $300 in cash from an ATM, and a few meals before it had been automatically canceled due to suspicious activity.

It would be easy enough for an investigator to check the credit card statement and see that I'd bought a ticket to Seattle. But what would have been the point in trying to hide my location? Where else would I have gone but Malice House? I had few friends from before Baker and I met, and even fewer from the three years of our pseudo-marriage. Little family besides my dad and Aunt Rose, who preferred the company of houseplants. I'd never known my mother. She and my father eloped right before I was born, and a few weeks later she'd disappeared with a bag stuffed with her clothes and all my father's medication. There'd been speculation about postpartum depression. The bag had been found weeks later submerged in the Potomac River. My mother's body was never recovered.

I waited a few tense moments. The phone remained silent. Just as I was about to shove it in my pocket and start unpacking the groceries, it rang.

I let out a shriek. But it wasn't Baker's number, and I hadn't transferred any other contacts yet except for Dahlia. It was an area code I didn't recognize.

Feeling a preternatural tingle, I answered the phone. "Hello?"

"Haven? Haven? It's Catherine. Listen, I spoke to Jonathan. He's tied up for a few days . . . he's actually at a hospital in Seattle, nothing serious, a scheduled procedure, but he'll have to be there until Wednesday. He said he'd come on Thursday to see the manuscript as long as there aren't any complications with the surgery."

She spoke so quickly that, still thinking of Baker, I barely remembered why she was calling.

"It isn't *that* urgent," I assured her. Though I was eager to sell the manuscript, a few days wouldn't make a difference. "Please, tell him not to rush if he's in the hospital."

"I promise, it's minor. You'll understand when you're older— bodies start to fall apart, these things happen. He's extremely anxious to see the manuscript. Can you meet Thursday? At the bookstore? Say, ten a.m.?"

I glanced at the dusty old wall calendar reflexively, but it was from 2020, and, regardless, I knew I had no plans.

"That should work."

"Excellent." She breathed a little heavily into the phone as though she had more to say, but then suddenly hung up.

I glanced back at the television screen.

Do your damn job. Finish the movie, Haven.

Instead, as though pulled by magnetic forces, I found myself opening the Werther's tin and fanning out the manuscript pages again on the library rug, getting lost once more in my father's strange world. The figures in my father's stories haunted me even more than the unanswered letters or the horror movie still paused on the TV. The mystery of those strange monsters and people, and of him—of why he'd written them. His characters had vivid backstories but only cursory physical descriptions, which had been a common criticism of his early works. After that, I guess critics assumed it was a "style choice." Now my fingers itched to give his characters shape, fill in the details my father had left out.

Then I remembered my conversation with the bookstore barista.

Keep looking for that right project . . .

An idea began to take shape behind my eyes. I found myself gathering the pages with an odd possessiveness almost as though I wasn't in control of my own body. What if *this* was the project? Was if it was fate that I, an illustrator, was the one to find *Bedtime Stories for Monsters*? An art director I'd been corresponding with in New York had told me that my illustrations were too dark for children's books. If I ever hoped to get a contract, I needed to stop drawing wolves and work on ballerinas.

"But kids love wolves," I'd argued.

"The kind who huff at little pigs," he'd answered. "Not one with the bloody corpse of a little girl mangled beneath their claws."

I thought he didn't know children at all—but apparently the entire world of publishing agreed with him, because I hadn't gotten a single reply from any of the agents I'd queried. *Bedtime Stories for Monsters* wasn't for children, that was for sure, but maybe my style would lend itself *better* to adult horror. I started to get excited thinking about the possibilities. If Catherine Tybee's enthusiasm was any indication, the manuscript would sell, maybe even for serious money. If I could attach my name to it as a sort of posthumous father-daughter collaboration, with me doing the illustrations, this could get my artwork out into the world in a major way.

A sudden dark mood descended over me as I considered the possibility that a publisher might want my father's words but not my drawings. *His manuscript is my property*, I thought with a fierce sense of possessiveness. Creditors had robbed me of all his other books, but they couldn't get their hands on this one. If any publishers wanted his words, they'd have to buy my illustrations, too. I'd sell it as a package or not at all.

Eventually, I managed to let go of the manuscript, though my palms felt sweaty and empty without it. I considered calling Catherine back to tell her about my idea but decided against it. It was an unusual idea, and I'd found that most people lacked vision when it came to things outside the norm. Better to go ahead and draw the characters. *Show* them what I meant to do.

When I'd first seen the sleeping porch off the bedroom, I'd thought it would make an excellent studio. Bundling up against the chill in one of my father's oversized wool cardigans, I dragged a short bookcase and a side table from the hall onto the porch. From downstairs, I grabbed the mugs and mason jars that my father had used to hold pens and dumped them all out, sorting through for any salvageable writing implements, finding almost three dollars in loose change and a silver ring with a Celtic knot design, a relic of some old affair. It was pretty—I tried it on, but it was too small for my ring finger, so I put it on my pinky. Ever since I'd taken off my wedding band and left it on Baker's dining room table, my hand had felt uncomfortably bare.

I used the now-empty jars to hold my graphite pencils and paintbrushes. I wiped down the desk and set out the rest of my supplies: sketchbook, teacup, laptop, paints. Once I got the internet set up, I'd find some online reference photos to use for the characters in *Bedtime Stories for Monsters*. Until then I had only the contents of my own imagination.

I considered making tea, only to find myself headed back for the Scotch. Drawing monsters called for stronger stuff than chamomile.

I poured a splash of booze into my teacup and sank into the heavy desk chair. It was cold in the shade of the porch. The salt in the air and the distant crashing of waves stirred my blood, making my fingers tremble. I took a deep breath. Unsteady hands and art were like oil and water.

Carefully, I rested the yellowed pages of *Bedtime Stories for Monsters* over my laptop's keyboard. They beckoned to me almost as though the characters were whispering from within the pages.

As a rule, I began preliminary sketches with the lightest pencil, H, so I could easily correct and redraw over it. But now I found myself grabbing the darkest, 6B, and attacking the blank page ferociously.

Soon the figure of a man began to take shape. Tall, lean to the point of being gaunt. Next, I snatched up a metallic Copic marker and summoned a curtain of silver hair to cloak his face, except for a smirk; only then did I realized I was drawing the Harbinger. My father had described the man as thin but strong, with a scar across his abdomen from where he'd pulled out his own spleen. The way the Harbinger moved in and out of the other characters' stories made me think of him as a creature of wind—slight and quick, his presence almost a feeling of déjà vu. He was a trickster; not as maleficent as some of the other characters, though still unquestionably a rogue.

In my fever dream of drawing, I barely paused to take a breath. Shapes just came to me. Bold lines formed the map of his shoulders. He hunched slightly as though walking into a storm. The more booze I poured into the teacup, the more feverishly I drew. At some point, I realized I was making the Harbinger everything Baker wasn't: If Baker was a gold-plated idol, the Harbinger was a pool of shifting mercury. *And they say art isn't therapy.*

I don't know how long I drew in that dazed state, but when the Scotch bottle was halfway empty, I looked up to find the sun setting. Shades of goldfinch orange burst across the horizon. I'd drawn the Harbinger in various poses, fantasizing about a two-dimensional man I could make to be everything I wanted. But when I got up to turn on the porch light and returned to my desk, I looked down at the drawing with fresh eyes and felt silly, a girl doodling her crush. I tore out the pages.

I moved on to other characters, drawing late into the night. Losing track of which nebulous forms I brought to life with graphite strokes, or if I was still even drawing defined shapes at all. The hours were a blur as the work pushed me further. Finally, sometime well after midnight, my hands refused to hold a pencil another second. I'd been working for hours with no food. My thoughts were still a tipsy rush, urging me to continue, but my body refused. It was all I could do to turn off the porch light and stumble inside the bedroom.

I stopped short.

The edge of the bedcover swayed. Something had ruffled it. I glanced back toward the porch, assuming it must have been a breeze from the open door. But the air was still. A dust bunny by the foot of the bed that I'd been meaning to clean up hadn't moved.

"Jesus, Haven. Not this again." I was letting my imagination get the best of me. Still, I knew I would lie awake all night wondering if I didn't check.

A chill tickled my bare feet as I took a step closer to the bed. The draft seemed to be coming from *under* the bed. A vent? Still, when I caught sight of a dusty golf club leaning against the headboard, I grabbed it.

Holding my breath, I knelt down to lift the bedspread with the tip of the club.

Shadows and . . .

Nothing—there was nothing there.

I started to ease my grip on the golf club, but just before I stood, my eyes fell on the china plate from before. It had been empty, but now there was a dark shape on the white plate. It wasn't until the smell hit me that I recognized what I was looking at.

Toast.

Fresh enough that it still smelled burnt.

*

I took Dahlia's advice and slept in the guest room. All night, I'd sat in the narrow guest bed with the covers to my chin, frozen like trapped prey, clutching the golf club with white knuckles. I had either drunk too much or had been seeing things because I damn sure hadn't made any toast, and I was certain I'd been alone in the house.

Wasn't I?

In the light of day, I finally got up the nerve to return to my father's bedroom and peek under the bed, only to discover nothing but the empty plate. No phantom toast. Clearly I had imagined it, and I felt utterly ridiculous—but my body still jumped at every creak in the house. My frayed nerves continued over the next few days as I finished setting up my studio and made a few trips into town for errands, until one night when I finally had enough of shrieking at every shadow and dialed a number I hadn't wanted to call.

A woman picked up on the third ring. "Yes?"

"Dahlia?" Nerves made my voice sound like I'd run a marathon. I cleared my throat. "It's Haven Marbury."

A grunt came before anything else. "It's late, Haven."

"Look, I know this might sound like an odd question, but I was hoping you could tell me a little more about the last years with my father. Specifically, about his delusions. I know he talked about a monster in the walls. . . ."

I trailed off, but she didn't fill in the missing line of thought as I'd hoped she would. I drew in a deep breath and asked, "What exactly did he say? About the monsters?"

There was a long silence on the other line, and then in a voice that sounded both cautious and a little mocking, she asked, "What has you asking about that man's delusions, Haven?" She paused before adding in a lower voice, "What happened?"

There was such a knowing weight to those words. In my gut, I felt certain that she knew what I was asking about already.

"Nothing," I said quickly, instinct telling me to hold my cards close. "I heard some pipes or something in the floor and wondered if that might have triggered Dad's delusions. Did the doctor ever say anything about that? About what might have led him to have these . . . odd notions?"

She grunted. "The mind is a strange beast. Isn't any more to dementia than that, is there?"

"Yes but . . ." I drew in another breath as an idea materialized in my head. "Well, you see, I'm writing a story about him. For a magazine. And I wanted to show all sides of him, not just the ones the usual publications profiled." I grimaced to myself—it didn't sound like a convincing lie. "A famous author hallucinating monsters makes for a great story."

Would she fall for it? There was some scrambling on the other end that I finally realized was a small dog scratching his nails on a linoleum floor when she chided, "MacGyver, *get down.*"

She returned to the phone. "There was a whispering."

Her voice was so loud in my ear that I nearly jumped. I swallowed and held the phone tighter. "Whispering?"

"An older man with a striking voice. Your father said he heard it mostly at dusk. Never heard what the man said, just an eerily enthralling voice. Sometimes coming from the woods."

"Did *you* ever hear it?"

Another grunt. "I left at five o'clock sharp every day."

That isn't really an answer, I thought, and felt a small tinge of sympathy for my father having to deal with someone so obstinate. "Did he ever try to investigate it? Or anything else about the demon in the walls? Or—"

"Ms. Marbury." Her voice was pointed. "I don't work for that man anymore, God rest his soul, and I don't particularly want to think back on those years. I have my hands full between the Lord and my grandchildren and my shih tzu. Now that's enough for your magazine article, isn't it? Oh—and I haven't gotten your check yet. Could it still be in the mail?"

Touché, Mrs. Whitney.

I tried to radiate confidence. "I'm sure it is. If you remember anything else . . ."

The shih tzu started barking again, and she shushed him before sighing. "Look, if you want to know more about your father, I suggest going through the attic. He kept secrets buried up there. I don't know more than that, I really don't. But I'll tell you this—and don't you dare put it in your article—there was one night I forgot my heart medication at his house. It was nine or ten o'clock when I went back for it. Your father didn't see me; he was up in the attic. There were dirty footprints on the stairs. A shovel sitting in the middle of the dining room table. It was weird—I got my pills and got out of there pretty fast, but when I looked back up at the attic window . . ."

She trailed off as though her voice had vanished.

"Dahlia?" I asked breathlessly. "Mrs. Whitney?"

She drew in an audible, shaking breath. "He wasn't alone up there. There were *two* people."

CHAPTER FOUR

She never bothered to comb her hair, but it didn't stop the men from coming. She could dress in men's trousers and a dirty white blouse with unwashed bare feet and still they followed her home, peered into her cottage window during the long night hours, showing up at Went's fish market and the bank and the five-and-dime whenever she happened to be there.

She was no great beauty. No songs were written about her eyes. Her thighs weren't smooth.

But there was something defiant in her. Something that sneered at the rottenest pieces of cruel men's hearts, and in return they wanted to hurt her, to break her, to eat out the defiance.

Let them try.

—From "Kaleidoscope" in
Bedtime Stories for Monsters

A HEAVY FOG rolled in overnight. In the morning, I found that Lundie Bay had disappeared into the mist. The waves crashed below as I drove down the winding cliffside road into town with my fog lights cranked up. The air was thick enough to taste: briny, forest-like. Town was all but deserted. Most of the wealthy second homers had already left for the season. They'd have flown their jets down to Southern California, where they could capture the last days of summer.

The battered old typewriter from the library sat in the passenger seat. I'd grabbed it first thing in the morning as an excuse to get out of the house—I was going stir-crazy. As soon as I'd watched Malice House disappear in the rearview mirror, I relaxed: Its ghosts hadn't followed me past the gates.

I parked along Boardwalk Street, and a few fishermen nodded to me as I scurried across the docks, typewriter awkwardly clutched under one arm, other hand holding my laptop case over my head, offering meager protection from the drizzle. Their faces were the same shade as the mist, their heavy raincoats slick.

The bookstore was quiet, having only just opened. A few employees were arranging books on the shelves, but there weren't any customers yet, and Catherine wasn't there. I found Kylie alone in the empty café, typing intently on her laptop. She looked up when my wet boots squeaked on the floor.

A smile spanned her face at the sight of the typewriter. "Is that what I think it is?" She slammed her computer closed and ran around the counter to help me lug the machine to one of the tables. "Oof! It's a beast."

I wiped the dust off my hands. "Seriously. And, hey, I'm pretty sure I remember my dad writing *The Desecration of Johnny Jim* on it. That has to make it worth more, right?"

Kylie had been searching the machine for a serial number, but at my claim, gave me the side-eye. "Hmm. If I'm not mistaken, *The Desecration of Johnny Jim* came out in 1985. When were you born, 1991? '92?"

I started to wonder how I would explain such an obvious discrepancy, when she leaned in with a wry smile. "Maybe your memory is off. Are you sure you don't remember him writing *Other/None Other* on it?" She thunked a heavy key. "That came out in 2000. You'd have been the right age to remember it."

I scratched my cheek. So, Kylie wasn't above a few white lies. Which made me wonder how authentic her literary memorabilia was—not that I cared as long as it got us more cash. "You know, I think it was *Other/None Other.* Yeah. I'm positive. I'd be happy to write up a letter verifying that."

She winked.

"How much do you think we might get for it?" I tried to sound casual as I ran my hand over the keys. I'd had no luck getting Comtek to come out to the house to install Wi-Fi; they required the steep installation fee up front before sending a technician.

Kylie gave me another knowing look. She was a barista in a town full of millionaires. She knew another broke person when she saw one.

"A thousand? Maybe more, depending on how old this model is." She grabbed a paper cup. "How about a coffee? On the house. Latte, right?"

She began filling the espresso machine, and I climbed up onto a barstool. Already, the café smelled like cinnamon and fresh-roasted coffee. I found myself comforted by the familiar whine of the process, the clanking of mugs. I could almost forget the phone call with Dahlia from last night. Clearly, she hadn't told me everything; I suddenly wondered if it had been neither my dad nor Dahlia who laid all the framed photographs facedown, but rather spirits. Poltergeists.

I chastised myself: Next, I'd have Dahlia trying to drag *me* to church.

Kylie handed me a latte in a to-go cup, then lifted her own. "To new friends."

Friends? I'd never been good at making friends. A mother gone by suicide, a childhood raised by nannies, a famous father—it didn't make for fantastic social skills. But I'd come here for a change, hadn't I? A fresh start? Baker was out of my life—I hoped—and so was my father.

I tapped her cup with my own and took a sip.

After leaving the bookstore, I dawdled around town, watching the tuxedo cat through the art gallery's window, ogling the pastries in the bakery's display case, though eventually I had no option but to return to Malice House. I needed to keep working on the illustrations so I could show them to Jonathan Tybee alongside the manuscript. A publisher would need a sample of at least three characters, I reasoned, to take my project seriously. And even if I held my father's manuscript hostage unless an imprint bought my accompanying artwork, I still wanted it to be the best I'd done. This was my one chance—my art had to be exceptional. I wanted leverage, not charity.

I sat in my car for a few minutes, using the bookstore's Wi-Fi to check my emails. Junk mail. Nothing from Baker. There had been no reply to my text, either. Sour memories came crashing back. That final night. The argument. I pressed the pads of my fingers into my bruised shoulder, testing the pain level, wincing.

I opened a new email and thought for a long time before writing:

Baker, I don't want any trouble. I just want my things back—the clothes in the bedroom and my paintings. They're in my studio, on the walls and in the storage drawer. You can ship them to Malice House. You know the address. I think it's best not to involve the police this time. Keep this between us.

I meant what I said when I left.

Haven.

My head was back in New York, back with Baker, so that when I pulled up to the Malice House gate and found it open, I had a moment of confusion. I'd closed the gate behind me, I was certain. Then I noticed a Dodge Charger with municipal plates parked in front of the front porch, half-hidden by a blazing red azalea.

The police?

Unfortunately, I knew all too well how to spot undercover cars. I'd done my research after my run-in with them in New York. For a moment I just sat in my car, idling in the driveway, forgetting it was even running until the windshield wiper suddenly swished, and I jumped. Hands shaking, I parked beside the other vehicle, which was empty.

It didn't take long for the officer to appear. She must have heard my tires on the gravel drive. She came around from the far side of the wraparound porch and stood at the top of the front steps and watched me get out of my car.

"Haven Marbury?"

She was a Black woman with a shadow of short hair, slightly longer in the front, wearing sunglasses despite the weather. She looked in her forties, though it was hard to tell with the porch's shadows obscuring her features. Instead of a uniform, she wore a black blazer and nice sneakers that could pass for dressy, though it was evident from the radio clipped to her belt and the badge hanging from her neck that she was official.

"That's me," I said uneasily, closing the car door.

"You're staying here? At Malice House?"

I nodded. From the bottom step, I didn't like how she towered over me, already looking down from on high.

"What's going on?" I asked. "Has something happened?"

She shifted her weight as she removed her glasses to reveal a face free of makeup. Not that she needed it; people paid a fortune for skin as clear as hers.

She pointed to one of the porch windows. "A break-in was reported."

Alarmed, I hurried up the stairs and took a closer look at the window. One of the lower panes had been broken, though the iron security bars embedded in the glass were intact. It looked like someone had tried to force the window open from the scuff marks on the sill but hadn't succeeded.

Dozens of questions filled my head. Was it related to the broken window upstairs that Dahlia had found? And why did a police officer know about a break-in at my house before I did?

"Dahlia Whitney called it in," the woman said, as though reading my mind. "She was driving past on her way into town and saw someone climb over the fence and run into the woods. She used the code to unlock the gate and came up here, saw the broken window, gave us a call."

She held out her hand. "I'm Detective Letitia Rice."

I must have taken her hand, though it was all a daze. Leave it to Dahlia to drag the police into something, make it a bigger deal than it needed to be, when she could have easily just called me herself. This was the kind of thing my father had always complained about—for all her Christian values, Dahlia delighted in drama.

"Sorry, this is all news to me. What did Dahlia say the person looked like?"

Detective Rice shook her head. "Couldn't tell if it was a man or a woman, just someone in a dark hoodie. This isn't the first attempted break-in, are you aware of that? We were up here a few times when your father lived here, and it got worse after he died. So many trespassers that Dahlia gave us the gate code so we could patrol by every so often."

That explained how the officer had opened the gate. I relaxed, but only slightly. I knelt to inspect the window again if only to break the awkward silence. "It doesn't look like anyone got in. Just broke this glass. I can't imagine why anyone would want inside the house. There's nothing there but old furniture and books."

Detective Rice folded her sunglasses and stashed them in her pocket. "As I understand it, your father's books are pretty popular. That kind of fame can draw out the weirdos. It could be an attempted burglary, but my guess is it's someone who just wants to get inside out of curiosity. For bragging rights. Take some selfies, post them online."

"You're probably right."

It felt like a natural place for the conversation to end, but Detective Rice didn't move.

"Well," I said pointedly, "I appreciate you keeping an eye on the place, but now that I'm living here, no need to patrol anymore. I'll be sure to call if I see anyone snooping around."

She scanned the porch from ceiling joist to floor, pacing as though she had all the time in the world—and in a sleepy town like Lundie Bay, maybe she did.

"Always liked this old house," she mused aloud. "Good bones. I bet the view from the upstairs is really something."

My patience was wearing thin, but like most people, the police made me nervous. I wasn't sure which upset me more, the attempted break-in or Detective Rice's unannounced visit.

"Striking," I agreed.

She rested a hand on one of the porch columns. "Nice to have someone living here again. Keeping the place up. Are you planning on staying or selling?"

"I haven't decided."

She nodded slowly, running her hand appreciatively along the rail. "Couple of good handymen in town. A fresh coat of paint and this place could be a decent B and B. What line of work are you in? A writer, like your father?"

I was jangling the house keys, but she didn't seem to get the message. If Detective Rice was looking to make a friend, or hoped I'd give her a deal on the house sale, she was out of luck.

"I'm not a writer," I answered curtly. Jangled my keys again, louder this time. "Again, thanks for—"

"Gotta be careful living so close to the woods," she said over me, turning sharply away from the direction of the coast to gaze out over the pines. "Are you familiar with the area? You might want to carry a can of bear mace. This time of year, the bears are getting ready for hibernation, gorging on all the food they can. They come down into town, sniff around people's property, cause all kinds of trouble. They can get aggressive, too." She gave me a long look. "You hear about the deaths?"

The keys went still in my hand.

"Last summer," she went on, seeing that she had my attention, "there was an aggressive bear. He'd been habituated by people leaving out birdseed and vegetables in their compost piles. Wasn't afraid of humans. He killed four people in a single season. A couple hikers from out of town and two local hunters. There was a massive search for him." She leaned back against the railing, arms folded over her chest as she slowly nodded. "A couple officers cornered him on the old quarry road just up the hill from here. I was the one who shot him, Remington eight-seventy."

Clearly, I wasn't going to be able to just unlock the door and go inside, though I wanted nothing more than to have Detective Rice off my porch with her talk about break-ins and bears and guns.

"It wasn't the bear's fault," she said, shaking her head. "But he couldn't be left alive. Too dangerous."

Lightning cracked over the trees, and the roll of thunder was so loud that it shook the porch and prodded the detective forward on her feet.

Grateful for the distraction, I quickly said, "I'm not a hiker."

She looked inclined to warn me again, but the rain started, and she squinted up at the dark sky and nodded. "Well, it's nice to meet you, Ms. Marbury." She handed me her card. "If you have any trouble, give me a call."

I stuffed the card into my pocket.

She took one more long look at the house. "Good bones," she repeated, nodding to herself. "Good luck fixing up the place. You'll get a lot for it. You can move back to New York, buy yourself a fancy condo."

She sauntered down the stairs, pausing by my trash cans to make sure they were the bear-resistant ones provided by the county, and then ducked into her car and cranked the engine.

My hands shook the entire time.

I never told her I lived in New York.

CHAPTER FIVE

The pups were hungry.

They'd been born a week ago. Premature pink little things that had crawled into the skin pouch around her belly, swelling it like a tumor as they grew. Their sharp canines came in even before their eyes opened. Their wet noses had nuzzled her hide, voracious, but when their snuffling mouths had latched onto her teats, they'd found no milk. Hellhound bitches were dry.

But the pups were so hungry.

She'd have to find warm milk somewhere. . . .

—From "Sweet Cream" in
Bedtime Stories for Monsters

✱

THE BELL ON the door to Lundie Bay Books chimed as I pushed it open. Entering a bookstore always reminded me of stepping into another world. It didn't matter where you started—you could be on cobblestone streets of a Greek island or the blustery sidewalk of Chicago's East Side, but the moment you stepped across the threshold, you might as well have been stepping into *every* bookstore. They all held the same feel, the same smells. Ink, paper—like dry tea leaves.

I glanced at the clock on my phone. Ten, right on time. I hadn't bothered to set my alarm that morning, as I'd stayed up the entire night working on the illustrations, just as I had for the previous nights, preparing for this meeting. Now, my palm was sweaty on my leather portfolio. My father's manuscript was tucked inside with its lingering smell of Werther's caramels and a handful of illustrations I'd finished with a light gray-blue wash, tying all the characters together with the same color palette.

"Haven!"

Kylie, behind the café bar, had spotted me first. She grinned as she wiped her hands on a towel and started around the counter, but then Catherine Tybee popped out from between two aisles, dressed in flowy black pants and a poppy-print shawl. Her sudden apparition made me jump.

"Oh! Catherine, you scared me."

Her eyes dropped to the portfolio clutched under my arm. She tugged on the shawl around her neck anxiously. "Is that it?"

"It is—" Before I finished answering, she pressed a hand against the small of my back and guided me down the aisle, away from the café area. I twisted around, frowning. "Aren't we meeting the other book club members—sorry, literary salon members—here?"

"I wouldn't dream of discussing your father's lost manuscript in the café. It's too public. So many busybodies in this town, not to mention aficionados of your father's works. If someone overheard what we were discussing, the news would be on the front page of *Publishers Weekly* by this evening."

I didn't think *Publishers Weekly* had paparazzi in Lundie Bay, but I didn't argue. Picking my battles.

"We'll speak in the back room," she continued. "We can talk freely there. It's the vault from when this building was a bank. The walls are so thick you wouldn't hear a bomb go off on the other side. The others are already here. Would you like something? Coffee? Tea?"

"A coffee, sure. Others? You mean more than Jonathan?"

An employee passed us with a pricing gun, and Catherine flagged him down and asked him to put in an order for us with Kylie at the café. Then she continued to steer me to the rear of the store. We passed the bathrooms and then entered a narrow hallway, made narrower by the cartons of books stacked head-height on both sides. The hallway finally opened up into an office. Here, it didn't smell like tea leaves and ink. A bookstore's back office lost the magic of the front portion of the store. There were too many signs of the mundane: dirty plates in the kitchenette sink, magnets on the humming refrigerator, cat-hair-covered coats draped on chairs. A wide worktable was filled with discount stickers and Bubble Wrap. An employee sat in a threadbare old swivel chair, reading a magazine and munching on a muffin. She didn't look up as Catherine ushered me through.

"A Wells Fargo," Catherine explained, motioning to the ugly, corporate green carpet. "We had to work with the existing building. Very expensive to renovate. Anyway, the vault is just here. We use it as a break room unless there's a staff meeting."

I thought of the girl with her muffin, who must have been kicked out of the room.

I barely had time to admire the antique vault door with its gleaming clockwork parts before Catherine led me inside the small chamber, barely more than a storage closet, with a slew of cell phone chargers plugged in one outlet and some purses and backpacks piled in a corner. Two people sat at a card table, paper cups of coffee in front of them. They stood at my entrance.

One was an older man with a shock of white hair and beard, dressed in a wool sweater, looking like a gentleman fisher straight out of an L.L.Bean catalog. The other man was younger, just a few years older than me, and wore a crisp white shirt with the kind of novelty bow tie that was meant to convey his quirkiness. I couldn't make out the pattern. LEGO bricks? I bet he was wearing "fun" socks, too.

Catherine gave a mock bow. "May I present our collection of misfits, the Ink Drinkers."

The older man immediately took my hand, giving it a strong shake. "Haven, such a pleasure. I'm Jonathan Tybee. I don't believe our paths ever crossed at any of your father's events. Wonderful to have you back in town."

The younger man, grinning a little goofily, was more deferential. "I'm Ronan Young," he said in a rush. "I oversee the library research department at Bainbridge University. Have you been? It's such a pretty drive, all along the coast the whole way, and a short ferry ride. I'd be happy to give you a tour of the library sometime. We've recently established your father's private collection there, you know. Anyway, it's such a pleasure to meet you. I so enjoyed getting to know your father—I'm sorry for your loss."

The room grew quiet except for one of the plugged-in phones, which beeped gratingly every thirty seconds or so. My father's ghost might as well have been hanging on a hook with the backpacks. If it wasn't for him—and his death—I'd have no reason to interact with any of these people.

Jonathan Tybee's eyes fell to the portfolio under my arm and he cleared his throat, breaking the tension. He sank into his folding chair and motioned to the one opposite him. "Please. Join us. That chair was your father's on the occasions that we met here. We usually gathered at Malice House—the library, of course—but after events in the shop, we'd meet here for simplicity's sake. It would be an honor to have you take his place."

It was only a folding chair, like all the others, but I felt like I was sitting on a dead man's throne.

I glanced at the vault door, not liking the idea of being closed inside like a tomb. Catherine must have read the apprehension on my face. She gave a small laugh. "Oh, the vault hasn't been closed in a decade. Hinges totally rusted. But don't worry, even with it open we won't be overheard. Ah! Kylie, thank you."

Kylie made a brief appearance to hand me a coffee, her eyes going to the three eager academics warily, then settling on me. She didn't look like she envied me.

"So you've kept up your . . . salon?" I asked, sipping the coffee once it was just us again.

Ronan's gleaming eyes dimmed. "No, unfortunately. After your father passed, we just didn't have the motivation. He was the heart and soul of the Ink Drinkers. The whole thing was his idea. I think he was bored up there, all alone, in Malice House. A mind as brilliant as his craves companionship, needs stimulation. He sought us out, starting with Catherine and Jonathan, and they were kind enough to pass along my name as the fourth member."

Catherine smiled benevolently from across the table.

"It's quite a drive from the university, isn't it?" I asked.

He balked. "Not even two hours if there's no traffic. And I confess, I get a little tired of the hustle and bustle there, all the students. I'm always happy for the excuse to come to Lundie Bay."

"Our salons were *legendary*." Jonathan leaned back in his folding chair, and I could picture him in the library's leather recliner, glass of Scotch in hand, as the fireplace threw shadows over his face while he and my father discussed obscure Portuguese poets. His striking beard gave him a sort of permanent scowl. I imagined that he'd been a match for my father's wit.

"The conversations we had . . ." Jonathan trailed off, shaking his head in fond memory. "When he spoke, you listened, because you knew that everything you thought you knew was about to shift on a seismic level."

I took another sip of coffee and fought the urge to roll my eyes. All my life, I'd heard people speak about my father like this, like he was some sort of literary guru instead of a guy who fell asleep and started snoring every time that he tried to meditate.

Jonathan laughed softly to himself at some secret memory. "Remember our discussion about Hesse's take on suicide not as an act of despair but a symbol of transcendence? The death of youth to prepare for the afterlife of middle age?"

Ronan nodded thoughtfully. "That was before his mind started to slip. The next week he didn't remember any of—"

Catherine slid her hand across the table, her elegant ring tapping loudly as she cleared her throat to silence him from talking about my father's decline.

Ronan went quiet.

Dachshunds. That was the pattern on his bow tie.

"It's fine," I started, but before I could say more, Catherine pressed her hands on the table with a dramatic flair.

"Enough about the past. Haven, we are all dying to see what you've brought."

A hush fell over the old bank vault. Jonathan toyed with his coffee cup, his unintentional scowl deepening. Slowly, I set the portfolio on the table and undid the leather tie. I'd stacked the pages of *Bedtime Stories for Monsters* on top with my illustrations in a manila folder underneath.

Suddenly, I felt like the room was too hot. There wasn't much ventilation in the vault even with the door open.

I could change my mind about the illustrations, I told myself. *I didn't have to show them.*

But when would I get another chance like this?

"Thank you for agreeing to meet with me," I said. "I'm sure Catherine told you about what I found. I think a lot of publishers could be interested in this and it isn't the sort of thing I want to handle casually. I'd appreciate your advice about particular imprints or editors who would best know what to do with it."

As soon as I flopped open the leather portfolio, the three of them leaned in as though pulled forward by an invisible string. They marveled at the manuscript like it was a gleaming oracle instead of just torn notebook paper with a coffee stain in the corner of page one.

"It's not like his other books," I explained. "It's a collection of short stories set in an interconnected world. It's called *Bedtime Stories for Monsters*."

A ripple passed between the Ink Drinkers. I could feel it in the way they almost intentionally didn't look at one another, and I suddenly got the odd sensation that they had discussed this new find at length among themselves before this meeting. They might have even come up with a strategy about how they'd approach the opportunity. How they'd *handle* me. Feeling a rush of protectiveness, I covered the pages with my hands.

Ronan must have sensed my anxiousness. He gave me a gentle smile and tented his hands, boyish excitement playing on his face. "May I see it?"

At my hesitation, he added, "It's all right. I've been trained as an archivist. I promise the manuscript is safe with me. I've come prepared." He removed a pair of white cotton gloves from his briefcase. I instantly felt guilty that I'd been handling the manuscript for the last week so carelessly, contaminating it with the oils from my fingers, hand lotion, and possibly a little spilled wine.

"Catherine said you found it in the attic?" he asked.

"Yes, locked in a drawer." I carefully slid over the yellowed pages, anxious not to have them more than a few inches out of my grasp. "I think they might be some of his early stuff from before he was published."

Ronan pored over the pages, inspecting the paper itself. He shook his head. "This is inexpensive paper. It oxidizes quickly, especially in a climate like this. I'm guessing the attic you found them in isn't climatized?"

"Right."

He glanced at Catherine and Jonathan. "They're four, maybe five years old."

I sat back in surprise. "That's all? He wrote these just a few years ago?" I thought of how my father had begun to lose his mind in those last few years, rambling about demons and hiding toast under the bed.

There was no point keeping that fact from the Ink Drinkers. Unlike his New York publishing contacts, they'd been around to witness his descent.

"That's when his dementia started," I said, echoing what we were all thinking.

Catherine made a small sound of agreement.

Jonathan slid the portfolio to his side of the table. He began reading the top page, eyes skimming over my father's handwriting. He paused where the writing slanted drastically to the left, the text growing loopy and unhinged.

I chewed on my lip and asked, "Does it make a difference when the manuscript was written? Or if he was in his right mind when he wrote it? The stories are different from his other works, but they're good. They aren't nonsense. Just . . . strange."

Jonathan paused while reading the introduction to look up. "I don't know, Haven."

I slumped back, feeling ill.

Ronan said more reassuringly, "All it means is that I'll need time with the manuscript. I need to compare the writing with other samples so I can authenticate the handwriting. That just a formality, of course—we take your word that it's his handwriting. But a publisher will require verification. The university's lawyers can help us ensure that this is a true Marbury original."

"And it doesn't matter that these stories are, well . . ."

He raised his eyebrows expectantly.

"Batshit crazy?" I finished.

His laugh was boyish. "If it's a Marbury original, it could be a recipe for banana pudding and still sell hundreds of thousands."

I relaxed back into my chair, feeling a little better.

Catherine leaned forward. "And the rest?"

I jerked upright, confused. "The rest?"

Her eyes went to the manila envelope under the yellowed pages. "Did you find something else? Another manuscript?"

"Oh."

It was now or never. I knew that if I slunk back to Malice House without having shown them my artwork, I'd be berating myself all night, probably after drinking myself sick. Malice House was so heavy with silence, yet I didn't feel alone there at all. Too many ghosts, and the only way out from under them was to get my own name out there, demand recognition for my own talent.

My palms itched, urging me to open the manila envelope. *Show the sketches. Let them breathe.*

I summoned my father's astounding ability to bullshit—surely, I'd inherited some of it—and said, "There is more. It's something I'm rather excited about, actually. The characters in these stories are practically demanding to be drawn. The way my father writes them, they almost leap off the paper already. Imagine if we did something that's never been done before within the Marbury opus: a fully illustrated volume. It makes sense when you think about it. The stories themselves are short, more of a novella length all together, so the publisher will need to flesh them out to justify a hefty price tag for the book. I'm an artist myself." I paused, clearing my throat. It was surprisingly easy to channel my father's magnificent ego. "And it's almost too perfect. Amory Marbury's posthumous stories illustrated by his daughter. A father-daughter collaboration from beyond the grave. The publicity hook alone is gold."

I don't know what kind of reaction I'd been expecting. To be honest, I hadn't really thought through the part where I'd show them my work. I knew I was pushing it with the talk of a publicity angle—an unpublished Marbury would sell just fine without me—but whatever I'd expected, it wasn't the look they gave me.

I might as well have tossed a lit match into dry pine needles.

Ronan blinked anxiously, almost a tic. Catherine opened her mouth to speak a few times, and then glanced at her ex-husband and took a deep breath. I wondered again what they had schemed before speaking with me, if this had somehow upset their plan, if I was wrong to trust them at all.

More forcefully, I continued, "Of course, my father's manuscript is my property, so I can sell it however I like, to whoever I like. I'm sure *some* publisher will be interested in a father-daughter pairing."

Catherine pressed a hand to her chest as though I'd misunderstood. "Haven, of course! It's a brilliant idea. I just don't think any of us were expecting this! I had *no idea* you were an artist. You wanted our advice on publishers and, well, this changes the situation substantially. You'll need to find a publisher with a reputation for illustrated works and an outstanding art department. . . ." Trailing off, she looked to her ex-husband for help, but he had his arms folded tightly.

Ronan saved me. "May we see the drawings?"

I couldn't very well say no now. I opened the manila envelope and slid out the stiff watercolor papers. I'd included only the illustrations I felt most confident about. The rest—the really strange ones—I'd stuffed into a different folder in my canvas shoulder bag.

Ronan didn't take off his gloves to flip through them, as though my sketches were just as valuable as my father's long-lost manuscript, and it softened me to him. He adjusted his glasses as he studied the watercolor-and-ink portrait of the Harbinger. In the story, the Harbinger got his name because he was the minder of monsters, or, at least, the one who got along with most of them the best. Some of the demons, like Pinchy, had no more sense than an oversized crustacean and had to be cleaned up after. The murders hidden. The corpses thrown into lakes or burned. That was the Harbinger's job.

Catherine and Jonathan watched carefully as Ronan flipped through the rest of the illustrations and, at last, closed the portfolio.

He took off his gloves.

The silence stretched. In the vault, with no windows and no clocks, it was impossible to keep track of time. I started to feel ill at ease.

"They're just preliminary sketches—" I started, already kicking myself for buckling under their stares.

"Is this all of the characters you've drawn? These three?" Ronan's voice had changed, wasn't quite as warm.

I hesitated before deciding not to tell them about the rudimentary sketches tucked into my bag's inner pocket, unfinished and raw. "I . . . haven't had time to do all the characters," I lied. "I thought this would be enough of a sample to show a publisher . . ."

"It's enough," Catherine said. There was an edge to her voice I didn't like. She wasn't smiling anymore.

I recognized that look on her face, and it turned my stomach. I knew what she was about to say. I'd heard it so many times before, from so many professors and art directors. I closed my eyes as she took a deep breath and launched into it.

"Haven, I certainly don't want to discourage you. Your artwork . . . well, it's fine, but it isn't right for this project. Your father was a Pulitzer-winning author. His readers simply won't accept these . . . doodles."

A dusting of static descended over my head. I could feel crimson heat spreading up my cheeks.

"I'm afraid, in a purely professional capacity," Jonathan added, "I have to agree with my ex-wife. I'm no art critic, so I won't make a judgement on your . . . talent. But as a rule, publishers don't want illustrated editions. There are the costs to consider, the added expenses of color printing . . ."

He stared at me expectantly as he so boldly dashed my dreams.

Ronan patted my hand kindlier, as though he knew they were ripping my heart out. "Not everyone has to make a career out of their hobby," he offered. "It's fine to make art simply for art's sake. Draw because you love it. Or whatever expression your creativity takes. Have you thought about pottery?"

Suddenly, I wanted out of there. I felt so stupid with my *doodles*.

Stupid that this man and his stupid bow tie had to soften the blow by suggesting I smash around fucking *clay*.

It had been a mistake to come to them. They were just as bad as my father's New York contacts—just as snobbish, looking down on anything with a whiff of genre.

Cheeks burning, I reached for my portfolio, but Catherine rested her hands on it before I could get out of there.

"Wait, Haven. I can see we've upset you, and that wasn't our intention. You asked for our advice and we're simply giving it. I think we forgot that we aren't speaking to your father. He was so direct, you know, he always wanted feedback without minced words. It wasn't a bad idea that you had, it just wasn't right for this. Leave the manuscript with Ronan so he can authenticate it. And your pictures . . ." She looked at her ex-husband with something akin to desperation. "Jonathan, maybe you could scan them and send them to someone from your imprint's old art department? Get a second opinion? We aren't art critics, as Jonathan pointed out. Maybe we have no idea what we're talking about."

I didn't like her hands all over my portfolio, but I could hardly wrestle it from her without looking like a crazy person. If they thought I was going to leave it with them after they'd bashed my artwork to within an inch of its life, they were even more delusional than my late father.

I'd cold-query literary agents. I'd call up my dad's former editors. I could even self-publish it. I didn't need the Ink Drinkers.

Besides, there was always Kylie's offer to consider—forego traditional publishing entirely. Sell the manuscript and my illustrations as a digital asset and maintain complete control of the entire process.

I grabbed the other end of the portfolio. There was a moment when I thought Catherine might actually wrestle me for it, but she let go with a tight smile.

I stood, the cheap folding chair squeaking beneath me, and held out a demanding hand for Ronan to give me the manuscript. He did so, hesitantly.

"Thanks," I muttered tightly, holding the pages close to my chest. "I think I'll go in a different direction."

"Haven . . ." Catherine called, but I ignored her.

I felt dazed, almost drunk, as I stumbled past the girl still eating the muffin into the narrow hallway lined with boxes of books.

"Haven!" Ronan ran after me. I got a glimpse of his socks—flamingos—and felt like I might throw up.

"Sorry, I have to go. It was nice to meet you," I called over my shoulder, not meaning a word of it.

The front of the bookstore was a welcome sight, even if just for the presence of its front door—an exit. Kylie typed away at her laptop in the empty café as I stumbled past a display for *Bodies of Water.* She gave me a questioning look, but I shoved open the door without pause and ran to my car.

On the drive home, the fog was even thicker than before, eating up the road just a few feet ahead of my lights. I felt woozy. *The stuffy vault. That stupid bow tie. Their smug faces.* How dare they suggest my father handled criticism better than I did. He *hated* criticism. He'd gotten editors fired from their jobs for the mildest comments. The worst was Ronan's painfully transparent attempts to make me feel better . . . calling my work a hobby . . . suggesting I take up *pottery*!

I couldn't help but open my portfolio where it sat in the passenger seat to look at my illustrations again. To verify that they weren't utter shit. That the Ink Drinkers were wrong, that I *did* have talent—

I only saw the person for a second before slamming into him.

I'd tried to press the brakes, but I hadn't been fast enough. He'd come out of the fog like he was made of it, standing in the middle of the road.

Skidding to a stop, I gripped the steering wheel like a vise and stared with wide eyes at the fog outside. The wipers swished back and forth, squeaking. The man must have fallen because I didn't see him anymore.

I killed a man.

I'm going to prison.

Unless I drive off . . .

A curse came up from the road.

Shit. I scrambled to open my car door and stumble outside. The fog lights shone on a man cradling his foot by the ditch. A stack of letters was scattered on the wet ground around him. He hadn't been in the center of the road, I realized. He'd been checking his mail, and I must have veered off the pavement. At least the mailbox had taken the worst of the impact, not him.

Hazily, the name on the overturned box registered.

Kahn.

Oh great.

I'd almost killed my wealthy neighbor, the one who kept secrets in the trunk of his car and lit three a.m. bonfires in the woods behind his house.

CHAPTER SIX

*In Malice, night was long, sundown was fraught, and day was short
and terrifying. When sunrise came, most things would slink back into
their hovels to digest whatever they'd managed to get into their bellies
as they awaited the next cool wash of night. Few things awoke during
sunlight hours, but beasts of sun were the ones to fear the most.*

—From "Beasts of Sun" in
Bedtime Stories for Monsters

I SANK TO my knees next to my neighbor. Reaching for my phone,
I hesitated. But what choice did I have? "I'll call an ambulance."

He shook his head, still clutching his ankle. "No, I'm fine."

I tried to assess the situation. What would a lawyer tell me to do?
Offer assistance? Deny blame? I settled on something in between. "I
think I should take you to the hospital."

He scoffed.

The road wasn't pooled with blood, it was true. His clothes weren't
torn. His limbs weren't mangled, except for a deep gash on the back of
one hand. The mailbox, though, was totaled.

I insisted, "Let me help you up. Or I can drive you back up to your house. We should"—I swallowed back a wave of uncertainty—"exchange insurance information?"

He laughed. There was an edge to it, but it wasn't aimed at me. Instead, his gaze scanned my body, making sure *I* wasn't hurt. For the first time, I looked closely at his face. My neighbor, Mr. Kahn, was in his late thirties. He didn't look like any tech investor I'd ever seen. No Patagonia vest, no button-up shirt. He was wearing black jeans and an oversized flannel shirt. I was getting less rich-nerd vibes and more ER doctor just off a forty-eight-hour call, shadows under his eyes and a vein of exhaustion that marred his otherwise handsome features. His complexion was on the darker side—he might have been of Middle Eastern or Southeast Asian descent, though I wasn't sure about his last name—and he had buzzed dark hair and the kind of eyelashes I'd have killed for.

"Not worth the hassle." He tried to stand despite my protestations. "Really, I'm fine. It's barely even a twisted ankle. Tell you what, I have no idea where my bandages are. Help me patch up this cut on my hand and pour me a double Scotch, and we'll call it even."

So, not a doctor then.

His eyes went to my gate just down the road. "You're his daughter, aren't you?"

A muscle twitched in my jaw. "Haven." I stared at him uneasily. In all my visits to Lundie Bay, I'd certainly have remembered if we'd met. "You knew my father?"

He gave a noncommittal shrug. "Enough to know he had excellent taste in Scotch." He toed the broken mailbox with his family name. "I'm Rafe."

"Well, Mr. Kahn, let me help you into the car."

Awkwardly, I wrapped a hand around his back, afraid to bruise him further and get sued double. He hobbled to the passenger seat, where I shoved my portfolio and laptop case and canvas bag into the back seat to make room. I had to lean hard against the busted door to get it to close. *Wonderful.* Something that was going to cost me even more money to fix.

The drive from his mailbox to my property was almost comically short. As I entered the code to open the gate, I glanced sidelong at him, remembering the bonfire from my first night back at Malice House. It was probably impolite to ask a man I'd almost killed what he'd been burning in the middle of the night.

"You're sure you don't want to go to the hospital?"

"I'd rather die on the side of the road. Hospitals around here are more likely to kill you than cure you." He paused before flashing me a guilty look. "Sorry. I wasn't thinking. I heard how your father died . . . an infection he caught in the hospital, right?"

I gave him a tight smile. My dad had been involuntarily committed to the memory care unit for study after a bad fall and had never left again. "That's what they tell me."

We went over a bump as we passed through the gate. He winced and clutched his ankle. I cringed. The last thing I needed after the hellacious morning I'd had with the Ink Drinkers was a well-lawyered neighbor suing me. I shot him a concerned smile.

Once I parked, I slung my bag over my shoulder and helped him hobble up the porch stairs and into the living room, where I urged him to rest on the sofa. A few drops of blood fell onto the fabric and he cursed and started to apologize, but I waved away the concern. His health was worth more than an old sofa.

"What's higher on your list of priorities?" I asked. "Booze or stopping the bleeding?"

"Blood can wait. I'll take the booze."

On the way to the kitchen, I shrugged my bag off onto the hallway bench. The portfolio fell partway out, and the anger and embarrassment from the meeting at Lundie Bay Books returned in a rush. On impulse, I snatched up the illustrations I'd shown the Ink Drinkers, crumpled them, and shoved them in the wastebasket.

I never wanted to look at those drawings again. All the characters I'd poured my soul into only to have a glorified book club tell me I was a hack.

In the kitchen, I grabbed the Scotch and a clean towel, then came back to the living room.

"Here you go. It's worth a little lost blood, I promise." I poured him a glass. "I'll see if I can find something upstairs to bandage that hand."

He wrapped the towel around the cut, then lifted the glass. "Much obliged, Ms. Marbury."

"Haven."

His eyes sparked over the rim of the glass. So velvety brown to evoke the fur of some soft, small animal. The same color as his band shirt beneath the flannel, which looked simple enough, though I guessed came from some couture nouveau-grunge designer with a Sorbonne degree.

I jogged up the stairs and dug around in the medicine cabinet until I found a bottle of hydrogen peroxide and Band-Aids. Every muscle in my body was aware of the stranger in the house. The possibility that he'd sue me—not that I was worth anything except, maybe, the lost manuscript. And then there was simply the odd sensation of having another breathing body under the same roof, especially one who was rather nice to look at. Even when I'd last visited my father, he'd had one foot in the grave, only half of him clinging to this world. As unnerving as Rafe Kahn's presence was, it was also oddly comforting. If there were ghosts here, at least for the time being, I wouldn't face them alone.

When I returned downstairs, I was alarmed to find the living room empty. I searched the powder room and the library, then found Rafe standing in an alcove of the hallway, his hand wrapped in the towel.

He held my crumpled illustrations in his other hand. He must have fished them out of the wastebasket. He was looking at them with his head cocked strangely.

"Oh. Those are trash." I grabbed them out of his good hand before he, too, advised me to consider ceramics.

"Did you draw them?"

I paused. "Yes." I was about to stuff them back into the trash can when he raised his eyebrows, interested, but I continued cautiously, "I'm an illustrator."

When he didn't laugh, I added guardedly, "My father saw the world in words. I see it in images." Then I cringed. "That sounded pretentious, didn't it?"

He took one of my hands, and the unexpected touch shocked me so much that I let him. "That explains this." It took me a moment to realize he was referring to the ink staining my fingers. He released my hand casually as though he often went around clutching neighbor's appendages. "And that pays the bills?"

"No. Monsters pay my bills." At his questioning look, I picked up a VHS cassette from a small pile on the hallway bench. Rob had written *Sophia's Third Grade Piano Recital* on it in purple Sharpie with hearts in place of the *i* dots, but it was actually a film called *The Silent Screams of Natty Gill.* I waved it in the air. "All these cassettes are horror movies. I recap them for a guy I met online. It isn't much of an income, either, but it's something. Everyone's hungry for scares: This one is about a girl possessed by a demonic force who sets fire to an entire mental health ward. All in all, it's one of the tamer ones." I tossed it back on the stack.

He scratched the back of his neck. "VHS?"

"Rob's kind of a conspiracy theorist. He doesn't trust modern technology. All his movies are super dark and obscure. A lot of foreign films, a lot that could probably get him arrested. So he records them on old VHS cassettes and sends them through the regular mail. Kind of a 'hidden in plain sight' thing. No one's going to be suspicious of some grandkid's piano recital." I shrugged. "Anyway, I haven't gotten internet installed yet, so no streaming anything for me anyway. Now sit."

I held up the bottle of hydrogen peroxide and motioned in the direction of the living room. He wouldn't let me help him out of his torn shirt, though he agreed to let me attempt a temporary bandage. He folded up the cuff of his sleeve so I could get to his hand. Even marred with blood, his tan skin made me realize how long it had been since I'd been this close to any man since Baker.

"And who exactly is the audience for your recaps?" His voice was as velvety as his eyes.

I dabbed peroxide onto a clean dishrag and then pressed it against the gash on his hand, expecting him to flinch as it bubbled, but he barely seemed to notice. "There's a subculture of people who read horror movie summaries online. The darker, the better. My boss calls them Bunny Lurks. I guess they can't stomach actually watching the movies, or else they can't get their hands on the films themselves, but they want to know what happens. It's like . . . an addiction to seeing how dark the world can be. I get paid more than most recappers because I can stomach the stuff most people can't. I don't *like* gore and violence, but, I don't know, it doesn't affect me. It doesn't bother me to watch."

"No nightmares?"

I kept my eyes on the blood. "Not from horror films."

I slapped on some gauze and started winding the bandage. He seemed to find my lackluster bedside manner amusing as his gaze drifted back to the crumpled illustrations I'd tossed on the table.

"Why trash those?" he asked. "They're brilliant."

A ripple of pleasure ran along my skin, but I quickly shook it off. I was still so hurt from the Ink Drinkers that I didn't dare expose my fresh wounds for more damage. I finished wrapping the bandage around his hand and inspected my shoddy work. No one had ever accused me of being a good nurse. Baker had gotten a black eye once, and when I'd come at him with a frozen bag of peas, he'd nearly run out the front door to avoid my care.

"Unfortunately," I mumbled, "you're alone in that opinion." I started dabbing the damp towel on the bloodstains on the sofa.

He cocked his head in an inquiring way.

I sighed. "It doesn't matter . . . I was hoping I'd get my first art contract from those drawings but got rejected. Once again." I gave a wry smile. "The life of an artist. Constant rejection."

"Really? Well, I'd like to see more of your work." He sounded so sincere that I honestly didn't know what to say.

I hesitated for more than one reason. First, he'd finished his drink and was no longer bleeding, so he had no reason to stay. Second, I was a stranger who'd nearly killed him. Third, for as much as I wanted my artwork out in the world, I was terrified to *actually* show it to people. Look at what had happened that morning. What if after a closer second look, Rafe Kahn laughed in my face, too? But I couldn't think of any explanation to get out of it that wouldn't paint me as a psycho with something to hide.

"My studio is upstairs," I said haltingly. "On the sleeping porch." I waved in the vague direction of the stairs as though it would be too much trouble to walk that far.

He stood, waiting expectantly.

I led the way awkwardly, all too aware of his presence behind me. His limp was already improving. He was tall enough that even a few stairs back he almost matched my height. He smelled like woodsmoke, and I thought again of the bonfire, wondering what kept a man like him awake.

We passed the large bed, which I'd convinced myself to start sleeping in again a few uncomfortable nights in the guest bed, and I blanched to see my skimpy pajamas and yesterday's lacy bra splayed out on the sheets; Rafe raised a curious eyebrow but said nothing. When we reached the sleeping porch, I looked at everything there with a worried, fugitive glance. The booze-ringed teacup. The almost-empty Scotch bottle, significantly more incriminating. The sketches scattered on the floor. My father's oversized sweater hanging from the back of the chair. I tried to see it all with a stranger's eyes. A stranger like him, who could afford anything, who could buy a gallery's worth of artwork only to keep it boxed up in an attic if he so chose.

"There." I was chewing on my thumbnail, my voice barely audible. He flipped through the sketchbook I indicated, whose silver binder rings were strained from being stuffed to the gills with decades of loose-leaf art pieces I'd slid between the pages for safekeeping. He stopped at the last few drawings, the wolves I'd worked on in New York as a sample for a children's book.

He handled each page with care. "I don't know what to say," he said at last. "These wolves look like they're about to step off the page. They're . . . *incredible*, Haven. Truly." He glanced for a moment at the woods beyond the porch screen, and I almost started to ask what he was looking at, but then he frowned and pulled out one of the unfinished sketches tucked between the pages. It was the Hellhound, the demonic dog from "Sweet Cream" with curving horns and square eyes like a goat. "And . . . this?"

"That is . . . something new I'm working on," I admitted awkwardly. "I was playing around with it last night."

He slid out the pages and flipped to the next one. It was a drawing of the Harbinger from "Beasts of Sun," the one where his long hair curtained his face and a scar marred his bare chest. I fought the urge to rip it out of his hand. My drawings seemed juvenile now, like fan art, and I didn't want my attractive neighbor to think I stayed up all night drawing shirtless men.

I laughed self-consciously. "I might have had too much to drink."

But he didn't seem to be listening. He picked up another sketch, this one of the Witch of Went from "Kaleidoscope," draped half in men's clothing and half in a gauzy black skirt with mud stains at the hem. He studied it even longer.

"You don't have to be polite," I blathered. "Like I said, I was just playing around. The wolves and forest artwork, that's for a possible picture book—"

"The wolves are good," he interrupted, then held up the illustrations of the other characters. "But these are *something*."

I paused, taken aback. "They're early sketches," I protested.

He shrugged off my humility.

"There's something here," he said again. Still studying the illustrations, he said, "There's a story here, isn't there? These characters are connected to one another. They share a world. A narrative. I can see it in the way you've given them life." He fixed a curious look on me as though just having realized something. "They mean something to you, too."

I hefted a shoulder. "Cash in the bank, hopefully." I wasn't about to tell him about zoning out while drunk only to discover I'd drawn the opposite of my ex-husband as some kind of sexy fever-dream art therapy session.

Now it was his turn to look slightly embarrassed. "Yeah, of course." He ran a hand along the back of his neck. "Sorry, I'm not a collector or anything like that. I just know what I like when I see it."

I smiled and accepted the drawings that he held out to me, but he didn't let go of them immediately.

His dark eyes searched mine. "Keep drawing, Haven. Your father had a gift. So do you. The kind of gift that demands to be shared."

CHAPTER SEVEN

The Night Market was only held for one out of the sixty hours of darkness, appearing amid the fog like a mirage of threadbare tents and wooden stalls and smelling of sandalwood. The Witch of Went was its mistress. She alone could make the market appear. Buyers stumbled out of the woods, disoriented, telling tales of circling back on themselves for hours until suddenly finding themselves in front of her stall. Whatever dark desire they sought, she had a cordial for it.

A heavyset young man with robin's-red hair lingered at her stall. "How much for a fuck?"

"That's not what I sell."

He gave a dark chuckle. "I wouldn't pay an ugly thing like you a cent. I meant how much would you pay me?"

The witch studied the red-haired man closely. He couldn't be older than twenty. He probably hadn't had time to damage his organs too much with drink and disease.

She smiled sweetly. "Come to my house tonight. The woods will show you the way."

—From "Kaleidoscope" in
Bedtime Stories for Monsters

RAFE'S WORDS LIT a fire in me. After the catastrophic meeting with the Ink Drinkers, this was the push I needed: Someone, even a stranger, to believe in me. Confidence renewed, I lost track of the days, drawing late into the lost hours of night as I completed more drawings of my father's characters, pausing only to scrounge quick meals from whatever I could find in the pantry, loathe to leave the house and go into town unless absolutely necessary. I even returned to the half-finished sketches of the crustacean monster called Pinchy, although, after the toast incident, I wasn't exactly fond of anything that had to do with the space beneath beds.

Back aching from hunching over my desk, I stood up to stretch and found myself peering through the screen into Rafe's yard, scanning the darkness for more bonfires, but the inky night was undisturbed. I hadn't seen him since the day of the accident. Maybe he had taken painkillers and passed out for days—I wouldn't have blamed him. If I had health insurance, I'd have stocked up on sleeping pills a long time ago.

Yawning, I debated going to bed, though I felt anxious at the thought of the empty sheets. Now that I was thinking about Rafe again, it only reminded of what it felt like to share a space with another person. Baker had always gone to sleep before me so he could rise at four a.m. to work out with his Instagram-famous personal trainer. I had become used to sliding into an already warm bed with the familiar weight of another person by my side, the rhythmic sound of him breathing. At Malice House, my father's bed was an ancient, groaning thing set so uncomfortably high that I had to actually *climb* in. And a chill never left it; no matter how well I sealed the windows with duct tape, a draft still snuck in.

Still, eventually, the lure of the bed won. As I stared at the ceiling, thoughts chased one another through my head. I had the illustrations now, but what to do with them? The Ink Drinkers were a dead end. I'd sooner bury myself alive under copies of *Other/None Other* than crawl back to them for help. I could still picture their faces. Catherine and Jonathan looking so smug, Ronan's pitying smile.

I'd cold-email agents, then. There had to be dozens of online agent databases I could search to find someone who represented both authors and illustrators. Tomorrow, I'd head into town to use the Wi-Fi at one of the coffee shops.

I fell into a restless sleep for a few hours, waking at the sharp poke from a graphite pencil that I'd forgotten in my pajama pocket. It was light outside. The bookshelf clock read 11:00 a.m. I wiped off my face, threw my hair into a ponytail, stuffed my laptop into its case, and grabbed my canvas bag.

Other than a few bikers and a police cruiser heading into town, Cliffside Drive was quiet as I drove past the Kahn house. Then again, the house was designed to be private—set back amid the trees, windows glazed with a reflective material, parking and garage around back so that from the road the house was only a wall of windows and timbers made to mimic the forest. It was only at night, with windows lit up, that the house announced its presence.

I slowed to a stop on the side of the road when I saw the mailbox at the end of the drive.

The broken pole had already been replaced with a new one. There was no sign of Thursday's accident except for some muddy tire tracks veering off the road. I wondered if Rafe was the kind of man to roll up his sleeves and install a new mailbox himself or if he'd paid a handyman.

Was he home? I tried to tell myself I was only interested because I had to keep him from pursuing legal action against me, but the truth was I couldn't stop thinking about what he'd said about my illustrations. It wasn't just the compliments—compliments were passed around to artists like discount Halloween candy. But he'd sincerely seemed to have seen something in my illustrations. Something in *me*.

I fished a pen out of my bag and ripped the back off a fan mail envelope. A grin tugged my cheeks as I remembered Rafe's smile, his dark eyes with that slightly mocking look. I sketched him shirtless, like the Harbinger, repairing his mailbox in the mud.

I like your work, too, I wrote beneath the drawing.

As soon as I'd stuck the note in his freshly repaired mailbox and climbed back in my car, I wondered if I'd made a mistake. A flirty sketch could be read several ways. What had compelled me to draw it? He *was* my type, a head taller than me with a touch of irreverence in his humor. Or was it just because I wanted him to compliment me again?

Praise was just so damn addictive.

Town was quiet, again. The day was damp and gray, again. I walked the long way around the docks to avoid passing in front of Lundie Bay Books on the chance that Catherine might be there and see me. But I kept glancing over my shoulder, feeling paranoid. What would I say if I ran into her? There was another café a few blocks away in a converted fisherman's cottage. Inside was a cozy maze of small rooms filled with sagging sofas and high school kids sipping hot chocolate.

"Do you have Wi-Fi?" I asked the barista, a guy with a blond goatee who had to slide his headphones off to take my order and give me the internet password.

I wound my way to an empty back room with only three tables and opened my laptop. Muttering to myself, I began an online search for literary agents who represented both writers and illustrators.

"Oh!" a voice said.

It took me a moment to place Kylie standing in the doorway. I wasn't prepared to see her here, outside of the bookstore, while my head was away in New York.

"What, you don't like my coffee?" she teased.

I quickly closed my computer. "Oh. No, I just . . . wanted a change of scenery. You aren't working today?"

Again, I had that nagging feeling of being watched, and I glanced out the window. It was a small town, so it wasn't exactly shocking to run into her here, but I couldn't help but wonder if she'd seen me on the street and followed me.

She sank into a chair at the table next to mine and opened her own laptop. "My shift doesn't start until noon. I wanted a change of scenery, too." She suddenly frowned. "I'm really sorry about Dahlia. She worked for your father, didn't she?"

"Dahlia Whitney? What about her?"

Kylie's eyebrows rose in surprise. Then she swallowed measuredly. "Oh, I thought you would have heard by now. The police will probably be getting in touch with you soon. . . ."

I thought of Detective Rice standing on Malice House's porch, talking about old bones.

"Why?" There was alarm in my voice. "What happened?"

Kylie hesitated. Then, in a soft voice, she said, "Dahlia's dead."

I wasn't sure what to say. Dahlia Whitney? The housekeeper? Last I'd seen her, she'd been as spry and grumpy as ever. It came as a shock, though maybe it shouldn't have been. She had to be nearing seventy years old, and she'd had a stroke a few years ago—I remembered because I'd offered to come stay with my dad while she recovered but she'd only barked that she was fine and had been back at work two days later.

"I'm so sorry to hear that," I said, mind stumbling a little to process the news. "Was it another stroke?"

Kylie chewed on her bottom lip anxiously. She glanced over her shoulder at the open doorway as though someone might be there listening before she turned around and practically whispered, "She was murdered."

For a few moments, I could only blink. *Murder* wasn't a word that belonged in a cozy coffee shop. *Murder* was a word that lived in my father's books or cable news. Not that I had known Dahlia well enough to be personally affected by her death, but murder was, well, murder.

I leaned forward and whispered back, *"What?"*

Kylie nodded reluctantly. "It's been all over the news this morning."

"I don't watch the news," I said, still reeling. "There's no internet or cable set up at my . . . *What* happened?"

"They thought it was a car accident at first. Hit-and-run. Some tourists saw her lying on the side of the road late last night and called 911. But I guess it was pretty clear she was gone. Her head wasn't, like . . . entirely attached."

I stared at Kylie, mouth parted.

"The news called it an accident, but the tourists who found her were down at the Salty Bite this morning talking about it to anyone who would listen. Grisly stuff. They tried to do CPR on her before they realized she was dead—it was so dark out they didn't see her wounds. The guy said when they looked closer, her hands and feet were severed, too." Her voice dropped even lower. "And there was blood all over her clothes, which meant it happened while she was still alive."

I pressed my hand to my chest. *Severed head? What the fuck?*

Kylie blew out a puff of air. "Stuff like that doesn't happen in Lundie Bay."

I sank back in my seat. I felt terribly guilty for all the unkind thoughts I'd had about Dahlia when she'd shown me around the house and before that, over the years.

"Who do they think did it?" I asked.

Kylie shrugged.

I let out a long sigh, which abruptly stopped as a new worry hit me. "Why did you say the police will want to talk to me? Because she used to work for my dad?"

Kylie rubbed the back of her neck anxiously. "No, not exactly." She crossed her legs, then crossed them again the other way. "The stretch of road where she was found? It was Cliffside Drive. The scenic overlook with that great view of the Mayfelt Islands."

I knew immediately which pull-out she meant. It was less than a quarter of a mile from my gate. In fact, Malice House was the closest residence to that portion of the road, with only a strip of forest separating it from the sea bluffs.

"You didn't hear anything last night?" Kylie asked.

Guiltily, I thought of how much I'd had to drink. I probably wouldn't have heard a siren if it had been blaring ten feet away.

I shook my head.

"Well, really, be careful. The police are still calling it a suspected hit-and-run, but I don't see how that's possible. Maybe one or two appendages could be severed in a car accident, but *all* of them? No way. Especially not how the tourists described it, like it had been done by an ax or something. Pretty precise." She shuddered. "Are you sure you feel safe up there? I finish work at seven. I could come up. Keep you company."

"Oh, no, it's fine—"

"I'll bring pizza," she insisted. "We can dig around for more memorabilia to sell. Take your mind off Dahlia."

In my mental fog, I found myself nodding. Maybe it would be smart to have another person in the house. Even with the security fence and extra locks, there was still a murderer out there if the tourists' rumors were to be believed.

Kylie stood and gave me a sympathetic smile. "See you at seven."

I nodded vaguely and then spent the next hour poring over local news websites for any more information about the murder. Social media didn't really have anything. Like Kylie had said, official news was meager, and the articles were basically repeats of one another. They were still calling it a hit-and-run, and they'd released Dahlia's name but gave no details about the mutilations.

I sipped my coffee anxiously while reading the news, and before I knew it, looked down to find a paintbrush in one hand, bristles dampened with coffee, tracing anxious umber circles on my paper napkin.

I hadn't even been aware of reaching into my bag and grabbing the brush.

Get your shit together, Haven.

I got the next coffee to go.

CHAPTER EIGHT

Elin's father stormed out of the house and slammed the door. Her mother put on a new record to hide the sound of her sobbing. Elin sighed up toward the ceiling. None of this was her fault. She wouldn't have been expelled if Ms. Tucker hadn't gotten suspicious and found the knife in her backpack and the note threatening Micky Dallinger. She wasn't even really planning to kill Micky, probably.

The heat was insufferable. She kicked away the covers. Then, slowly, something else gave them a tug from the bottom of the bed. The sheets slid downward one inch at a time, exposing her bare arms and nightgown. Something at the foot of the bed was pulling the sheets off her.

Elin swung her feet off the side and touched one toe down to the braided rug. Some living thing skittered in the dark cavern beneath the mattress.

"What the hell?"

The rug was wet with slick, oyster-like glop.

—From "Extremities" in
Bedtime Stories for Monsters

●

ON THE DRIVE home, I kept checking the rearview mirror, unable to shake the feeling that I wasn't alone. Followed by Dahlia's ghost, maybe, or else some more corporeal threat. When I finally reached the gates to my house, I stopped the car abruptly.

The gates were open, and a familiar car waited in the driveway.

I squeezed the steering wheel and exhaled a *"Fuck."*

Detective Rice climbed out of her Dodge Charger as soon as I pulled in behind her. A male officer wearing a uniform got out the other side. Their doors slammed in unison, making me jump.

I switched off the local news station on the radio and took a few deep breaths before getting out myself. Detective Rice wasn't wearing her sunglasses today, and her eyes were bloodshot from what I assumed must have been an extremely difficult past twenty-four hours.

"Ms. Marbury."

"Detective Rice."

"I'm afraid I have upsetting news."

I squeezed my keys hard enough that their ridges bit into my palm. "About Dahlia Whitney?" I glanced at the other officer. "I heard."

She nodded as though this didn't surprise her. It was a small town, and small towns loved gossip. The male officer, whose boyish, clean-shaven face didn't fit with his thinning salt-and-pepper hair, began to circle my car, inspecting it casually without making it too obvious what he was doing.

Detective Rice pulled a notepad out of her jeans pocket. "Okay if we ask you some questions?"

I froze. "Um . . ."

She interrupted, "Why don't we go inside? It looks like rain."

I silently cursed under my breath—the heavy clouds overhead were on her side, urging us out of the open.

"Sure," I said tightly.

The police hovered too closely to my back as I unlocked the door. Inside, their eyes immediately drifted over the bookcases in need of dusting, empty wine bottles, the stack of VHS cassettes. The younger officer went to the table full of framed photographs, which had somehow fallen face down again, and began turning them over just as I had done my first day back.

"I heard that Dahlia was found close to here," I said, anticipating the line of questioning I was sure would follow. "I didn't hear anything last night, sorry. I was home, but working on a project with my headphones on."

That hadn't been true about the headphones, but it felt innocent enough. I *hadn't* heard anything.

Detective Rice paced the short length of the foyer, notepad in hand but not writing anything down. She seemed more curious about the knickknacks covering every flat surface than probing my recollections of the previous night.

"Did you see any cars coming or going around ten o'clock?" she asked in a perfunctory way.

"No. I was on the second-story porch, working, as I said. You can't see the road well through the trees."

"No one stopped by? No visitors?"

"It was just me."

She raised an eyebrow as though she doubted me, then pulled a black envelope out of her blazer pocket. "Do you have many visitors who know the gate code? I ask because this was tucked under your door knocker when we arrived."

Frowning, I grabbed the black envelope. Was it *legal* for police to take someone's mail? Granted, she hadn't opened it. The envelope was addressed to me, but only my name with no address, which meant someone had hand-delivered it to the front porch. Which also meant they'd gotten past the gate.

Instantly, I thought of the broken windows. The trespassers I'd assumed were just kids being dumb.

Detective Rice looked pointedly at the envelope, waiting.

Jaw clenched, I ripped open the envelope and pulled out a creamy white card. My pulse was doing strange things. Turning my back to the detective, my eyes devoured the note.

Believe it or not, I occasionally make myself useful with a post hole digger. The portrait is flattering, though I noticed that you left off the shoddy bandage job you did on my hand. Don't worry, I won't sue, but I might stop by for another drink.

—R

P.S. Don't you have a mailbox?

My shoulders eased as I turned around to face the officers. I held up the note with a dismissive shrug. "It's just from my neighbor. It's . . . an inside joke."

Detective Rice looked visibly disappointed by this news. She jotted something down on her notepad and then, scratching her nose, sighed.

"Right. Well, are there any security cameras on the property? There's a chance cameras might have caught something on the road or picked up movement if anyone crossed the grounds." She glanced toward the tree line as she muttered, "Or the woods."

I'd only been thinking of a car on Cliffside Drive going after Dahlia, not a person on foot. Now I had fresh reason to worry about the recent attempted break-ins.

I shook my head. "No cameras."

Detective Rice exchanged a look with the other officer, who had moved to the bookcase and now slid out a volume. He handed it to the detective wordlessly. She weighed it in her hand for a while and then held it up. "You've read *Feast of Flowers*?"

I started. A woman was *murdered*; why on earth . . .

"Yeah." The word stumbled out. "When I was a teenager. Why? What does my dad's book have to do with Dahlia?"

The officer returned to the bookshelf, running his hands along the spines, and I felt an unpleasant shiver at the way the two of them kept looking around like they were searching for something.

"Are you, like, a fan?" I asked.

It came out more confrontational than I'd intended. I couldn't imagine why else she'd be asking.

"No, no, nothing like that." Detective Rice seemed to realize her words might have offended me, so she added, "I'm not much of a reader in general. But it's been brought to our attention that there are some commonalities, for lack of a better word, between Dahlia Whitney's case and certain elements of this particular book your father wrote. I'm sorry to involve you, but I'm guessing that you're the closest thing we have to an expert on his works."

I blinked. I thought they'd come to question me because of the proximity of the murder to the house. Now it seemed that wasn't their true motive at all. I didn't like the feeling that Detective Rice held all the power, and I was just a plaything for her to poke at and see if she could make squeak.

"What kind of commonalities?" I asked warily.

Before she could answer, the radio hooked to her belt blared with a hiss of static. She snatched it up, listening to police-speak and numerical codes that meant nothing to me. But it must have meant something to them because she immediately handed me the copy of *Feast of Flowers* and shoved her notepad in her pocket.

"Let's continue this conversation," she said, distractedly. "I don't think we need to meet at the station. I just need some background information at this point. You still have my card?"

"Of—of course," I stammered, relieved at the interruption. "I'll call you."

"Good. I'll follow up if you *forget*." She paused, already moving toward the door. "I suggest you keep the doors locked." She slowed and the shadows caught her sunken eyes. Thoughtfully, she added, "It would make me nervous, living so close to a recent homicide. After the break-ins, too. You might consider returning to New York for a while. Taking a vacation. Getting away from Lundie Bay."

Her eyes met mine, and I wasn't sure what I read there. Fear? For me—or *of* me? If she was advising I leave town, she must not suspect me of having anything to do with the crime.

She nodded stiffly. "Have a good day, Haven."

I walked them to the door and watched as they climbed into their car and backed out of the driveway. The gate closed automatically behind them. I made a mental note that I needed to figure out how to change the gate code.

My hands were shaking as I closed the door. How long had it been since I'd had anything besides caffeine? In the kitchen, I made a quick cheese sandwich and washed it down with Chardonnay while re-reading Rafe's note on the counter. Once some food was in my belly and I'd calmed down from the police visit, I couldn't help but smile at his note. I'd be lying if I said a little flirtation wasn't welcome.

As rain pelted the windows, I settled in for the afternoon with one of the movies I'd been meaning to watch for Rob. *The Shadow of Us* was better than I'd expected. Right from the start, it was clearly more sophisticated than a typical jump-scare slasher. It opened on a thirtysomething woman jogging through the woods. It could have been the same Pacific Northwest forest right behind Malice House, which made me a little uneasy, thinking of Dahlia's body. *Severed head. Severed hands. Severed feet.* The movie camera kept cutting to a car driving along the coast, the angle obscuring who was behind the wheel. There was something wrong with the car—at first, it looked like a pristine luxury sedan, but as the camera zoomed around to the other side, it showed shattered windows, a hefty dent in the driver's side door, blood dripping from the tailpipe.

I made notes, jotting down the character's names and sequencing the events. The woman came home to find a stranger dead on her porch with a deer antler through his eye socket; different enough from recent events that I soon forgot all about Dahlia.

Afterward, it took me less than half an hour to write up a grisly synopsis I knew Rob's clients would salivate over. I was just finishing when the intercom buzzed, and I jumped and cursed aloud. For a moment, I barely knew where I was. Not my apartment—my father's house.

The intercom buzzed again, and I shoved myself to my feet, rushing over to the box beside the front door. I mashed the button.

"Yes?" My voice sounded strangely high-pitched.

For a moment, there was silence, then a familiar voice blasted over the speaker, "I've got the pizza!"

Shit. Kylie. I'd completely forgotten. Well, it was too late to turn her away, especially in the downpour outside, when it was obvious that I was home.

"I'll buzz open the gate," I called.

In another few moments, she was standing in the open door-way, smiling beneath her oversized raincoat hood. She held a damp pizza box.

"It's really coming down," I observed, hoping I didn't look too flustered.

She stomped her boots and handed me the pizza while she uncoiled herself from her jacket. She shook out her hair, then scrunched it back into shape. "Miserable, isn't it?"

This surprised me. Most people in Lundie Bay had come to accept, even love, the weather. *Meteorological Stockholm syndrome victims*, I'd called them to Baker.

"You must not be from here," I said.

"I grew up in Tucson."

"Yeah? What brought you to this tiny place?"

She painted a vague gesture in the air. "You know."

What did that mean? A boy?

She kicked off her boots, revealing knee-high athletic socks, and took back the pizza. "Kitchen through here? I'm starving."

We ate dinner sitting cross-legged on the Oriental rug in the library, along with the Chardonnay and some cookies I'd found in a recent box of fan mail from a reader who apparently hadn't heard my father had died months ago. I told Kylie about Detective Rice's visit and her question about *Feast of Flowers* being connected to Dahlia's murder. Kylie had slogged through the book for a college English class, and neither of us could figure out how it could be connected. Once the pizza was finished and we traded what little new information we knew about Dahlia's case and then gossiped about the goings-on of Lundie Bay, Kylie stood up, stretched, and perused the room. She picked up the framed photograph of my parents' wedding.

"Is this your mother?"

I nodded. "She died when I was three weeks old, back when we lived in Maine."

She made a small sound of condolence and set down the photo. "I'm sorry."

I shrugged, though my eyes lingered on the photo and how happy they looked. How different would our lives have been if she'd lived?

Kylie ran her hand along the bookshelves. "Have you read them all?"

"The ones my dad wrote?" I took a bite of crust. "No."

She slid out a book, only to slide it back in. "His work never grabbed me if I'm being honest. I had to read *The Desecration of Johnny Jim* when I started working at Lundie Bay Books. It was a book club pick. Nothing ever happened in it, you know? I like books with twists and surprise endings. And what was with the elms? Jesus, the elms. Every page, the elms, the elms, the elms."

I wrinkled my nose, thinking. "There was an elm tree outside his window in our old house in Maine."

Her eyes went wide. *"Seriously?"* She snorted. "One lady in the book club went on for an hour about how the elms were some deep sexual symbolism."

I laughed as I licked grease off my finger. "People give authors too much credit. It was just the first thing he saw."

Kylie wandered around the room, pausing at the photograph of the Ink Drinkers that the police officer had set upright. She must have recognized her boss, Catherine, but she said nothing.

Instead, she looked up as though an idea had just struck her. "Did he keep journals? Personal diaries? Those would be worth a fortune to my online buyers."

I remembered his office in the Maine house, how I'd knock on the door to say good night and more often than not he'd be writing in a thick blank book, leather-bound, custom ordered from a bookbinder in Italy.

"Yeah. Pretty religiously. But he donated all of them, along with most of his personal library, to the rare book collection down at Bainbridge University."

Kylie's face fell. I stood up and wiped pizza grease on my jeans. "They're cataloged and stored in some basement there." I tried not to think of Ronan Young and his silly bow tie.

I found a David Bowie record and played it on my father's vintage record player, while Kylie roamed the shelves and pulled out a few volumes, stacking them on the coffee table. It felt good not to speak about Dahlia, about the break-ins, and just chat about books and scheme things we could sell for quick cash. Her eyes lingered on the bar cart full of awards, but she had enough restraint not to ask me about those, giving me the benefit of the doubt that I was above selling my father's awards. Not entirely deserved—I probably would have.

She was surprisingly knowledgeable about his works. Then again, she worked in a coffee shop named after one of his books with his portrait assailing the walls.

"I'll take these if you don't mind," she said at last, pointing to a pile of books. "I'll list them online and see if we get any bites. Here, I'll take a picture of the stack and email it to you. I'm not going to steal one, but you don't know that about me yet." She winked jokingly as she snapped a picture, but then frowned down at her phone. "No internet?"

"Not yet."

"How long are you going to stay in town, anyway?"

For a moment—either it was the wine or the uncharted territory of hanging out with a potential friend—I almost told her about Baker. About the fight. About how I couldn't go back, even if I wanted to. Which I *didn't*.

"I haven't decided."

Almost as though she could read my mind, she asked, "So there's no boyfriend back in New York?"

I ran my hand up my left arm over the sleeve. Had she seen the bruises? My sleeve might have ridden up—but bruises could have been made by anything. Suddenly, I wondered if she'd googled me. I hadn't purged my relationship with Baker from social media yet. There must be hundreds of photos of us together at bars throughout New York and on vacation. What would the smart thing to do be: leave them up or try to erase any evidence of us having been together?

"No boyfriend. I was actually married, but that's over now. He, well, wasn't a good guy." I chastised myself for saying anything at all. Kylie gave the shoulder I was cradling a narrow-eyed look before I dropped my hand. After the awkward silence stretched, I blurted out a little fast, "But I do have a cute neighbor here."

She kept her eyes on my shoulder and seemed on the verge of saying something about it, but then glanced out the window in the direction of Rafe's house, the only house bordering my property. "The Kahn place? Rafe Kahn? I thought he was old."

"If he is, he ages *extremely* gracefully."

She lifted a blasé shoulder, which I hoped meant she'd moved on from questions about my ex-husband. "The cashiers at the bookstore gossip about everyone in town. Apparently, he's only in town a few weeks out of the year. He's never come into the café or bookstore while I've worked there. Did you know his money is in peanut butter? An old family business."

I almost laughed aloud. My grunge-clad neighbor, who I'd assumed was a tech trader? "He's a *peanut butter* mogul?"

"Yeah. A peanut butter mogul."

She shoved a cookie into her mouth and was reaching for another when a sudden scraping sound made her freeze.

Our conversation halted.

The sound seemed to come from the other side of the wall, like someone was dragging a rusty dishwasher down the hall. So loud that both of us immediately pushed to our feet.

The sound stopped as suddenly as it began. For a few long moments, all was quiet. Then a slow squeal built, louder and louder, and ended with a clatter.

Kylie nearly coughed out her cookie. "What the hell was that?"

My face must have told her I was just as clueless. At a loss, I mumbled, "It must be old pipes—"

The sound squealed again, louder.

Closer.

The squeal moved down the wall and to under the floor—*do crawl-spaces work like that?* It was headed in our direction with the speed of a sidewinding snake.

Kylie and I scrambled up onto the sofa as the sound passed right beneath our feet. A shiver licked my back—this must be what people meant when they said a ghost walked through them. Kylie's eyes were so wide I could see the whites circling her pupils.

"Pipes?" she echoed doubtingly.

The sound rumbled beneath our feet and continued to the opposite side of the room, where it started slowly up the far wall like it was moving behind the plaster.

A pale crustacean, my father's voice echoed in my head, *the size of a small person.*

I indicated the iron fireplace tools near Kylie's side of the sofa. "Grab that shovel," I gasped. "And hand me the poker."

Without stepping on the floor, she leaned over the sofa arm and reached the tools. Clutching the poker, I climbed down from the sofa and started cautiously toward the wall.

"Don't! Are you crazy?" Kylie warned.

I pressed a finger against my lips as I took another step toward the wall. *Something* was there. A raccoon, maybe, or a possum. Could it be a person? I remembered the broken windowpanes and the phantom toast under my bed. What if it hadn't been a dream but a prank? The old walls were probably thick enough for a thin person to slide between.

The slithering began again, and I didn't think. I swung the fire poker at the wall as hard as I could. It embedded into the plaster, sending chunks to the floor. Chalky dust clouded the air, and I coughed and waved the dust away, then pulled back the crumbling plaster until I could peer into the hole.

It was too dark to see anything inside.

"I need a flashlight!" I yelled.

Still standing on the sofa, Kylie turned on her phone and tossed it to me. I caught it and shone the light inside. The space behind the wall was about twelve inches deep, filled with tufts of disintegrating yellow insulation.

No raccoon.

No person.

No *demon*.

"See anything?" Kylie called.

My heart hammered. "It's empty." I tossed Kylie back her phone.

We stared at each other. If she hadn't been there, I don't think I would have believed any of it happened. Just like with the toast. But she'd heard the sound, too. I wasn't imagining things this time. I wasn't becoming my delusional father, hearing whispers at night and slithering in the walls.

"Pipes," Kylie said again, flatly.

Neither of us believed it, but I nodded back. "Pipes."

CHAPTER NINE

She'd been wrong about the red-haired man. Too much beer and hard liquor had rotted his liver. But his heart was good and strong. What was left of him was stretched out in the middle of the table, wrists and ankles bound to each of the table legs. Seven bowls of blood lined the perimeter for the seven body parts worth harvesting: spleen, kidneys, eyes, liver, heart, tongue, teeth. It took days to process the ingredients. Drying the organs in her electric oven and pulverizing them, measuring out the blood into bottles, polishing the teeth in a rock tumbler that she turned with a crank. She'd taken a lock of hair from the man but not for her potions. Hair ruined a potion. These strands she cross-stitched into a fire-flower brooch, which she pinned to the lapel of the oversized button-up shirt she wore, smiling sweetly when another man complimented her on her skill with a needle.

—From "Kaleidoscope" in
Bedtime Stories for Monsters

AFTER KYLIE LEFT, I spent a long, anxious night with a horror movie I'd seen a dozen times playing on TV in the background. That probably wouldn't be a comfort for anyone other than me, but then again, I'd always had unusual taste. I kept the golf club by my side, just in case, as I toyed with the Celtic ring on my pinky, thinking.

The sounds hadn't started again since Kylie left. I tried telling myself it really *had* been pipes, or some component of older home maintenance that I, an apartment dweller, had never encountered before.

But sleep never came.

It must have been around two or three in the morning, moonlight seeping through the windows, when I remembered Kylie asking about my father's journals. I hadn't thought about them in years. But now I realized those entries, buried in the university library basement, might offer some clue to the strange phenomena that had been happening since I'd arrived. If Dad had experienced anything similar, he would have documented them there.

I'd always been running away from my father's biography, not toward it, but now, rattling around between the walls where he spent his life, I was becoming significantly more curious about the man I called Dad.

It was almost a two-hour drive to Bainbridge University, and I had to time my arrival to the ferry. I left in the morning after a breakfast of frozen waffles and cheap coffee. The scenery on the seaside drive along rolling hills looked torn from the pages of a travel magazine. The sea spray, the fog, the glimpses of the ocean between towering pines were like life as in a daydream. The road wound dangerously close to cliffs, and I was glad it wasn't peak tourist season, when the drive would be bumper-to-bumper.

As I neared Seattle, more signs of civilization began to pop up: sprawling gas stations, shopping centers, housing developments where there had once been forestland. I hadn't spent much time in the city. Baker and I had come out to the Pacific Northwest once to visit my father and stayed in downtown Seattle—Baker claimed he needed access to the airport if something came up with his work, though in reality, I think the idea of being confined in Malice House with my father was as unappealing to him as it was to me. We had taken a few extra days and bounced around from coffee shop to coffee shop and ridden a ferry to the San Juan Islands, where we'd rented mopeds and eaten fresh-made caramels at the bakery next to the ferry terminal. It had been a happy trip, until we'd driven out to Lundie Bay to visit Dad.

He and Baker hadn't gotten along. Dad didn't like how Baker was always touching me, guiding me, making suggestions for what I should wear and eat. Dad called it for what it was—controlling—though I hadn't wanted to admit it at the time. At the beginning of our marriage, I'd adored the attention from someone I thought of as far out of my league. On that particular trip, I remember tension snapping in the air, my father storming out and getting lost in the woods, Baker and I outside all night with flashlights, our voices hoarse, until we finally found him, muddy and disoriented, sleeping in a bed of pine needles.

Bainbridge University was located on an island—technically a peninsula—northwest of the city, most easily accessed by a car ferry. I'd been expecting a campus similar to Rhode Island School of Design, where I'd gone for my undergrad in visual arts, with brick buildings from the seventies updated with glass atriums and students hurrying to classes or sitting in circles on the quad with murky pot clouds over their heads. But once I'd made the ferry crossing and followed the signs to campus, I was surprised to drive beneath an imposing stone archway and find that the buildings were more like something I'd expect to find at Princeton or Duke University: heavy, ecclesiastical gray stone structures, slate rooftops, ancient trees whose gnarled roots tore up the brick sidewalks at a glacial speed.

It was a small campus, and it didn't take me long to follow the signs to Clifford Library and find parking. The few students, dressed in wool scarves and Patagonia jackets, didn't glance my way. For them, anyone over twenty-five barely existed.

The library was the jewel of the campus. Bainbridge was a small but prestigious university focusing on literature and theater. My father had no particular connection to it other than a few keynote addresses over the years—but what university *hadn't* he spoken at? I don't know how the administrators at Bainbridge convinced him to bequeath his personal library; I suspected a woman was involved. A library studies grad student, young and fawning, sent as bait. Or else a sophisticated older librarian. When it came to women, my father didn't have a type other than preferring them to be smart—but not more so than him.

I hugged my coat tighter and jogged up the library's stairs, tugging open the heavy oak door. Impossibly, it felt colder *inside*. There was an antique fireplace in the foyer that didn't look like it had been lit in a hundred years. My shoes clomped over the stone tiles as I opened the antechamber doors into the central library. My eyes were immediately drawn upward. The reading room was stunning, and I had been in a lot of libraries, dragged along as a child to my father's lectures.

Clifford Library's reading room was covered by a glittering glass dome that supported an enormous chandelier. Ten long tables spanned the room, each with leather-upholstered chairs and brass reading lamps. Shelves lined the walls, supporting imposingly thick books, a ladder ready to fetch those from the uppermost shelves. These were the prettiest books, I imagined, not necessarily the most in-demand. The reading room, while beautiful, was only one portion of the library. There would be basements, storerooms, and workrooms deep inside that held the boring, dog-eared, well-used books.

Only one seat was occupied, by a student with a lazy ponytail and gray yoga pants. I approached the circulation desk and cleared my throat.

The librarian, a heavyset woman with deep marionette wrinkles, wearing a chartreuse wool jacket, blinked up at me. "How can I help you?"

I shivered in the empty room. "It's kind of quiet today, isn't it?"

She blinked again. "It's fall break. Most of our students are gone until Monday."

My shoulders relaxed. Fewer people meant fewer prying eyes. "Oh. Well, my name is Haven Marbury. My father is—was— Amory Marbury."

There was no flash of recognition on her face, though she surely must have known the name. I plowed on, "About six months ago, he passed away and bequeathed his private collection here."

She still only stared at me. What had I expected? A parade?

I cleared my throat. "I was wondering if it would be possible for me to look through his donated items."

She folded her hands. "The general public is not allowed in the stacks. Patrons are welcome to look up specific titles in our database and request them, and a library aide will bring them to you. All materials must remain within the reading room, of course."

General public? He was my father.

"Haven?"

I turned toward the sound of my name. Ronan had just stepped out of swinging double doors, holding a small stack of books. He set them down on the counter, looking surprised. "What brings you out here?"

When I explained what I wanted, he patted the circulation librarian on her chartreuse shoulder. "I'll handle this, Angie. Haven's an old friend."

He beamed at me with that goofy smile.

I was nothing of the sort, though since he seemed inclined to help me, I didn't argue. He grabbed a plastic keycard and handed me a visitor sticker.

"I wish you'd let me know you were coming! We could have had lunch—but in any case, I'll show you to the stacks."

I slapped the visitor pass sticker on my shirt, then followed him through a set of double doors into the librarians' workstations, which were filled with binding glue and typewriters, a few outdated computers, and mounds of books in need of cataloging or repair.

"So," he said, a little too animated, "what are you thinking about the manuscript? Catherine said she's been trying to reach you. I'd still really like to examine it. I discussed it with one of the library's authentication specialists. He agreed to give it a look. . . ."

I wasn't about to let Ronan believe that there was a chance in hell

I was going to let any of the Ink Drinkers so much as breathe on the manuscript after what they'd said about my art. If I didn't need Ronan and his keycard to get me into the restricted area of the library, there was no way I'd even be talking to him right now.

"Yeah, I've sort of put the whole project on hold," I answered. "I've been distracted. I don't know if you heard, but my father's former housekeeper died."

His smile fell. He nodded curtly as he led me through another set of double doors and down a flight of stairs. "Yes." His voice was a whisper. "Just awful. Are you all right? Did you know her? I never had the chance to meet her. Our literary salons always met in the evenings after she'd left for the day."

"I didn't know her well. Still—you know."

He made a sympathetic sound in his throat.

The bottom of the steps opened to the warehouse-like stacks, where ten-foot-high shelves spanned the dark recesses. Labels at the end of each shelf told their contents.

Dolby Collection.

Freedom Bridge Documents.

Penwright-Field Collection.

At last, we stopped at a small unit tucked into an alcove.

Marbury Collection.

I offered a smile, even though it didn't seem to fit within the dark warehouse walls. "Thanks again."

"Take your time," he said with sympathy. "Not everything has been cataloged yet, so put anything you take off the shelves on this cart. I'll reshelf it for you." His eyes ran along the titles. "What exactly are you looking for? Is it related to the manuscript?"

"No." I answered too quickly. "Just some family history."

I waited for him to leave, but he kept looking over the spines as though they were old friends he rarely had a chance to visit. "And your art? Are you still drawing?"

I bristled at the mention of my art. As much as I wanted to tell him

I hadn't and would never take up pottery, I also didn't want him to know how badly the Ink Drinkers' comments had stung me.

"Like I said," I lied, "it's all on hold."

He smiled, and then after another moment of awkward silence, cleared his throat. "I'll be upstairs. Unless you'd like company while you browse?"

I forced a smile to soften my words: "I don't."

As soon as Ronan was gone, I shed my coat and set to work. Glancing over my shoulder every few minutes, I perused the books. My father's collection comprised four massive shelving units with six shelves each—a few thousand books in all. Some I recognized. I remembered them lining my father's study in our Maine house as I'd sat on the floor and drawn brier roses and shifty-eyed foxes in the margins of my children's books. There were copies of his own works annotated with personal notes and maps that he'd sketched for updated future editions, most of which had never happened. A Marbury collector would kill to hold one of these, with my father's handwriting scrawled in the margins. Kylie could probably auction these for a few hundred dollars each.

I briefly wondered what kind of security Clifford Library had. Scanning the corners, I saw a camera with a blinking red light. It was aimed at the stairs—tracking who entered and exited—but for all I knew, there could be more cameras pointed toward me.

I reshelved the books dutifully. The last thing I needed was to be chased down by campus police for stealing a book, which, I could argue, should have belonged to me in the first place.

I moved to the next shelving unit, running my finger along the spines. Expensive collectors' editions of the classics. My father had been partial to the German fin-de-siècle poets, Rainer Rilke and Hugo von Hofmannsthal, as well as Portuguese books-in-translation. What little Portuguese he'd spoken as a child he'd quickly lost after the death of his grandparents. He'd always maintained that the Portuguese side of our family was the most notorious branch (the other side being unremarkably English), painting them as bohemian ne'er-do-wells. *Winemakers*, he'd say with a laugh. *Occultists. Artists.*

After sifting through the classics, I finally reached a set of leather-bound journals. *Bingo.* They were fat, pretentious things that I'd loathed as a child since my father had spent more time with them than with me. Every night, while a nanny tucked me into bed, he disappeared to his office to catalog his day. I slid one out at random. It had been processed by the library, stamped on the inside cover with the name of the collection. Something soured in my mouth to see his personal writing made so . . . institutional. I couldn't imagine handing over my innermost musings to a library where anyone could read them. Then again, my father had made a career out of baring his soul in thinly veiled autobiographical fiction.

I read a few pages and, as I suspected, he'd heavily curated his entries to portray a particularly favorable version of the truth. Amory Marbury wasn't about to reveal all the sordid details of his many affairs and unwise investments. I imagined these journals had been an exercise in planning an autobiography or else leaving the right information for a future biographer to discover—with just enough scandal and self-doubt to spice things up.

I started with the most recent ones, from 2015.

June 4, 2015

Had a call with Julia over the foreign rights for Righteous Sweetheart. *She hadn't read the contract—isn't that an agent's main job? She explained that we sold world rights to Theroux-Gould instead of limiting it to North America, and now that everything is signed, there's no renegotiating the deal. She insisted that we discussed this, and I called her on the lie. She was mortified, but I forgave her and reassured her that mistakes happen even to the best of agents.*

June 18, 2015

This morning began at 5 a.m., when a car came to take me to Dulles. The flight to Austin was uneventful enough that I managed to edit a chapter of a work in progress. The literary festival opened with a reception that someone at Theroux-Gould had promised I would attend, so I couldn't remain a hermit in my hotel room, scribbling out my little stories, as I wanted. Met James Guice, the biographer, and a charming young woman who wrote teenage dramas that I gather are quite popular. But the words call . . .

I selected a different journal, from 2011, when he'd bought Malice House, but there was no mention of anything odd happening. No poltergeists. No randomly appearing toast. It seemed any unexplained phenomena hadn't begun until around the same time as his dementia diagnosis. If he kept journals after 2015, he hadn't donated them to Bainbridge University.

Disappointed to find nothing that could explain the sounds from last night, I ran my finger further back in time along the journal spines until I reached one from 1992. My birth year. I thought again of how he didn't have any pictures of me in the house.

March 9, 1992
Haven cries and cries and cries.
She wants her mother. The nanny is a poor substitute, and I'm even worse. The police say they aren't giving up on Clara's case, but with no body after two weeks, it's obvious they don't expect to find anything. They're keeping the bag of her clothes found in the river as evidence. Sergeant Lewis said it's a clear suicide case and gave me a grief pamphlet. The jackass. I have nothing of her left. Not a single piece of clothing, not even her wedding ring . . .

I closed the journal, feeling deeply unsettled. Real life wasn't like one of my horror movies. There were real answers, real evidence. It wasn't as though a demon had burst out of the wall and swallowed my mother thirty years ago. *Something* must have happened to her body.

A knot formed between my shoulder blades. I stood, pacing in the cavernous hallways. I might as well have been the last soul alive down here in this bunker of words. I imagined I could get trapped for days before someone would finally need an obscure book and come down here to free me. And where was that buzzing sound coming from?

I grabbed another volume off the shelf, a first edition of *Feast of Flowers*, and fanned through the pages. I'd hoped to glimpse some notes jotted in the margin that might give me some clue as to why Detective Rice thought there was a connection between this book and Dahlia's murder, but other than his signature on the title page, my father hadn't inscribed anything. I closed it and hunted for another copy of *Feast of Flowers*.

It didn't take long to find a UK edition of the book with a forget-me-not on the spine. As soon as I pulled the volume out, I noticed that the binding had been re-glued. As part of my degree at RISD we'd studied bookbinding, and I could tell that a few of the saddle stitches beneath the shoddy glue job had been cut. When I opened it to check the condition of the pages, I nearly dropped the book.

The pages were gone.

Well, not *entirely* gone. Someone had carefully cut out the interior portion of the pages to make a book safe. I'd made one as a little girl out of a thick *Lord of the Rings* hardback, using a boxcutter to cut a hole in the pages big enough to hide valuables—costume jewelry when I was little, marijuana when I was a high schooler. In this edition of *Feast of Flowers*, the pages had been cut to accommodate a medium-sized box the size of a pencil case. The box was made of dark wood and beautiful ivory inlaid pieces depicting a hunting scene. I recognized the style—my father had similar boxes on the Malice House shelves, which he'd brought back from his travels in Portugal during his mid-thirties.

I shook the box. It rattled softly with a mystery object.

I glanced over my shoulder, feeling watched. The stacks were empty, though I couldn't shake the feeling. Moving quickly, I extracted the inlaid box from the pages and opened it. Inside was a key with a plastic tag attached. In my father's handwriting it said:

I stared at it blankly.

A key to the basement of Malice House would have been strange enough to find in a book safe. But the truly puzzling thing was that the house *had* no basement. There was barely even a crawl space. I knew with complete certainty because I had crawled down there years back, checking for termites, thinking they might be the cause of the strange sounds my father claimed to be hearing. The house was built near a limestone cliff. After a few feet of dirt, there was only solid rock. No cellar. No basement.

So, what the hell was this a key to?

The buzzing sound came again, this time in shorter bursts. *Buzz. Buzz.* I searched for the source of the sound and found myself staring into the black lens of the security camera. The red light blinked at me. Slowly, the camera panned up an inch, then down again.

It was aimed directly at me now.

"Shit," I muttered. Maybe it was the circulation librarian making sure I wasn't stealing anything. Which, I realized, was *exactly* what I was going to do.

I turned my back to the camera, heart pounding, and stuffed the key into my canvas bag. Dangerous, I knew. There was a chance Madame Librarian or Ronan would come to inspect everything after I'd left. But since they hadn't finished cataloging the collection, it was likely that no one would ever know there had been a key.

I grabbed the other books I'd been rifling through and stacked them on the shelving cart with the book-safe copy of *Feast of Flowers*, then, clutching my bag, jogged up the basement stairs. The lights, set on a motion sensor, shut off one by one behind me.

"Did you get what you needed?" the chartreuse-sweatered librarian asked from her desk.

I scanned the area behind the counter, looking for a computer or monitor from which she might have been watching me, but there was none. So if it wasn't her behind the camera, who was it? Ronan?

"Mr. Young wanted to speak with you before you left," she said. "His office is through that door, up the stairs."

"Sorry, I can't. I'm running late."

She picked up the phone receiver. "I'll just give him a quick call. He'll be right down."

"Really. I can't."

I got out of there before she could finish dialing his number.

The entire drive home, through the mist, my eyes kept sliding to the stolen key that I'd fished out of my bag and tossed on the passenger seat, as if staring at it enough would miraculously reveal what the tag meant.

As soon as I was home, I tried the key on each door in the house, but as I suspected, it didn't fit any of them. I was debating putting on rain boots and climbing down to the crawl space again when my phone rang, and I cursed.

An unlisted number.

"Hello?" I paused, feeling like I was speaking to a ghost. Almost inaudibly, I whispered, "Baker? Is that you?"

But it was a female voice—not a pleased one. "Haven? It's Letitia Rice with Lundie Bay PD. Is now a good time to continue our talk?"

CHAPTER TEN

The Hellhound waited and watched from across the street. Inside the yellow house, a baby cried. The father left as the clock struck the twenty-third hour of night and disappeared into his growling black vehicle. The scent of sweet mother's milk wafted through the open windows. The Hellhound trotted across the street and crawled under the wire fence into a yard cluttered with signs of human young: a wooden box filled with sand, a rope swing. The back door was cracked open.

Inside the house, the baby cried and cried until it didn't.

—From "Sweet Cream" in
Bedtime Stories for Monsters

●

I COULDN'T PUT Detective Rice off forever. That was the thing about police. They had a way of finding you wherever you ran.

I was still fumbling with the mystery key, trying it unsuccessfully on the back door while balancing the phone on one shoulder. "Now? Um, sure." I opened the junk drawer and dropped the key inside.

There was a click on the other line. Was she recording this?

"Great. As I mentioned before, it's been brought it to my attention that there may be a connection between Dahlia Whitney's homicide and *Feast of Flowers*." There was a ruffle of paper on the other end like she was checking her notes.

Looking through the copies at Bainbridge University had refreshed my memory slightly; I recalled it was a bildungsroman set in the seventies about a wholesaler who ran a floral mart in Chicago, but that was about it.

"I'm afraid I don't see the connection," I said.

More flipping of pages on her end. "Apparently, there's a plotline about a serial killer. The main character sells flowers, and one of his clients winds up dead the day before her wedding. Does that sound right? You'll have to forgive me—I have the book, but I'm only a few pages into it."

It started to come back to me. Yes, there was a serial killer in *Feast of Flowers*, though as I recalled, it was only mentioned briefly, a few paragraphs at most.

"I don't remember any details," I said. "If you're asking if I know why my father put that in his book, I have no idea other than serial killers *sell*?"

She didn't laugh at my joke, not that I'd been entirely joking. "Is it true that the serial killer in the book cut off the victim's hands?"

I felt a chill. The news still hadn't confirmed the rumors about Dahlia's hands, feet, and head being removed, but Detective Rice's question implied it was more than a rumor. "I really don't remember."

She continued, "It's an ongoing investigation so I can't get into details of the case, but the victim had some mutilations that, I'm told, echo certain plot points. I gather that a lot of his fans are, well, fanatical—"

I gripped the phone harder. "You think a fan killed Dahlia? Like a copycat or something?" I glanced at the heavy-duty lock on the back door, even more worried about the recent break-in attempts.

"I'm just asking for your thoughts."

She had to know as well as I did—I'd seen enough horror

movies—that it wasn't uncommon for killers to remove hands or fingers to get rid of fingerprints to make victims harder to identify. The *Feast of Flowers* connection felt like a stretch.

However, Detective Rice couldn't have known that one of my father's works *did* have an eerie connection: *Bedtime Stories for Monsters*. In it, the human-sized crustacean called Pinchy was known for, well, *pinching*. He used claws the size of garden shears to snip off body parts. Head, hands, feet—he pinched them all. Neat and clean. And always while his victims were still alive.

Feeling sick, I sank to the kitchen floor. Did I owe it to Detective Rice to tell her about Pinchy?

"Ms. Marbury?" she prompted.

"Yeah." I swallowed, feeling suddenly dizzy. "Um, I'd be happy to go through my father's old files and see if he kept anything on *Feast of Flowers*. Research notes or whatever."

She was silent for a moment. I heard a pen scratching on paper. Then she came back on with a breezy weariness. "Great. Thanks." She paused. "I take it you decided to remain in town?"

I squeezed the phone tightly. "That's right."

She made a small grunt before hanging up.

I spent the next few days trying to distract myself from Detective Rice's call and Dahlia's death by working on my illustrations and poking around the house looking for any hidden locks that would lead to this mystery basement that didn't seem to exist. On Saturday, my phone rang, but as soon as I set down my paintbrush and saw the number was from Lundie Bay Books, I let it go to voicemail. It could be Kylie, who I had no reason to avoid, but Kylie probably would have called me from her cell phone. And I didn't want to take the chance that it was Catherine. Sure enough, when my voicemail beeped, I poured myself a glass of wine, sat back down at my studio table, and listened to Catherine's tight optimism.

"Haven! I was just speaking to Ronan Young. He mentioned you were down at Bainbridge University on Wednesday. I wish you'd let me know. I would have loved to drive down with you. Get some time alone to talk about the manuscript. Call me back as soon as you can. Jonathan has an interested editor. The advance they're talking about is *substantial*."

I twirled my paintbrush as I considered what to do. I sure as hell wasn't going to call back. So what if that was rude? I didn't trust for a second that Catherine and Ronan just happened to talk right after he'd run into me. Ronan had called her. Spied on me—I felt sure he was behind the security camera.

Why were they so obsessed with the manuscript? Did they think I was going to give them a cut?

I looked down at my sketchbook to find that while my mind had been on the phone call, I'd inadvertently doodled the unfinished clawed foot of some monstrous being. I set down my paintbrush and rubbed my face. *Pull yourself together.*

A knock came at the front door. Jesus, what was the point in even having a security gate?

I closed my sketchbook over the strange unfinished drawing and went downstairs, still feeling off. What time was it? Twilight breathed against the windows. My heart was racing as I approached the door slowly, trying to peer through the beveled glass.

To my relief, it was Rafe, replete in designer flannel shirt, black jeans with a threadbare rip on one knee, and hiking boots.

I broke out in a smile and pulled the door open. "Oh! It's you."

"It *is* me." He looked a touch embarrassed by my enthusiasm, until I frowned.

I asked, "How did you get past the gate?"

"Oh, I have my ways." Grinning sheepishly, he held up a chunky VHS cassette. "I've been thinking about you and your monsters. I've been wanting to watch this movie for months but couldn't muster the courage. Took me forever to find a VHS edition online. You still don't have internet, I take it?"

I shook my head.

"That's what I thought. Want to watch it with me and hold my hand if I scream?"

A date? For a second, I felt like a flustered teenager instead of a thirty-year-old with a failed marriage under my belt. Should I be trying so soon after Baker? Then again, Rafe was exceedingly pretty to look at. And I *was* lonely, not to mention possibly losing my mind, drawing terrible things without even realizing it.

The title on the VHS case came into focus. *Dark Night of Seoul*. A Hitchcockian Korean-language movie that had come out a few months ago and made a splash for a particularly gruesome scene involving a sewer grate. Even though it was mainstream, it was dark enough for Rob's clientele, so I'd written about it, cashed my three-hundred-dollar check, and never thought of it again.

"Hmm . . ." I teased.

He grinned, leaning in the doorway, then produced a package of microwave popcorn from his other pocket, waggling it temptingly. "If the movie isn't enough of an enticement, maybe a snack?"

"You'd have more luck with a bottle of wine."

He leaned in with a smirk that made me feel bubbly, his eyes going to my wine-dark lips. He grazed his thumb over my chin. "Something tells me you have that covered."

His charm was undeniable. My instincts told me to come up with an excuse to send him away. There was the manuscript to sell, the crawl space to scour, movies I actually needed to watch to get paid for. Not to mention the illustration project that could change the entire course of my career.

But he smelled good, like woodsmoke.

I stepped back, allowing him entrance. "Don't get me wrong, this is *only* so you won't sue me for hitting you with my car."

He followed me to the living room, where he tossed the cassette and popcorn on the coffee table, his eyes going to the sofa, the scene of the crime. I was glad I'd cleaned off all the blood.

"Are you trying to swap sexual favors for indemnity?" he asked.

I laughed in surprise. "All I agreed to was holding your hand through a scary movie."

He rubbed his chin, grinning. "We all have our kinks."

I made the popcorn and poured us both wine, then we settled on the sofa, and I grabbed the remote. He sat on the far end, and for a moment, I was felt the distance too keenly, a heartbeat of wondering why he hadn't sat closer.

"You don't have a sewer phobia, do you?" I asked, pressing PLAY.

He laughed. I wondered what Rafe Kahn was afraid of. The next time I was at the café with internet connection, I'd have to google him, find out more about this peanut butter empire of his. And if there was anyone else in the picture. An ex-wife. A girlfriend. I hoped he didn't have kids—I wasn't great with kids.

The movie opened with a scene of a posh couple checking into a hotel. Rafe sipped his drink and seemed riveted to the television. I was over-aware of his presence. The woodsmoke smell on his flannel shirt. The sofa's sigh as he crossed and uncrossed his legs. His genuine laugh when the couple got stuck in the elevator with an incontinent old man.

My phone buzzed, and I checked it as subtly as I could. A message from Jonathan Tybee.

Good news, Haven. Empire Publishing wants to make a preempt offer on the manuscript. It's going to be the deal of the year. But they need to see it first. Can you drop it off at the bookstore tomorrow?

Biting my lip, I texted back a quick:

Tomorrow's no good. I have plans.

After a moment, my phone buzzed again.

I promise this is more important. We're talking a high six- or even seven-figure advance. I'll come pick it up first thing in the morning. Are you at home?

I nearly growled in frustration. As far as I was concerned, Jonathan Tybee was never getting past the gate.

Rafe glanced at my phone but didn't ask who I was texting. He motioned to my empty glass. "More?"

"God yes. Next time, don't ask."

I texted Jonathan back quickly.

Nope. Out of town for a few days. I'll call when I'm back.

Rafe took our glasses to the kitchen and came back with them filled to the brim. He sat closer to me this time, resting an arm on the sofa back. For a second, a memory came to me of watching movies with Baker. He hadn't known about my side gig recapping horror movies. He wouldn't have approved; Baker preferred car chases and men in capes. He considered himself a public figure—which *I* considered a stretch, given that it was a long-dead relative who'd been famous, not him—and was obsessed with me "acting accordingly." Before we'd been married, I used to poke around at oddity and curiosity art shows, paint my face like a skeleton for Halloween, and of course, draw wolves I hoped would one day make it into a children's book. Baker had tried to put an end to all that once I'd moved in—I only watched horror movies when he was away on a documentary shoot, when the apartment could be all mine.

Other than Baker, I hadn't been with anyone in years. But Rafe's presence filled every corner of the house. He was like a light that cast a glow beyond the limits of his body.

My lips were dry. When I licked moisture into them, I tasted popcorn butter. *Sinfully good.*

The sewer grate scene came, and Rafe made a show of grimacing, though it was clear he was only pretending to be frightened. I patted his arm with exaggeration.

"There, there. It's just a movie."

He leaned his head into my shoulder to hide his eyes, and I laughed and shied away at his breath on the side of my neck even as goose bumps erupted across my skin. His lips grazed my ear. An accident? I found myself leaning into him, giving the slightest of sighs. His lips found my ear again. *Not an accident this time.*

His hand fell around my waist, tugging me imperceptibly closer.

I turned to face him and saw dark eyes studying mine, set amid those to-die-for lashes. His lips were wine-darkened, too, parted just enough to show the edges of his teeth. For a second, I shivered with a premonition. *Someone walking on my grave.* The lights seemed to dim. *You're wrong,* a voice whispered in my mind. Rafe wasn't like a light filling the room. He was everything that wasn't light—he was the darkness, he was moth wings at the window, he was mist.

But it was only a fleeting thought, and then he grinned, and I grinned back, and nearly laughed at myself for being so dramatic.

Even before he touched my chin, I leaned in to kiss him.

On the television, the couple drowned in a sewer filled with blood.

CHAPTER ELEVEN

In the next room, a cowboy warbled a slow ballad on the record player. Pinchy looked up at the moon through the window in Elin's bedroom. Pinchy loved the nighttime. Pinchy wished days, short as they were, would never come.

Bleeding out on the floor beside him, Elin screamed and screamed and screamed.

—From "Extremities" in
Bedtime Stories for Monsters

●

I WOKE TO fingers of light reaching through the window. My head ached. I felt parched. Why had I drunk so much? Maybe I'd been showing off for Rafe. Or maybe I'd wanted us both to be a little out of sorts, filled with liquid courage.

I kicked off my bed covers and sat up.

I was alone in the bedroom.

I checked for messages—still no responses from Baker, which was hardly surprising, though Catherine and Jonathan and Ronan had blown up my phone with texts. I groaned, then closed my eyes and listened for sound from downstairs. Where was Rafe? We'd made out long after the movie credits on a sofa that had once been splotched with his blood. It must have been after midnight when I'd jerked awake, realizing that both of us had passed out at some point. I was lying on top of him. His hand under my shirt. Most of my clothes still on. Popcorn in every crevice.

I'd stumbled upstairs to bed, not bothering to wake him. I'd half expected him to come up too, to finish what we'd started downstairs. I was apprehensive about sleeping with another man, but he wouldn't have been unwelcome. But the other side of the bed was untouched. Was he still asleep downstairs? Maybe he'd woken in the night and gone home.

He'd better not sue me now, I thought wryly.

I swung my legs down off the tall bed, ankles dangling in the cool draft, then took a step down.

A scuffling scramble came from under the bed. Still half-asleep, it took me a split second to register that a wild animal might have gotten inside.

The golf club—where?

As I swung my gaze around the room, something clamped onto my ankle.

I cried out as lightning bolts shot up my shin. My hands twisted in the sheets, desperate for something to cling to that would help with the sudden pain.

I heard screaming—my own.

Footsteps pounded up the stairs as my legs started to buckle. Rafe? It had to be. He must have stayed the night. *Thank god.* My thoughts couldn't pull themselves together. I leaned forward toward my ankle. Blood was dripping down my skin onto the floor. And . . . what else? What was that *thing* poking out from under the bed? Sickly and pale, clamped around my ankle like a claw.

My legs went slack from shock, and I collapsed to the floor just as Rafe skidded into the doorway.

He stopped short, eyes going wide.

My hip throbbed from where I'd hit the floor. The thing had punctured my ankle, but at the appearance of another person, let go and scrambled back into the shadows. From my position, I could see under the bed. It was dark under there, and panic blurred my vision. But the thing was moving a little. What *was* it? There weren't words to describe it. It was a person; it had to be. A person in a costume or with some sort of severe deformity.

Two flannel-clad arms grabbed me around the torso, dragged me into the bathroom, and set me down on the toilet. Rafe wrapped the bath mat around my ankle as tightly as he could.

"Haven." He shook me. When I didn't respond, he grabbed my chin and forcibly jerked my head to look at him. "Haven! Don't move. Stay here and try to stop the bleeding. I'll be back as soon as I can." He swiveled back to face the bedroom, where I heard that awful scurrying noise again along with a plaintive, soft squeal. "Where's your phone?"

Phone? I could only stare at the dots of blood on the tiles. "Um . . . The nightstand . . ."

He left in a rush, pulling closed the bathroom door behind him.

For a few seconds, the pounding of my heart eclipsed all other noises. Blood roared in my ears. Once my light-headedness cleared, I listened to a scuffle in the other room, followed by more of that high-pitched squealing like some sort of protest. Then the *thunk-thunk* of something being dragged down the stairs. Had Rafe killed it— whatever it was?

The front door slammed. Then, silence.

I jolted back into my body.

When I peeled back the bath mat, blood trickled steadily from the puncture wounds on my ankle. *Fuck.* At least the bone didn't seem broken. I needed a towel, but my dad kept them in the steamer trunk in the primary bedroom since the bathroom was so small. I'd have to venture back out there.

It took me a moment to find the courage to open the door. I cracked it slowly, relieved to find the room empty. Splotches of my blood stained the rug and pooled on the hardwood floor. The sheets were tangled, ripped off the bed. A briny smell permeated everything.

My phone was gone from the nightstand.

I crawled over to the steamer trunk and grabbed a towel. The lid slammed back down, making me jump. I wrapped the towel tightly around my ankle, tucking in the end to hold it in place. Still reeling, I managed to move on hands and knees to the top of the stairs.

"Rafe?" I called in as loud a voice as I dared. No answer. Louder, I called again, "Rafe?"

How much blood could a person lose before passing out? The wound wasn't going to close up with a Band-Aid and some Neosporin. I had to get to a hospital, but how? Maybe I could hobble downstairs and get into my car, but I didn't see how I could drive myself down a steep cliffside road with an unusable foot.

Where is Rafe?

Whatever that thing under the bed was, it was incredibly dangerous. Had it attacked him? For all I knew, he was lying in the front yard right now, bleeding out from hundreds of picture wounds.

I crawled to the bedroom window. The portion of the front yard and driveway that was visible looked perfectly normal. No monsters or half-dead neighbors sprawled in the grass.

My head slumped down as my vision blacked out briefly, then shot back upright.

What was that thing?

Words responded in my brain as clearly as if someone had been standing over me, speaking them out loud.

You know what it was.

Yes. I did. I'd known when I'd fallen and seen it with my own eyes, even cast in shadows, barely more than a shadow itself. *I'd drawn it.* Sketched those fleshy claws, that deformed body that was at the nexus between man and beast and sea monster.

The black pinpricks blinding me slowly evaporated, and I blinked back to myself. No. That was impossible. *Pinchy isn't real.*

A voice in my head reminded me I should be calling 911.

I searched around the chaotic bedroom for my phone before remembering that Rafe had taken it—*why?* He had his own phone, surely.

I crawled back into the hallway, where an ancient touch-tone phone sat on a side table on top of an outdated phone book. But as soon as I grabbed the handset, I froze. What would I say to the 911 operator? I couldn't tell them about Pinchy. I'd be committed, especially with a family history of early-onset dementia. Besides, a paramedic would take one look at all the blood and, without me able to give an explanation, report it to the police. And my history with the police not believing my claims made me more than skittish. It had gone very badly before, an arrest on my record. A night in jail.

I thumbed through the phone book with badly shaking hands. There was no listing for Rafe Kahn. Hardly surprising—Rafe probably hadn't had a landline home phone in ten years. Instead, I found the number for Lundie Bay Books.

I punched in a number with bloodstained fingers, and the dial tone gave way to someone picking up on the other end.

"Lundie Bay Books, this is Orion."

"Kylie." I gasped. "I need to speak to Kylie."

There were scuffling sounds of a phone being passed around and then after what felt like an eternity but was probably only a moment or two, a pleasant voice said, "This is Kylie."

I clutched the phone like it was the one thing linking me to sanity. "Kylie? I need you. *Now.*"

CHAPTER TWELVE

At the edge of the forest, the silver-haired man came to a road and followed it to a sad little town with a sad little sign that read TOWN OF WENT. *Blue smoke rose from the chimney of a white clapboard house.*

He didn't bother to knock. After all, she had been following his bloody trail every step he'd taken through the geometric forest.

"You'd better have brought me something good, Harbinger," she purred from the shadows behind him. "And you'd better have dug it out of your flesh yourself. More potent that way."

He turned to her and opened his bloodstained hand.

The Witch of Went's lips pulled back in a sickle smile.

—From "Beasts of Sun" in
Bedtime Stories for Monsters

●

WHO ELSE COULD I have called but Kylie? The idea of Detective Rice listening to me rave about slithering creatures made me laugh a little deliriously, and then I started to cry. It came on in the same unstoppable way that it had when I was a girl, with an ugly twist of the face and stinging eyes.

On the phone, Kylie hesitantly responded, "Haven?"

Her voice gave me a solid shake. I gripped the phone handset hard and explained, "I need you to come to my house." I gazed glassy-eyed at the bloody marks on the floor. "Something's happened."

From the other end came the beep of a credit card machine, the soft hum of chatter, the placid Celtic music they played on an endless loop at Lundie Bay Books.

"Uh, I'm at work right now." I could feel questions pressing in from the other end of the phone. I could imagine how Baker would have reacted if I'd called him for help. He'd ask a rapid-fire barrage of questions: exactly what had happened and where I was and if I was alone. That was the researcher in him, needing to gather every piece of information and control every variable.

After a second, Kylie said, "Let me tell the manager I'm leaving early. I'll be there in fifteen minutes. Are you okay until then?"

A small pool of blood found a groove in the wooden floor and began flowing toward the top of the stairs. "Yes. But hurry."

The handset slipped out of my fingers. The phone started beeping and I fumbled to put it back on the base. I leaned back against the wall, wincing. My vision was swimming. The furniture in the hallway blurred into dark, nebulous shapes. Blood rushed in my ears, *shhh-shhh*, like waves beneath a full moon.

Once I knew she was on her way, I had a rare moment of calm during which reality trickled back in, and I took stock of my situation.

I felt immensely grateful that Kylie hadn't asked more probing questions. I'd sensed from our first meeting that beneath her warm smile was a person who had dealt with enough trouble to know when to ask questions and when not to—and when to drop everything for a near-stranger's call.

A mucous streak stained the bedroom floor, mixed with drops of my blood. Everything reeked of the ocean. My heartbeat kicked up harder as I slid my gaze to the now-empty space beneath the bed.

Had it really been Pinchy? Was I losing my mind? Now that some time had passed, my certainty in what I'd seen was fading. *Something* had attacked me, but I'd had a lot to drink and had still been half-asleep when it had happened.

I closed my eyes, but the image of the hairless, fleshy appendage with sharp claws lingered. It didn't *feel* dreamlike. My brain didn't want to believe what my eyes had seen. The pale body the size of a small person. Spindly limbs, and too many of them. The face with no nose, a lipless maw for a mouth, too-big oily eyes reflecting my own screaming face.

Think, I urged myself.

The thing under the bed could have been a person in a costume, albeit a *very* good costume, complete with a custom claw-shaped weapon. It didn't seem likely, but what other explanation was there? Someone had to be messing with me—someone who knew about my father's manuscript. Maybe whoever had been trying to break into the house. But the costume—the thing—had looked uncannily like *my own drawing* of it from a couple weeks ago . . . which I hadn't shown to hardly anyone. Not enough time for anyone to manufacture such an elaborate disguise.

Then a new thought struck me. The night when Kylie had brought over pizza, we'd heard scrambling under the floorboards. . . . Had *that* been the same thing? A monster inches from us the whole time?

Wincing, I pushed myself up and hobbled on my good foot to the sleeping porch, where I peered out at the driveway, anxiously awaiting Kylie's car. Clammy sweat rolled down my temples. The road was quiet. The gate was closed. There was still no sign of Rafe on my property or on his own. The lights were off in his house; it looked like no one had been home for days.

My eyes fell on my sketchbook. It was fat, overstuffed with a lifetime of drawings. Frantically, I clawed through it, letting the loose pieces I'd tucked in fall to the ground. I needed to see my illustration of Pinchy to know how close the resemblance really was. Finally finding it, I pinned it down with a stapler as if it might try to crawl away. In my father's manuscript, Pinchy's story was titled "Extremities" for reasons that were now painfully obvious. It was about a preteen girl who turned out be a raging psychopath. The muggy bayou heat started to get to her, and just as she was sneaking of out bed to murder her parents, a demonic lobster-thing hiding under her bed pinched off her feet, causing her to bleed out. My father hadn't described Pinchy other than to call him pale and crustacean-like. I'd added the oversized black eyes. The gaping mouth. The trail of mucus he left behind.

As I stared at my own drawing, I wondered: What if it hadn't been a costume? What if my father wasn't demented when he talked about demons in the walls? Maybe some preternatural being really had been slithering around inside Malice House for years, giving my father night terrors and terrifying Dahlia Whitney into never spending the night.

But if that were so, why hadn't it ever attacked Dad or Dahlia? Why had only *I* seen it?

No. Rafe saw it, too.

A piece of me was relieved I wasn't the only one, but a larger part of me itched with questions. Rafe still hadn't come back.

I heard the front door open downstairs and flipped over the drawing of Pinchy, wishing I could hide it forever.

From downstairs, Kylie called out with a note of worry, "Haven?"

I hobbled back into the bedroom. "Up here!"

Her footsteps charged up the stairs. She stopped short in the doorway, staring wide-eyed at the blood. "Holy shit." She dropped her messenger bag and ran to my side, scanning my body for wounds. "Did you call for an ambulance?"

I shook my head.

"Do you want me to?"

I shook my head again. "It's not, um, that bad."

She raised her eyebrows in disagreement but didn't press.

"I need to keep this between us, okay?" I stammered. "It was an accident. One of those . . . one of those animal traps, you know? A bear trap. The kind with spikes that clamp onto your foot. My dad must have left it out in the garden. I stepped on it by accident."

She sucked in a breath, but a moment later, a sheen of doubt shaded her eyes. Her lids narrowed. "Where is it?"

An image of pale flesh and oily eyes flashed in my mind. Hoarsely, I asked, "Where's what?"

"The animal trap."

Oh.

"I . . . I managed to pry it off downstairs."

Her line of vision followed the growing puddle of blood to the landing and the stairs beyond, which were perfectly clean. Not a single bloody footstep. Clearly, I'd been wounded in the upstairs bedroom, not outside.

"Are we alone?" she asked quietly, eyes darting nervously.

I was relieved she wasn't going to press me for harder answers. We *were* alone, which was terrifying in its own way. Where was Rafe? Where was the thing that attacked me? But to Kylie, I only said, "I think I need to go to the hospital."

"No shit." She stood. "Let me change out that towel first for a new one."

She threw open the bedroom steamer trunk and grabbed a towel, then disappeared into the bathroom and came back with a rattling bottle of painkillers.

She knelt beside me, offering me a few pills. "Worth a try—they might help."

I swallowed the pills dry as she replaced the towel, and together we managed to get me to my feet, down the stairs, and into the beat-up old Subaru that she had parked on the far side of the gate. She must have hopped the fence to get to the house.

We were halfway to the hospital, pain throbbing in my ankle, when it hit me: Kylie had immediately known where my father had kept his towels.

CHAPTER THIRTEEN

The Decaylings enjoyed dragging things deep under the lake to see what would float back up. Small rocks and bits of wood. Silverware and napkins. Shoes. Whenever one of the picnickers brought an egg, they delighted with their silent giggles that sent out cascades of bubbles. Eggs were fun: They sank if fresh, floated if rotten. But no picnickers had come for weeks. Ice formed at the edges of the lake each morning, melted by afternoon, only to return the next day. Winter was coming. Winter meant cold days and colder nights beneath the ice, toying in their underwater kingdom with desiccating picnic baskets and the fish-nibbled bones of those who had brought them. At long last, one of the Decaylings saw a figure moving on the other side. A man. He wore all black, not like most of the picnickers who came in checkerboard shirts and flouncy dresses. They wondered if he would float. With sharp fingernails, they chipped up at the ice.

—From "The Decaylings" in
Bedtime Stories for Monsters

AT THE HOSPITAL, I was relieved to learn my ankle wasn't broken. It had a mild sprain, and three of the punctures required stitches. The rest needed only adhesive butterfly closures, and as the on-call doctor wrapped the whole thing in an Ace bandage, she warned me to expect bruising to appear over the next twenty-four hours but gave me permission to walk on it as long as I wasn't in too much pain.

Kylie drove me home. Pumped full of painkillers, I kept nodding off in the passenger seat of her SUV. I vaguely remembered her helping me into the house and into bed. I must have finally fallen asleep because when I woke up, it was dark outside. The bloodstains had been mopped up, though a red tint clung to the wood, which I doubted any amount of scrubbing would remove. Steady rain pelted the window. The television blared from downstairs.

I limped down the stairs, wincing whenever I put weight on my ankle. The back of Kylie's head appeared over the living room sofa like it had been separated from her neck and placed there like a jack-o'-lantern. Then there came a crunch of popcorn as she lifted a handful to her mouth. On the screen, the summer camp caretakers stumbled through the woods away from the figure chasing them.

"Kylie." My voice was hoarse, so I tried again. "Kylie?"

She snatched up the remote and paused the movie almost guiltily, then wrapped her cardigan around her thin frame, looking me over in concern.

"You're awake. How do you feel?"

"Groggy."

"Yeah, that doctor was generous with the painkillers." She handed me some printouts. "They gave me your paperwork when we checked out." Her next look was sharp enough to slice me in half. "They said they would have expected a lot more damage from a *bear trap*."

As a creep of red came over my face, I bought time by sipping water from a glass on the side table. I wiped my mouth with the back of my hand. "Thanks. Rafe didn't stop by, did he? Did you see a car or anything at his place?"

"Your neighbor?" She shook her head. "I haven't seen him."

My mood fell into a dark place, filled with worry.

Kylie raised her eyebrows at my silence. "Does this mean you went out with the peanut butter mogul?"

I grimaced. "He came over for a movie."

Her eyes glimmered with curiosity, but again, thankfully, she didn't ask more questions.

"Can you call my phone?" I asked. Rafe had taken it but forgotten to tell me where he'd left it.

She dialed my number and reported that it was ringing, but we didn't hear anything in the house. Maybe the battery was dead.

"Can you look up his number and try to call him?" I asked.

She pulled out her phone and typed in some queries but then shook her head. "Nothing comes up on a search. Sorry. Rich people always wipe their numbers from the internet." She shoved her phone back in her jeans pocket. "Want me to go next door?"

I shook my head a little too emphatically, imagining what might be lurking in the woods between my house and his. "I'll, uh, follow up with him later."

I desperately wanted to know that he was alive and get verification that he'd seen what I'd seen—that I hadn't imagined it.

I put a little weight on my ankle, gingerly testing it out. Luckily, the creature had let go of me before doing too much damage. Other than the few punctures, its attack had resulted in mostly scratches that didn't turn out to be as bad as the blood loss had initially suggested.

Kylie leaned back against the sofa. The television suddenly sprang to life again. The camp director's wife screamed. Kylie cursed and fumbled with the remote, which she'd accidentally sat on. When she paused the television again, the silence was oppressive.

"Sorry." She gestured to the stack of Rob's tapes on the coffee table. "I didn't feel right leaving you here alone, so I thought I'd flip on the TV. You have some seriously twisted taste in movies. And what's with the old cassettes? My *mom* used to use those."

I rubbed my forehead, feeling weary even though I'd just slept for hours. "Long story."

"I don't mean any offense about the movies. Actually, I think it's kind of cool." She gave me a half-smile and picked up her messenger bag. "Call me if you need anything, okay? I'd stay longer, but I have a deadline for a writing contest tonight. . . ."

"It's fine. Go. And thanks."

She hovered at the door as though she wasn't sure she should trust me to be alone but then gave a soft nod and left.

I turned the lock behind her and collapsed against the door, pulling up the leg of my yoga pants to better examine the wound. The Ace bandage they'd put on at the hospital was clean and well-wrapped; hard to believe that this morning, my blood had been spilling out everywhere. I raked my fingers through my hair and almost started laughing in a nervous way again. *Monsters. Demons.* I took a few deep breaths and looked around for another glass of water.

Come to think of it, where was the wine?

As I hobbled into the kitchen, a blinking red light caught my attention. The ancient answering machine attached to the kitchen phone.

I wanted to ignore it. The last thing I needed was a collections agency calling to tell me a check bounced or, worse, Detective Rice peppering me with more questions. I hated to think of what she'd do if she heard about the mysterious "bear trap" accident after she'd warned me so emphatically about wild animals.

But also, it could be Rafe calling, so I jabbed the answering machine button.

"Haven. Jonathan Tybee here. Call me back right away. I tried texting you. I have an editor at Empire extremely interested in acquiring your father's manuscript. They want to see it right away. I'd love to come by today and pick it up so I can scan it. Call me."

Frustrated, I nearly ripped the phone out of the wall and threw it into the sink. I needed money but not badly enough to work with

Jonathan Tybee. Besides, I had bigger problems. I was tempted to call him back and tell him to come on by whenever he wanted and snoop around the woods while he was at it; maybe something would leap out and eat him.

Now that Kylie had left, I had a moment to think further about how she'd known that my father kept the towels in an unusual place. I couldn't see any way that a person's first instincts would be to look for towels in an old trunk in a different room. If she'd never been in the house before, wouldn't she have looked for a linen closet or opened the bathroom vanity drawers first? But no, she'd gone straight to that trunk.

Conclusion: Kylie had been here before.

Which meant she'd lied to me the night she'd come over with pizza and said she'd always been curious about the old house. Could she have been that mysterious other person that Dahlia had seen with my father in the attic? What business would Kylie have with my father, and in the attic, of all places? She'd made it clear she wasn't a fan, though she did sell literary memorabilia. There was a chance she'd approached him to ask about selling some of his typewriters, but if that was the case, why wouldn't she have simply told me?

Then it occurred to me that *Kylie* could be the person attempting to break into the house. There had been the broken window the first day I'd come, when Dahlia had shown me around, and then again when Detective Rice showed up. What if Kylie had seen—or thought she had seen—something valuable and wanted to get her hands on it without having to pay me a percentage?

Maybe she knows about the manuscript.

The thought struck me out of nowhere and swept through me like a summer storm, leaving me clammy.

I hobbled up the attic stairs and turned on the light. It looked much the same as it had the last time I'd climbed the stairs: the single light bulb, the hoarded boxes, the mildewing stacks of books. It still held that earthy, raw smell that was part ever-present damp of a Pacific Northwest fall and part something else.

If my line of thinking was correct, what could Kylie have seen up here that was worth lying to me about?

The boxes of dirt were where I'd left them, pushed up under the eaves, and they made me feel more unsettled than ever. It was colder in the attic than in the rest of the house. I wished I'd worn a sweater. I felt a sudden compulsion to look behind me, afraid I wouldn't be alone.

But the air was still. It was so quiet I could hear the waves crashing at the base of the cliff far in the distance.

Then a light through the window caught my eye.

I sucked in a breath.

The light was coming from Rafe's house. It was a downstairs light that hadn't been on just hours ago when I'd last checked.

Rafe's alive.

Relief flooded me as I limped back downstairs, anxious to see him, to grill him with questions. Neither Dahlia nor the cleaners from Seattle had thrown out my father's heavy rubber rain boots, which, fortunately, were large enough to fit over my bandaged ankle. I slid them on along with a raincoat, grabbed a flashlight, and limped into the yard toward Rafe's house.

But I paused in the yard as my thoughts caught up to my impulses.

Just because *someone* was home next door didn't mean it was Rafe. Whatever had attacked me could be there, could have attacked Rafe, too.

Was I walking into a trap?

I pressed on, though more apprehensive.

The trees looked bigger at night. I couldn't help but shine my flashlight along the edge of the woods, half expecting reflective animal eyes to peer back at me. It was pouring again. Did the rain ever truly stop in Lundie Bay or did it just take a breath and start again? The rainfall masked all other sounds, hiding whatever else might be with me in the woods.

A privacy fence separated our two properties, so I had to walk down the driveway, enter the gate code, then head down to the road and go back up his driveway. The front of his house, facing the ocean, was nothing but a wall of glass, so I hobbled to the back of the house to locate the entrance. Rafe's garage door was open, showing off a cherry-red electric sports car that seemed too flashy for his style. I passed my flashlight quickly over the garage, curious, but there was nothing inside other than a few gardening tools and a pair of road bikes. My boots splashed in puddles as I passed an ancient shed that looked like it dated back to the time when only fishermen frequented this bay.

Then I came to his fire pit.

I paused, remembering my first night here, when I'd seen Rafe take something out of the back of his car and burn it. I'd always wondered what he'd been burning. I took a step closer to the pit and shone my flashlight over the ashes. Old logs, glistening in the rain. I glimpsed something shiny but then a gruff voice behind me made me spin.

"Haven?"

And then there he was, inches from me. He'd come from the direction of the woods holding his own flashlight. He wore a dark raincoat, the hood of which did a poor job keeping off the rain. It streaked his face and neck and disappeared into the collar of his wool sweater.

"Rafe. My god." One night of making out didn't warrant me throwing my arms around him, but I was immensely glad to see him, if anything to know I hadn't been responsible for his death. I stared into the woods he had come out of and swallowed. "What are you doing out here?"

He didn't look back at the trees. It was always dark in those woods, even during the day. Too dark for me to ever take more than a few steps in any direction before feeling a chill and hurrying back inside.

His face remained stoic, though his eyes mirrored relief to see me in one piece, too.

"Come inside," he said. "Let's get you dry. And then we need to talk."

CHAPTER FOURTEEN

"What is it you seek, Harbinger?" the witch asked.

"What makes you think I seek anything?" The Harbinger took the green glass bottle of milky potion she'd given him in exchange for his spleen.

"Rumors spread. You were at Fathom Lake last week and Fordstown before that." She pointed a long finger at his bag. "You paid dearly for milk that can only be consumed by Hellhounds. You're traveling the country in search of monsters. I'll ask it again: What is it you seek?"

"Not what," he said evenly. "Who."

—From "Beasts of Sun" in
Bedtime Stories for Monsters

❧

THE KAHN HOUSE was just as modern and minimalist on the inside as its exterior promised. Floor-to-ceiling industrial windows that likely granted a breathtaking ocean view during the day instead only threw our reflections back at us. Giant sequoia timbers supported the great room ceiling and framed a slate fireplace that might have been copied from one of Colorado's luxury ski resorts. There wasn't a single piece of artwork on the walls, which felt intentional, as though the house itself was meant to be the aesthetic statement. A compact rowing machine was positioned to afford a view of the pines.

Rafe led me to the kitchen, which was the size of most New York apartments. It had concrete countertops, and appliances that were seamlessly hidden amid the cabinets. He pulled out a metal stool beneath the massive kitchen island.

"Sit. I'll get you a towel."

"And my phone," I asked anxiously. "Do you still have my phone?"

"Wait here."

He disappeared into a cavernous hallway, and I heard his boots climbing to a second story. I drummed my fingernails nervously on the countertops. It occurred to me that I knew almost nothing about my neighbor. Listening for sounds of him returning, I slid off the stool and opened a few drawers, feeling somewhat justified for snooping. *Eco-friendly bamboo napkins. Minimalist silverware.* I opened a large cabinet that proved to be a pantry and stopped abruptly.

Peanut butter.

There were hundreds of plastic jars of peanut butter stacked on the pantry shelves. I took out the closest. I didn't recognize the brand, but it looked as cheap as anything you'd find in a budget supermarket. Judging by the care put into the house and his taste in fashion, I would have guessed that the Kahn family business would have produced some small-batch, pollinator-friendly nut butter in glass mason jars. I was still staring at the jar when I heard him clear his throat.

"Hungry?"

I slammed the pantry door closed. I hadn't heard his footsteps coming back down the stairs. But he could hardly fault me for looking through a pantry.

I held up the jar. "So it's true. All this"—I motioned to the house—"is peanut butter money. Kylie told me, but I didn't believe it."

"Kylie?"

"She works at the bookstore café in town."

He raised a wry eyebrow as though he understood the ridiculousness of the source of his money. Then he opened a drawer and handed me a spoon.

"Thanks." I scooped out a bite of peanut butter, surprised to find I was suddenly ravenous. But it stuck uncomfortably in my mouth, and I felt like a child, naive and sticky, and that was the last way I wanted to feel around Rafe.

I set down the jar and gave him a probing look. "What were you doing out there, just now? In the rain?"

He closed the silverware drawer slowly. "Same as you, I'm guessing." His brown eyes sought out my own. "Looking for *it*."

I don't know exactly what I felt more of: relief that I hadn't imagined the attack or terror that it had really happened. I swallowed down a lump. "When you didn't come back, I was afraid you were dead."

He shook his head, running his hand over the stubble coming in on his chin, his thoughts somewhere distant. "Once I got it outside the house, it ran into the woods. I've been out looking for it all day. Or, more accurately, its body. It was bleeding pretty badly from when I threw it down the stairs. I don't see how it could have survived."

I could barely get my breath above a whisper. "I think I might know what it was."

Was I really doing this? I had been rehearsing this little speech in the back of my mind all day, but now it seemed insane to tell somebody that a drawing came alive.

But he saw the thing, too, I reminded myself.

Just as I was about to say more, he sighed and said, "So do I."

I wasn't expecting this at all, and the shock of it rendered me temporarily silent. Then I remembered that he had seen some of my sketches of the *Bedtime Stories for Monsters* characters. Had the Pinchy sketch been among them? No, I was sure it hadn't been. But he'd also mentioned my father's excellent taste in Scotch—he had to have known my father, at least a little. Maybe Dad had told him about the manuscript.

"You do?" I asked slowly.

His hand fell away as the distant look in his eyes telescoped back to the here and now. Troubled, he grabbed a spoon and took the jar of peanut butter from me but didn't take a bite. He drew in a deep breath.

"Alopecia."

The way he said the word made it sound like the name of some demonic creature. When I only stared at him, he continued, "It's a disease that leaves people entirely hairless. Animals can get it, too. Have you ever seen a hairless bear? It looks like something out of a nightmare."

I knew what alopecia was, but I could still only stare at him. "You're serious?"

"I think it was a diseased wild animal. I saw a sea turtle once without its shell. Terrifying. Whatever it was, it must have gotten into the house last night while we were watching TV. I thought I'd closed the front door, but maybe I hadn't."

I pushed off the stool like it had suddenly caught fire and limped around in tight circles. "A wild animal? Really? But it *reeked*. It smelled . . . briny."

He waved his spoon toward the now-dark windows. "Everything smells briny. The ocean is a hundred feet away."

"I don't think it was an animal."

He cocked his head as he asked evenly, "Then what was it?"

For a moment I detected an undercurrent of challenge in his voice, but I couldn't trust that paranoia wasn't getting the better of me. When I didn't answer, he scrubbed his hands over his forehead and said, "Look, we both drank a lot last night."

"I wasn't *that* drunk."

"How good of a look did you get at it? It was under a dark bed, and you were freaking out. I promise you; *I* got a good look. I wrestled it out of the house and chased it through the woods. It *was* strange looking, but I don't know what else it could be."

I stared at him. Maybe only my distorted mind, pickled in horror movies, could have gone to monsters instead of a more logical explanation.

"Did you ever go up to the attic of Malice House with my father?" I blurted out.

The accusation surprised him enough that he dropped his spoon and had to bend to pick it up.

"The *attic*? No. Why?"

He sounded sincerely baffled.

I folded my arms tightly. The taste of peanut butter on my tongue was starting to turn. Too salty. Almost *briny*. "And my phone?"

He pulled it out of his pocket guiltily and set it on the kitchen counter. "Yeah. Sorry."

"Why did you take it?" I checked the battery—five percent—and quickly scanned for new texts or messages. There were several from Jonathan and Catherine Tybee, one from Ronan Young. I slid it into my jacket pocket, relieved to have it back.

"I was going to call for help," he said. "I'd left mine on the sofa downstairs. Honestly, I forgot I had it until just now."

I probably was being paranoid. *Had* it been a diseased animal? I certainly was no expert on Pacific Coast wildlife. And it was true that I'd been half-asleep and hung over. There was also the possibility of impending dementia to consider . . . but that was the most frightening of all, even more than demons.

"What do *you* think it was?" he pressed.

I bit my lip, debating whether I should tell him about my illustration of Pinchy, my father's delusions that the house was haunted, his habit of leaving out toast to appease them—a snack that still seemed to be haunting me even after his death.

I briefly closed my eyes. What I knew of Rafe, I liked. I liked that he could repair his own mailbox, and I liked his flirty notes, and I liked that this tall, attractive guy would pretend he was afraid of horror movies to make out with me. Hell, *I even liked his peanut butter.* There was a good chance I was going to lose any shot I had with my handsome neighbor if I said what I really thought.

But I said it anyway.

"I think it was a demon."

To Rafe's credit, he didn't laugh. He just cleared his throat and said slowly, "You're going to need to explain."

Fiddling with the peanut butter jar label, I told him in stutters about *Bedtime Stories for Monsters* and the character from the "Extremities" story and how I'd illustrated it to look uncannily like whatever had attacked me from under the bed. When I finally looked up, I couldn't read the cryptic expression on his face.

He cleared his throat and said in a deep voice, "Haven, I haven't been honest with you."

Alarm danced up my spine.

"I know about Pinchy."

Of all the things I'd thought he might confess to, this wasn't even a possibility. I was waiting for Rafe to admit that the manuscript was, in fact, his own writing. That my father had stolen the idea from him and that he was owed the entire Marbury fortune, unaware that creditors had already beat him to it.

"I didn't know your father well," he explained, settling onto a stool as he tapped his spoon anxiously on the knee of his jeans. "I'm not in town often, and I keep to myself, and it seems like he did, too. But one night when I was taking out the trash, I noticed him on the other side of the fence, in the forest back behind your house. He was digging in the pouring rain, which seemed a little odd. I asked if I could help. He invited me in for Scotch." He paused here to get a glass of water and gulp it down. "After a few drinks he started telling me about the demons that lived in the walls of his house. He mentioned that one. Pinchy. Hard name to forget. He said he had to leave it snacks every few days or it would start misbehaving and turn the faucets on, or push books off the shelves. He seemed . . . a little out of it."

"He had dementia," I said in a whisper. "He never publicly announced the diagnosis."

Rafe nodded as though he'd expected the truth was something along these lines. "When you showed me your illustrations, I didn't realize that they were connected to the same monsters he talked about." He paused. "So, what are you saying, that you think he didn't make them up?"

I wasn't sure *what* I thought. My father hadn't described Pinchy in as much physical detail as I'd given him in my illustration, and the thing under the bed had looked like *my* drawing. Which begged the question: Did my father create Pinchy, or had I?

But I couldn't dare tell Rafe any of this. It was already too unbelievable. So I said the easiest thing that would get me out of the conversation. "Maybe you're right. It must have been an animal."

I was shivering visibly now. My hands left damp prints on the kitchen island countertop. Outside, the woods pressed in, but the windows only reflected my own pale face.

"Hey, are you all right?" He came around the island and rested a big palm reassuringly on my shoulder.

I gave a weak nod.

"Did you report it to the police? I heard about that older woman who died near here."

I expected another long reminder about the history of bear attacks in the region, but thankfully, Rafe didn't launch into the lecture. Maybe he hadn't been in town often enough last year to have heard the warnings.

"Yeah, I will, for sure," I lied, sliding out from his touch.

A muscle jumped in his jaw. He leaned back against the concrete countertop, dark eyes fixed on mine. "There's something else about that night I stayed up drinking with your father before he died."

I wondered if he was going to tell me more about my father digging in the yard. I hadn't had a chance to investigate those boxes of dirt in the attic yet. I'd meant to search the grounds for signs of where he might have removed the dirt. There was definitely no basement beneath the house, but for all I knew, he could have dug a shallow pit in the yard and buried a lock box or something. Maybe that was what the label on the key referred to.

However, Rafe said simply, "It's about you."

My jaw slacked in surprise. I sank back down onto the stool, wary.

"He told me that you were an artist. He said your work was . . . inspired. That you found the soul of your subjects in a way that eluded a normal artist's eye. He told me he'd wanted to be an artist himself as a boy. Create comic books, but his father discouraged it and said it was beneath him, that he should write something worthy instead. 'Serious fiction.' Amory was a little jealous of you, I think, but not in a bad way. Maybe it was more like . . . he was in awe. You were creating artwork that felt true to yourself, and you were actually good at it, too."

I listened, riveted, deeply touched—and more than a little confused. It was almost as though Rafe was talking about a complete stranger. My father, a comic book writer? I'd never heard Dad mention any such thing. There were no comic books or graphic novels on his shelves—I knew, because as a kid I would have loved to have stumbled upon something like that instead of dull, leather-bound editions of the classics. I'd never seen him draw as much as a stick figure.

It made me wish I'd spent more time in the basement of Clifford Library, reading through his old journals.

It made me wish I'd spent more time with the real man.

Now, of course, it was too late.

"He would have wanted you to continue your project," Rafe said softly. "Illustrating his manuscript. Even if it came from a confused mind, he wasn't confused about his feelings toward you. He loved you, Haven."

CHAPTER FIFTEEN

"You look tired, sweetheart. Take my seat."

The man in suspenders had boarded the bus on Harrow Street. He smoothed his tie over his potbelly as he stood.

Anita pressed a hand on her blue button-up dress just above her own belly. At nine months pregnant, her belly was only slightly more swollen than his, though judging from the broken veins on his red face, liquor was the culprit in his case, not Danny Grape in the bed of his dad's pickup truck.

"No, thank you." The man made her skin crawl. The baby kicked suddenly as though it, too, sensed something wrong with him.

"Sit," he repeated with a yellow-toothed smile.

The young mother found herself bending at the knees and resting back on the metal bench. She didn't want to be staring at the man's gut and groin. Didn't want to be anywhere close to him.

But he kept smiling down at her, and ever since he had spoken, she found that she couldn't move a muscle.

—From "Everyone's Favorite Uncle" in
Bedtime Stories for Monsters

THE PAPERWORK FROM the hospital prescribed rest and elevating my foot for at least three days. I normally wasn't the type of person to listen to doctors, even though I begrudgingly knew they were right, but it did give me time to work through the stack of movies Rob had sent in his latest shipment. I watched the films one after another. Silly jump scares. A few clever twists. One was an older "rediscovered" film starring an A-lister in his first role as a budding teenage actor; he falls into a septic tank and literally drowns in shit. It made me giggle in dark delight—Rob's clientele would be pleased.

I typed up my summaries and had Rafe drive me into town so I could email from the library's parking lot. While Rafe hunted us up some coffees, I sat in the cramped passenger seat of his sports car with the heater on and the windshield wipers going, checking first my bank account, then my email.

Still nothing from Baker. It was like he had disappeared off the face of the planet. I hesitated to do an online search for his name even with private browsing mode on, knowing that Detective Rice already had an eye on me. I didn't want her combing through my browser history at some point.

I spotted Rafe heading back across the parking lot, carrying two paper cups of coffee, and I dashed out one last message to Rob.

A few years ago, you told me about a German documentary on poltergeists. It was supposed to be the definitive source on true hauntings. Do you still have it? Can you overnight me a copy?

Dots appeared to show he was writing me back. I shouldn't have been surprised that Rob was online—Rob was always online.

You being haunted, Haven? I didn't think horror movies got to you.

I looked down at the Ace bandage around my ankle and thought of phantom toast and boxes of dirt in the attic.

They don't, but other things might.

I shoved my phone back in my pocket as Rafe climbed into the car and handed me one of the coffees. We puttered around town a little longer, swapping stories of our first impression of Lundie Bay, and when he dropped me back off at my house, I couldn't help but wish I'd concocted more imaginary errands to stay with him a little longer.

Good to his word, Rob deposited nine hundred dollars in my account the next day. My ankle was feeling well enough to drive myself into town, and I sat in the library parking lot with my laptop, staring in shock at the numerical figure in the bank statement. Money had always been a point of contention between Baker and me. In the three years we'd been married, I'd never seen a bank statement. I had no idea how much he was worth, but whenever an eye-watering check came at a sushi restaurant or bar, he didn't blink. He funded his own research expeditions to the tune of hundreds of thousands of dollars and gave me a generous clothing and food allowance—though never direct access to funds. Except for the small, secret amount I made from Rob, it was still always *his* money.

Funds in hand, the first thing I did was get Wi-Fi installed by a Comtek technician who grumbled incessantly about the poor wiring in the old house. Soon after, I rediscovered the joys of online shopping. After splurging on my much-missed face creams and power bars, I searched for security cameras. I didn't want anything that would be monitored by an outside company; I suppose I'd inherited more of my father's paranoia than I'd like to admit. Small, unnoticeable cameras were expensive, but I bought three of them, and when they were delivered the next day—along with another package from Rob—I debated where to install them.

I ended up climbing on a stepstool with my good foot to mount one in an eave of the front porch, aimed at the front door and window where someone had tried to break in. I put the second one inside, on the table in the entry hallway, where it could record everything from the library to the stairs and a portion of the dining room, though I had to turn off the notifications for this one or else my laptop app would beep every time I moved near it. The last one I hid in a slipper in the primary bedroom, pointed under the bed.

After a few days, nothing showed up on the cameras except for a nighttime opossum that kept wandering up to the front porch, and Rafe dropping by to visit me, letting himself in with a copy of the house key I'd made for him. Still, I checked the feed religiously.

With internet at home, I soon fell down a rabbit hole of searching for literary agents who might be interested in representing an illustrated *Bedtime Stories for Monsters*. I was still wary of the older, entrenched New York agents, who I guessed would be more interested in my father's writing than my artwork, but I found an up-and-coming agency in Los Angeles that was actively signing graphic novelists. I sent them an email before the voices of the Ink Drinkers got in my head and I lost my nerve.

Dear SunBurst Agency,

I am an illustrator based outside of Seattle, WA, and a graduate of Rhode Island School of Design's visual arts major, seeking representation for my own work as well as a posthumous collection of short stories by my father, the late Amory Marbury (winner of the Pulitzer Prize and the Booker International Prize). I've been working on a collaboration that would pair my father's writing with my illustrations of his characters. I think your agency might be the right fit for this bold, innovative project.

Due to the confidential nature of the manuscript, I cannot forward a copy, but if you are interested let me know and we can arrange a video call.

Sincerely,

Haven Marbury

There wasn't much I could do with my ankle, but I didn't need to walk to be able to draw. I set up a makeshift studio on the dining room table, bringing down a set of graphite pencils, my sketchbook, a few tubes of paint. It felt good to draw again after the attack. Something about creating order out of nothing but a blank page cleared my mind in an almost addictive way, and I'd drawn for hours without even realizing that time was passing. Rafe's words echoed in my head every time I touched the pencil to the page: *He would have wanted you to continue your project.*

This was the piece of my father that had been missing my entire life. While my father had never insulted my artwork, he'd never exactly encouraged it, either. He had watched me sketching in book margins as a little girl with an unreadable expression beneath his heavy brows. I had always taken that look to mean he thought little of my talent and only tolerated my aspirations. But after Rafe's story, I wondered if that look was more about himself than me. Wanting art, bullied into literature.

It made me regret that my father and I had never talked about these things. Always sticking to banal topics: the perpetually grim weather in Lundie Bay, logistics of where we would eat for dinner, what books we were reading. Hard to believe a father and daughter could spend their entire lives skirting around any deeper truths, but we had managed.

I was so engrossed in my latest sketch, this one of the were-bird, Kestrel, that I barely noticed when Rafe let himself in the house with a bag of groceries that I'd asked him to pick up in town. He glanced over my shoulder on his way through the dining room to put away the food in the kitchen.

He chuckled at the drawing, though not in a cruel way. "You really have a thing for drawing naked men, don't you?"

Feeling heat at my cheeks, I slammed the sketchbook closed. "My father made up the characters! I'm just drawing them."

He grinned adorably. "Uh-huh." He reached out for the sketchbook. "Let me see."

I handed it over reluctantly, though secretly, I longed to know what he thought. Negative criticism had a way of sticking with me, and

I hadn't been able to shake the feeling of Ronan Young's dismissal. An artist's insecurity was ever-present, an insatiable beast voracious for more and more praise.

He spent a few minutes studying the illustration. "Which character is this?"

"Kestrel. He's a demonic bird who can turn into a human."

In "Sundown Coming," Kestrel was something like a reverse were-creature. Instead of a person being bit by a wolf and turning into a werewolf under a full moon, a plain kestrel had been eating a mouse when a rabid human had bit *it* with bare teeth. The bird got away but changed into a maleficent were-person soon after. In his human form, he was still essentially a bird—still had the mind and instincts of a raptor, but the body of a man.

"So I guess the real question is, why did your *father* write about so many naked men?" Rafe asked.

I took back the sketchbook as I rolled my eyes. "Trust me, my father didn't have any secret homoerotic desires. If he had, he wouldn't have kept them secret. That man was not ashamed of his libido—he used to brag about his affairs to anyone who would listen."

"Well, it's good. Really good, Haven."

I grinned like a little kid; I couldn't help it. My laptop, open on the coffee table, dinged with an email alert and I dragged my eyes over to the inbox.

A response from the SunBurst Agency.

I grabbed my laptop so quickly that I nearly smacked it into Rafe's knee as I pulled it into my lap.

Hi, Haven,

My name is Eddie Chase. I'm the founder and senior agent of SunBurst, and I wanted to respond to you directly. The minute one of our junior agents received your email she forwarded it to me, sensing a hidden gem. While I admit that I haven't read your father's books personally, many on our team are huge Marbury fans. But more importantly, what we are really interested in is you. I googled you and found some of your work on SkitchPad.usa, and I speak for all of us in saying that we love what you're doing. Your idea to freshen up a literary figure's writing with your unique style really speaks to SunBurst's mission. I'm ready to fly up from LA to meet with you in person. You in?

Eddie

I wasn't crazy about Eddie Chase's cool-guy LA vibe, and I knew better than to believe a word of praise from anyone in the art industry, but I couldn't help but feel an electric shock.

Grinning, I began typing a response immediately, telling Eddie I'd love to meet with him and suggesting some times.

While I typed away, Rafe picked up Rob's latest manila envelope on the coffee table and frowned at the note Rob had scrawled on the back in purple Sharpie.

Don't let the bedbugs bite, H.

Rafe held up the package as a question. "What's this?"

I closed my laptop and snatched it out of his hand, ripping open the package and shaking out the VHS cassette inside. Rob had written the documentary name on it with the same deep purple: *Poltergeistia—2007.* I guess this one didn't need to be disguised as a dance recital.

"Another horror movie?" Rafe asked.

"Well, yes," I said, grabbing the remote control. "But this one isn't fiction."

CHAPTER SIXTEEN

When the Decaylings tap-tap-tapped on the underside of the ice, the Harbinger crouched low and tapped back. They grinned with algae-stained sharp teeth. It was rare that their victims played with them. They chipped away until they could press their blue lips against the hole.

They whispered, "Do you float?"

The Harbinger leaned down to the hole. "No games today, lovely ladies. I seek a creature with the power to tame chaos. Have you heard of such a one? A name. That's all I need."

They hissed among themselves in the cold lake waters, tails swishing through the muck, and then one swam back to the hole and bared her teeth.

"Come closer and get your answer."

—From "The Decaylings" in
Bedtime Stories for Monsters

"I'M NOT SURE what I think about your employer," Rafe said five minutes into the *Poltergeistia* documentary.

The opening credits alone would have made most people switch off the TV. It was filled with seizure-inducing quick cuts of cheesy B-roll images that looked like they'd been made by high schoolers. And the subtitles translating the German into English didn't appear to have been run past a native speaker, judging by the bizarre syntax.

"Rob's a strange guy," I said, "but he's okay."

I had never actually met Rob. I didn't even know his last name. The packages he sent came from a California address that I suspected wasn't his real one. More than once, I'd stumbled upon inconsistencies that made me think he might not be based in the United States at all. For the first couple years we worked together, he'd written that he loved my "sense of humour." Lots of his tapes had timestamps based on a twenty-four-hour format, not a.m. and p.m. Once, out of curiosity, I'd paid a guy to trace his IP address, but it came back as located in a different country each time he ran it. Barbados. Switzerland. Canada. Rob was good at covering his tracks. For all I knew, Rob was actually a Venezuelan grandmother.

Once I got used to the documentary's choppy visual style, I found it riveting. With my notebook by my side, I jotted down some of the more salient points that the narrators, a pair of tousled-haired twin brothers, noted about the history of poltergeists.

"Poltergeists are among the most well-researched yet least understood species of ghost lore," they reported. "Coming from the words *poltern*, 'to knock,' and *Geist*, 'spirit,' poltergeists were initially identified as 'noisy ghosts,' known for their rumbling, knocking, and slithering sounds. Now, they are more often known for an ability to move objects and manipulate simple machines such as turning on faucets or the oven."

In an attempt to present sound scientific methods, the twins went on to identify other possible explanations for poltergeist phenomenon. There was a skeptic in the 1950s who had studied apparent cases of poltergeists and deduced that downdrafts from uncovered chimneys were able to move objects as heavy as wooden chairs. Geologic researchers had suggested that seismic activity was responsible for knocking pictures off walls and making doors slam shut. Then there was the behavioral psychology team of researchers at the beginning of the 1900s—all of whom were men—who came up with an icky explanation they called the "naughty little girl theory," which suggested it was mischievous girls moving objects and making noises to get more attention.

What I found most interesting about the documentary wasn't the real-world explanations, most of which were common sense, but how similar some of the reported paranormal phenomena were to what I'd experienced at Malice House.

In one scene, the documentary hosts described a family whose framed photographs were facedown every morning when they woke up. Every time they set up the frames, it was the same way the next day, though nothing else on the shelves had moved. Then there were the interviews with homeowners who claimed to hear slithering beneath the floorboards and inside the walls. When exterminators had come to check for pests or animals, they'd found nothing.

But the piece of information that stuck with me the most was when the hosts spoke with an old Scottish woman who claimed to have a poltergeist that followed her when she moved houses. After some research, she had determined that the spirit was tied to the soil, and when she'd potted up her lavender plants and taken them to her new house, she'd transferred the ghost, too.

It made me think of the boxes of dirt up in the attic. What if my father had come to a similar conclusion, that the ghosts he believed were haunting him were tied to the dirt? And he was . . . *what*? Trying to trap them in boxes?

When the documentary ended, Rafe flipped off the television and rubbed a hand over the back of his neck. "You're in a strange line of work, Haven."

I was loathe to tell him that this particular film was not for a gig. Rafe had looked at me oddly enough when I'd told him about Pinchy and how my drawing had seemed to come to life. He was still mostly a stranger, for all the times he'd driven me to town or brought me groceries, or for that one night of making out that I replayed in my head more times than I wanted to admit. He was a *normal* person. Not like me or Rob, or even my father, who'd been haunted by demons whether they were real or just of his own making. Even Kylie struck me as having one foot outside of the normal-person realm of annual dentist visits and kickball leagues. Not only was she selling literary memorabilia that I suspected were forged, but there was something about the way she showed up where I was and didn't ask questions about obvious lies that told me she'd seen the kind of things people didn't just casually bring up over cheese plates.

I tucked one of my feet under me on the sofa and tapped my pen anxiously again my notebook. "What do you think of what they said on the documentary? Poltergeists and hauntings?"

Rafe's gaze went to the blank TV screen, which even though it was switched off, still hummed. "Unexplainable phenomena?"

I shrugged. "Yeah."

"I guess I haven't thought about it very much." His hand fell over mine, quieting the tapping pen. He left his hand here, stroking the back of mine softly. "But it sounds like you have."

There was an invitation in his voice to tell him more.

I took a deep breath. "I never thought much about it either, though ever since I was little, I guess I've had a sort of sense that there is more out there than we can see. Whether it's ghosts or religion or dreams, I mean, it's all kind of fucked-up when you think about it, right? Do we really understand reality at all? We think we know everything there is to know, but people have *always* thought that. Back when doctors bled people to get rid of disease, and when everyone thought the earth was flat. What if we're there now, the modern equivalent of thinking the earth is flat, and we just don't know what we don't know?"

I was fully aware that I sounded like a teenager who'd gotten high for the first time. Thirty-year-old divorcées weren't known to talk like this, especially not to their hot neighbors who they had half a mind to seduce.

Once Rafe understood that I was asking him a real question, he settled back into the sofa as though he was giving the issue serious consideration, and this was one of the things that drew me to him. Whenever he looked at my artwork, he *truly* looked. If I asked him a serious question, he gave it serious thought. So many times, Baker had glanced at my sketchbook when I'd shown him one of my pieces and given me a quick enthusiastic nod, only for his attention to immediately slide back to his phone.

Rafe's glass of wine was in one hand, resting on his knee, half-forgotten as he stared at the blank television screen.

"I know that feeling you're talking about," he said after a moment. "I've felt it, too. A vague sense that something is missing, for lack of a better word. That this world might not be the only world."

Having Rafe acknowledging a sense of the unknown wasn't the same as him believing that a monstrous lobster had come to life and attacked me, but it was a start. I traced my hand along the back of the sofa between us, and as though he could read my mind, he leaned in.

Our second kiss was slower than the first had been. This wasn't the same wild tangle of two people punch-drunk on a giddy flirtation. Rafe scooted closer so he could slide his hand around my waist. My body sighed into his palm. I tasted my father's wine on Rafe's mouth along with salt from his skin and the sea air. My hand slid around to the back of his head, running over the sandpaper of his short hair.

My computer dinged with an alert. I ignored it. Rafe was much more interesting than the latest celebrity tweet. It wasn't until a few minutes into the kiss that I remembered that particular alert tone was for the security camera app, not social media.

I broke off the kiss and grabbed my laptop, muttering a quick, "Hold on. Sorry."

My first thought was that it could be Jonathan Tybee making good on his threat to come to the house to get the manuscript. Or maybe

Detective Rice with new questions about the connection between Dahlia's murder and my father's books, or even whoever it was who kept trying to break into Malice House.

The app was set to rotate among the three cameras: the one on the front porch, the one in the hallway, and the one in the bedroom. There was nothing on the front porch. No Ink Drinkers, no crazed fans. The live feed of the hallway camera caught the back of my head in an eerie way that made me feel like I was outside of my own body. Then the feed rotated to the bedroom camera that was aimed under the bed. This screen had a red dot in the corner that indicated activity. But there was nothing there.

"Is everything all right?" Rafe asked.

The angle of the camera was off—it was pointed higher now, showing some of the bedspread. Then I saw my pajamas on the floor and relaxed somewhat—it looked like they had slipped off the bed and knocked the camera out of alignment.

"Yeah, um, false alarm." Though a voice urged me to go check, I set my laptop on the coffee table and grabbed Rafe's shirt, pulling him back into a kiss.

But after a few moments, it was no use. I couldn't shake the unsettling feeling of the camera alert going off when nothing was there.

I broke the kiss and sighed. "No."

"No?"

I glanced toward the stairs. "I just have so much work to do before this literary agent comes. Do you mind if we . . . pick this back up later?"

Rafe belonged to that particular breed of man who was so good-looking that he never appeared to feel rebuffed; he simply took me at my word. His eyes lingered on my lips, but then he shrugged a little boyishly. "Sure."

After he left, I did a thorough check of the primary bedroom, relieved to find nothing amiss and that the pajamas had simply fallen as I'd suspected. Then, since I could hardly invite Rafe back over after kicking him out, I decided to limp my way up to the attic to dig around the boxes and see if Hans and Frans from the documentary were right about poltergeists.

I pulled on a pair of faded old garden gloves as I knelt by the box of dirt. The back of my neck felt chilled, but I didn't take down my ponytail so as to not have to continually brush the hair out of my eyes with dirty gloves. As my hands rested on top of the box, I felt a sudden compulsion to look behind me, afraid I wasn't alone. Peering back into the quiet, I could hear the house creaking in the wind.

I opened the first box and began to comb through the clods of dirt. Even with the gloves on, the soil was cold, almost freezing. I raked my fingers through it, breaking up chunks, fishing out tiny seeds that looked like they'd come from a birdseed blend. Every moment I expected my fingers to catch on something hard, like a bone. I hoped for an animal bone. I wouldn't like it, but I could handle discovering that my father's dementia made him kill small birds or buy hamsters and forget to feed them—just as long as the dirt didn't hide long strands of blond hair, human teeth, a partially decayed skull.

But the box was empty save for the soil, like my father had simply wanted the dirt itself. Why? Where on the property had he gotten it from?

The birdseed.

I remembered seeing an old broken feeder in the woods on the far side of the security fence. My father must have dug up this soil from that area of the forest. Which was near where Rafe said he'd once seen my father digging.

I glanced outside the attic window.

It was late. The rain had stopped long enough for the moon to make a brief encore through fractured clouds. I could only imagine what one of the hospital's ER doctors would say if they knew I was about to hobble outside on a still-bandaged ankle with a shovel, ready to dig for god-knows-what.

CHAPTER SEVENTEEN

*The Hellhound dragged the mother by the wrist from the yellow house
to a den where her pups waited. She'd left the human baby to grow
into a larger meal. For now, she only needed the grown one. Now that
her pups' eyes had opened, they were two twin whirlwinds chasing
each other's tails and growing hungrier by the day. They smelled her
approaching the den and barreled out, panting, climbing all over the
cadaver, already trying to nurse from the dead woman's breasts. The
Hellhound growled to order them back into the den. Her jaw ached as
she dragged in the cadaver and finished preparing their meal.*

*The den was getting crowded with bodies. After the pups sucked
a dead mother dry, the Hellhound would gnaw on the bones, but not
even she, with her ample appetite, could eat that much meat before it
turned. . . .*

—From "Sweet Cream" in
Bedtime Stories for Monsters

I LIMPED INTO the backyard, where I freed a ladder in the
garage from endless spiderwebs, nature's booby traps.

Clouds rolled back over the moon. The only light came from the back porch and the flashlight I'd left balancing on a log. A light shone in an upper room in Rafe's house. What did he get up to when he wasn't nursing his helpless neighbor or making multimillion dollar nut butter deals? I never had asked what he'd been burning in his fire pit that first time I'd seen him—it was too odd of a question, and he already thought I was strange.

As I carried the ladder to the far end of the property fence that bordered the woods, I noticed how decades of fallen pine needles had blanketed the rear portion of the driveway so completely that it was practically gone, eaten by nature, with only a few patches of gravel as evidence that it had existed. The pines pressed in so closely back here; it had been irresponsible of my father not to have removed them. A strong storm could easily blow one onto the roof, smashing the attic and second-story bedrooms to ruins. A forest fire would leap from trees to house effortlessly. The six-foot privacy fence didn't even do a good job keeping *people* out—it would never stop nature.

I leaned the ladder on the fence and went back for a shovel, which I tossed over first so I'd have my hands free to climb. Dropping down carefully on the other side, I made sure to land on my good ankle. Immediately, I shivered. There was a reason I never went beyond the fence. At home, I could convince myself the world was a civilized place, but back here, the truth was bare: We were only borrowing time and space from the trees. This forest would persevere much longer than us.

I moved toward the area where I'd seen the birdfeeder and spotted it at last. Hanging from a tall rusty pole, long empty of seed. There was no sign of overturned soil, but Dad must have dug back here months or even years ago, and the forest had a way of growing back over anything that tried to damage it.

I picked a spot and plunged in the shovel. It was slow going with my wounded ankle.

As the rain grew, so did an uncanny sense that the trees couldn't have been cut down even if my father had tried. They towered over the house like sentinels—but on the lookout for what?

Shivering, I returned to my work. Plunging the shovel into the damp soil again and again. Dig, scoop, dump. Trying not to fuck up my ankle any more than it already was.

If this was one of Rob's horror movies, my shovel would connect with a glistening human skull . . . a skull that, after an examination by the county morgue, might match dental records belonging to my vanished mother. Only this wasn't a movie, and my mother's disappearance wasn't particularly mysterious. Young and mentally ill, known to have substance abuse issues and a documented case of severe postpartum depression. Just because her body had never been found didn't mean anything paranormal was involved. Although, if this *was* a horror movie, paranormal activity would only be a red herring for the real murderer: her husband.

It was always the husband in Rob's words.

Before my delusions got the best of me, I reminded myself that my mother had died in Maine. Malice House might as well have been Narnia for all my father had known about it at the time. He hadn't found and bought the house until nearly twenty years after her death, and even with my twisted mind, I couldn't believe that he would have kept her stuffed in some freezer for decades only to transport her body here to bury it.

The ground was turgid. My father's too-big rain boots sank into it, sucking me into the mud.

What was I even looking for?

There was nothing here, nothing buried, no bodies, certainly no hidden basement. As much as I didn't want to admit it, the truth was staring me in the face: The boxed-up dirt in the attic didn't mean anything. My father was demented. He probably thought he was collecting rock samples on Mars.

With a crash of thunder, the clouds opened into a drenching downpour. The shallow holes I'd dug filled with runoff.

Defeated, I threw the shovel to the ground. "Damn it!"

To my shock, the sound of a person laughing came from the other side of the fence. A dark, low kind of laugh that I first thought might just be the distant rumble of machinery or a truck on Cliffside Drive.

Was someone on my property?

I went still.

"Rafe?" I called hesitantly.

But *my* house was on the other side of the fence, not Rafe's. To get there, he would have had to scale the fence, too, or else come up the driveway. There was no answer, but I could have sworn I heard footsteps smashing the dead grass on the other side of the fence.

Dahlia Whitney had been murdered just a few hundred feet from here. Her body cut apart in the same way Pinchy attacked his victims. The thing under the bed that attacked me might be out there, too. Whatever it was, it was dangerous, and since Rafe had never found its body, it might not be dead at all.

A puff of steam rose into the air on the other side of the fence, followed by another, and after a terrified moment, I realized someone was *breathing* over there.

Could I run? Not likely, on my ankle.

Through a few hairline gaps between boards, a shadow moved slowly, blocking some of the ambient light from the house.

A line of frigid rain found its way down the back of my neck. I was too frightened to shiver. I wanted to be anywhere but here; tucked into a warm afghan with a cat on my lap and paintbrushes at my fingertips.

I squeezed the shovel harder.

The rain began falling in heavy sheets. The thin clouds of breath stopped for a few seconds. Then something smashed hard against the fence.

I shrieked.

The wood cracked. The fence held, but barely.

I staggered backward, brandishing the shovel. Adrenaline took me over like a puppet master, and I gave myself to it, surrendering to a primal self that knew better what to do.

The world had darkened to the color of the clouds, a tenebrious gray that swallowed soil and sky and everything in between. The downpour rushed in my ears. I thought I heard dark laughter again.

I moved backward until I felt the press of the birdfeeder pole at my back and twisted around, breathing hard. Something crashed into the fence again. In another second, it was going to shatter.

I'd left the ladder on the house side of the fence. My plan had been to use the shovel to hinge it over to the forest side when I was ready to climb again, but the movement would give me away. Regardless, the person was *on* the house side. Improbably, I felt safer in the woods.

I moved with painfully slow, silent steps away from the fence, moving toward the lights of Rafe's house broken by the span of trees separating our two properties. I used the shovel as a crutch as I ran limping toward his house.

My ankle felt tender but strangely painless, which meant adrenaline had kicked in. I was making the sprain worse, but in the moment I didn't care. It was all I could do to stumble forward in the meager moonlight, hoping I didn't smash into a tree branch. I thought back to Baker and me with our flashlights, arguing with each other, searching for my father all night.

Who would come looking for me?

As soon as Malice House's lights faded behind me, I stopped running and bent over to catch my breath. I closed my eyes and listened. The rain had lightened. The night was filled with dripping water from trees and the distant sound of the ocean, but no footsteps besides my own.

I threw a glance back in the direction of my house. Who the hell was there?

Following the lights of Rafe's house, I limped over fallen branches and brambles. Frigid rain rolled off the branches overhead and fell on me in gelatinous drops. It was only a few hundred feet through the trees to Rafe's driveway. Not that far at all. *Keep going.* My boot caught on a root, and I crashed down, landing on hands and knees in the rotting leaves. Pain shot through my ankle. My hand had landed in something slimy—in the dark I couldn't see what it was. Some kind of fungus. It smelled like death.

When I pushed to my feet, I stopped, confused.

Where was Rafe's house? The lights had vanished.

At first, I thought he must have turned off every lamp in the house, but when I twisted in a circle, there was his house behind me, lights still blazing. I must have gotten turned around when I fell. I shook my head and headed for the glow of his home.

The leaves were slick under my boots. So much rain had gotten into them that I felt it sloshing around, miniature oceans drowning my toes. I climbed onto a rotting log, balancing carefully, and when I stepped down, Rafe's house was gone again.

I turned, and there it was behind me.

"What the *fuck*," I breathed.

A branch snapped somewhere close, and terror overcame me. I didn't have the safety of the fence now. For all I knew, I was out here in the open with whatever had killed Dahlia.

I tried to move toward Rafe's again, but impossibly, the lights appeared to grow more distant the farther I went. What was happening? Panic must have disoriented me. The strip of forest between our two houses wasn't that wide; I could probably throw a softball from one end to the other. But now his lights were barely a twinkle between the farthest branches, as distant as a star. When I looked behind me, there was no sign of Malice House at all.

Instead of crossing the narrow strip of trees between our properties, I had managed to wander far into the deep of the woods.

I climbed a small rise and twisted in a circle, scanning the trees.

No lights anywhere.

I wasn't a hiker. New York hadn't prepared me for the type of absolute darkness beneath the trees. The city streets glimmered with lights at all hours, from traffic signals and headlights, bars and twenty-four-hour bodegas. It was only now that I felt the absence of the city—its crowds, its sounds—that I realized I'd never been in the woods alone. A few short hikes as a child, a single camping trip with Baker and his college buddies. That was all. My father had grown up exploring the woods of Maine, catching salamanders and building pine-bough forts—or so his biographical journals claimed. But he hadn't deemed it necessary to expose me to the great outdoors. My childhood years had been spent in bookstores and libraries, boarding school, long car rides with nannies.

It was so quiet that I could hear the waves in the distance.

"Cliffside Drive," I muttered, whipping my head toward the sound. That was how to get out of the woods. The road hugged the coast from Seattle as far north as Canada. If I just followed the sound of the waves, I couldn't help but hit the road eventually.

The hair on my arms stood up like electricity was building somewhere close by. I hugged the shovel close. Its solidity was the only thing I had to cling to. I felt something brush the back of my neck and shuddered, wiping frantically at my neck. A spider?

Something was stuck to my shirt. I tugged it free and stared in the faint light.

A feather.

Even in the almost complete dark, I could tell this was no ordinary feather. It didn't take a naturalist to know any owl or hawk feather wasn't a foot and a half long and ending in a razor-sharp point.

A branch snapped somewhere close, and I yelped. I wasn't alone. A figure moved through the underbrush about thirty feet away from me. My mind started to spin out of control: *Kestrel. It's a goddamn demon.*

The figure moved like a person, walking confidently over the underbrush and so quietly that I could almost convince myself I was imagining things.

The wind made the trees sway overhead. Laughter mixed with the sound of dripping rain, and I spun in the opposite direction. Who was there? I didn't see any more movement, until my eyes adjusted more. Something was glowing faintly like phosphorescent fungus. Maybe it was a trick of my eyes. I blinked, trying to make sense of the dark shapes.

Was that a face there, behind a tree about twenty feet away, looking out at me? It didn't reflect moonlight but was actually glowing on its own in the darkness—unless my mind was playing tricks on me. For all I knew, that laughter belonged to the trickster, the silver-haired man in black, the Harbinger.

I spun around and hobbled as fast as I could toward the coast, ignoring the pain in my ankle. A root caught my toe. I stumbled, barely catching myself before falling. I'd never learned how to move through the woods, especially without following a trail. Suddenly, every patch of pine needles hid a divot and every root conspired to trip me. The branches of the lower canopy whipped my face, their rubber hands urging me backward, back toward Malice House.

I reached a clearing where the fog had lifted, though not enough to expose the moon or stars. The darkness started to make me doubt myself. If I continued toward the sound of the ocean, then I couldn't help but come across Cliffside Drive, which I could then follow back to the house. But the trees were filled with echoes, and I couldn't be certain anymore which direction the ocean was. As I plunged toward what I hoped was the sound of waves, a premonition crept over me. *Something was wrong.* In the time I'd been in Lundie Bay, sleeping with the windows cracked, the rhythm of the waves had settled into my unconscious. This was different.

The sounds weren't waves, I realized.

They were whispers.

Luring me in the opposite direction from the road.

I stopped cold. Branches caged me in overhead, but at least I could see a few feet on either side of me. A massive fallen tree, smelling of rot, opened the canopy and formed a sort of pathway through the woods. At the very end of the cleared space stood a figure.

She was too far away to make out any features, but I felt certain it was a woman. She was short, with a smear of shadows below her waist like a skirt made of night. Whispers crept like smoke along the underbrush. A terror I'd never felt before prickled up my skin. Rob had sent me a movie once with a note attached: *Haven, this one is DARK. My other recappers couldn't make it past the bathtub scene.* The movie had been violent and sickening, and I'd watched it while eating chocolate-covered pretzels, jotting down notes, pausing at the climax to hunt for my nail clippers. Rob's movies never scared me. Not even that one.

But I was scared now.

My lungs were too empty to scream. My legs seemed to know what to do, though, and they stumbled backward and then began to run in the opposite direction. If my ankle hurt, I didn't feel it now. Pine needles scratched my cheeks as I pushed into a copse. A branch caught me in the middle, and I doubled over. I dropped to my knees, scrambling under it on all fours. The forest floor was damp and earthy as my fingers dug into pine needles.

Then, ahead: *a light*!

It was high enough that it had to be one of the streetlamps illuminating Cliffside Drive.

I got up and—at last—my feet hit solid road. The sound of shoes on pavement had never been more welcome. I paused beneath the streetlight to catch my breath. On the other side of the road, the cliff gave way to the ocean a hundred feet below.

I limp-jogged down the road, wincing at the pain in my ankle and in my chest from colliding with the tree branch. It had to be around midnight. I had no idea where I was on the road. I didn't recognize any landmarks. Somehow, I had wandered miles from Malice House in a forest that had kaleidoscoped around me.

Around the next bend, a car was parked in a scenic view pull-out, its engine still on, headlights blazing out to sea.

I sobbed out loud in terrified relief. "Hey, I need help!"

I threw myself against the driver-side door. There were two people inside, one in the driver seat, the other in the passenger. I pounded my fist against the foggy window.

They didn't move.

Were they asleep? Passed out on drugs?

"Help, please!"

I tugged on the door handle, surprised to find that it was unlocked and swung easily open.

Well, that's why they didn't answer my call.

Dead.

Both of them.

Blood and brain matter stuck to the insides of the windows. Their faces were so badly damaged that I couldn't even tell if they were women or men, old or young, strangers or someone I knew.

I doubled over and threw up onto the pavement.

CHAPTER EIGHTEEN

The Decaylings left the Harbinger sopping wet and bruised, but that was no matter. Clothes dried. Bruises healed. They'd asked a smaller price for their secrets than the Witch of Went had—the angry scar on his abdomen like a receipt for services rendered. And now he had what he needed. A name, or at least a moniker: the Salem Dreamer.

Next, he had to find that dog from hell.

—From "Beasts of Sun" in
Bedtime Stories for Monsters

"LET'S GO OVER this one more time."

The shadows under Detective Rice's eyes suggested she'd had a very long night, though it was nothing compared to the night *I'd* had. Morning glow was starting to filter through the forests, burning off the fog that still blanketed Cliffside Drive, thick and wet, making me shiver. The police hadn't offered me a blanket.

A guy driving home from a late shift had found me by the side of the road puking my guts out and, after hearing my panicked babbling about the bodies, had called 911. The police had come, gotten a statement and ID from the guy, but kept me longer. We'd been at it for hours. All I wanted was to crawl into bed and pull my covers over my head. The bodies were gone. The coroner had shown up around three in the morning and double-bagged the cadavers after the police had taken a slew of crime scene photographs. Officers were still going over the car, collecting and bagging evidence, while I sat in the back of Detective Rice's Dodge Charger with the door open.

Down the street, a journalist paced on the far side of the police tape like a jackal, trying to get information out of the cops.

"So you left your house intending to visit your neighbor but got turned around in the woods." Letitia Rice consulted her notes. "And this was around twelve o'clock?"

"The best I can recollect." She had supplied the timeline, not me. Sometime around two in the morning I'd managed to calm down enough to help her estimate the events of the night before, though naturally I'd left out the fact that *ghosts* were stalking me. I wasn't even sure *I* believed that.

"You said you weren't a hiker."

"I'm not, *clearly*." I threw out a tired hand toward the forest. "I got lost in a quarter mile of trees."

A police officer waved the detective over. They spoke quietly for a few minutes near the victims' car, then Detective Rice gave the lurking journalist a withering glare and returned to me.

"Any information on who they are?" I asked.

She shook her head. "We ran the tag, but because it's a rental car it'll take some time to track down their identities. Probably tourists. Neither of them had ID on them. Any wallet or purse they had was taken."

The police had refused to tell me anything about the victims, but when the coroner had removed the bodies, I'd been able to tell that it was a man and a woman in their late twenties or thirties, judging by their trendy clothes. I'd heard the words *murder-suicide* muttered between officers.

Detective Rice sighed. "We'll need to confirm with Mr. Kahn that you were with him yesterday evening. We'll see if he saw anything or can verify when you were home." She scratched her nose and then flipped her notebook closed. "Can I be straight with you, Haven?"

I gave a weak nod, exhausted.

"This doesn't look good for you. Your father's former domestic employee is found dead just up the road from here, and now you just happen to find two dead bodies in the middle of the night. Do *I* think you had anything to do with it? No. The way I see it, you're a victim here, too. Whoever has been trying to break into your house could be connected to these attacks. But with the tip about your father's books mimicking Dahlia Whitney's murders—and my gut's telling me more connections might come up with these, too—the coincidences are stacking up against you. So the more help you can give us, the better it will work out for you. I'm on your side here."

I didn't believe her, and from her tired voice, I don't think she really expected me to. I had no reason not to trust Detective Rice personally, but I'd had my own run-ins with distrustful cops, and I had seen enough horror movies and true crime documentaries to know how police operated when they were investigating a murder. And this felt like a classic tactic to warm me up and make me feel comfortable in hopes that I would let details slip.

"Got it," I said tightly, then added unconvincingly, "Anything I can do to help."

Detective Rice looked like all she wanted to do was crawl into bed, too. She shoved her notebook in her pants pocket and squinted up at the rising sun. "You're free to go, though I expect we'll have more questions once these bodies are ID'd. Shame you didn't head back to New York when I told you to. Now I'm going to have to ask you to stick around town for a few days; after that, I wouldn't blame you if you threw up a For Sale sign and got the hell out of here."

A car pulled up, headlines shining in the early morning fog, and stopped at the barricade. A police officer began speaking to the driver, then yelled Detective Rice's name. "Ride's here."

Detective Rice nodded before turning back to me. "It's probably not a good time for you to be alone. I've seen bodies damaged like that before, and I can tell you that it starts to get into your head. Gives you nightmares."

"I'll ask my neighbor to come over."

She gave me a stiff pat on the back. "I went ahead and called someone for you. Figure you'd need a ride back to the house anyway."

She motioned to the cop, who said a few words to the car's driver, who turned off the headlights and cut the engine.

To my horror, Catherine Tybee stepped out of the car. She was wearing jeans and leather boots with a shawl wrapped around her torso, but she hadn't had time for makeup in her hurry to get here.

The police officer lifted the tape for her to duck under.

"Haven! Oh, this is a *nightmare!*"

I shoved up from the back seat of Detective Rice's car. Catherine was as welcome as a bee sting. I threw an alarmed look toward the detective. She called *Catherine Tybee*? What on earth made her think we were close? Catherine must have been spreading gossip around Lundie Bay, telling everyone about me moving back into Malice House and my *deep connection* to the Ink Drinkers.

Catherine approached me in a rush with her arms open for a hug, but the look on my face must have warned her off. She let her arms fall. If she'd tried, I didn't trust myself not to slap her away and bite and kick like some rabid animal. Adrenaline still shot through me, stringing me out. I hadn't slept. I'd just seen people with *their faces shot off.*

A rare moment of uncertainty crossed Catherine's face, but then she rewrapped her shawl around her chest and pressed a hand against her cheek. "You poor thing. I'll take you home. This is just awful. I can't imagine what you must be feeling."

The unfortunate truth was, I *did* need a ride home. I'd ended up miles away in my delirium. It would be a long, miserable walk in the mist with my bandaged ankle, and bumming a ride off Detective Rice or another police officer was equally unappealing.

I briefly debated calling Rafe to pick me up, but I was too tired to argue. The one thing Catherine had going for her was that she was here now. The sooner I could be in my bed, the better, and I was caring less and less how I got there.

Catherine shepherded me into her car, where she dug a second wool shawl out of the back seat and forced me to wrap it around myself. Her fingers stretched anxiously over the wheel as she drove, leaning forward in her seat, face pinched.

". . . hate to think what their loved ones will do when they find out . . . really not safe, you know . . . bear attacks from a few years ago . . . don't think bears can open car doors, can they? Do they have thumbs?"

I didn't know if her anxious chatter was meant to fill the silence or if she really wanted to have a conversation about the capabilities of bears, but I didn't even pretend to listen. I closed my eyes and tried not to picture blood splatter.

When she pulled up to my gate, she rolled down her window at the keypad box. "I'll need the code, sweetie."

This was the jolt I needed to snap out of my stupor. I looked between the keypad and the house through the gates and then grabbed the door handle. "Here is fine. I'll let myself through the gate. Thanks for the ride."

As soon as I opened the car door, Catherine scrambled after me, practically climbing over the gear box until her seat belt stopped her. "Wait! Let me make you some coffee! You shouldn't be alone."

"I'll call a friend."

"But I'm right *here*! You've got to be going through so much right now. First Dahlia, now this. Your poor father only died a few months ago. And we still need to talk about the manuscript. You know, Jonathan has been trying to call you. He has an offer on the table from Empire Publishing. What about your illustrations? Are you still working on them?"

How had this woman managed to steer concern for my wellbeing into an opportunity to needle me about the manuscript? Her gall was stunning. Grimacing, I muttered a quick thanks for the ride and slammed the door.

I made sure to block the keypad from her sight with my body while I typed in the code. I was half-afraid she was going to hit the gas and barrel straight forward once the gates slid open, but she just sat in the driveway, chewing on her lip, her knuckles white on the steering wheel.

The house held a musty, unpleasant odor, like I hadn't taken out the trash in a few days. Two empty wineglasses sat on the living room coffee table next to the open VHS box for *Poltergestia* and the notebook where I'd jotted down research about soil and paranormal sightings. Contrary to Catherine's exclamations, I didn't feel *alone*. Whether it was the remnants of my evening with Rafe or something else, I felt watched. My eyes fell on the hidden camera on the entry table, and I again got that topsy-turvy feeling that I *was* being watched—by myself, or some future version of myself.

On my way to the stairs to take a shower, already peeling off my dirty, sweat-soaked shirt, I passed the archway to the library and noticed that all the framed photographs on the table were facedown again. The German accent of those twin documentarians snuck its way into my brain, whispering about unexplained phenomenon merely being science that we didn't yet understand.

"Hello?" I called to the empty house, feeling a little ridiculous. Naturally, only my voice echoed back.

Stripping out of the rest of my clothes, I cranked up the shower as hot as it could go and stood under the water, letting it scour me. I wanted to burn off the thin film of gore from what I'd seen in that car. The heat stung in a good way, both numbing me and waking me up.

Alone in the shower, drowned in scalding water, I finally let forbidden thoughts come.

There could be a logical explanation for the slithering sounds and the overturned photographs. Pipes. Down drafts. *Sure*. There could even be an explanation for that thing that attacked me, like Rafe said, a diseased wild animal that, in the dark, my mind twisted into Pinchy.

But what about the figures I had seen in the woods? Those were no wild animals. I supposed that it could have been crazed fans in costumes trying to scare me out of my house like an episode of *Scooby-Doo*. But this wasn't television. As disorienting as the woods at night could be, was it really possible to get lost crossing a few hundred feet from my house to Rafe's? The way his house lights had moved wasn't natural. In *Bedtime Stories for Monsters*, the Witch of Went's ability to bend reality like a kaleidoscope—it was even the title of her story—felt eerily identical to what I'd experienced.

What if . . .

"Don't think it, Haven," I growled aloud at myself.

What if . . . they're really all fucking real?

Kestrel. The Harbinger. The Witch of Went. All the characters that my father had created and that I had given form to were here, in this world, far more than mere poltergeists.

Or else I'm truly losing my mind.

I finished in the shower, threw on some clothes, and crashed into bed for a much-needed nap, more exhausted than I'd ever been in my life. But my mind wouldn't calm down. Why had Catherine Tybee had to bring up my father's death? Wasn't it bad enough that I was surrounded from the moment I woke to the moment I fell sleep by his novels and his awards, his old Werther's tins and his sweaters still draped over chair backs like he'd just stepped out to get the mail? I was the only family he'd had other than his sister, Rose, but their relationship had barely extended to birthday cards. For years he'd been shuffling around in this old house on his own. Sure, he had Dahlia, and invitations to conferences and award ceremonies, and book readings, and ample affairs even at his age, but I knew how hollow all of that could feel. I'd been married, supposedly sharing my life with another person, and had never felt more alone than when I'd been with Baker.

I must have fallen asleep at some point because I woke up some time later in a groggy post-nap haze, wondering if it was even still the same day. I grabbed my phone from the nightstand to check the time and saw a text message from Kylie.

Haven. Holy shit. I heard about the deaths. Are you okay?

I didn't want to spend years trapped in this house spiraling into paranoia like my father. I could see my future like the water swirling down the tub drain, and what I saw was grim: I might look put together from the outside but inside I'd completely lose my grip on reality. Descend into an obsession with a fictional world whose borders bled off the sketchbook in ways that made the hair raise on the back of my neck.

I *wouldn't* end up like my father, haunted by demons of my own making. I might've been barely clinging to sanity, but that meant I hadn't yet let go.

I had to get out of this house. I had to get away from my father's ghosts.

I texted Kylie back with shaking fingers.

Want to get a drink?

CHAPTER NINETEEN

From high above the trees, people looked like mice skittering beneath his shadow. Kestrel took his time picking out the slowest, plumpest target before descending.

—From "Sundown Coming" in
Bedtime Stories for Monsters

●

KYLIE SUGGESTED WE meet after her shift at five o'clock at the bar at the Mayfelt, a historic hotel perched on the cliffs overlooking town. The minute I opened the inn's door and saw the cozy antique fireplace, a bar that looked like it had been transported straight out of a British pub, and more empty tables than not, I felt instantly better. This is what I wanted. Quiet. Normalcy. The biggest pour of merlot the bartender would give me.

A couple shared a slice of chocolate cake drizzled with strawberry sauce at a table near the windows, which must have a beautiful view when the weather was clear. At the moment, heavy fog padded the glass like the entire hotel was about to be packaged up and shipped off. Sipping my wine, I toyed with the Celtic ring from my dad's pen jar, spinning it like a top on the counter, letting the rhythm hypnotize me.

Kylie was still wearing her bookstore name tag when she showed up. It declared her favorite book to be *Get in Trouble*. She slid onto the barstool next to me and hung her messenger bag from the hook beneath the bar. She caught the bartender's eye and said, "Malbec, please?"

Then she twisted sharply toward me and cupped her hand over her mouth, whispering, "What the *fuck*, Haven? Dead bodies? Are you okay?"

I nodded shakily as I replaced the ring on my pinkie and polished off the remainder of my wine. When the bartender brought Kylie a drink, I asked for a second.

"Actually, no. I'm not."

"No shit. I can't imagine coming across something like that. What were you doing out on the road by yourself so late?"

I picked up the ring and twisted it around my finger, wondering how much to share with Kylie. Her sense of humor drew me to her. There weren't many young people in Lundie Bay and almost no Black people, which meant she was comfortable being an outlier or more likely, simply didn't have a choice about it. She reminded me of someone I would have met in New York City, not here, like we were both castaways who had washed up in this place against our will. At the same time, though, I knew in the back of my head that Kylie was being cagey.

Granted, so was I.

"I got turned around in the woods trying to go to my neighbor's house." I gave a shrug I hoped looked casual, while hiding my shaking hands in my lap. "I didn't think I'd had that much to drink, but I guess I did."

Kylie nodded sympathetically in a "been there" way, but then the nodding transformed into a head shake as her expression turned grim. She gave an involuntary shudder. "People are saying that it's a bear again. Apparently, this happened summer before last. There was, like, a rabid bear that killed a few hikers. The forest service closed off all the trails this afternoon. They're warning people not to go into the woods."

"No way it was a bear. Blood was sprayed everywhere like from a gunshot." That was horror movie logic 101. "The police were whispering about a murder-suicide."

She shook her head at her glass of wine. "I guess rumors are just rumors."

I suddenly pressed my hands flat on the counter. "Hey, can I ask you something?" I wasn't sure where my impulsive openness came from—maybe the wine. "Something . . . strange?"

This stoked her interested. "Sure."

"Well, first off, I can't tell you how much I appreciated you taking me to the hospital. But, when you came over, you took a towel out of the trunk in the bedroom. It's just something weird I noticed. How did you know that's where a towel would be?"

She rubbed her eyebrow like her piercing was itchy, digging her fingers into her forehead like she had to think about it. "Oh. I did look around. Remember? I couldn't find any towels in the bathroom, and it made sense that because it was so small that they'd be somewhere right outside."

"Oh." I forced a small laugh to break the tension.

Did I believe her? It was true that I didn't remember much about that day other than completely freaking out, but it still didn't seem right. I didn't remember her looking anywhere else. I was thinking of ways I could push for more answers when another idea wormed its way into my brain.

"Yeah, the house is so old that there are all kinds of quirks, like having to store towels in weird places," I said. "I actually found a key the other day that referenced a basement, which is strange, because the house has no basement." I watched her closely, looking for any tells.

But if she knew anything about a mysterious basement, she certain didn't show it as she scrunched up her face in genuine puzzlement. "That's weird. What else could it refer to?"

I shrugged. "No idea. I've been trying to figure it out. My dad was kind of a hoarder. The attic is filled with more boxes than I could ever go through. I wonder if the basement is, like, really an offsite storage unit somewhere where he kept more things. Maybe things he didn't want people snooping through after his death."

She sipped her wine. "Maybe."

Her reaction didn't strike me as that of a criminal mastermind brilliantly covering up a scheme, so I lost the nerve to push harder.

"Sorry. I've been a little out of it."

Her lips formed a small, sympathetic pout. She motioned to the bartender to refill both of our glasses. "Well, I have news that might make you feel better." She plunged a hand in her messenger bag and fished out her wallet. She took out five hundred-dollar bills and laid them down dramatically on the counter. "I sold the typewriter. Almost eight hundred dollars, so that's your cut. Not quite as much as I'd hoped, but I got the sense immediate cash would be better than spending time waiting for a higher bid."

Money, especially cash, had been so foreign to me that I pounced on the bills like we were doing a drug deal and quickly stashed them in my pocket. "That *is* good news."

"How's work going? Your artwork?"

My eyes snapped to her suspiciously. Catherine had practically snarled that same question at me that morning with a feral hunger. But Kylie seemed like she was just making conversation, and I reminded myself that she didn't even like my father's books, let alone know about the manuscript.

Hunching forward over my wineglass, I chewed on a nail. "My art?" There were plenty of things I could say about my artwork but nothing that wouldn't make me sound like I was following my father down the long road to dementia. "To be honest, I've been thinking about art in general a lot. Like, if it holds a kind of . . . power."

"Yeah? Like what?"

I straightened as I toyed with the candle the bartender had set out on the bar. "Well, you're a novelist, right? Do you think what you write has an impact on the world? Not just after a book comes out and people read it and either love or hate it, but the *actual writing* of it. You're making something out of nothing. In a way, you're creating a new world."

"Like writers playing gods?"

"Yeah. Yeah, exactly. Who is to say that by creating a story, that story isn't actually happening somewhere? On a different dimension or a parallel universe? Or that you aren't writing fiction at all but just channeling a world and characters that already exist on some other plane?"

She leaned back as she considered this, and her eyes shifted to the three empty wineglasses in front of me. Just when I was expecting her to tell me to slow down on the booze, she rested her elbows on the bar and her chin in her hands. Her forehead wrinkled in thought.

"There is a kind of strange feeling that happens when you get really into the writing," she said. "It's probably the same for you when you're drawing. The flow. The muse. That zoned-out state where it does almost feel like you're touching on some, I don't know, magic."

I nodded, staring into the candle flame. Was it just being "in the zone"? Sometimes when I drew or painted, especially recently, I felt entranced. I would spend hours working and have little memory of it, like phantom driving, suddenly being parked in front of my destination and not remembering how I got there.

"When I was a kid," I said, "I thought art had to be beautiful. That the prettier you could make a drawing, the better it was. Until one day when I was digging around a bookstore while my father was doing a reading. I must have been nine or ten. I found a book of 1960s-era Colombian art: really ugly, grotesque stuff. And I just *got* it. It unlocked this deeper understanding that art didn't have to be pretty to be valid. I mean, I wouldn't want bullet-ridden albatrosses on my bedroom walls, but I realized that the dark, strange, ugly works were the most powerful. No one ever overthrew a government because they read a book on ponies, you know? It's because they read about monsters, war, darkness—and were inspired to change things."

Kylie wore an amused look as she tapped her painted fingernail on the bottom of her wineglass.

"Do I sound crazy?" I asked.

"You found two dead people this morning and got questioned by the police. I'd probably be mulling over life and death and creation, too." She chewed on the inside of her cheek before asking, "What's got you thinking about all this? Is it . . . related to your father's books?" Her voice dropped. "People at the bookstore have been talking about the connection between *Feast of Flowers* and Dahlia's murder. Do you think, like, a copycat killer took inspiration from his book? Between you and me, I don't buy the bear thing either."

I shifted uncomfortably. "I've just had a lot on my mind."

Kylie leaned back on the barstool, swiveling it back and forth as she thought. "If there was a murderer copying a plotline out of *Feast of Flowers*, there's nothing you can do about it, right? The genie is out of the bottle. Once a story is out there and into the common conscious-ness, it can't be taken back."

Her words lodged in my brain like a thorn. She was right. Once a book was published it couldn't be taken back even if it was banned or retracted; its ideas spread like a literary virus. But not all my father's books had been published and let loose on the zeitgeist. *Bedtime Stories for Monsters* only existed in the mind of the sole living person who had read it—me.

We shifted to other subjects: to the bookstore and how Orion was trying to get Kylie to join his fiction writers critique group, and then she had to take off because she had early shifts solid for the next week. By the time we left, the sky was clouded over again but, thankfully, it wasn't raining. Driving down Cliffside Drive gave me the disorienting feeling that I was in my own horror movie, being in the place where just the night before I'd stumbled out of the woods and found the dead tourists. When I got home and my headlights projected striping black shadows on the house through the gate's bars, I stared at it in dread.

Next door, blueish lights flickered on and off in Rafe's windows. He was watching TV; alone, I hoped.

I pulled out my phone and texted.

Feel like company?

At some point I would have to stop avoiding my own home, afraid of those mysterious spaces between the walls, but tonight wasn't the night.

When he texted back inviting me over, I backed out of my driveway and pulled into his. There was no way I was going to risk cutting through the trees on foot again.

When I closed my car door, I glimpsed the eaves of Malice House towering over the pines. The fog devoured everything in sight except for the structure. It looked like I'd wiped my hand over a fogged-up mirror and the house, in the center, was crystal-clear, like it was the only real thing and we were all just walking dreams.

CHAPTER TWENTY

Malice was chaos, and chaos was malice. There had been order once. Kings ruled over countries, mayors over towns, tiny dictators at home. But in a land where no one truly knew anyone and everyone conspired, order was anathema, and forging any system of cooperation that would suss out greatness from the bedlam would take a devil's trade.

—**From the Introduction to**
Bedtime Stories for Monsters

RAFE'S BED WAS a massive Japanese-style beast that faced the floor-to-ceiling windows oriented toward the sea. Beside me, he snored in his sleep. After we'd watched TV and made out a little, I'd snacked on peanut butter out of the jar and ended up eating the whole container. Now it sat heavy in my belly. There was a chance I'd be sick. From this angle in bed, all I could see outside was sky and water, giving me the strange sensation of being out at sea.

I wasn't sure what instinct made me roll out of bed and shuffle into his slippers when I couldn't find my own shoes. All night, I had replayed the conversation with Kylie at the Mayfelt in my head: art and power. *Bedtime Stories for Monsters* had been a curse ever since I'd found it. The manuscript seemed to possess a power over anyone who knew about it: The Ink Drinkers were desperate to get their hands on it, crazed fans were trying to break into the house, and somehow, I knew the manuscript was tied to my father's downfall. I wasn't sure which had come first, the manuscript or his dementia, but I wasn't interested in chicken-or-egg riddles. There was something dark about that book. Malignant. One way or another, in some form, Malice had crept into Malice House.

Wearing Rafe's slippers and his robe, I tiptoed out to my car and drove the absurdly short distance back home, still not trusting myself to make it through the strip of woods in a straight line. Now that the clouds had shifted and the moon was out, some of the house's dazzling terror had faded, and it looked more like what it was: just wood and nails, tar paper and insulation.

I moved anxiously, like I was being pursued. In the library, I dropped to my knees and tugged off the lid of the Werther's tin and pulled out the rubber-band-bound pages of the manuscript. This was the only copy in existence. Written by hand, not saved on a hard drive anywhere. I hadn't made photocopies and I sure as hell hadn't let Jonathan Tybee scan it.

I stuffed it back into the tin and brought it with me as I hobbled upstairs.

The windows rattled as the wind picked up outside. I threw a look over my shoulder, feeling like a stranger in my own home. Ever since I'd felt that kaleidoscope sensation in the woods, I couldn't shake it—a certain alienation had attached itself to me. Reality felt inverted. Like I was the crazed fan breaking in, not the resident.

Upstairs, I began throwing my sketches of the *Bedtime Stories* characters into the tin along with the manuscript. All my finished illustrations in ink and watercolor. Hours had gone into each of them. I tossed in all my preliminary and half-finished sketches, too, and even dropped to my knees to fish crumpled, rejected sketches out of the trash can. Everything went into the Werther's tin. I swept the rest of my supplies into a cardboard box and crammed it into the corner of the bedroom.

I only felt safe once I'd driven back to Rafe's property and stepped out onto the back patio sheltered by two sides of his house. From here, the ocean wasn't visible, only the forest. But Rafe maintained his property better than my father had, and there was a low stone wall and a tidy row of Leyland cypresses as a border between his house and the wilderness. The wild pines didn't press in here like they did at Malice House.

His bedroom window on the second floor was still dark. I wasn't sure what time it was, but it had to be the early-morning hours of night.

I set the Werther's tin on an Adirondack chair facing the fire pit.

Matches.

I'd forgotten to grab a box of matches. Rafe would have some inside his house, but I didn't want to wake him by rustling around like a ghost in his kitchen. The old shed was just on the far side of the patio. I tried the door, but it was locked. The glass window was dirty and covered in cobwebs; it didn't look like anyone had been inside for months. An old, forgotten relic from an earlier time. The ancient foundation disappeared deep into the ground. The whole thing stuck out like a bruise against Rafe's otherwise sleek and well-tended house. I was surprised he hadn't bulldozed it and put in a koi pond.

I was about to head inside the house when I glimpsed a lighter tucked in a chink between the rocks surrounding the fire pit. Before I could lose my nerve, I grabbed it and began tossing pages into the fire pit. Words and images tried to snag my attention, but I wouldn't listen. Their siren song wasn't going to sway me.

With a flick of my thumb, the lighter birthed a flame. I crouched low, holding the flame to the corner of the Harbinger's finished illustration.

"Come on, come on."

It didn't want to catch. I'd painted his portrait on thick, expensive watercolor paper. A gust of wind made the flame dance away. I flipped the lighter on again and held it there, determined, until the paper finally surrendered. The flame smoldered slowly around the edges, but then once it hit the oil-based ink, it started roaring. I watched the fire consume the Harbinger's black boots and pants all the way up to the crown of his silver locks. By then all the papers were burning.

I tossed the lighter on the edge of the pit and collapsed back onto the Adirondack chair, studying the flames.

Weeks of work, gone. Not to mention however long my father had worked on the stories. And all the lost money, too; I was burning hundreds of thousands of dollars in royalties.

But all I felt as I watched the pages burn was immense relief.

Ever since I'd found the manuscript in the attic, a curse had been following me. Crazed fans trespassing at all hours of night and trying to break into the house. Dahlia and the two tourists brutally murdered on Cliffside Drive. Worst of all was what the manuscript was doing to *me*. Making me suspicious of everyone I came in contact with, from the Ink Drinkers to Detective Rice, even to Kylie.

Making me think ghosts are real.

The highest eave of Malice House was visible over the Leyland cypresses at the edge of Rafe's patio. With a jolt, I realized I was looking at the same small attic window that I had looked through nearly a month ago, my first night back in Lundie Bay, when I had observed Rafe burning something in this same fire pit at three in the morning.

Curious, I pulled out my phone and checked the time.

3:01 a.m.

A shiver ran over my skin. I hugged Rafe's robe tighter as I slipped the phone back in my pocket. Again, I had the feeling that reality had inverted. Could there be a world where I'd seen *myself* through the window, at the fire pit now, burning the manuscript?

The fire was thriving now. Small scraps of paper floated on the updraft, carrying sparks skyward like they were trying to escape.

It occurred to me then that I was kind of fucked when it came to Eddie Chase.

Our meeting was scheduled for later that day. We planned to meet at the Mayfelt Hotel bar at four in the afternoon. He probably wasn't planning to fly into Seattle until later in the morning, so maybe there was still time to call him and tell him not to come, that the manuscript was gone.

Still, as the last scraps of paper crumbled to ash, I felt like I'd shed some awful, heavy, smelly coat. *Bedtime Stories for Monsters* was gone, as were my illustrations, but I had an entire portfolio of other artwork that I'd done back in New York. Illustration pieces that had nothing to do with Malice or demons or my father. Artwork that was truly my own.

I'd thought that the only way to launch my career was to tie my work to my father's fame, but Eddie had said SunBurst was more interested in *me*. Maybe my artwork was good enough on its own. Eddie might not like the bait-and-switch, coming all the way out here only for me to show him an entirely different project, but I had the head of a literary agency interested in my work, and I needed this fresh start. I'd be an idiot not to at least try.

I watched the fire smolder until only wispy ashes remained, then filled Rafe's watering can from the outdoor tap and doused the coals. The last thing I needed was to inadvertently start a forest fire. Steam rose as the ashes sizzled. The water revealed something shiny in the ashes—I'd glimpsed it before. I set aside the watering can and poked through the ashes to pick it up.

A dog tag. The kind that belonged to an actual dog, not a soldier.

It was attached to a scrap of melted plastic orange collar. It read TOSCA on one side and had a phone number on the other.

Did Rafe ever own a dog? I didn't recall seeing any water or food dishes inside or photos of a dog on his refrigerator, though maybe the dog had passed away long ago.

Something whispered in my ear not to dig around further, to let things lie; yet I found myself reaching out tentatively with a piece of kindling. The end of the stick grazed something else hard amid the smoldering ashes, and I fished out a second dog collar. This one was leather and almost entirely burned except for the silver tag. *Max.*

I started to feel ill as I dug through the fire pit and came up with more dog tags. Some were still attached to burned collars, some were just the tags. They were all sizes and shapes.

Ronaldo. Zeus. Pepper. Bella.

"What the fuck," I whispered, my voice clouding in the cool night.

I glanced up at Rafe's bedroom window. Still dark.

This was what Rafe had been burning weeks ago? I'd seen him carrying something larger than collars out of the trunk of his car, but there were no bones amid the ashes. Whatever had happened to Tosca and Max and Ronaldo, they weren't cremated in this fire pit. So where were the dogs? What kind of a person burned dog collars?

I peered up at his house, unnerved.

If I asked him about it, there could be a perfectly reasonable explanation. But what if there wasn't one? I barely knew him. We'd only spent a few nights together. Did I want to confront him about his weird bonfire collection, alone in his house, when no one knew where I was?

Shit.

I wasn't sure what to do, but I knew that I didn't want to go back inside. So, I did what any smart woman would do and began to snoop around. I went to the shed again and tried the door but couldn't get it open. I peeked into the window, but it was too dark inside, the glass too dirty. I fished out my phone and used the screen light to look inside. Old, broken clay pots. A rake. Bags of fertilizer and mulch that looked years old. It really didn't look like anyone had been inside for ages.

White Rabbit—a horror movie Rob had sent. In it, a boy found out his grandfather was a murderer by going through his trash. What people threw out told a lot about them. Rooting through Rafe's garbage felt like a pretty serious invasion of privacy for a guy I was starting to like, but then again, burning dog collars wasn't boyfriend-able behavior.

He had the same bear-proof municipal cans I did, but I was surprised to find the garbage inside was a mess. We were supposed to bag everything in specific bags, but Rafe had just tossed random things in there. Fast-food bags. Beer bottles clinking together—*Jesus, what kind of monster doesn't recycle?*—and stacks of unopened junk mail. I used a stiff cardboard envelope to riffle through the rest, all of which seemed normal detritus for a single bachelor, until I saw a box of hair dye: L'Oreal number 4, dark brown.

Rafe was in his mid- or late-thirties. It was possible he wanted to cover a few gray hairs. But from a cheap drugstore women's box of dye? The whole thing thoroughly creeped me out.

I sent Rafe a quick text telling him I'd had a great evening but decided to go home, and got back in my car.

There might be demons here, but it was starting to seem that there were demons everywhere.

CHAPTER TWENTY-ONE

A whistle pierced the night.

The Hellhound raised her jowls from the dirt floor of her cave. The pups slept soundly, smelling of warm ripe milk, curled on the cadaver of her latest kill. The whistle outside raised in a three-note melody—it was him.

She trotted to the mouth of the cave, sniffing the air. When he came before, dressed all in black, he'd brought a thick cut of meat wrapped in brown paper, but today he smelled of sweeter treats.

He crouched down, calling to her. She came forward on rippling muscles and pressed her head into the wide palm of his hand.

He laughed as he scratched her scruff. "Fleas. Yeah, I have them, too."

He took a green glass bottle from his pocket and set it on the dirt. "Cost me dearly to get this. It's no normal milk. It'll keep those little devils of yours satiated until they're old enough to hunt on their own. But there's a catch. I need you to track someone for me."

—From "Sweet Cream" in
Bedtime Stories for Monsters

I JOLTED AWAKE to a ringing phone.

Aggressive light streamed through my windows.

A couple days had passed since that terrible night at Rafe's when I had burned the manuscript and my illustrations and found dog collars in his fire pit. The weather had consistently been gray and wet and cold since then, making me only want to spend longs days in bed as I tried not to think about what I'd found.

Squinting from the light, I answered the phone on instinct, which soon proved to be a mistake. "Hello?"

"It's Detective Rice. I'm sorry it's so early."

I held the phone away from my ear long enough to check the time. Eight thirty in the morning. My heart began stomping around on my insides. A call from Rice had, in my experience, never led to good news.

"I wanted to let you know that we identified the bodies from the Cliffside Drive attack."

I sat up, scraping the hair out of my eyes. "Really?"

She cleared her throat. "Can you come down to the station?"

A cannonball plummeted into my belly. My mind wheeled around, trying to come up with some excuse, but I couldn't think fast enough. I wasn't even sure I could refuse, legally.

"Is something wrong?" Besides the many, *many* things that were obviously already wrong.

"Ask for me when you get here" was all she said before hanging up. *Fuck.*

As soon as the call clicked off, a text message notification popped up from Rafe. He'd been texting me frequently since Monday morning, when he woke up and found that I'd left, and I hadn't answered any of them.

I wasn't about to answer this one, either. I tossed the phone onto the bed and went to take a shower. Rafe had been the one good thing that had happened to me since coming to Lundie Bay, but now it seemed even that burgeoning relationship was cursed. *Dog tags in a fire pit. So fucking weird.*

I could ask him about it, somewhere safe and public like at a busy restaurant in town, but I was afraid of the answer. I was getting my normal itch to run away. But this time, I didn't have anywhere else to go. Malice House was all I had.

Once I was showered and wearing relatively clean clothes, I drove down the dizzying road into town. I'd forgotten to bring my sunglasses since it was usually overcast, and the bright morning sun stung my eyes. The good weather had roused the shoulder-season tourists out of their rental houses, and town was bustling. Every parking spot was taken downtown and along the docks, though the police department had plenty of spaces open.

Inside, a young male receptionist smiled in a way that didn't mesh with the drab 1970s architecture of the building, like it was his first day and he was used to working at a hotel front desk.

"I'm here to speak with Detective Letitia Rice?"

He spoke into a phone and in a few minutes, she came around the corner with a manila file in hand. She was wearing slacks and a tan sweater that had largely escaped the iron that morning. She jerked her head toward the hall. "We can talk in one of the interview rooms."

A warning traipsed up my neck. I blurted out, "Am I in trouble?" It hadn't occurred to me that I might need a lawyer.

"Nothing like that, Haven. You aren't being officially interviewed." She wrinkled her noise at the state of the lobby. "So noisy in this place. We want somewhere quiet."

I followed her uneasily to an office with a table and two chairs that looked more like a budget corporate break room than the kind of interrogation chambers in the movies. She motioned to one of the chairs. "Coffee?"

"No, thanks."

She cleared her throat and went to pour herself a cup from a coffee maker, then sat down and opened the manila folder. My eyes were immediately drawn to printed photographs of a man and a woman, but at a glance, neither looked familiar.

"The Cliffside Drive victims you found." Her lips folded together like she'd tasted something bitter. "We were able to ID them from the rental car agreement."

She slid the folder around to me so I could see the photographs clearly. They looked like they'd be taken from social media profiles. A young white couple around my age, both of them strikingly attractive in that LA botoxed way.

"Recognize them?"

I shook my head.

"Their names are Francesca Myers and Eddie Chase."

I think I forgot to breathe for a few seconds. I'd seen a photo of Eddie Chase on SunBurst's website, but he'd looked totally different in button-up shirt and slacks than rumple-haired and wearing athleisure as in the detective's picture.

"Eddie Chase?" I raked a hand through my hair. "I was supposed to meet with him later this afternoon."

Detective Rice nodded. "I know. Once we ID'd him, we contacted his office manager who gave us his itinerary and email login. He and his girlfriend arrived in Seattle day before yesterday and were taking a vacation day before driving up to Lundie Bay."

I still couldn't connect the smiling face in the photo with the cadaver I'd seen in the car. I squeezed my hands together under the table, trying to funnel my nervous energy there instead of letting it show on my face.

"I had no idea. I promise. I assumed he was flying in this morning."

She slid the photographs back around as though she knew she'd tortured me enough. "It's okay, Haven. I believe you. I've read your emails to Mr. Chase and there's nothing out of the ordinary there. But you have to help me out. You arrive in town and your father's housekeeper is murdered a few days later, and now two more victims who were tied to you. Can you give me any leads that I can follow? Anyone want to mess with you for some reason? Or make *you* appear suspicious?"

"I thought it was a murder-suicide."

She scratched a place on her scalp, keeping her mouth shut.

I shook my head. "Maybe whoever is trying to break into Malice House? What about this bear? There are rumors it's another bear."

She took a slow sip of her coffee and didn't bother to address rumors of wild animals. "Tell me about this ex-husband of yours."

"Baker?" The name slipped out like I'd choked on a bite of sandwich. "How do you know about him?"

"TLO database," she said smoothly. "Tells us everywhere you've ever lived, who you've lived with. It only took a few phone calls to find out about your ex-husband. Or, sorry, ex-boyfriend, right? You were never actually married?"

I didn't like the way she dangled that information over me. She seemed to be suggesting that if she could dig that up, she could unearth a lot more. And no doubt had—including the prior police reports I'd made in New York and my own arrest record.

But she didn't mention those, and I wasn't about to volunteer trouble.

I squeezed my hands together harder. "You think *Baker* did this?"

She rubbed a hand over her mouth. "We haven't ruled out a murder-suicide. There was no indication of mental illness or strain in their relationship, but you never know what could make someone act unlike themselves. The truth is, everything's on the table now, including a jilted husband. Think about it: A wife suddenly moves away, then there are signs she's being stalked, and, finally, people close to her wind up dead. It's as plausible as anything else."

Rob's favorite phrase returned to me again: *It's always the husband.*

"Then why don't you ask him?" I said dryly.

She studied me carefully, searching for something, then drew in a long breath. "That's the thing. We tried. Can't get in touch with him. It seems he's disappeared."

Her eyes bored into me.

That look told me that she had *definitely* read my arrest record: *Haven Marbury. Domestic violence.*

"He's often gone on documentary expeditions," I said carefully.

"He tends to go places where there isn't good reception. The Galapagos, that kind of thing."

"Uh-huh. You don't seem too disturbed to hear your husband is missing, Ms. Marbury. Most spouses would be alarmed, even if the relationship ended on rocky terms." She waited, studying me to see how I'd react to that "rocky" comment. I suddenly wondered how much snooping she'd done, if she'd had New York contacts interview neighbors from our co-op, if anyone had heard the yelling from the night I'd left. "Have you had any communication with him?"

"I've sent texts. I can show them to you. He hasn't responded."

"And that didn't worry you?"

"Like I said, he's sometimes hard to reach."

"Uh-huh."

Now it was my turn to clear my throat. "Look, I have no idea who killed Dahlia or Eddie and his girlfriend. I also know you don't have any DNA or evidence tying me to either murder because I had *nothing* to do with it. And as far as the connections to my father's books, I can't help you. I haven't even *read* all his books. So, I'd really like to go."

A flash of annoyance crossed her face, and I knew I was right—they had no evidence.

She pushed aside her coffee like it had offended her and then stood. "Fine, Ms. Marbury. But stay in town. I might call again." She opened the door for me.

I practically stumbled out of the police department, blinking into the bright sunlight. I couldn't have been in the police station for long, but it felt like days had passed. My stomach had turned queasy from hearing Baker's name. I was suddenly very thirsty, even a little light-headed. I stumbled toward my car, but a voice stopped me.

"Oh, Haven! Hello!"

I stopped in my tracks. It was Catherine.

Jesus Christ, can't I get a break? It felt uncannily like she was following me. The timing was too perfect to be a coincidence—I had only just stepped out of the police station.

I faced her reluctantly, keys in hand, so close to having gotten in my car and escaped. She was hurrying down the sidewalk, her silk scarf trailing behind her, smiling widely as she held out a hand to signal for me to wait. The bookstore was only a few blocks from the police department, so there was a chance she'd just been out walking or maybe seen me drive by. But I *really* hated how often Catherine was popping up unannounced.

Preparing for a confrontation, I said quickly, "Catherine, I don't want to talk about the manuscript."

"Oh, no, that's not what I wanted to talk about." She waved it away as though she'd never been interested in *Bedtime Stories*, never practically stalked me to get her hands on it. Her smile melted into a concerned frown. "Kylie Nance never showed up for work yesterday or today. She's never this late. Orion can't get a hold of her. He even stopped by her apartment, but it was locked and didn't look like anyone was home. Is there a chance you've heard from her?"

I gripped my keys harder. "Kylie is missing?"

I'd had drinks with her over the weekend. She hadn't mentioned any vacation; she'd even talked about her early work shifts all week.

"I don't know if I'd use the word *missing*. I don't think it's that serious yet. At least, I hope not." But Catherine certainly looked shaken, toying anxiously with her jangling beaded bracelets. "I just wondered if she'd been in contact with you."

"We met up on Sunday, and she seemed fine then."

"Oh. Dear, I hope nothing's happened." Catherine petted her silk scarf anxiously, but I didn't like the hint of theatricality in her gestures.

"What's her address? I'll go by her apartment myself."

"Goodness, I don't know off the top of my head. Call Orion at the bookstore. Or better yet, why don't you come by the store now and ask him? You can have a coffee on the house. Ronan is here, up from Bainbridge University."

She tried to herd me back toward the bookstore, but I stood my ground, holding my keys the way I'd been taught in self-defense class, as though this elegant, slightly heavy older woman was an attacker in a black ski mask.

I frowned. "How do you know that Kylie and I are friends, anyway?"

Her eyebrows rose. "I didn't realize you were. I just assumed it was likely she'd reach out to you sooner or later."

"Why?"

She held her hands out palm-up as though it was obvious. "Well, because Kylie is a *huge* Marbury fan. She's read all your father's books at least a dozen times. She wants to be an author herself, though between you and me, I think her stuff is a touch too dark. Sometimes I worry her interest in your father borders on fanatical. She's joked around about 'finding what Amory Marbury kept in the proverbial attic.' I'm sure she's harmless, of course, but it wouldn't surprise me if she'd approached you."

I gave Catherine the strangest look, as though she was talking about someone completely different.

I blinked slowly.

"Kylie is a *Marbury* fan?"

Catherine adjusted her scarf, glancing over her shoulder in the direction of the bookstore. "Oh, yes. That's what brought her to Lundie Bay. She moved here three years ago because your father had a home here. She begged me for a job so she could be near the place where he wrote. I even warned him about her preoccupation once, but his mind was already going. He wasn't concerned about twentysome-thing girls."

My body was starting to feel strangely hollow. Nothing Catherine said made any sense. From the moment I'd met her, Kylie had made her *lack* of interest in my father's books abundantly clear. She was like me, tired of and more than a little puzzled by all the attention on him. Sure, she sold his memorabilia online, but that was only about cash, because Marbury fans—not *her*—were obsessed.

"Come have coffee with me and Ronan," Catherine pressed.

"No. Thank you." My tone sharpened. I threw my shoulders back, trying for a power stance. "And I should let you know that the manuscript is gone. I burned it. So there won't be any book deal. No money. You can tell Ronan and Jonathan to stop calling."

She stared at me—eyes wide, head cocked like a pigeon—and then blinked slowly. "*Burned* it?"

Talking to Catherine made me anxious, so I opened the car door and tossed in my canvas bag. "That's right. It might as well have never existed. Bye, Catherine."

I slid in before she could say anything else and then slammed the car door.

That jolted her out of her shock, and she ran around and knocked insistently on my car window, yelling through the glass, "Wait! Why were you at the police office?"

I started to back out, but she still knocked on the window, trotting out into the parking lot.

"Why were you at the police station? Haven!"

I enjoyed watching Catherine Tybee disappear in my rearview mirror.

⚜

I texted Kylie and left voicemails for her, and when she still hadn't responded by noon the following day, I called the bookstore and got her address from Orion, who warned me that Kylie didn't live in the best area.

I punched the directions into my rental car's GPS and followed the map to a road that skirted town and dropped into a valley where a few aging, less than picturesque duplexes hugged the road alongside a liquor store and Lundie Bay's closest thing to a fast-food restaurant, serving soggy-bun hamburgers.

As I stared through my windshield at Kylie's door—badly in need of paint, a neglected pot of petunias to one side—I wondered if I was wrong to have come. For all I knew, this was the home of one of my father's most unhinged fans, and inside I'd find pictures of him plastered on the ceiling, some demonic candelabra on a shrine dedicated to his books, stolen used towels nestled by her pillow.

She lied to me.

Maybe I shouldn't have been surprised; she sold forgeries. Her entire business model was based on dishonesty. But this felt different. Some deep-seated part of me still wanted to believe that despite everything, Kylie was just a quirky recluse in this town. Like me.

So why lie about having read my father's books? What did she hope to gain?

She'd mentioned that she thought it was cool that I liked horror movies and that she was an aspiring novelist herself with dark taste in fiction. So, had she befriended me to gain access to my father's house? His belongings? Or was it *me* she wanted for some reason?

Then, plunging down an entirely different line of thought, I wondered if it was possible that she hadn't lied to *me*, but to Catherine. The older woman's enthusiasm for my father's work was easy to see, and Kylie could have seen it as an easy con to get the job.

I ran through the drizzle, glancing with paranoia at the parked trucks nearby. But everything about the duplex seemed utterly unremarkable. If something nefarious was loose in the world, it wasn't to be found between the dying petunias of 14 Bay Lane.

No one answered my knock, which was hardly a surprise. Peeking in the window revealed a dark, empty sitting room/dining room combo. I again looked around the parking lot. Two guys in ball caps with a Confederate flag bumper sticker on their truck were unloading a cooler. The lowered tailgate gave me a glimpse of a camouflage-colored ammo rack holding a couple shotguns. I waited until they carried the cooler into their duplex and then dug around my bag until I found my paint scraper. Now that I was sure I didn't have witnesses, I jabbed the sharp end against the window lock and jiggled until it broke.

I slid open the stiff window and, standing on the petunia pot, ungracefully climbed inside.

I was relieved to find a typical twentysomething's living room with plates left out, TV remote on the sofa, shoes kicked in a haphazard pile by the door. No pictures of my father plastered to the walls. Rather, her IKEA bookcase was filled with an impressive variety of novels, mostly horror and fantasy. I found one battered copy of *Other/No Other* on the bottom shelf, but one book hardly made for a shrine.

The dining room table was covered with paperwork and a laptop that, when I checked, had a dead battery. Judging by a sour-smelling bowl of cereal, she'd been gone several days.

My stomach twisted. Was I worried *for* her or *of* her?

I found a charging cable on the floor and booted up the laptop. After a moment, several word-processing documents popped up. Novels she'd been working on. From what I gathered after skimming a few pages, one was about a nurse being haunted by the ghost of a patient. Another was a young adult fantasy about a faerie lord.

Also on the table were pay stubs from Lundie Bay Books; a shopping list that looked eerily like my own: wine and frozen pizza; a stack of library books, mostly biographies. Shirley Jackson, Ray Bradbury, Robert Heinlein. In a nearby notebook, Kylie had written down the make and model of the typewriter each had used, along with notes about commonly used expressions and quirks in their communications. Research for her forgeries.

I went to the kitchen, where I threw on the tap and searched through cabinets for a glass. I filled it with water, gulping it down.

Think, Haven.

Had Kylie said anything strange when we'd met at the Mayfelt? Not really—*I'd* been the one acting odd.

I started going through her kitchen drawers and stopped suddenly. With a trembling hand still holding one of the drawer pulls, I found myself looking at *my own face*. A younger version of myself from back when I used to bother straightening my hair. It was a paper photocopy of my old RISD student ID photo. Behind it was a printout of an obscure article about a small university art show I'd been in.

I knew for a fact I had almost no online profile. Someone, presumably Kylie, must have dug *very* deep to find these traces of my past.

The glass slipped out of my hand and clattered loudly in the sink. I flinched, then pressed my fingers against my eyes, pushing until I saw stars.

What the hell was Kylie up to?

I took her laptop and cord, let myself out through the front door, and then got into my car. I shakily tossed her laptop into the passenger seat—when I had more time and privacy, I'd comb through it. But for the moment, I just sat there in the parked car, staring. My hands were white-knuckled on the steering wheel.

If Kylie was stalking me, as that ID photo suggested, then I didn't owe her anything. But I couldn't shake the feeling that she was missing because of me. Just like Dahlia and Eddie Chase and his girlfriend. Everyone who was disappearing or dying was tied to me.

How long until I was next?

On a whim, I glanced in the rearview mirror. The asshole Confederate guys hadn't come back out of their place. The whole apartment complex parking lot was eerily quiet.

I climbed quietly out of my car, ducking low as I ran along the length of parked cars until I got to their truck. I snaked my arm into the truck bed and felt for the uppermost shotgun. It wasn't locked to the ammo rack; they must have just returned from a hunting trip and hadn't yet squared everything away. Or maybe they were the careless types to never lock up their guns.

I grabbed the shotgun and a half-full box of shells, then darted back to my car. I stashed the gun on the floor of the back seat and covered it with my cardigan before starting the car with shaking hands and pulling out as fast as I could, checking my rearview mirror the whole time, praying that Bay Lane Apartments didn't have security cameras.

CHAPTER TWENTY-TWO

"Sit on the sofa, honey. Go ahead."

Anita blinked up at the overweight man in suspenders. Where was she? Someone's house. His house, probably. Standing in a living room with a rust-red sectional sofa and a boxy TV set. Suddenly, her legs ached. She wanted to sit very badly. She couldn't think of anything other than sitting just like he had said.

"Good girl. You look warm, too. Take off your sweater, doll?"

She did. Undoing the buttons one by one over her straining belly. She couldn't imagine anything she wanted more than to take off her sweater. He'd told her to call him Uncle Arnold and assured her he was a good man, like family.

Anita was sure of it.

He was a good man. He was like family.

—From **"Everyone's Favorite Uncle"** in
Bedtime Stories for Monsters

IT WAS POURING when I pulled into Malice House's gate. My umbrella and raincoat were inside, hanging on the hook by the kitchen door, so I dragged Kylie's computer into my lap in the driver seat and connected to the house's Wi-Fi while I waited out the weather. Her files were even more disorganized than my own. I had no idea how she found the documents she needed. Temporary downloads cluttered the home screen. It seemed she had a habit of screenshotting: snippets of text conversations, offensive tweets from celebrities, typewriters for sale on eBay. It would take me days to comb through every file. I scrolled through her applications list and stopped on Find My Phone.

The app had to update before it would open, and given how many programs Kylie had running, her computer was sluggish. I didn't dare reboot the machine and lose the files she'd been working on, so I clicked on her photo album while I waited.

Most of her recent photos were shots of typewriters, books, and ballpoint pens for her online business. She had a few selfies that she'd taken on the Lundie Bay boardwalk, and a few more in what looked like her apartment's bathroom, testing out different colored lipsticks. I had to scroll back nine months even to see another person in a photo: a cute, twentysomething Southeast Asian guy with curly hair and two-day stubble. Their pose together implied they were more than friends, but seeing as he didn't appear in any recent pictures, it wasn't hard to guess that the relationship hadn't worked out.

The rain finally let up. I left her laptop open so that it wouldn't pause the application's update-in-progress and jogged across the driveway with it to the front porch.

A black envelope was pinned under the knocker.

I glanced over my shoulder with a shiver.

Rafe's house loomed on the far side of the privacy fence that separated our properties. I still hadn't responded to his texts asking why I'd left so suddenly the week before. Whenever I thought of the dog collars, I felt ill. There was no ignoring those scorched silver tags and the owners who must be frantically wondering what happened to poor Tosca and Pepper and Zeus.

I grabbed the envelope while scanning the tree line. *He still has a house key.* Rafe had never told me how he'd gotten past the gate to leave the first envelope—probably climbed over with strength alone or used a ladder, as I'd used to get into the woods. It didn't matter now. He had both the gate code and a front door key. He could traipse in whenever he liked.

I made a mental note to call the security company that installed the gate keypad. After Detective Rice had shown up unannounced, I'd fiddled with it, but it hadn't been immediately apparent how to change the numbers. I suspected there was an instruction manual somewhere in the house, buried in my father's labyrinthine files, but I'd yet to find it.

Inside, I set up Kylie's laptop on the library coffee table and plugged it in to continue charging, and then ripped open Rafe's envelope.

So the girl who doesn't get scared by horror movies gets scared off by . . . what?

I tossed Rafe's letter into the hallway trash can with an aggression that surprised me. The note hit too close to home. For so long, I had thought there was something wrong with me; I was an unbaked cake missing the right proportions of disgust and fear to make me bake up into a proper human. But now I *was* afraid. Those dog collars. Kylie missing. Eddie Chase murdered.

Kylie's Find My Phone app was about one-quarter of the way through the update. I took the time to rifle through the entry table's drawers, looking again for the gate keypad instruction manual, but found only old bills and editorial letters my father used as kindling for the fireplace. I knew the manual wasn't in the kitchen—I'd already torn through all those cabinets searching for booze.

When nothing turned up, I climbed the stairs and dragged file folder boxes out from under the guest room bed. They were caked with dust a quarter-inch thick. Inside were manila folders labeled things like *conferences* and *magazine publications*. My father had saved his correspondence with the various awards committees who had lauded his work, yet I didn't find a single saved rejection letter—not that I could blame him. Any rejection I got for my artwork was immediately banished to my computer's trash folder, promptly emptied.

There was no folder for manuals or warrantees, so I shoved the boxes back under the bed and stood, dusting off my hands. My eyes fell on a side table in the corner, partially hidden behind the room's overstuffed recliner. It had a single, small drawer.

It was the only place I hadn't looked other than the endless boxes in the attic, so I slid the drawer open. Inside was a palm-sized spiral-bound notepad. Not a cheap grocery store notepad, but a pretty one with soothing abstract swirls that had probably been a gift from an expensive stationery store.

I sank into the recliner and flipped it open. My father's handwriting filled the first few small pages; the rest was blank.

Easier to see a star if you look beside it, not at it. That phenomenon is called is averted vision. Try averted writing.

Altered states: Drug and alcohol. Meditation? Breathwork? SLEEP DEPRIVATION. So, what is the opposite? How to stay outside of the trance?

There were no more entries, though the thoughts felt incomplete.

I went downstairs and booted up my own laptop while I waited for Kylie's to finish, all the while wondering about my father's strange notes. When my computer turned on, an alert flashed from the hidden camera program, indicating movement on the front porch. But that was no surprise—it was just me coming home. However, when I checked closer, there were actually two recordings. One from eight minutes ago—that was me—and another from nineteen minutes ago. Cautiously, I hit PLAY.

The second video cut with a disorienting gap to Rafe standing on the front porch; the camera's motion sensor had a slight lag, so it hadn't picked him up until he was suddenly *there*, right at the front door. He knocked, waited, called my name. When there was no answer, he turned to look at the empty driveway and then used his key to let himself into the house. For a few minutes, the camera only recorded the open front door. Then he reemerged and locked the door, leaving the black envelope under the knocker.

A chill fell over me. Rafe had been here *nineteen minutes ago*—we had just missed each other. He'd been inside my house, presumably looking for me, but I had no way of knowing what else he had done while inside. And then he left the card outside to hide that fact. I checked the hallway camera's feed, but it only showed him walking upstairs and returning a few minutes later. The only other video was of myself entering just minutes later.

As a little girl, I used to tap my fingers when I was nervous. A mild obsessive-compulsive urge that mainly had gone away as an adult. But now I found myself tapping thumb against index finger, middle, ring, and back again, and then repeating it on the opposite hand.

Old habits don't die hard—they don't die. Ever.

Kylie's Find My Phone program still had about seven minutes left in the update. I paced in front of the coffee table, debating my options. If Kylie didn't show up in the next day or two, someone from the bookstore would probably file a missing person report, if they hadn't already. She was over eighteen, and there was no evidence of abduction as far as I could tell, so I guessed her case wouldn't be a top priority. Besides, missing Black women didn't exactly get prime attention in America. Though, with Detective Rice, another Black woman, on the force, maybe that was different in Lundie Bay? If the police did look into Kylie's case, they would notice that her apartment had been broken into and would likely find my fingerprints, so I should probably get ahead of this and surrender Kylie's laptop to them and explain why I'd taken it.

But then again, I didn't need any more scrutiny right now.

I returned to scrolling through Kylie's photo album, hoping to see a picture of family or a friend that would give me some clue as to where she might have gone. The images were the flipbook of a lonely life: few people, few photos in general. So when a familiar building suddenly popped up with a gaggle of grinning coeds in front, I stopped in sheer surprise. It took me a moment to place the building, but then it hit me—Clifford Library at Bainbridge University. I'd assumed the group of students sitting on the steps were friends of Kylie's, but now I realized that they were posing for another photographer who Kylie had captured off to the side. She'd been taking a picture of the building, not the girls.

When I checked the date of the photo, it was from Monday, three days ago.

"Why were you at Clifford Library, Kylie?" I whispered.

The answer seemed obvious: She wanted something from my father's personal library—but what?

I stared at the photo for a few minutes until I got up the nerve to call Ronan Young. He was among the last people I wanted to talk to, but also the only one who might be able to give me answers.

"Haven?" He must have had my number saved in his phone, which I found disturbing. "I'm glad you called."

I winced. "Hi, Ronan. I'm wondering if you can help me with something."

"I'd be happy to try."

"I'm trying to track down a friend of mine. I think she was down at Clifford Library on Monday. Did you happen to meet with her? Her name is Kylie Nance—she works with Catherine at Lundie Bay Books. You might know her."

"Oh, yes. I do. Kylie has visited our reading room a few times— she collects rare books as a hobby. A nice young woman. She has a special interest in your father's work. I helped her myself."

Goose bumps rippled over my arms as I thought of Catherine insisting Kylie was a Marbury fan. And now Ronan was verifying Catherine's words.

"Did you happen to see what books she was looking at? Specifically?"

He paused as though I had asked a strange question, which I suppose it was. But I was rapidly moving beyond the point of caring if I came across as suspicious.

He cleared his throat awkwardly. "We usually don't share that kind of information." I could picture eager-to-please Ronan Young, probably in an avocado-print bow tie, squirming at the impropriety of my question. "Perhaps you could—"

I interrupted, "I really need to know."

The way to deal with Ronan was to needle at his anxious spots until he simply couldn't help but give in and be helpful.

"I assume you have a good reason," he said slowly. "I'll have to look up the call request to know for sure. I remember it was a relatively small stack of books."

"What collection were they from?"

"Your father's—I assumed that's why you were calling."

I closed my eyes briefly, not sure if I should feel betrayed by Kylie or frightened for her, and when I opened them, I was staring at a map of Lundie Bay on her computer screen. The application had finally finished updating, but a PHONE NOT FOUND emblem blinked in the bottom right corner.

Shit. Her phone was turned off.

"Pull the books she looked at," I told Ronan. "I'll be down there right away."

"We close in five minutes, Haven. I'm sorry."

Damn it. At this time of the day, it would take at least two hours to drive down to the university. "What time do you open in the morning?"

"Ten o'clock, but it's only library aides until two in the afternoon, when I come in. They won't be able to pull a previous client's requests."

"Fine. I'll be there at two. I really need to see those books, Ronan."

I left the next day a few minutes before noon so I'd catch the ferry. As my rental car hurled down Cliffside Drive, a strong, wet wind kept pushing me toward the seaside cliff. Water stretched as far as I could see below. Rain pelted every window. It leaked in through the broken passenger-side door that had never quite closed right after the collision with Rafe's mailbox.

I kept an eye on the tree line as the car hugged the forest edge. This time of year, wild animals were particularly active, harvesting what they could before winter's scarcity. Every flickering shadow seemed to hold a face, though they were only branches shifting in the wind when I looked closer.

Traffic thickened as I approached Seattle's outskirts, but after the ferry, the island's roads fell eerily vacant. My car thunked rhythmically over the sections of pavement. My heart jolted in time with the sound as I glanced at Kylie's laptop, open in the passenger seat. It still flashed the PHONE NOT FOUND message, but since the computer wasn't connected to Wi-Fi, that meant nothing.

Once I was past the towering oaks lining the campus entry, I slowed. Classes must have just let out because college students clogged the sidewalks. They looked so painfully young. Backpacks slung over one shoulder, travel mugs of syrupy-sweet coffee in hand. The air was cool enough that packs of scarves were out, wooly things that swallowed girls' necks.

I had to circle the parking lots several times before I found a spot. Finally, I jogged up the stairs to Clifford Library, holding the door open for a pair of students who barely glanced at me as they stared at their phones. The reading room was packed, and the noise and activity made me anxious.

"Haven?"

Ronan was waiting for me by the circulation desk, wearing a pinched face and a plain navy bowtie. It almost made me a little sad not to see him with a fun print. A small stack of books sat next to him on the counter, along with a white call slip. His fingers nervously drummed on the uppermost book.

"Hi, Ronan. Thanks." Now that he was facing me and not just a voice on a telephone, I felt my tension soften enough to apologize. "I know it's a strange request. Kylie and I are working on a project together. It's related to her memorabilia business. When I couldn't get a hold of her, I wanted to see what she was working on."

"Are you worried about her?"

He must not have talked to Catherine; this seemed to be the first he'd heard of Kylie's disappearance.

I quickly shook my head and lied, "No, no, nothing like that." I cleared my throat and looked pointedly at the books. "This is what she pulled most recently?"

"Yes." His shoulder eased as he shifted into librarian mode like slipping into a worn sweater. "She didn't request anything rare, just a few copies of *Other/None Other* from your father's personal collection."

All four books in the stack were indeed different editions of the same title. A first edition hardback, a paperback with a bonus introduction by some hot-shot professor, a book club edition, and a Spanish-language translation. I smiled and scooped up the books. "I'll bring them right back."

He looked like he had more to say, but I plunged into the sea of library tables and sank into a chair before he had the chance.

I opened the paperback edition and checked the copyright page: 2003, third printing. *Other/None Other* was an outlier among my father's books. His one foray into literary horror and the closest thing any of his published works came to touching on paranormal themes. It dealt with a fireman who'd suffered from disturbing visions ever since he was a small child, when his best friend died in a house fire. Later, as an adult, his visions began to play out in real life. Desperate for an explanation, he searched New York City's seedy underbelly of psychics and voodoo priestesses. It turned out that everything was just in his head. The seemingly paranormal visions were actually the fantasies of a drugged-up patient in a psych ward who'd been badly burned in a chemical accident. Frankly, I thought the ending was a cop-out, but readers ate it up.

My father's familiar handwriting was sprinkled throughout the margins of this edition. Pencil mark notations to himself. Lines he'd underlined to pull for marketing quotes. Ideas for a possible sequel that had never happened. I checked the Spanish-language edition and the first edition hardback; they were also personally annotated. When I flipped open the last volume, the book club edition from 2004, a call slip fell out. It was dated Monday, so it had to be Kylie's call slip. She'd written numbers on it: 59, 178, 221, 403.

I flipped to page 59, where my father had underlined a single passage: *The spark began in the basement. The furnace. Someone had left the coal door open.*

On pages 178 and 221, there were no marks, and I wasn't sure why Kylie had noted those, but on page 403, my father had underlined: *The original farmhouse had been built in 1890 on disputed land and moved thirty years later, lifted onto logs by a system of pulleys, then pulled by horses into the neighboring valley. Decades later, a boy fell into the old house's foundation and broke his leg, just as Bartley had foreseen.*

My father had written in the margin: *Malice House move of 1947— open foundation accident 1950.*

It took a moment, but when it finally hit me, I pushed up from the table and hurried past the students reading quietly at their library tables to the circulation desk, breathless.

"Ronan. Do you know how to access property records?"

CHAPTER TWENTY-THREE

The Lord gives words and the Lord takes words. We are the curators. We are the collectors. We are the minders of words written and spoken, thought and not yet thought. Give us your stories, and your stories will live forever. Offer them not freely, and we will take them just the same. This is the creed of the Robber Saints.

—From "Late Fees" in
Bedtime Stories for Monsters

RONAN'S OFFICE WAS on the second floor of Clifford Library, a tiny closet of a room that, judging by the shelving that spanned two entire walls, probably *had* been a closet. Now those shelves were packed with books and reams of printer paper and a few bobbleheads of *Doctor Who* characters. A novelty wooden plaque on his desk read MY WEEKEND IS ALL BOOKED. I peered over his shoulder at his desktop computer screen, tapping my fingers anxiously. He pulled up the state's GIS mapping service and logged in with the university's account.

"This should get us the data," he explained. "Property records aren't housed in any central system. County tax offices hold some, as well as GIS databases and the MLS real-estate system. Private companies hold others. But the university has special access that should get us into the major databases. Let's see. Forty-Six Cliffside Drive . . ."

I flinched when he rattled off Malice House's address off the top of his head. He'd been to the house a few times as part of the Ink Drinkers literary salon, but the house was nearly two hours from Bainbridge University. Odd that he would remember the address so readily.

"Okay, this is the current listing. It looks like it was updated in 2017. Does that look like the correct property boundary?" He leaned to the side so that I had a better view of his computer screen. It showed an aerial view of Lundie Bay with Malice House's property outlined in a jagged red box. A narrow portion of the property extended back into the woods like the blade of a knife; I hadn't known that was part of the parcel.

"Yes." The house and fence looked accurate to the current condition. I couldn't take my eye off that thin red line. It gave me the eerie sense that Malice House was bound by a supernatural force; that everything within was its own universe, one step outside of our world.

Ronan toggled to a database screen filled with GPS coordinates, dates, and addresses, and ran his cursor down the list.

"It looks like the earliest record for the address at Forty-Six Cliffside Drive is from 1999, when the county renumbered the homes on that street. Probably because of all the new development. Before that, it was Eight Cliffside Drive, dating back to 1960."

"The house was built long before 1960."

"Yes, I see that in the records. You were right—Malice House was moved to its current location in 1947. It looks like it was a much smaller structure at the time—it's listed as a one-room fisherman's cabin. Wouldn't have been too hard to move with a team of horses. Believe it or not, it was fairly common to move houses back then. The original mobile homes, huh?" When I didn't respond to his joke, he adjusted his glasses and went back to reading. "Let's see, at the time it was owned by Alice Halliday, who then added onto it substantially to create the current floor plan." He twisted in his chair to look at me curiously. "You said you read about this in *Other/None Other?*"

I fluttered my fingers like his question was a buzzing gnat I couldn't be bothered with. "Yeah, the main character has a vision about an old house that was moved and the open foundation left behind. I think my father got the idea for that plotline from Malice House's true history." The numbers and codes on the spreadsheet were frustratingly incomprehensible to me. "Does it list the house's original location?"

"I'm checking now. Unfortunately, the GIS database doesn't have that information, but I'll log into a private property service we have access to. Ah, there. Yes, Forty-Eight Cliffside Drive. Right next door."

He swiveled the monitor so I could see the marked-off property, but it was unnecessary. I already knew the house at 48 Cliffside Drive. Its mailbox was the reason my car door wouldn't properly close.

Malice House initially resided on Rafe Kahn's property.

Rafe's house was only five or six years old; before that, the land had been unoccupied. My house's original foundation had been lying there all this time, waiting. The limestone bedrock beneath Malice House's current location made a full basement impossible, but Rafe's property was a little farther inland, so there must be a few feet more topsoil before hitting rock.

"Malice House's basement," I muttered aloud.

Ronan raised his eyebrows. "Sorry?"

My throat had gone dry. I shook my head, not answering. No wonder I'd never found the door that the key would unlock. The shed on Rafe's property with desiccating bags of potting soil inside must have been built on top of the original Malice House foundation by Alice Halliday, or whoever owned it before her.

I remembered my conversation with Kylie at the Mayfelt, when I recalled my conversation with Kylie at the Mayfelt, when I'd told her about the basement to see if she was lying. She must have filed away that information and come here the very next day to do her own research about it.

Why? What does a missing basement matter to her?

In any case, the notations that Kylie had marked on her call slip suggested that she had figured out the basement's location before I had, which made me whisper, *"Fuck."*

What if Kylie went to Rafe's house to try to get into the shed? Rafe, who did something disturbing with dogs and God knows what else. I was hesitant to trust Kylie, but she was missing, and I didn't think I could take another dead body showing up that was connected to me.

"Haven?" Ronan adjusted his glasses at my profanity. "Is everything okay?"

I grabbed the printout he'd made for me and shoved it into my canvas bag. "Thanks, Ronan." My mind tug-roped in different directions as I moved toward the door, when he suddenly stood up from his chair with enough force to send it wheeling back across his office.

"Wait."

I almost didn't stop. Ronan Young was a footnote on my story now. But the tremulous look on his face gave me pause.

He wet his lips anxiously as he wrung his hands. "Catherine mentioned that you burned your illustrations and your father's manuscript. I know that must have been hard for you. You probably won't believe me, but it's for the best. Your father's work only would have held you back. Take my advice. Sell the house. Move anywhere but Lundie Bay. You have talent; you'll find your calling on your own."

The lines in his face had deepened, betraying a strange intensity. Unsure what to make of the urgency in Ronan's voice, I took a hesitant step back, nodding. "Right."

As soon as I was back in the rental car, I scrubbed my hand over my face, trying to make sense of everything. I decided to use the university's Wi-Fi while I was here to check my email, but when I opened my laptop, the first program that popped up was the Find My Phone app.

And now, a green dot blinked on the Lundie Bay map.

The error message was gone, which meant that Kylie—or someone else—had turned on her phone.

And I knew exactly where she was.

✳

This time of year, sunset came early, and though it was barely seven o'clock when I made it back to Lundie Bay, the sky was already bruise black. Streetlights hanging over Cliffside Drive cast nets of light around the car, snagging my thoughts. I'd spent the entire drive debating what to do now that I knew the location of Kylie's phone. She'd been missing for three days. I knew from movies that was an eternity in a missing person case. If she was in trouble, every minute counted.

I pulled into a scenic overlook not far from my house while I thought it through. I could call the police. But Detective Rice was already suspicious of me. Besides, from what I could tell, the location of her phone was in a suburban neighborhood a few miles inland from the bay, where many of the locals lived. If it had been an abandoned warehouse or a meat packing facility, I wouldn't have hesitated to tip off the police anonymously. But life wasn't a horror movie. Kylie was probably just crashing with friends or some guy, maybe even the cute guy from her photo album.

"Shit," I said aloud.

I threw my car in reverse, turned around, and drove the opposite direction from home, following the GPS through downtown Lundie Bay and inland until I finally reached a modest, older subdivision labeled Water's Edge despite its distance from the coast. The houses here were older brick ranches. The kind of place with faded floral patio furniture and dated brass fixtures, though some of the houses had added on Craftsman-style porches or pergolas to dress up the old structures. A few swing sets indicated young families lived in the neighborhood. It must have been a private subdivision because street-lights were almost nonexistent, and the few they had barely put out light. I had to squint at the numbers to verify the address that matched the one on Kylie's Find My Phone app.

I rolled by the house slowly, not wanting to stop in front and announce myself. It looked like any other ranch home, with an attached single garage, a tired carport, and dusty, sparse boxwoods in the front yard.

I parked a few doors down and sat in the car with the headlights off, debating what to do. I'd tried calling Kylie several times, but she didn't answer. Maybe she was watching television or taking a long bath. Still, all the lights were off in the house, even the front porch light. No TV flickered through the windows. At seven o'clock, I would have expected *some* sign of life. Instead, it was completely hushed.

The shotgun I'd stolen from the pickup truck guys still rested on the floor in the back, covered by my cardigan. I considered taking it with me to the house in case Kylie was in danger, but then I realized what a colossally stupid idea that was. This was a family neighbor-hood. A lady in sweatpants walked an arthritic old black lab a block away. I couldn't go bang on a stranger's door with a shotgun in hand. Besides, I knew nothing about guns. I didn't know if it was loaded or even how to check.

I toyed with the car keys, pressing my finger pads into the sharp edges, the pain strangely satisfying. As soon as the dogwalker turned the corner, I got out and strode to the house as quickly as possible while trying to act natural. Away from the road, it was even darker. The ranch's windows were closed. The shades drawn. A buzzing hum came from inside the house that I thought might have been an old appliance.

No one answered my knock. I tried again, shifting my weight from one foot to the other. I kept my phone in hand, ready to dial the police if needed. My latest movie recaps played on a screen behind my eyes. Scenes just like this where, watching the main character from the comfort of my sofa, I'd jotted down in my notebook the shorthand *TSTL*: Too Stupid To Live. But now that *I* was starring in my own fucked-up storyline, it wasn't so simple. Who was I supposed to have brought with me? Creepy Catherine? Rafe, who might be a dog killer? A police officer who suspected me of murder? If anything had happened to Kylie, every minute was crucial. If I waited until daytime tomorrow to come back, it could be too late.

The door was locked. Whoever lived here clearly wasn't home. Glancing over my shoulder to make sure no neighbors were watching, I slipped along the back of the house. The yard was made up of overgrown grass and one of those fake wishing wells. A small deck led to a sliding glass door. I approached as quietly as I could and tested the door, surprised when it slid open, unlocked. I hesitated before inserting my head through the narrow gap.

"Hello?" I called in as loud a voice as I dared. "Kylie?"

The house was quiet except for the chugging sound, which was coming from the refrigerator. I forced my feet in, limping slightly, shining my phone's bright screen around until I found a desk lamp.

I switched it on and found myself in a living room with a sagging velour sofa and an older television set. Bookshelves held kids' board games that had been popular in the nineties: Battleship, Hungry Hungry Hippos, Jenga, and a collection of well-worn Louis L'Amour paperbacks.

A hallway led to a bedroom, then, around a corner, a bathroom and another bedroom. All were vacant, with similar worn furniture as the living room; everything dated but kept clean.

How did Kylie know whoever lived here?

As I returned to the living room, I stopped with a ripple of foreboding at a framed photo on a bookshelf. Someone had laid it facedown just like the photos at Malice House the first day I'd arrived. With a shaking hand, I set it upright. It showed an older smiling white couple who looked like someone's grandparents, but probably not

Kylie's unless she was adopted. She hadn't mentioned grandparents living nearby

I made my way to the other side of the house, which held the small kitchen and a pantry. An exterior door next to the trash cans led to what I assumed was the garage.

Kylie wasn't here.

"Well, shit," I said aloud.

Between the wilted flowers rotting in a vase on the dining table and the smell of trash that should have been taken out a while ago, I got the feeling the house had been unoccupied for several days. So why did the app say that her phone was here? I made my way back to the bedrooms for another look. Maybe her phone was in a drawer or hidden under the pillows. The hallway seemed darker and longer as I passed through it the second time, and I wondered if a streetlamp had gone out. I passed the bookshelf with the framed photo, feeling watched by the two sets of drooping eyes, and turned into the first bedroom, only to smack right into the doorjamb. *Ow.* Confused, I massaged my nose and frowned at the hallway. I could have sworn the bedroom was closer to the living room.

I'm distracted, I told myself. *Fear starting to distort reality.*

Or *had* the hallway gotten longer?

I limped down it, hands easily touching both walls this time—it certainly seemed to be narrower, or else I hadn't paid close attention before. When I finally reached the bathroom and turned the corner, I stopped like the soles of my shoes had been sewn into the carpet.

The remainder of the hallway was at least twice as long as it had been before, and instead of ending at the second bedroom, turned sharply again. *How the hell did it change?* Hairs rose on the back of my neck. I thought briefly of the shotgun still in the backseat of my car. Even if I didn't know how to use it, it would have made for a good threat. *I should have brought it.* The beige carpet was so soft underfoot that it was unsteadying, like walking on pillows. I followed the curving hallway around the corner, but ahead, it turned *again*. A nautilus spiral in faux-wood paneling. There had been a second bedroom here, I was sure. I remembered it. But now, the hall turned and turned again in a maddeningly impossible way.

My mind scrambled for answers as I backtracked out of the hallway maze back into the living room, relieved to be on stable ground. I was breathing shallowly. The desk lamp shone on the same dated furniture as before. Everything was so perfectly mundane here, so unchanged, that I had to question myself.

What the fuck is going on?

The refrigerator chugged away loudly, drowning my thoughts. An ancient thing from back when manufacturers made machines that lasted—this one would probably outlive a brand-new model. I jerked open the fridge door, thinking that the contents would tell me how long the house's residents had been gone. If it had fresh leftovers and unexpired milk, they might be back any moment.

There *was* a jug of milk and a few condiment bottles in the door, but every other shelf was packed with clear Tupperware and Ziploc bags. Each one held a cut of meat I couldn't immediately identify; chicken breasts, maybe, and something that had the bruised color of liver. There had to be enough meat in here to feed a family for weeks. *But only two elderly people live here.* I slammed the door closed and took a few unsteady steps backward.

On the edge of panic, I dug out my phone from the tangle of my pocket. It took me three tries to dial Kylie's number correctly. Her phone was supposed to be here. *She* was supposed to be here. It started ringing on my end and, about two seconds later, a phone rang somewhere in the house.

I spun, attempting to follow the sound. It was coming from beyond the kitchen door in what I'd assumed was the garage. I hung up and, in the sudden quiet, could hear my breathing almost as loud as the refrigerator.

Something clunked in the garage as though someone had dropped a tool; a long dragging sound followed it.

My lips parted in a silent cry for help.

A block of knives sat on the counter, and I grabbed the biggest one, then inched toward the garage door. My palm was slick on the cheap brass doorknob. I mustered my courage and cracked it open. The door gave a squeal that made me cringe.

A light was on in the garage coming from a single bulb hanging over a worktable. Meticulously arranged handyman tools lined the walls on pegboards. Plastic storage bins stacked along the wall held Christmas decorations. This was the garage of a person with old-fashioned values, cleanliness next to godliness. I could picture the older man from the photograph diligently repairing a wobbly chair in here.

Now, though, a young man lay on the worktable. Naked. Sickly pale. His wrists and ankles had been tied to either end of the table. A deep gash cut across his abdomen, though there was no blood.

"Jesus fucking Christ," I whispered.

Someone had positioned various vessels from the kitchen around the table. An organ that I couldn't immediately identify rested in a vintage green casserole dish.

I did a quick count. *Seven bowls.*

I took a shaky step closer to press my hand against the man's neck to check for a pulse, but I didn't need to. The minute I made contact with his cold, hardened skin, it was evident he was dead.

Fuck, fuck. I looked closer at his face and jolted with recognition.

Orion, the bookseller.

A slight scuffing sound came from the far end of the garage. Something moved next to the storage bins. Shadows hid the figure until the tip of a sneaker moved into the light.

A person moaned softly.

I nearly tripped over an extension cord as I scrambled to the far end of the garage. Kylie leaned against a stack of cardboard boxes labeled *Elementary School Memories.* Dried blood and a dark bruise obscured her face. Her hands were bound with paracord. A silver stripe of duct tape covered her mouth.

"Kylie. Hey!" I shook her urgently. She moaned again.

I ripped off the tape and started sawing through the paracord with the kitchen knife, throwing worried looks toward the doorway. We were alone, but for how much longer? The seven bowls behind me kept ringing in my ears. The number itched at me until I remembered "Kaleidoscope."

It was the tale of the Witch of Went, an overlooked middle-aged woman who got her revenge on abusive men by cutting them up and using their blood and organs for potions that she sold in a mysterious market. As terrifying as she was, she was my favorite character in the collection. There was something so satisfying about watching a quietly cunning woman slash up psychopaths who deserved what they got. She had an erstwhile romance with the Harbinger, and I was always surprised and a little glad that he never turned on her, and that she never slit his throat. In any case, the text made it clear that she used seven bowls to harvest the organs from her victims.

"Kylie?"

She blinked open one swollen eye. Her pupil was dilated. "Haven?" She licked her dry lips, gummy with the remnants of duct tape adhesive. "What day is it? Jesus. We have to get out of here." Her voice was weak, but her resolve was unmistakable.

I glanced at the garage door, but someone had padlocked the release lever. "Can you stand?"

She slid her feet under her, and I strained to help lift her. She must have been drugged or dazed by her head injury because she walked like a foal taking its first steps. As we passed the table with Orion's body stretched out, a whine escaped her mouth.

"My car's outside," I said urgently. "Just a few more steps."

She kept whining in a way I didn't think was entirely conscious. We limped into the kitchen, shoes scuffing on the linoleum, past the trash cans and humming refrigerator, to the sliding glass door that led to the backyard.

Only, the sliding door wasn't there anymore. It was simply *gone*. Where it had been was now another wood-paneled hallway with beige carpet, identical to the hallway that led to the bedrooms. I looked between the two hallways, feeling like I was losing my grip on reality. My panic bubbled up all over again.

"Do you smell that?" Kylie whispered.

The mustiness of the carpet and old furniture had swelled. Beneath the scent was the stinging smell of pine, so strong it scraped through my sinuses. The authentic scent of the woods, not some cloying cleaning product.

I heard a rasping sound at the end of the bedroom hallway and stared into the shadows. Something moved there, slowly and deliberately, coming from the direction of the second bedroom. A sound like dry leaves brushing against one another. Then I saw the gleam of two eyes reflecting the desk lamp's glow. A woman was moving slowly toward us, wearing a dark skirt that rustled against the wood paneling. Her hair and clothes were the same color as the shadows, and I could have easily told myself it *was* just shadows, that fear was making me see things that weren't there.

"The front door!" Kylie gasped.

We hobbled to the front door as fast as we could, and Kylie began twisting open the locks with what little strength she had. I pointed the kitchen knife toward the encroaching shadows, squeezing the handle so tightly that my hand numbed. Kylie jerked open the door at last, and we fell into a wave of fresh night air.

I didn't even remember getting into the car. Suddenly, we were there, me in the driver seat, Kylie in the passenger, and I was shoving the shotgun into her hands. I'd left the house's door open, and as I cranked my keys in the engine, a shape that moved like a cloud of shimmering charcoal dust slowly descended the front steps, and the foot of a woman emerged from its midst.

CHAPTER TWENTY-FOUR

Arnold told everyone to call him uncle whether they were five years old or fifty, but the truth was he had no blood relations. At least not anymore.

—From "Everyone's Favorite Uncle" in
Bedtime Stories for Monsters

●

"WATER?" I ASKED Kylie hoarsely, standing in Malice House's library. "Coffee?"

"Fuck that. Where's the booze?"

After speeding away from Water's Edge, we'd decided to park in the scenic overlook pull-out just down the road from Malice House in case anyone came looking for us, and walk the rest of the way. As soon as we were inside, we locked every door and window, drew the curtains, and checked and rechecked the security cameras. The shotgun sat heavy on the coffee table, which was empty now of everything else save a few damp towels Kylie had used to wash the blood off her face.

I grabbed a wine bottle out of the kitchen and twisted off the cap for Kylie. She took a long sip without flinching and then passed it back to me.

"We can't call the police," she said, wiping her mouth, which was still sticky with tape residue. "That woman, Haven—the things she did. The way she moved. It wasn't *right*. They'd think I was making it up." Confusion haunted her eyes as she tried to make sense of whatever she'd seen. Finally, in a barely audible whisper, she asked, "You saw her, too, didn't you?"

I took a deep drink from the wine bottle before sinking onto the sofa next to her. My fingernails clawed at the bottle's label, anxious.

"I need to tell you something, Kylie. And I need you to listen until I'm finished. Maybe it will be more believable if you pretend it's just a story. Like I'm recapping a horror movie for you. Okay?" My lips trembled a little.

Eyes glassy, she nodded.

I cleared my throat. "Our story starts with a girl coming home to her dead father's house. In the attic, she finds a forgotten manuscript called *Bedtime Stories for Monsters* and decides to illustrate it. Strange things begin to happen. The girl's father always thought the house was haunted, and after staying there awhile, the girl starts to think maybe he was right. The former housekeeper ends up dead. Mysterious people try to break into the house. Something attacks her from under the bed. So the girl starts investigating. She watches weird German documentaries about poltergeists. She does research at university libraries. She realizes the things that are happening are identical to what's in her father's manuscript—the way people are getting murdered and even the way she was attacked. Our heroine begins to think that she somehow brought the book's characters to life by illustrating her father's words. Her father always said their family was cursed, and now she begins to understand—whatever this curse is gives her the ability to create monsters. And now, the monsters are loose."

Kylie had listened from the other end of the sofa with a steady gaze, hugging a pillow to her chest, dark shadows under her eyes.

"Do you get what I'm trying to say?" I asked.

She took a ragged breath and briefly closed her eyes as she hugged the pillow tighter. With cracked lips, she whispered, "I've never been the kind of person to believe in ghosts or curses—hell, not even astrology—so give me a minute, okay?" There was no telling what thoughts were tumbling through her mind, what traumatic memories from the past few days.

Finally, she opened her eyes. "I would've said you were crazy a week ago. But that woman—*she* was real. She came out of the woods like she was made of them, a drop of liquid separating from a puddle. It happened, um, Tuesday, I think. What day is today?"

I hesitated. "Friday."

She let out a long breath as she clutched the pillow so hard that I thought it might tear. *"Fuck."* After gathering herself, she continued. "I was about to drive to work for an early shift, it was still dark outside. She was just suddenly there, next to my car. Smelling like rotting mushrooms. Paracord in hand. I tried to run but got turned around in my apartment complex. It didn't matter which direction I went, I kept going in circles."

The confusion in her eyes was familiar.

Kylie clawed her fingernails against the pillow, making a grating sound on the ribbed fabric. "Something knocked me out from behind. I don't think it was her. Maybe an accomplice. I only got a quick look, and it was still dark—a white guy who was shirtless or maybe even completely naked. When I woke up, I was tied up in the garage of Orion's grandparents' house. Orion was still alive. She was draining his blood into a plastic milk jug."

Kylie's eyelids fluttered closed. Her lips moved in a silent prayer or reassurance to herself, and then she said, "This is what you were getting at when we met at the Mayfelt, isn't it? About how artwork has the power to tap into other worlds? I thought you were just being artsy and ruminative . . . but then that woman messed with my mind somehow to make it seem like the woods were bending. It happened again in Orion's grandparents' house. The hallway . . ."

"I saw it, too," I said quietly. "The hallway turned in on itself."

She flopped back against the sofa, tossing the throw pillow aside, and dug her hands into her eye sockets. In a deathly quiet voice, she asked, "So, this horror movie . . . How does it end?"

I shook my head for a long time, wishing I had an answer.

My mind kept turning back to Orion's lifeless body in that suburban garage. And to Eddie Chase's and his girlfriend's blood spatters on the windshield. It seemed undeniable now that my ink pen had opened a Pandora's box that could never be closed. Burning the manuscript and illustrations hadn't changed anything. The characters from *Malice* had bled like watercolor from their world into ours and were out there now in the woods and town, enacting their grisly story lines on the population of Lundie Bay.

Dad wasn't crazy.

Dementia might have skewed his reasoning toward ghosts instead of the very real Marbury curse, but the result was essentially the same: monsters at the door.

My father had known about the curse; maybe not the specifics, but certainly *something*. He'd mentioned a family curse a few times when I'd been a little girl but had always made it sound like a tall tale from our colorful relatives. Now, in hindsight, those strange musings I'd found in the spiral-bound notepad in the guest room seemed like an attempt on his part to figure out how it all worked. Yet, for some reason, even though he had to have known the danger of the curse, he'd continued to write. Why? Had he figured out how to tame it?

I suddenly recalled Detective Rice's warnings about the rabid bear from the summer before. My father had been alive then and in the depths of dementia. *Maybe it wasn't a bear at all,* I thought darkly.

Kylie picked up a copy of *Righteous Sweetheart* from the floor, running her hand over the cover like she was brushing away a sheen of dust.

"Hey, Haven?" There was an odd hitch in her throat. She met my eyes with piercing intensity. "I have a story to tell you, too."

I begged a moment of reprieve to get a glass of water from the kitchen, taking tight little sips to steady my nerves. When I returned with water for her as well, she took a sip then wiped her mouth.

She cleared her throat. "So, my story is less of a horror movie and more of a family drama," she said, setting the glass on the coffee table and not meeting my eyes. "A fucked-up Lifetime Original."

She opened the copy of *Righteous Sweetheart* and dragged a fingernail in a slow circle around the author's name printed on the title page: Amory Marbury.

"But our stories start the same way. Mine opens with a girl moving to a tiny town on the Washington coast after her mother's death. A vacation town. Famous for a certain fish-and-chips pub and its resident reclusive author. Not exactly the first place a Black girl from Tucson would think to go."

She flipped a page, letting the paper's edge gently slice across the pad of her finger. "She had planned to move to Los Angeles and try to get a job in a writers' room, or waitress and write novels on the side until she got her big break. But a strange thing happened after her mother died. Her aunt sent her a letter. It told a different story, this one about a trip her mother—an arts and culture reporter out of Nashville—took twenty-five years ago to cover a literary festival. In the festival's green room, she met an older, charming, venerated author. After a few cocktails, they went back to his hotel. You can probably guess where my story is going. It's not the most original plot twist, but it has the benefit of being true."

She shut the book and tossed it onto the coffee table. "Nine months later, I was born."

All my questions and doubts about Kylie began to coalesce into one coherent answer, like finally seeing the hidden picture after hours of staring at an autostereogram.

"My father . . ." I started again. "You mean he was your father, too?"

She dragged in a deep breath. "I wasn't sure at first. That's why I came to Lundie Bay, to find out if it was true. I got a job at Lundie Bay Books because I figured they'd know all the dirt about him. I found out Dahlia Whitney worked for him, and one day after she'd left for the evening, I went to his house. I told Amory that Dahlia had sent me to help clean as an excuse to look around. He figured out pretty fast that I wasn't a house cleaner when he caught me going through stuff in the attic. I confronted him about my aunt's letter."

She picked up the wine bottle but didn't take a sip.

So she was *the second person Dahlia had seen in the attic.* I was shaking slightly.

"What did he say?"

"He wouldn't confirm it, but I saw how much the news shook him."

Finally, it all made sense. The girl before me wasn't an obsessive fan like the *Other/None Other* stalkers who left twists of paper in the Malice House gates. She *hadn't* been lying when she told me that she didn't see the appeal of my father's books. The reason Kylie knew where my father had kept the towels was because she'd been inside the house before, pretending to be a house cleaner.

A half sister I never knew about.

I pressed my hands against my face, claiming a moment of crude solitude, flooded with feelings I'd never experienced and didn't know what to do with. I'd known about my dad's affairs, so maybe it shouldn't have come as a shock to learn that one had resulted in offspring, but the possibility had never occurred to me. I'd always assumed it was just me and him. As an only child, I would have killed for a sibling. How different would my life have been if my dad wasn't the only family in it? If I'd had someone to share the loneliness? Maybe I wouldn't have so easily fallen for Baker's promise of a new family to cancel out the trauma of my real one.

After a second, my hands fell. "I don't know which story is crazier."

Kylie—my *sister*—gave a small, unfunny laugh before turning to face me. "Do you really think the Marbury family is cursed? That some kind of occult magic brought fictional characters into reality?"

I hesitated, still shaken by the news, then gave a single nod.

She stared at me as though waiting for me to waver, then took a deep breath when I didn't. "So that's it, then. I'm cursed, too, I guess." She ran a shaky hand, glittering with rings and tattooed with a Victor LaValle quote, down her face. "How does it work?"

It felt so strange to be speaking to her now, knowing that she was just as much my father's daughter as I. There was a mountain of questions between us, but for now, I focused on the present. "I honestly don't know. As far as I can tell, none of the characters in his other books have been brought to life, only the ones from that particular manuscript. It's the only one of his books I illustrated, so I think maybe it takes physical representation as well as a written description. Like the story gives them soul and artwork gives them physical form. For years, Dad talked about poltergeists in the house. My theory is that it was those characters somehow rattling around, formless, making little mischiefs by knocking down framed photos and stealing toast, until I came along and finally drew them into completion."

I explained what I'd learned from watching the documentary, my encounters in the woods, and my burning of *Bedtime Stories*. Kylie listened with a sharp ear, taking everything in and filing it away.

She asked, "Do you think I can do it, too? Manifest characters? If our father could, and you can, I don't see why not. I could try—"

I slammed the wine bottle on the coffee table harder than I'd intended, cutting her off with the loud smack of glass on wood. My ankle throbbed with phantom pain. "It's a curse, Kylie. Not a gift—it has only ever created monsters."

The wine sloshed in the bottle a miniature blood-tinted storm at sea. Once it had settled, I said, "I think Dad was trying to figure out how the curse worked, too. Before I went to look for you, I took a trip down to Clifford Library. I found the same underlined passages in *Other/None Other* that you did.

"I think Dad was trying to figure out how the curse worked, too. Before I went to that house in Water's Edge, I took a trip down to Clifford Library. I found the same underlined passages in *Other/None Other* that you did."

Kylie's eyebrows rose with interest, and the shifting muscles of her forehead caused a small section of dried blood to flake off and land on her neck. "About the original basement?"

"Yeah. The librarian helped me figure out the house was moved in the 1940s. It used to be on Rafe's property, so that's where the original basement is. I think I know: beneath an old shed with a very old foundation. There could be anything down there, but I wouldn't be surprised if that's where my father kept whatever information he knew about the curse."

Kylie picked anxiously at the wine bottle's paper label. "So, then, let's find out. Call Rafe. Tell him that we're curious about the old structure. He won't mind if we look, will he?"

My skin prickled in apprehension, thinking about the fire pit and dog tags. Kylie didn't know about my disturbing discovery about Rafe. I still hadn't spoken to him since we'd hooked up, though he'd sent me a handful more texts after leaving the black envelope on my porch, all of them asking what he'd done to scare me away. It was only a matter of time before he came back with another letter or to try to speak with me in person. I would have to confront him sooner or later about what I'd found and hope that he had an explanation that wouldn't reveal yet another psycho in my life.

"Okay, but we should take the shotgun," I mused, toying with the ring on my finger.

Kylie cocked her head. "Just to go to Rafe's? Aren't you . . . friends?"

The silence stretched as the clock on the mantel ticked away the long minutes of night. I could hear the trees shifting outside, branches creaking, and imagined I could even detect the crash of waves far in the distance, though it might have just been in my head.

My open laptop suddenly trilled.

My immediate fear was that Rafe somehow sensed we were talking about him and had sent an email, but it was the camera app. I snatched up the computer and saw that the feed for the front-porch camera was blinking red, signaling recent movement other than our own.

I pressed a finger against my lips for Kylie to be quiet, then pointed in the direction of the front porch just behind us. The drapes were drawn so anyone standing outside wouldn't be able to see us, but they didn't do much to muffle sound, given how well I could hear forest sounds outside.

I angled the computer so that Kylie and I could watch the feed together. It had that grayscale night-vision that inverted the world into a photo negative. The porch was empty now, though the porch swing at the far end swayed as though someone had just bumped into it. The front light cast a painfully bright glare down on the grass, painting the rest of the yard in too-sharp contrast.

Something rustled on the far side of the wrap-around porch, which the camera's angle couldn't catch. We heard the sound in real life *and* on the camera's disorienting split-second lag. Kylie grabbed my arm and motioned to the windows at the far end of the library. We both listened as footsteps slowly crossed on the other side of the wall. Whoever was out there was moving slowly, trying to be quiet. We followed their sound until they turned the porch corner and walked outside the same windows we sat beside.

The camera feed picked up a steel-wool-toned figure with glowing pinprick eyes moving toward the windows, crowbar in hand.

CHAPTER TWENTY-FIVE

Had the forest changed? Holding a lantern up to the long night, the Harbinger turned to look back at the path from which he and the Hellhound had come. Somehow, they'd gotten turned around.

Music filtered through the trees. The Hellhound stopped to look up, ears perked. Twinkling lights appeared in the darkness ahead. A clearing had opened where there had been no clearing moments ago. The air carried the smells of roasting sausage and barley beer.

They hadn't been traveling to the Night Market, but the Night Market had found them just the same.

—From "Beasts of Sun" in
Bedtime Stories for Monsters

●

IT WAS CATHERINE Tybee.

Even with the camera's distorted infrared feed, I recognized her swept-back hair and bulky raincoat. The camera gave her eyes a demonic sheen that suited her a little too well.

Kylie looked at me and mouthed, "What the hell?"

I held up a finger for her to remain quiet. The house was locked, and the windows barred. I didn't know how Catherine had gotten past the gate, but there was no way she could get into the house without a key. My rental car wasn't in the driveway, so she probably thought the house was empty.

Kylie and I huddled together in silence to watch the camera feed on my computer. As long as we remained quiet, Catherine had no reason to believe we were home. The shotgun on the coffee table was reassuring, though I couldn't imagine any world where I would pop a cap into an aging bookseller.

Kylie eased a pen out of the jar on the side table and opened the copy of *Righteous Sweetheart* to the blank back page. She wrote:

Were you expecting her?

She passed me the book and pen, and I jotted down:

Dad's new manuscript + Catherine's Ink Drinker Club = STALKERS

Kylie read my note and then asked:

Do they know about the curse??

She tapped the pen insistently against her question. Ever since my first meeting with the Ink Drinkers in the bookstore's bank vault, I had taken their obsessive interest in the project as a chance to make money off the manuscript's publication or a possible desire to gain renown through the discovery of a literary secret. They were librarians and professionals committed to logic; I doubted they'd believe in a curse.

Albeit a little uncertain, I shook my head.

She pointed the pen at the shotgun, then wrote:

Loaded?

I shrugged and Kylie rolled her eyes and pantomimed a silent groan. I started to write an explanation, but then Kylie tapped my arm urgently and pointed to the computer screen.

Before I could focus on the feed, the glass behind us shattered. Shards fell against the drapes and rained to the floor.

We hugged our legs tightly on the sofa, not daring to move a muscle, sharing the same self-preservation instinct. The camera feed showed Catherine smash the crowbar against the windowpane again to break off the remaining jagged pieces of glass still attached to the iron bars. Then the feed displayed her grayscale hand reach through the broken pane, and in a disorienting collision of realities, her *actual* hand reached through the drapes behind us, warm tan flesh with maroon-painted fingernails, feeling along the interior windowsill for a lock.

Kylie tugged on my shirt urgently, motioning to the stairs with a silent question. I shook my head. Better to stay perfectly still. Catherine might hear our footsteps if we tried to go upstairs and hide. I doubted Catherine knew that the decorative wrought-iron panes were actually a security feature. She could get her hand through, but that was all. And there was no lock within reach—my father had designed it for maximum safety.

The woman's grotesquely disembodied hand felt around the drapes and the windowsill then finally disappeared. We waited as the mantel clock ticked too loudly, too slowly, like time was skewed. Then an object flew in through the broken pane and landed on the rug.

Kylie started to twist to look behind the sofa at the object, but I shook my head, signaling for her to wait. We remained motionless until the feed showed Catherine leaving the porch, recording the roar of her car's engine, followed by the crunch of wheels on gravel.

We waited another few minutes out of caution, and then I carefully pulled back the drapes and peeked through.

Catherine was gone. The front porch and driveway were empty. I unfolded myself from the couch and walked around it carefully, mindful of the broken glass, to pick up the object Catherine had thrown in.

I immediately went cold.

It was an oversized blue coffee mug with BOOKMARKS ARE FOR QUITTERS printed in a pretty calligraphy font.

Kylie eyed the object with distaste, like roadkill. Even though we were alone, she still spoke in a hushed voice as she said, "My boss just tried to break into your house. With a crowbar. And left you a *mug*?"

The mug was ice-cold in my hands. There was no coffee stain on the rim; it was a brand-new mug. It wasn't *my* mug. It *wasn't* the mug that I'd picked up at a little used bookstore in the Lower East Side that I used to keep on my studio table in our Chelsea apartment with its perpetual inch of day-old coffee in the bottom. But it was identical to that one.

"I had one like it." My voice was shaking. "When I lived in New York."

"Okay, so that's weird."

No one knew about that last night in New York with Baker—the night I fled. Detective Rice had hinted that she'd looked into my arrest record and Baker's disappearance, but there was no way she could know the exact details—for example, the mug's role in it all.

"Remember I told you about my ex-husband?" I said shakily.

She bobbed a slow nod as her eyes drifted knowingly to my left shoulder.

"We got into a fight on the night I left." An image of blood soaking into the carpet hit me, and I fought to keep my voice steady as I said, "This mug ended up broken in the fight. I mean, obviously not the same one. One like it."

Her eyes swept over me, wary. "You think your ex is here? Like, he told Catherine about the mug?"

I shook my head in a swift arc. "Not possible. He wouldn't come to Lundie Bay." The way I had left things, I would never be seeing Baker again. I said hesitantly, "The police told me he's missing."

She took her time biting her lip and then said slowly, "Don't take this the wrong way, but did you off your husband? Because it's starting to feel that way given how jumpy you are when you talk about him and how certain you are he didn't do this. And, hey, no judgement. I get the sense he was a bad guy."

"Don't be ridiculous," I said evenly.

It was clearly what Detective Rice suspected, too, or at the least, the possibility had crossed her mind. I wondered what she'd made of my explanation that Baker could be on an expedition—her look had suggested she'd though it more likely he was stuffed into a sewer grate somewhere. But if the detective didn't know about the mug, how the hell did Catherine Tybee know about it—and understand its significance—when no one but Baker and I did?

"Right," Kylie said flatly.

A conclusion struck me. "Catherine is the person who's been trying to break into the house. She wants the manuscript or wants to scare me out of here—I guess so that I'll move? She told me she once tried to buy the house from my father."

Kylie unfolded her legs and picked up my canvas bag from where I'd let it slump to the floor. She started going through it until she pulled out my jangling car keys.

"What are you doing?" I asked.

"We have to follow her. She knows something."

I dragged my nails through my hair, thinking. My heart was galloping. "It's the middle of the night. You've just been through hell and back. We both need rest and a clear head. We'll go into town in the morning and talk to Catherine, okay? If we confront her when we're both strung-out, she'll have the upper hand." I held out my hand for my keys, which she surrendered. "Take a shower and some Advil. You can sleep in the guest room and borrow some of my clothes."

Kylie's eyelids were half-sunk with exhaustion already. Crusty blood caked her hairline where she hadn't managed to clean it all with the towel. I couldn't help but study the shape of her features, looking for an echo of my father. Watching her movements for a glimpse of his mannerisms. All my life, I'd been alone. No mother. An absent father whose ivory tower was so high its shadow always kept me in the cold and dark. I'd spent years trying to get into the sunlight and build my own structure, even just half the size of his. And here was someone doing the same: reckoning with her past, yearning to carve her own mark.

"Fine, we'll wait until tomorrow," she agreed. "But give me that gun. We need to know if it's loaded."

I handed her the gun and the box of shells. She held a shell up to the light, reading the tiny markings on it. "I think this is buckshot. Effective for shooting people, not so much against monster crustaceans or whatever that thing you told me about is." She rifled through the bag again. "I don't see any slugs, though, so buckshot is the best we've got."

"You use shotguns a lot?" My voice rose in alarm.

"No," she admitted. "I've never actually used one. But I'm a novelist. My work in progress is a thriller. I've watched dozens of online tutorials about loading and firing guns. I'm kinda surprised the NSA hasn't shown up at my door yet."

It was a common joke among novelists; during his speaking events my father had often recounted something similar about being monitored by government watchdogs, and it always got a chuckle. Neither of us was laughing now. I'd never been so thankful for well-researched fiction if it meant Kylie could shoot.

"I should have said this sooner," I told her, briefly feeling the embarrassing sting of tears, then getting control of myself again. "I'm glad about what you said—to have a sister. I wish there were a better inheritance to share with you than a family curse, but I'm really happy to find another Marbury."

Her smile was exhausted but genuine. She gave a small salute as she headed up the stairs. In a few minutes, the upstairs shower turned on.

Now that I was alone, I let go of my tightly held facade and collapsed into a shaky mess on the library floor. The events of the past few hours eclipsed everything that had come before it, even back to the night I had fled New York. The mug felt heavy in my hands. *Someone knows about what happened.* Someone must have ordered this exact mug online because they knew how badly it would rattle me. Identical to the one that had been smashed to pieces. Lying on the carpet next to a puddle of blood.

Glancing up the stairs to make sure Kylie was still in the shower, I pulled out my phone and texted Baker's phone, feeling the unsteady insanity of reaching out to a ghost.

Where are you? Who else knows?

There was no answer, not even the three dots to show he'd seen it and was writing back. My mind skated around, trying to find its way out of the fog. My body shook, at the brink of collapse. I dragged myself up the stairs and changed into pajamas, then crawled between the smooth sheets, but not before checking under the bed.

I had a feeling that for the rest of my life, I'd look under the bed before going to sleep.

CHAPTER TWENTY-SIX

Their lovemaking had been quick and unexpected. Too much barley beer and the hard smile of a hard woman. As she was lacing up her boots, the witch asked him, "Have you found what you were looking for, Harbinger?"

—From **"Beasts of Sun"** in
Bedtime Stories for Monsters

AFTER DECADES OF bearing my father's weight, the primary bedroom's mattress sagged in his permanent shape of my father, so no matter how I turned or tried to claw my way out, I always slid back into his imprint. In the morning, I ached from my bandaged ankle all the way to the base of my skull. Over bowls of dry cereal—the milk had expired—Kylie and I looked like specters of who we'd been weeks ago. But I felt a defiant cry in my marrow. We were together. I was no longer alone. *I had a sister.*

She leaned over her laptop, which I'd given back to her after explaining why I'd taken it, tapping on keys as she read the news. She sucked in a tight breath and turned the screen toward me.

"They found Orion."

It was a social media post linking to an official statement from the Lundie Bay Police Department. The news must not have made it yet to the more prominent media outlets of Bellingham and Seattle. The statement reported that a dog walker had noticed the house's door left open all night and called the police, who found Orion's body in the garage. There was no mention of seven bowls arranged like a satanic ritual or a milk jug full of blood or organ meat in the refrigerator. The house belonged to Orion's grandparents, who had moved into an assisted living facility the previous week after the husband suffered a bad fall. The perfect place for the Witch of Went to set up her grisly operation. The house hadn't been that different from her own clapboard house on the outskirts of a small town, so well described in her tale.

My phone lay on the kitchen counter, the screen black. I chewed on a lip. "Great. Detective Rice is probably going to call me down to the station again."

"But you barely knew Orion."

"It might be enough that he worked at a bookstore that sold my father's books and that we'd crossed paths a few times. I'm already an unofficial person of interest. And I *was* in his grandparents' house where he was killed. They might find my DNA."

Kylie scooped a handful of dry cereal out of the box. "So don't answer if she calls."

I sighed as I slumped against the countertop. "Sooner or later, they'd come here. I'm not hard to find. It isn't like I have anywhere else to go. The police department even has the gate code—Dahlia gave it to them before I moved in. I haven't found the instruction manual to reset it and the security company that installed it went out of business a few years ago."

She finished chewing and swallowed. "Who else has the code?"

"Only the police and Rafe, as far as I know. Catherine must have gotten it from one of them because when she dropped me off the other day, I made sure she didn't see me enter it in."

I went to the kitchen window and stood on tiptoe to peer over the property fence at Rafe's house, tapping my fingers anxiously. His car was in the driveway, and several lights were on in the house. A shadow passed behind sheer drapes on an upstairs window; he was home.

"We'll have to wait to investigate the shed on Rafe's property." I said uneasily as I rinsed my bowl in the sink. "I'm not keen on the idea of running into him. We shouldn't do anything until he's gone."

Kylie folded her arms and didn't press about Rafe, maybe assuming our date had gone bad. "So then, town? Talk to Catherine?"

I nodded, still distracted by the shadow in Rafe's windows and the memory of his note. *So the girl who doesn't get scared by horror movies gets scared off by . . . what?* As far as I knew, he had no connection to Catherine Tybee, and it didn't seem like he would give her my gate code. For some reason, I still wanted to trust Rafe. My stupid heart was involved, or at least my lust. As long as I didn't confront him about the dog collars, he could continue to exist in my mind as a sexy condiment tycoon who kissed me during horror movies and praised my art.

We got dressed and continued to read online news coverage as it came in on Orion's murder, though there was no significant new information. Before we walked down to the overlook where I'd left my rental car, I carefully fit the loaded shotgun into a long bag meant for a yoga mat and slung it over my shoulder. We were artists, not fighters, but creation and destruction were like a photograph to its negative: essentially, the same story.

Lundie Bay seemed unexpectedly busy until I remembered it was the weekend. The leaves were starting to change, and though town was sleepy during the week, it transformed into a popular day-trip destination on Saturdays and Sundays. The news of Orion's murder, along with Eddie Chase, Francesca Myers, and Dahlia Whitney, hadn't deterred the leaf-peepers. We parked several blocks from the bookstore and walked the rest of the way, keeping our heads down and slowing as we rounded the corner. I didn't want to risk Catherine seeing us before we saw her. But as soon as the bookstore came into sight, our caution was irrelevant. A red CLOSED sign hung on the front door.

We ambled closer for a better look. A hand-written note under the sign explained that the bookstore and café would be closed all week for personal reasons. Someone had drawn the constellation of Orion surrounded by a heart and written a quote:

"You, only you, will have stars that can laugh!" —*Antoine de Saint-Exupéry,*
The Little Prince
Love you, O.

"An employee died," Kylie said. "Of course, they'd close it. I should have thought of that."

"As far as anyone knows, you're still missing, too. Tough times for Lundie Bay Books' employees." I stuffed my hands in pockets. "Do you know where Catherine lives?"

Kylie shook her head.

While we figured out what to do next, we crossed the street to a bakery to get coffee and pastries to make up for the dry cereal we'd had that morning. After taking seats facing the window, I couldn't help but notice the guy next to us was reading a battered copy of *The Desecration of Johnny Jim*. He'd highlighted about every other line—either a lit student or an intense Marbury fan. As soon as Kylie started to talk, I elbowed her and motioned toward the guy. The last thing we needed was a fan in earshot of us talking about Malice House. She went silent.

Out of the other corner of my eye, I glimpsed a young man in a wool sweater and bow tie pass in front of the bakery window. I sat up straight, barely believing my own eyes. *Ronan Young.* He'd been looking down at his phone and hadn't seen us sitting in the window seats.

I grabbed Kylie's sleeve. "Hey! Quick. We need to follow that guy."

She shoved the last of her scone in her mouth and washed it down with coffee. We tossed our cups in the recycling bin on the way out and hurried into the street.

"Who was it?" she asked.

"Ronan Young from Bainbridge," I said breathlessly.

"The librarian?" Her head bobbed from side to side as she tried to keep sight of him while he passed a couple pushing a stroller.

"He wouldn't have driven up to Lundie Bay unless it was to meet with Catherine and Jonathan."

We kept our distance as we followed Ronan. He walked past the bookstore, barely glancing at the CLOSED sign, and turned left at the end of the block. He shoved his phone in his pocket and entered the narrow alley that ran behind the row of shops.

We stopped at the alley entrance and watched from there. He jogged up to a white set of doors and knocked. In a moment, someone opened a door for him.

"That's the bookstore's back entrance," Kylie whispered. "Where we get deliveries."

"Catherine must be inside. The Ink Drinkers have to be meeting there." There were no windows or fire escapes in the alley or other ways that we might get into the bookstore besides the front and back entrances.

"I have an employee key, but it's at my apartment," Kylie offered.

After a brief debate, we decided to go get her store key, even though it meant we might risk missing the Ink Drinkers leaving. I drove across town like a banshee. At her duplex, I waited with the engine running while Kylie ducked into her apartment and returned with both the key and a change of clothes, since mine were two sizes too big for her. By the time we drove back to town and parked, less than half an hour had passed. We had no way of knowing if the group was still inside the bookstore.

"We should go in the front," Kylie said. "The back entrance opens to a narrow hallway, and if they're in any of the office rooms, they'll see us immediately. But the front of the shop has more places to hide."

Kylie silenced her jangling keyring as we approached the front door, trying to go unnoticed by the nearby tourists on the street. We slipped inside, leaving it unlocked in case we needed to get out quickly and hoped that no curious tourists would try the door and find it open.

"Stay low," Kylie mouthed, motioning to the display tables stacked high with new releases. We crouched as we listened for signs of life. I'd never been in a closed bookstore. It reminded me of a time in high school when I'd left some medication in my locker, and the school janitor had let me in to get it: The empty hallways and dark classrooms were jarring, the echoes of student life from hours earlier still somehow present.

I'd never realized how many stark, haunting women's faces graced the covers of crime thrillers and historical romances and literary fiction until they were all staring at me from the shelves in the darkness as though begging for help. Women trapped in their stories. I expected the lights to come on at any minute, for us to be caught between Poetry and Local Interest. The old bank-teller stalls, converted to cash registers, were eerily quiet. Somewhere back there, Orion's name tag still pronounced his favorite book to be *Steppenwolf*.

Kylie motioned for me to follow her through the aisles. Once we moved beyond the new releases and bestsellers, the shelves grew to ceiling height. The books were packed spine-to-spine here instead of face-out. There had to be thousands of titles. She led me past the graphic novels into the children's section, with its startling flat-eyed stuffed animals seated around pint-sized tables and chairs, and then toward the entrance to the hallway that led back to the office, bathroom, and vault.

We heard voices coming from the open vault as soon as we reached the puzzle display. Jonathan Tybee's rumbling professorial voice made an emphatic declaration I couldn't make out. Then Catherine's softer lilt asked a question. Kylie and I leaned in to hear better.

"This isn't what Dahlia had in mind when she did what she did," Catherine said. "She thought she was putting an end to it."

"We all thought it ended there," her ex-husband snapped. "No one thought the violence would continue or that we'd have to be a part of it."

"Please, let's calm down," Ronan urged.

"Orion is dead!" Catherine said. "I'm allowed to be upset! That sweet boy worked here for four years. You've never met a bigger bibliophile. He was working toward being a manager, and now he's in the morgue!"

Their voices faded as one of them must have moved to partially block the doorway. Kylie ran a hand along her throat, scratching nervously at the hollow at the base of her neck.

"That's practically a confession," she half mouthed, half whispered. "If they didn't kill those people, they know who did."

"We *know* who killed Orion," I whispered back. We had both seen the shadowy figure of the Witch of Went in Orion's grandparents' house. "And I think other creatures from Malice are probably responsible for murdering the others."

"Then why are the Ink Drinkers talking like *they're* somehow involved?"

"Shh." I signaled quickly as footsteps came out into the hallway.

We pulled back into the children's section, pressing ourselves flush against the puzzles, but it was only Ronan going to the bathroom for a tissue. He soon returned to the vault, and they continued arguing.

"Orion makes four deaths since she's come to town," Jonathan added somberly. "How many more is it going to take? And on top of the deaths from last summer, too. I think we can agree it's out of control."

"Of course it's out of control!" Ronan yelled. "It's been out of control since Amory first told us about his diagnosis. It was out of control when Dahlia killed him!"

I flinched as though someone had slapped me. Kylie went deathly still. Her wide eyes shifted to me.

The puzzles pressed into my spine with dozens of sharp corners like claws. Nothing could have prepared me for hearing that my father was murdered. *By Dahlia*. Dahlia Whitney, shih-tzu owner and member of a megachurch. Cranky old lady. Devoted grandmother. Ronan's words replayed through my head like the resounding toll of a church bell, but they somehow never stuck; I simply couldn't believe it. There was no way what they'd just said could be true.

"What the fuck?" Kylie mouthed. Her lips curled like she was about to be sick.

I dragged a shaky hand down my face but felt nothing, numb. But then Kylie squeezed my knee hard, digging in her fingers until I finally felt an energizing sting of pain.

"They're in the vault," she whispered. "There's no way out of there but the vault door. We can corner them there with the shotgun and demand they tell us what's going on."

"What if they call our bluff?"

"It's no bluff! They just said Dahlia murdered Amory! I'll shoot their knees or their feet—I don't care. There are monsters out there and people who are just as dangerous *here*. I'm not letting myself get tied up in some garage again, watching someone else die."

She tugged the strap of the yoga bag off my shoulder and quietly unzipped it. The barrel of the shotgun gleamed in the low light.

The distinctive sound of someone cocking a gun came from the aisle behind us.

We both went motionless. Catherine, Jonathan Tybee, and Ronan were still arguing in the vault. *So who else is here?*

Stepping out of the shadows, Detective Rice moved to stand beside a display of gardening books with her police-issued pistol aimed at us. In the darkness, her face was unreadable, but the outline of her shoulders was tightly coiled, a woman who wouldn't hesitate to shoot.

"Breaking and entering, Haven? Stand up slowly," she ordered. "And kick that shotgun over to me. Carefully."

CHAPTER TWENTY-SEVEN

They longed for the thaw. For spring when the picnickers would
return. Yet April came with no visitors to Fathom Lake. Then
May. Come June, they crawled out with blackened fingernails and
waterlogged skin, pulling themselves over forest and meadow until they
dragged themselves to the feast and gorged their fill. Wherever they
went, Fathom Lake seeped along with them.

—From "The Decaylings" in
Bedtime Stories for Monsters

●

I STOOD SLOWLY with my hands held out in front of me. Kylie
used her toe to push the yoga bag across the carpet until Detective
Rice could reach it.

"It isn't breaking and entering," I insisted in a hushed, urgent
voice so the Ink Drinkers wouldn't hear me. What was the detective
doing here? A tourist in town must have seen us sneaking around the
closed bookstore and called the police. "We have a store key."

Detective Rice didn't lower her gun as she moved slightly away
from the shelves, where a ray of grayish light fell on her face. She
looked even more exhausted than she had before and far too grim

for just catching a pair of bookstore trespassers, which objectionably wasn't *that* severe a crime, especially given everything that had happened over the last few weeks.

Kylie motioned to the hallway that led to the back offices and said, "Those people back there just confessed to murder."

Detective Rice's eyes flickered to the hallway and the lilting voices still arguing in the vault. Her eyes narrowed a hair. "Who are you?" she asked Kylie with a thrust of her chin.

"I work in the bookstore café. The owner, Catherine Tybee, just tried to break into Haven's house. We saw it happen and have it recorded on a camera feed."

Detective Rice let out the sigh of an overworked, overstressed woman who was nevertheless still sharp as a knife blade. She motioned with her pistol toward the hallway. "Go. Head back there. Both of you."

I felt my eyes go wide, and I started to argue, but it was clear from the detective's expression that she wasn't in an argumentative mood. Kylie and I exchanged a glance but had no choice except to do as she said. The light was on in the vault, spilling out into the rest of the hall.

Ronan was the first to see us. He jumped up from the card table like he'd seen a ghost. Catherine and Jonathan twisted around and stared at us, wide-eyed.

"Kylie?" Catherine said, pressing a hand to her chest. "What are you doing here?" Her watery blue eyes fixed on me with a sharp accusation like this was all *my* fault, like they hadn't just been reminiscing about my father's murder.

Detective Rice answered, "I found them in the front of the store. They'd let themselves in with an employee key and were listening to your conversation."

The Ink Drinkers stared at us with utter bafflement and something that almost resembled fear. Finally, Jonathan took a deep breath and pinched the bridge of his nose. Then he said to Detective Rice, "Thank goodness you were running late."

Running late?

From the way Kylie sucked in a sharp breath, she must have realized a second before I did that no tourists had called the police on us. No, Detective Rice was an *Ink Drinker*.

Catherine pushed forward, wrapping her shawl around her chest like she had a sudden chill. "I don't understand, Kylie. You were reported as missing—"

"I heard you talking just now," Kylie interrupted in a sharp voice. "You said Dahlia killed Amory Marbury."

Jonathan held up his hands like a high school principal. "Settle down now, everyone. *Christ*. Letitia, step back so they can get in. Haven, Kylie, sit down."

We shuffled awkwardly in the tight space, all six of us keenly aware of the pistol in the police detective's hands and keeping our careful distance from one another like we had the plague. Kylie and I hovered over the empty chairs until Jonathan jabbed a finger at us.

"*Sit.*"

We did as commanded.

Detective Rice holstered her gun—I suppose we weren't much threat trapped in a vault with the four of them blocking the doorway.

Catherine pressed a hand to her cheek, shaking her head. "This is awful. Just awful. Kylie, you shouldn't be involved in this. And, Haven, I'm sorry you had to learn about your father this way. We never meant for you to find out."

"*Our* father," I said hollowly.

"What was that?" she asked.

I had to wet my dry lips. "*Our* father."

Kylie's head bobbed in a slow nod. It took the others a minute to understand what I meant, and then once the realization hit, they all got a little wide-eyed.

Detective Rice's eyebrows tented in surprise. "No shit?"

Catherine combed a wrinkled hand through her gray-streaked hair as she tried to make sense of it. "I see." She seemed to war with herself for a few moments and then muttered in a showy way, "That man. A tortured soul. A sinner as much as a genius."

I wasn't in the mood for dramatics. I leaned forward, my hair falling over my eyes, and demanded, "Why did Dahlia kill my father?"

Catherine shook her head while her fingers still nervously threaded through her hair like it was all too complicated to explain.

Ronan said quietly, "Because we asked her to."

"Ronan!" Catherine scolded.

The librarian rested his hands on his hips as he faced her. "Well, we did, Catherine. There's no reason to hide it anymore. Amory was only a few weeks away from dying anyway. It was awful there at the end. You didn't see it, Haven, but we did. He was a shell of himself. Terrified by his own house. Rambling about monsters. We debated for a long time before finally asking Dahlia to put rat poison in his coffee. And now Dahlia is dead because of what we asked her to do."

"I don't understand," Kylie said, slowly shaking her head. "So it was, like, a mercy killing?"

Jonathan Tybee's scoff was heavy with condescension. "No, Kylie, it wasn't. The fact that Amory was near death anyway only made it easier for us all to go through with. Your father broke with reality in his last few months, Haven. He was convinced his house was haunted. Naturally, none of us believed him. We're all rational people here. He became desperate—thought he had to prove it to us. He did something strange. . . ."

Jonathan's face, normally ruddy and full of expression, fell pallid. I read the nauseating fear behind his eyes and could only imagine how this *rational* man had warred with his reason when faced with undeniable preternatural forces.

He took a deep breath, no longer looking professorial but like a jittery teaching assistant on the first day of class. In a voice he had to fight to keep steady, he continued, "We never knew how it worked, but somehow, he created an aberration. Pulled it out of his worst nightmares. We all saw it. It got loose from the house and killed some hikers and deer hunters before Letitia and several other officers shot it. We managed to keep it quiet from any official reports, but the truth was, your father was able to bring a fictitious *thing* to life." He ran a shaky hand over his brow like he needed a drink to calm his nerves as he muttered, "The rational became irrational. And we, the innocent, became complicit."

Ronan turned to me almost apologetically and added quietly, "When you came to town, we were afraid you might have the same ability and would use it to the same ends."

They're right. That was my immediate thought, instead of trying to defend myself. They were right to fear me.

Kylie—my *sister*—and I, we were just as dangerous as they thought. My ignorance of what I'd been doing with my paintbrushes didn't make me guiltless.

"We're not murderers," Ronan insisted. "It was an impossible situation to be placed in. People in town were dying, and we felt we were the only ones who could do something about it. It was the lesser moral evil."

The room started to fracture into kaleidoscoping lights, but it was no curse, no dark magic this time, only my mind. The booksellers and librarian in front of me hadn't been psychopaths at all; they'd been trying to protect their neighbors from *me*.

Somehow, *I* was the villain here.

"So what?" Kylie asked hotly. "You're going to kill us?"

"Of course not," Catherine said. "We don't want anyone else hurt. There have already been far too many victims. But I'm afraid we are going to have to keep you here while we discuss how to proceed."

Kylie rolled her shoulders back. "Yeah, *we're* the threat. Sure."

Detective Rice pivoted to face me and asked point-blank, "You did it, didn't you? You pulled more characters out of his fiction. Creatures that slaughtered Dahlia and are out there right now, hunting down others."

She looked like I disgusted her. Try as I might, I couldn't find a reason to blame her. Nausea pooled in the back of my throat. My thoughts turned to the pale-faced woman in Orion's grandparents' house moving down the hallway with the ability to bend reality. The refrigerator full of organs in Tupperware. Eddie Chase's destroyed face.

My voice came out hoarse. "I didn't know what I was doing."

Jonathan barked a bitter laugh. He muttered something low I couldn't make out, and Catherine gave him a sharp look.

Jonathan nudged Ronan. "Search the room for any paper or writing implements." As Ronan edged his way into the vault like a mouse hunting for seeds, taking pens from the table, gathering our purses along with my keyring, picking up the few books stacked along one wall, Jonathan explained, "We don't know how it works other than it involves art combined with the written word. We can't leave you with anything you could use to create more aberrations."

Catherine watched Ronan distractedly as he finished clearing the room, her fingers twisting in her shawl's fringe.

Detective Rice disappeared for a moment and returned with two bottles of water from the bookstore office's kitchenette. She set them on the card table and then rested a hand on the vault door. "You have water," she said. "The vault is ventilated. We'll be back tomorrow after we've talked this through with the others."

"*Others?* Who else is involved in this?" I demanded.

But she ignored me, and I had to assume she meant the other police officers who had cornered and killed my father's monster last summer.

"Wait!" Kylie yelled. "You can't leave us in here. That door doesn't even close anymore."

"Oh, sweetie. It works fine. I made that up so the cashiers wouldn't be scared to use it as a break room," Catherine explained apologetically. "Jan gets so claustrophobic."

It took Jonathan's and Detective Rice's full weight to ease the vault door closed. Kylie and I both jumped up from the chairs as we watched the crescent of freedom thin until the door slammed closed with a thud. Gears moved on the complex machinery as the lock clicked into place.

Kylie tugged uselessly on the gears. "It's twelve inches thick. No one will hear us screaming." She pulled out her phone and her face fell. "And, there's no reception with the door locked."

My fingers tapped against each other maniacally; I didn't even try to stop the tic. "We sat at this same table," I said, coiling my hands into fists, "and they told me my artwork was terrible. They tried to stall on publishing the manuscript or take control of it away from me. God, I get it now. I can't even blame them. They must have been terrified when they found out I was an illustrator. History repeating itself."

"Don't feel bad for *them*," Kylie said, thrusting a finger toward the front of the bookstore. "They killed our father! And locked us here! They can reassure themselves all they want that they're conflicted heroes—it doesn't make it true. If they had just told you what happened last summer when you first arrived, no one else would have died."

I dragged my nails over my lips, wondered if she was right. Why hadn't they been honest with me from the start? To be fair, I couldn't imagine that I would have believed them if they'd started talking about curses and monsters crawling off a page.

I let my hand fall away from my mouth. Maybe they were simply afraid that if they told me, I wouldn't care and manifest demons anyway.

"When they come back in the morning," Kylie said, pressing her fingers against her temples, "we'll tell them about the key to Malice House's basement. There must be answers there. You said that Amory was trying to figure out how the curse works—maybe he discovered something. We'll convince them that we want to stop all of this as much as they do."

A grim shadow worked through me. "I don't think that's how curses work."

"What do you mean?"

"It's a curse, not a choice. Curses have an inevitability to them.

They attach themselves to a place or a family and work malevolence through them. At least that's how curses work in the movies." I'd seen enough horror flicks to have a PhD in terror. And even though movies were fiction, all fiction was based in reality; it was reasonable to believe that at least some horror-movie lore was rooted in truth.

I stretched out my hands, still ink-stained from the last time I'd drawn, studying the familiar lines and grooves to remind myself that I was real, not fiction. "Remember when we talked about the flow state? The muse?"

Kylie nodded.

"Well, whenever I worked on the illustrations from my father's manuscript, it was like I entered a dissociative space where some other self took over. Like when you're in a crisis and a subconscious part of you just knows what to do. I'm not sure I was ever in control—the curse was. I couldn't have resisted it, and I'm guessing that when Dad succumbed to dementia, he couldn't resist it anymore either."

Kylie sank down to the ugly gray-green Wells Fargo carpet, then grabbed a water bottle and twisted it open. "Fuck."

I joined her, cross-legged, on the vault floor. The only light came from a single harsh fluorescent bulb. Ronan had removed all the books, so there was nothing to read to distract ourselves. My mind kept running through the list of characters I had illustrated. Pinchy seemed to be gone, but the others were very much alive: The Harbinger. The Witch of Went. The Hellhound. Kestrel. The Decaylings. The Robber Saints. Uncle Arnold. Each of them atrocious in their own way, whether human-like or bestial. Each bound to a story line that hadn't turned to ash along with the pages that birthed them. Story lines that they would bring to their grisly conclusions again and again unless I found a way to stop them.

Eventually, exhaustion overtook me. I lay flat on the vault floor with my raincoat draped over my head to dim the light. It wasn't long before Kylie stretched out next to me. After a nebulous amount of time, she started talking in her sleep. Strange, sharp words I couldn't quite make out. Was Detective Rice right about the vault being ventilated? Or were we slowly suffocating, falling into delirium?

With such questions in my head, I surrendered to the dark nothingness of repose until a soft clanking sound reached me even in my dreams. After fading in and out of sleep's realm, I finally stirred awake and found myself staring at the bank vault door.

It was wide open.

CHAPTER TWENTY-EIGHT

It was thirty hours into night, and Ricky was in the attic, pounding on his typewriter. A dark, unfinished space, but with the baby downstairs still waking every hour, it was the only place he could get a modicum of privacy. And this story was pouring out of him like he was channeling it from God. His fingers couldn't move fast enough over the keys. This would be the one, he knew it. They'd finally be able to move to a house with enough room for the baby, maybe even for a little brother or sister in another year or two, and he could stop those long, sticky hours cleaning the movie theater.

He didn't hear the footsteps on the stairs until the people were right behind him, filling every corner of the tiny attic. Too many to count. Men and women in brown cloaks that hooded their eyes. Two of the largest men grabbed him, stuffing crumpled manuscript pages in his mouth to silence his shouts, while a woman came up with a long silver straw-like extractor that she placed into his ear canal. She sucked and sucked, drew a phlegmy mass through the straw and into her mouth, then spit it quickly in a brown glass bottle.

"Catalog it," she commanded to another cloaked women.

—From "Late Fees" in
Bedtime Stories for Monsters

●

I IMMEDIATELY SHOOK Kylie awake.

After staring at the open vault door, she whispered, "Do you think Ronan opened it?"

It had also occurred to me that Ronan might have returned to the store without the others and unlocked the vault. Of all the Ink Drinkers, he seemed the least malicious. His life was comprised of beloved old books and quirkily printed bow ties; he wasn't the type to lock terrified women in bank vaults.

I raised an uncertain shoulder.

Kylie pushed to her feet and moved cautiously toward the open door. A premonition scratched along the back of my neck, forcing me to my feet.

"Wait. It feels too easy," I said. "Something isn't right."

The long hallway beyond the vault was night-dark. I had no way of knowing what time it was, but I guessed it was past midnight. The eerie feeling of being inside a bookstore after hours enveloped me. Beneath the smell of new books and printer ink was an unsettling trace of pine, though I couldn't be sure of its origin—the bookstore sold candles, so the smell might simply be wax. But I didn't like the sense that the trees had found us, even here.

Kylie cautiously eased the vault door open the rest of the way. In the middle of the long, narrow hallway, the shotgun rested on the carpet alongside our purses. There was no sign of the yoga bag. The gun was aimed away from us, like a gruesome offering that a cat had delivered to its owner's front door.

We stared at the shotgun for a few seconds before Kylie knelt and picked it up. No one jumped out at her. I think we'd both suspected a trap, but the bookstore remained dark and still. She checked the gun quickly. "It isn't loaded. The Ink Drinkers must have taken out the bullets."

I darted forward and grabbed my bag, verifying everything was there before slinging it cross-body over my chest. I tossed her the other bag, which she slid on her shoulder.

"Why would they give us our stuff back?" I asked.

"No idea. Everything about this feels off." Clutching the shotgun, she took a few cautious steps down the hallway. Without the normal soft music playing, every movement we made sounded amplified. She tilted her head in my direction and asked in a hushed voice, "What exactly did you pull out of that manuscript that I should be worried about?" She hadn't gotten the chance to read *Bedtime Stories for Monsters* before I burned it.

"You met one of them already," I whispered as I followed, keeping my gaze on the open doors to the break room and bathroom. "Besides the Witch of Went, there's a trickster called the Harbinger who goes from town to town in search of an ultimate villain who can bring order to Malice. He's called the Salem Dreamer."

"Sounds like a brand of mattress for witches," Kylie murmured.

"*I* didn't name him."

She peered cautiously into the bathroom, continuing when she seemed confident it was empty. "And the rest?"

As we moved slowly down the hallway into the front portion of the bookstore, I summarized Malice's nefarious residents and their story lines. She grimaced at the Decaylings' taste for flesh and shuddered to hear of Uncle Arnold's attraction to impressionable young women.

"So how does it end?" she asked.

"It doesn't end. The final page— Wait. Hang on." Something had fallen and clattered loudly in the store. "Did you hear that?"

The store was so dark that I couldn't make out the books' titles. Kylie was barely an outline in front of me. Something fell again, making the same tumbling *thud*.

"That was a book falling," Kylie whispered. "Someone knocked a book off a shelf." She curled her fingers around the shotgun's barrel. Even unloaded, it could still be used as a blunt weapon. "I don't think we're alone."

"There," I whispered, pointing to a display table of fall-themed picture books in the children's section. "Get behind it."

We scrambled across the aisle and into the children's section. The picture books were bulky enough to mostly hide us, but my back and sides felt exposed. Besides, whoever had opened the vault door clearly already knew we were here, so there was little point in hiding.

In the next aisle over, another book fell.

Shit—we definitely weren't alone.

A musty smell began to permeate throughout the children's section, heavy with notes of rotting grass and sulfur. I pressed a hand against my nose. *That* was no candle-wax scent. A dark stain slowly spread across the carpet. I might have assumed the roof was leaking, except for the fact that it wasn't raining. When I pressed my hand against the stain, the carpet was waterlogged and muddy. I jerked my hand back.

One of the picture books on the display table fell over. Kylie flinched hard and threw me a confused look. *It's just the two of us—no one knocked into it.* I chewed on the inside of my cheek. In the following instant, the picture book next to it fell, too, like a ghost had nudged it over.

The sounds of more books falling began to ricochet throughout the store.

"Go!" I gasped. "The front door."

Kylie scrambled down the children's section aisle, keeping low. I'd never realized how labyrinthine Lundie Bay Books was. During the day, with Irish music playing and the presence of other customers, it was pleasant to get lost in the meandering sections. But now, in the dark, I quickly became disoriented. A gardening book tumbled off the shelf next to me, landing right where I had been about to set my foot.

Kylie took a sharp right at the end of the aisle, then hesitated before turning right again. She stopped almost immediately and looked behind us, uncertain. "I know the store layout—this is supposed to be travel guides."

Instead of travel guides, the children's section was once more in front of us with the same teddy bears sitting around the same miniature table.

Fear gathered at the back of my neck as my mind recognized this familiar disoriented feeling. I stepped forward, hyperaware of any flicker of movement or hint of sound. What appeared to be a lurking, motionless figure caught my attention from the corner of my eye, and I pivoted sharply, shrinking with terror.

But nothing jumped out at me. The figure remained immobile.

One deep breath, and I realized it wasn't a person but several cloaks hanging from a spinning display rack. I approached the garments cautiously, afraid of what or who might be hidden within the folds but found only grayish-brown wool. There was no one there, only the cloaks. One of the cloak's pewter brooches bore the emblem of an open book.

I knew that emblem from "Late Fees."

"Those robes weren't here before," Kylie said in a low voice behind me.

"I know."

Another book tumbled off the shelf behind us, a heavy collectors' Christmas pop-up book that fell open, launching paper tin soldiers upward. I scrambled away from it.

"This way," Kylie hissed. She plunged down the next aisle into Sci-Fi and Fantasy. The shelves had somehow grown; they were taller now, reaching almost to the ceiling. The altered reality made my brain splinter. Was Kylie seeing this, too?

The books displayed on every end cap had fallen facedown, just like the photographs in Malice House and the house in Water's Edge. Books throughout the store continued to fall—thuds came from every section. We turned down any aisle we came to, only to find another corridor twisting into more mazelike passageways.

How many stories had I read where a girl longed to be trapped in a bookstore? *None like this.* My foot sank into a soggy portion of the carpet, and I recoiled as the frigid water soaked my shoes.

The puddle stretched around the corner and into the next aisle. The rotting grass smell was more intense here, almost gag-inducing. A shadow moved low to the ground about ten feet in front of me. A hand slowly emerged from behind the nearest shelving unit. Its fingernails dug into the carpet to give it traction. The pale, brackish skin was wrinkled from submersion and held a slight green cast. The black fingernails were two inches long.

I backtracked but then stopped when my back hit a shelf—there was nowhere to go.

Kylie hadn't seen it. She knelt beside a pile of fallen books. She picked one up and opened it, flipping pages slowly at first, then more frantically. She grabbed the next book, flipping anxiously through it, too.

"The pages are blank in every single book," she muttered in confusion. "The stories are gone."

"We have bigger problems. *Go.*" I grabbed the book out of her hands and threw it to the floor, then shoved her away from the thing crawling toward us from the puddle at the end of the aisle.

We raced the opposite way down the aisle. The bookstore had transformed into an actual maze now. Terror numbed my mind as I limped behind Kylie, afraid of what lay around every corner. Kylie accidentally collided with a spinner rack of bookmarks, and I fell into her, knocking the whole thing to the ground. I let out a shriek and she cursed as we crashed to the floor in the bookstore's central aisle, a tangle of limbs, until we finally separated and looked up to see a figure standing directly in front of us.

Ronan Young held a set of keys in hand, staring at us with an open mouth but no words.

"Ronan?" I shrieked.

Other than the two of us splayed on the floor with a shotgun, he didn't act like anything was amiss. *Like a paranormal force had overtaken the bookstore.* Behind him, Lundie Bay Books had returned to normal. The former bank-teller stalls, new release tables, and front door were exactly as they should be, without a single overturned book or soggy spot in the carpet.

My eyes latched onto the front door behind him. An exit. *Our escape.* Heart pounding, I yelled, "What the hell are you doing here?"

He scrubbed an uncertain hand over his forehead, the key ring dangling flaccidly from the other. When he spoke, his voice was high-pitched from nerves. "How did you get out of the vault? And get the gun back?"

I didn't have time for Ronan's questions. Kylie pushed to her feet and reached down a hand to help untangle me from the spinner rack. Ronan continued to stare in bafflement at our breathlessness and sweat-streaked faces.

Once on my feet, I grabbed Ronan by the upper arm and started dragging him toward the door. "We all need to get out of here. Now."

"That's why . . . that's why I came back." Digging in his heels as he tossed a look back toward the dark shop. "To unlock the vault. I don't know how you got out, but the Ink Drinkers all discussed locking you in there and decided we aren't prepared to hurt anyone else. . . ."

"Shut up," Kylie snapped.

Ronan pushed up his glasses, pressing his mouth into a flat line.

I gave Ronan a firm shove toward the front door, not caring if I hurt him. His weight pushed it open, and the three of us tumbled out, the bell jangling behind us.

Kylie and I hunched over to catch our breaths beneath the streetlights and the swollen moon. We were out. My mind registered it, but my body refused to believe, still coursing with adrenaline.

Ronan locked the door behind him, testing the handle. Through the glass, the bookstore appeared completely normal. Ronan didn't seem to have witnessed any of the terrifying events that we had.

He slid a disturbed look at the shotgun in Kylie's hands. "So how did you get that gun back? Jonathan took it with him." Then he shook his head. "You know what? Never mind. It doesn't matter. Keep it. Look, too many people have already suffered. Whatever ability you have and that your father had, Haven, we just don't want it around Lundie Bay. Catherine and Jonathan and Letitia are prepared to forget everything if both of you leave town by tomorrow. I know it's short notice, but you need to pack up and be gone."

I let out a bitter laugh. "You're a real hero, Ronan."

He took the insult bravely. "I'm sorry, Haven. You would do the same if you were in our place."

Kylie let the shotgun barrel droop threateningly toward Ronan's knees. There was a chance *he* didn't know it wasn't loaded. "You want us gone? Fine. We'll be gone. I don't want to stay in this shitty town anyway. Now, get out of here, bookworm."

Ronan started moving backward, unnerved by the shotgun and the crazed look in Kylie's eyes, until he got up the nerve to turn and hurry down the street until he disappeared around the corner.

Kylie leaned against the brick wall outside a real estate office, breathing hard. After a moment, she pressed her fingers to the bridge of her nose and asked, "So, if Ronan didn't let us out of the vault, who did?"

"One of *them*," I said in a flat voice. "I don't know why. To terrorize us. Taunt us."

She stared at the gun in her hands as if it had the answers. "If Ronan hadn't shown up and broken that distorted reality or whatever it was . . ." She trailed off. She didn't need to finish.

I leaned against the brick wall, relishing the cold solidity of the material. "I don't know what would have happened, but I agree with Ronan. Neither of us should have ever come to Lundie Bay. We were both chasing a ghost. There's nothing for us here. No legacy. No inheritance. You and me, Kylie, we're the authors of our own stories, and getting the fuck out of Lundie Bay is page one."

She snorted a laugh that threatened to turn into tears. I wrapped an arm around her back and, together with my sister, hobbled toward my car, ignoring the strange looks of a couple stepping out of a bar who stopped dead upon seeing our two makeup-streaked faces—and the shotgun.

CHAPTER TWENTY-NINE

A few hours into the long night, the Harbinger and the Witch of Went stepped through the tangled weeds of the geometric forest at the Hellhound's heels.

"Can she truly track any scent?" the witch asked.

He grunted in the affirmative.

"And she is leading us to this Uncle Arnold you spoke of?"

He slowly shook his head "No. I would only seek out Uncle Arnold if I had no choice. He frightens me more than any creature here, even more than you." A teasing smile touched his mouth as he returned to following in the Hellhound's path. "She's leading us to the library."

—From "Beasts of Sun" in
Bedtime Stories for Monsters

●

AS SOON AS the front door of Malice House slammed closed behind us, Kylie set the shotgun on the library coffee table and began pulling my father's awards off the bar cart. The Pulitzer. The Booker. The awards filled the basket of her arms as she searched for a container to put them in.

"Boxes," she muttered. "We need boxes."

I let my canvas bag slump to the floor by the entry table. "What are you doing?"

"Packing, obviously! Taking anything valuable that we can sell online to finance a future as far away from this place as possible."

There was an unhinged gleam in her eyes. After all she'd been through in the past few days, I was surprised she was even standing.

I eased the Pulitzer out of her arms and set it back on the bar cart. "Listen. Ronan Young isn't going to show up at the break of dawn with a pitchfork and chase us out of town. The Ink Drinkers said they wanted us gone by tomorrow, and we'll do that. But take a few deep breaths. Let's be strategic about what we can take and where we're going to go."

Kylie bit nervously on her lip, still looking shaken. But she pulled in a slow inhale and after releasing it with even slower speed, said in a steadier voice, "I'm less worried about the Ink Drinkers than I am about whatever was after us in the bookstore. The way the aisles twisted like a labyrinth felt like the time I got turned around right before the Witch of Went abducted me." She clutched the Booker award harder, eyes widening. "And I don't think the witch was the only thing in the bookstore."

I remembered the pale, water-wrinkled hand stretching around the corner of a shelving unit. The skin on my ankles prickled into gooseflesh, still damp from the puddles that had soaked the bookstore carpet.

"I know," I said as exhaustion caught up with me, and I sank onto the sofa arm. "I saw other creatures, too. Characters from the manuscript I illustrated before I knew about the curse. Back when I thought I was just making pretty pictures to sell." I gestured weakly with my hand, letting it fall into my lap. "All those books falling down? And how the words were erased from them? That was the Robber Saints' doing." My ear suddenly started twitching as I thought back to their tale.

I continued, "It's what they do—steal stories off the pages of books, even out of writers' minds before they're written. Erase literary legacies. Then they lock the stories away in their library where no one can ever get to them. Those were their cloaks in the children's section."

Kylie seemed to turn a shade paler. I grabbed her wrist and tugged her down to sit next to me on the library sofa. "Listen, I'll move the security cameras. I'll aim one toward the woods and one toward the driveway. That way, we'll be warned by my computer's alerts if anything approaches the house while we're packing. My rental car will only fit a few boxes, so we can't take much. And you'll probably want to go to your apartment, too, and get anything you need."

"Bold of you to assume I have anything worth taking," she muttered, but I knew she'd have clothing and items that couldn't be replaced.

I squeezed her angular knee through her jeans. "Drink a glass of water, okay? I'm going to the garage to get some post office cartons that we can use for packing."

Her eyes stretched wide enough to reveal white ringing her light-brown irises. "You're going back outside?"

"I'll be right back." I marveled at my own bravado, though it was always easier to feign strength in front of an audience. I rested an unexperienced hand on the shotgun barrel, hoping it wasn't obvious how much it trembled. "Can you reload that?"

She fell into a calmer breathing rhythm now that she had a task. "Yeah, where'd we put the rest of the shells?"

I told her where she could find them, then went around the house to gather the security cameras in the entry hallway and the upstairs bedroom. As soon as I stepped onto the front porch and was exposed to bare night again, fear caught up to me. All I could think about were the grisly parts in that damn manuscript. It didn't matter that I'd burned it—I could recall its lines with almost preternatural accuracy. The characters had worked their way under my skin. I felt infected, a host to monstrous parasites that depended on me for their very lives.

Shuddering, I tried to focus on the task at hand. The security camera in the porch eave came down easily, and I reset it so that it now aimed down the length of the driveway. I placed the second camera to point at the garage, and the third angled toward the woods beyond the fence. Then, gathering my courage, I climbed down from the porch into night-dewed grass and tromped toward the garage, arms hugged tightly across my chest.

My limbs quivered as I ducked into the open garage door. I'd barely touched the mountains of fan mail since I'd first brought them home from the post office. Now, I dumped carton after carton onto the oil-stained concrete floor, feeling strangely satisfied. My father had never responded to them in life, and he certainly wasn't going to in death.

Once I had several empty cartons, I started back toward the house but paused as a light in the distance snagged my attention. The pines swayed behind me in their rustling dance, casting strange shadows, emitting the eerie sounds of wind and friction.

Rafe's house loomed over the privacy fence with its giant sequoia beams. His back porch light was on, but all the interior lights were off. In these early hours of the morning, almost all Lundie Bay must be asleep now except for a few early-bird fishermen and night-shift workers. But Rafe and I, we were three o'clock people. Denizens of the witching hour.

I'd have to leave without saying goodbye. I hadn't known him very long—logically, I knew that I'd get over him, though at the moment, my heart and body didn't quite agree. But leaving without saying goodbye meant I could ignore all the red flags that had waved prominently before my eyes over the past weeks, and remember only his woodsmoke smell, his soft lips, his velvet eyes; none of the more troubling details.

I kept staring into the light with almost hypnotic fixation. Ghosting Rafe was one thing, but I didn't see how I could leave Lundie Bay without ever learning what secrets my father kept in that basement beneath the shed.

The notion haunted me as I went back inside, making sure to lock the door behind me. Kylie was in the library, teasing the most valuable books off the shelves and adding them to a growing stack on the sofa.

I dropped the postal bins on the floor and rested my hands on my hips. "There's one more thing I have to do before we leave."

The ridge of her backbone straightened. "What now?"

"Hang on." I went to the kitchen and returned with the basement key from the junk drawer.

Understanding settled into her face. "You want to see inside the basement."

I was worried she might try to warn me away from leaving the safety of the house, but Amory had been her father, too. She'd been searching for answers almost as long as I had. Instead of talking me out of it, she simply picked up the shotgun with a tight sigh, digging deep for an extra ounce of energy, and said, "Well, you can't go by yourself."

I felt an unexpected grin pull my face despite the danger we faced; I was getting an inkling of what it was like to have a sibling who would conspire in perilous schemes, and I liked it.

"Did you reload?" I asked.

"Yup."

We took a few minutes to pull on warmer clothes before venturing outside, taking only the shotgun and the basement key with us. The night had grown bitter cold. Gravel crunched beneath our shoes as we walked the driveway's length. I punched in the code to open the gate and watched as the primary source of the house's security rolled back, exposing us to all the night's dangers.

Shivering, I led Kylie through the gate, down to Cliffside Drive, and back up Rafe's driveway to his patio. The fire pit remained untouched since I'd raked my fingers through it, their tracks still there forming moats amid the coals. The moon gleamed off a portion of an exposed silver dog tag. I averted my gaze quickly as my heartbeat galloped.

"That's it," I whispered to Kylie as I motioned to the shed. "We need to do this without Rafe's knowledge."

Kylie studied the dark windows of his house for any sign of movement. "I'll keep lookout, on the far side of the shed, in case he's awake and looks out a window. Don't take too long down there, okay? This place gives me the creeps almost as much as *your* house."

"How will you warn me if someone's coming?" I asked. "Should we have a codeword?"

"How about I just text 'get the fuck out and run'?"

"That works."

The key slipped into the lock easier than I would have expected for such an old structure, but then again, my father had only been gone six months. Maybe he'd come here often before he'd died, during the months-long stretches when Rafe was out of town.

Kylie suddenly grabbed my arm. "If you find anything down there, bring it back, okay? I want to see it. He was my father, too."

I ducked my chin in understanding. "I know, Kylie. I will. I promise."

I eased the shed door open, fearful of rusty hinges. The interior smelled of damp stone and freshly churned dirt, layered with an undertone of rotting wood. I flipped open my phone to use the screen light. I located a gas lantern and a matchbox as well as a canister of gas among the dusty equipment, then switched off my phone and filled the lantern's tank, operating by moonlight alone.

The entire structure was barely the size of a single-car garage. I doubted whether Rafe had even ever set foot in here—his designer clothes didn't scream "fertilizer." Most of what was there looked like it dated from the 1970s or 1980s back when the property belonged to old Alice Halliday, with perhaps a few of my father's things from the years when he'd bothered to hire a landscaper. A sun-faded rug on the floor had a faint chicken pattern. I toed the rug to the side, releasing a cloud of dust, which revealed uneven boards underneath.

Bingo. Trapdoor.

A heavy iron ring lifted the boards. Beyond was a wooden staircase so steep it could almost be called a ladder. It was pitch-black in the basement, not a single stray pinprick of light. With the unlit lantern and match in hand, I started down the stairs. They were thick with cobwebs, the detritus of beetle husks, and desiccated mud clods from someone's boots. Darkness swallowed my feet and then legs and still, I descended. Once I was partway down the ladder, I closed the trapdoor overhead. I didn't want a glimmer of light to escape and give away my presence.

The darkness was entire.

There was no telling how deep the stairs went, how vast the basement was. It was only me and the darkness, the intense musty smell of soil, the creak of my boots on the step.

The match sputtered. I lit the gas lantern, turning up the flame as bright as it would go.

I was nearly at the bottom of the stairs. There were only two more steps before giving way to the packed dirt floor of the basement. The geology in this part of the region was mostly limestone bedrock; there was barely enough soil to dig out a basement, so the ceiling was scarcely taller than me, forcing me to stoop to avoid the cobwebs padding the joists. The space was roughly the same size as the shed atop it, maybe ten by ten. A one-hundred-year-old foundation of limestone boulders held the earth at bay.

Next to the stairs was a small desk, and beside that stood shelves fabricated out of cinder blocks and wooden boards. A creaky three-legged chair was pushed tidily up to the desk and held a mangy thing that I first thought was the desiccated carcass of an animal, but, upon closer inspection, was one of my father's old cardigans. On the desk sat a white china mug from the set in Malice House's kitchen.

The most striking thing, though, was that almost every surface was covered in papers.

Individual pages had been fastened to the foundation with glue; many of them had lost their hold, and dozens of papers now littered the ground, coated with dust and debris. I walked in a slow circle around the perimeter, holding up the lantern to the pages. Almost all contained a drawing. They had been done in either ink pen or pencil, most simple contour drawings of common subjects: faces, fruit, furniture, though some attempted more advanced subjects. During my program at Rhode Island School of Design, we had learned all the foundational artistic techniques: line theory, shading, contour drawing, negative space. These illustrations displayed none of that academic training, though the artist who'd drawn them hadn't been without talent. One course in my program had been Folk, Outsider, and Self-Taught Art, and this bore all the hallmarks of someone who'd diligently honed a style outside of artistic convention.

I pulled out the wobbly three-legged chair and clutched my father's moth-eaten cardigan in my lap as I sat, marveling and soaking up a lifetime of his artwork in the flickering lamplight. I felt certain my father had never shown this artwork to a living soul. Why else would he have made a studio down here in an ancient hole? The basement had a sense of being located out of time; part of me felt like I could remain here for days and reemerge to find no time had passed at all, or else years had, like a night spent beneath a faerie hill. My fingers itched to hold a pen myself. To connect with my father in this wordless way, the language of shapes and lines.

I gathered a few of the better drawings and stacked them up to show Kylie. I glanced at my phone to make sure she hadn't texted. Though the basement might feel timeless, time *was* moving forward aboveground for my sister, and I needed to hurry.

I quickly scanned the books on the makeshift shelf, most of which dealt with occult practices and symbology. *Magick* by Aleister Crowley. *Three Books of Occult Philosophy* by Henry Cornelius Agrippa. A battered copy of *Macbeth*. A big old soapbox tin, rusted at the corners, sat next to the books. I pried open the lid and stared down at a miscellany of papers, letters, and a five-by-seven journal. Dread and a tiny but persistent prickle of curiosity needled my skull.

I picked up the journal. It was of the same provenance as the ones I remembered my father writing in when I'd been a little girl. He ordered them from a convent in Italy whose nuns used three-hundred-year-old bookbinding techniques, and I was sure each one cost a small fortune. I had assumed all his journals were now housed in Clifford Library along with his personal book collection, but as soon as I skimmed over the first few entries, I realized these were very different in tone from the carefully curated biography he had documented in his official journals.

Here, entries were dashed out with little or no organization. Few included dates. Instead of tidy rows of writing, these pages were filled with sketches, lists of ideas, or book titles he wanted to research. My father's *actual* thoughts. He'd written here for his eyes only, not future biographers or adoring fans. As much as it felt like an invasion of privacy, Amory Marbury's mortal shell was gone. There was no *him* anymore to be offended. There was only my own need to know.

Time wasn't infinite; Kylie was outside, and I needed to return to her. I could read the journal in full back at my house.

And yet I found myself opening to the first page . . .

CHAPTER THIRTY

I feel I am halfway to understanding. Some truths are evident . . .

The curse is hereditary and on the Acosta side. Of that, I'm certain. Martim and Della say it all happens at dawn, always underground—the emergence; that's what they call it. The manifestations surface from a cave or basement or simply rise out of the bare soil. I have no reason to doubt them other than the fact that they are liars through and through . . . ha! Oh, I'm sure they have answers, but I don't trust them to tell me the truth.

. . . he was a drunk, but he thought himself so dignified. It ate at him that his relatives were artists and vintners. "No son of mine," he'd say to me. "No son of mine." It took me years to draw again. By then I knew better than to leave my sketchbooks anywhere he might see them. I wonder to this day if the poor hearing in my left ear is from the blow. Seven years old and scrawny as a hen. "No son of mine will draw comics." Well, fate laughs at his ghost. His granddaughter is going to art school. She wants to be a picture book illustrator! Ah, but it frightens me. What if she can . . . But I have no indication of that. None whatsoever.

Maybe fate laughs at me. If I encourage her art, I risk opening the door to the Acosta curse. So do I do what my father did to me?

I'm developing a new theory after the soil hypothesis went nowhere. The samples I gathered came back from the lab with no foreign fungus found, no anomalies. Extremely disappointing. After reading the entry in La Candileja *about fungal infections, I'd been so hopeful that microbes would prove capable of triggering the state of ecstatic creation and, thus, terminating the state as well. I need to stop looking for a miracle cure. The answer will be, like everything else, discovered through toil and patience.*

A writer is compelled to shape stories. An artist compelled to build images. A philosopher compelled to think. It happens in our subconscious. The curse knows this. We cannot avoid it. But maybe we can redirect the impulses with training. Averted writing—we write, yes, but not what the curse wants us to write. Feed the beast a few bites here and there and it won't demand a feast.

After reading a random sampling of entries, I sat in shock. Dad had spoken very little to me about his parents, both of whom had died before I could know them. He'd loathed his father, a history professor with a drinking problem, though I'd never heard a word about my father being forbidden from artistic pursuits. He'd always acted strange when I'd mentioned my artwork—turning gruff and changing the topic—and I'd assumed I was a disappointment to him, but now I wondered if the reality was more complicated.

Maybe Rafe was telling the truth.

The idea struck me hard and made me reconsider Rafe's trustworthiness. He had told me about the conversation that he'd had with my father, where Dad confessed to greatly admiring my art. Maybe my dad really had seen my talent—only feared encouraging me.

The other entries would take time to examine thoroughly and understand exactly what he meant. I assumed the bit about soil had to do with the boxes of dirt in the attic, since it seemed my father had at one point hypothesized that psychoactive fungus played into the curse. It was eerily similar to the concept in Rob's *Potergeistia* documentary, that fungus was responsible for poltergeists. One theory pointed toward a mind-altered state and the other toward paranormal activity, but the mere coincidental similarity of "answers found in dirt" left me uneasy, like I was walking on a path my father had already blazed and would be as unlikely to ever reach the end.

My phone lit up. It was a low battery alert, not a text from Kylie, but I noticed the time while the screen was on. Nearly 3:30 a.m. I had to get back.

I flipped to the last entry in the journal.

Diagnosis today. Alzheimer's. After so many tests and questions, it's a relief to have an answer. I'm going to keep it from that old bitch Dahlia as long as I can, though she and the Ink Drinkers are such nosy gossips. I'm sure they've been going through the house when I'm not there. Trying to steal from me. They're the reason I sit in a dank hole, hiding my truth from prying eyes.

Christ, the cold down here . . .

It was hard to read about the paranoia that later consumed him. My own fingers were growing cold and stiff. Kylie was waiting for me aboveground where very real dangers lurked, but now that I had a taste of answers, I was hooked. There were too many drawings and documents to take it all back to the house with me, and I didn't dare leave behind the most revealing ones.

Just a few more, I told myself. *Then I'll go.*

I grabbed one of the yellowing envelopes. It was addressed to Amory Marbury at our old Maine address. The postmark was faded, but I could make out *1992*. The year of my birth and my mother's suicide. The return address was for a location in Portugal.

Amory,

Cousin, I owe you an apology for how we left things. If you had stayed to let me explain, I would have told you that this isn't the first time such things have happened in our family. We have ways of dealing with these occurrences. You really should have stayed. You don't need to carry this alone. Indeed, Della thinks it may be dangerous to do so. There is no shame in what you have achieved.

Your final words to us were speaking of a curse, but we have never seen it that way. To us it is a blessing. I urge you to open your mind and embrace the possibilities.

Tell me, how will you explain this—explain her—to your American friends?

Martim

I'd heard stories from Aunt Rose about travels my father had taken to visit relatives in Lisbon in his younger years, shortly before I'd been born. He'd never told me about the trip. I'd assumed it was filled with embarrassing misadventures that didn't fit his carefully cultivated literary persona, or else youthful scandals that a father wouldn't share with his daughter. So, what exactly had happened in Portugal with these mysterious cousins, Martim and Della? The letter only bred new questions, and I found myself almost uncontrollably stuffing the letter back in the soapbox and rifling through the rest before stopping abruptly. At the bottom of the tin sat a sealed manila envelope.

It was marked *Sanctuary: A Short Story. 2007.*

I stared at the envelope as tingles scaled along my exposed skin. When I'd been a sophomore in high school, I'd helped my father run a weekend writing course for the local college in Maine. It was on creative writing as a tool for therapy and personal growth. The students were supposed to turn their traumas into a fictitious narrative to see their experience from a new perspective. My father had joked that he would write about every single father's worst trauma—his teenage daughter—and that he'd title his narrative "Sanctuary," an obvious play on my name.

It had only been a joke. Just an unoriginal and, frankly, sexist joke about hormonal teenagers.

But here was the story. He had *actually* written it.

The world shrank to that cold basement and the envelope. I forgot about Kylie. Time lost its meaning as I took out the unfinished draft of a handwritten short story, most of it crossed out and much of it rewritten in the margins, whole sections skipped, and names so negligibly changed that it was obvious that the characters were based on him and his cousins, Della and Martim.

With dread, I began to read, skimming the lines hastily.

SANCTUARY

When the traveler stepped off the plane in Évora, the cousins were waiting for him. There were two of them: Dores, her lean elegance marred by a pair of cheap oversized red sunglasses, and Madu, in a straw fedora and two weeks' beard. There was no sign of the numerous children both of them claimed to have.

As soon as the traveler collected his bag, Madu draped a necklace of slender olive leaves around his neck.

"Is this a Portuguese custom?" the traveler asked. "Like getting lei'ed in Hawaii?"

Dores took a long drag of her cigarette and didn't answer.

Madu grinned coldly. "No, cousin, it's an Acosta family one."

. . . one of the older children disappeared into the warehouse and returned with a black-and-white photograph of his grandmother, and, yes, the traveler was certain. These people were his. He was theirs.

"When is the funeral?" he asked.

The casket was made of marbled olive wood, nut brown and caramel, that the traveler felt must be of tremendous value, which made it all the more unnerving to see his grandmother's body, clean but unpreserved, with none of the attention to makeup that one would find from an American undertaker. She had been dead seven days, and the late summer heat was not kind.

. . . once night had come, Dores and Madu walked the traveler to the far edge of the olive grove where the woods began. They reached the ruins of the original

olive mill, now a gaping doorless entry built into the hills. Dores lit a torch with her cigarette lighter, and they escorted him through the threshold.

Grave-faced, Madu plucked out a pencil that had been stabbed into the dirt wall and held it out to the traveler. "It is time to add your entry to the Acosta family book. Draw."

Very well, the traveler would play along. He asked, "What should I draw?"

"Anything you wish. A cat. A spider. An earthworm."

The traveler had sketched in the privacy of childhood bedrooms and college dorms, drawing his own hand or copying photographs out of magazines until he'd convinced himself he had talent. His father, however, had pushed the writing career. If he couldn't be convinced to attend law school, he could at least contribute to the literary canon.

. . . began to sketch the most challenging thing for any artist to master: a baby. The telescoping proportions of chubby arms and legs, the bulbous head, smooth skin that made lifelike shading impossible.

"Well done, cousin," Madu said quietly. Dores said nothing, but her cigarette did the talking.

Time to go home. Time to get out of here. How much had he had to drink? The traveler lurched for the ladder, but a sharp sound from deep in the cellar stopped him.

A baby's cry.

Somehow, he'd known it, hadn't he? Known what he was doing when he'd taken that pencil. He'd felt the fizz of magic like carbonation in his blood.

It was a girl child with a dense patch of hair at the crown of her skull and peculiar ears. The left one folded at the upper rim, but the right one was smooth. Identical to the drawing . . .

"You said it takes both words and art," the traveler protested, near the edge of panic, *"but I wrote nothing."*

Madu said steadily, "But cousin, you did."

One final loose page peeked up from behind the handwritten story. I knew what it would be as soon as I saw the yellowed age of the paper, the curve of my father's contour pencil line in the same style as the drawings pasted around the basement.

Inch by inch, I pulled out a sketch of a baby with a thick patch of hair and peculiar ears.

In the corner: *Amory's baby, 1992.*

Fate, apparently, had a way of being literal.

Two words were enough to make a story.

They were enough to make a soul.

Certainly, my father meant the notation as shorthand for his *drawing* of a baby, but that wasn't what he had written. That simple semantic twist meant that when my father left the cave in Évora, it was with his biological child in his arms.

He'd taken her home—

Taken *me* home—

And raised me as his daughter, instead of what I truly was: a mistake pulled off a page, born of a curse.

A monster.

CHAPTER THIRTY-ONE

And yet, despite my better judgment, I too wish for something more.
Not for me—it's too late for an old man's castles in the sky—but for
the one who comes after me. Like the characters in these pages, I
hope for a world where confusion finds purpose; where hard women
triumph; where seekers find, at the end of a too-long night, the answer
to the most malignant question. An answer I never found. Why?
Christ, why?

—From the Introduction to
Bedtime Stories for Monsters

A NOVELIST'S PROFESSION was one of lucrative lies. My
father traded in fictional worlds. Yet I held no doubt that every word
of "Sanctuary" was real. He'd changed a few details, but it was closer
to a confession than a work of fiction.

I had been his trauma. At least, my genesis had.

I sat back in the rickety chair, staring at the ancient limestone boulders in front of me. My mind felt oddly blank as I took in the strum of a
cricket somewhere, the rustle of paper under my feet. Then, as though
waking from the longest sleep of my life, I sucked in a deep breath.

I dragged my jagged nails along my scalp until it was painful.

The unspeakable truth written in the short story was almost too excruciating to face. I scrubbed my hands over my forehead, telling myself to focus on the facts, to force the senseless to make sense.

For one: What did this mean about the woman I'd been told was my mother? Naturally, it hadn't occurred to me that my mother *might never have existed*. She was yet another fiction.

I found myself digging through the tin for more clues until I located a rubber-band-bound set of photographs that had been taken at my parents' wedding. One was a copy of the same photograph framed in Malice House, but I had never seen the others, which were all various poses of my parents in a garden back in Maine. I flipped through the photographs as fresh questions materialized. Was she a friend of his? An actress he'd hired?

The last photograph was a closeup of the woman's hand clasped in my father's, adorned with a silver Celtic knot ring. My gaze dragged from the photograph to my own ring finger. It was the same ring I wore, which I'd found amid the trinkets in one of my father's mugs of pens and loose change.

A strange sound clawed out of my throat. I leaned forward, clasping my hands. I couldn't break down here, now. I breathed into the bowl of my hands, then pressed my fingers into my eyelids until I saw stars.

A tremor raked my body from shoulders to fingertips.

Any other person might have felt horror at the knowledge that they were a figment of a stranger's imagination. Yet in my mind's cavern, I felt a twisted sense of relief. All my life, I'd felt disconnected from other people: classmates at grade school, roommates at RISD, friends in New York. Even from Baker; maybe mostly from Baker.

A tear blazed a trail down the hill of my cheek. I wiped it away with a shaking hand. The basement had grown frigid. My toes were numb.

I am one of them.

Pulled from a page.

A baby crying in a cave.

Yet my father—and I still thought of him that way—hadn't run from the crying thing. He had taken me back to Maine, raised me as his daughter, even made up a dead mother so that no one would question my creation. Once, in kindergarten, I'd brought home a drawing of a dragon that he'd put on the refrigerator for one solitary day before banishing it to what I assumed was the garbage can—*but now I understood.*

He was afraid I had the curse, too. Despite the horror of all of it, I was left with an unexpected but staggering sense of tenderness toward the man. Amory Marbury had never been a doting father, but neither had he been neglectful. He'd never made me feel less than human. Never once looked at me with fear in his eyes. He had accepted and raised me. Loved me in his way.

I started sobbing, mourning a man six months' dead more than I had at his funeral. How easy it would have been for him to have left me with dubious relatives. To have run from the truth of what he'd done. *But he hadn't.* It was perhaps the greatest thing that Amory Marbury had ever achieved. Forget the awards, the MacArthur genius grant, his literary reputation. *This* is what mattered. That deep in some forgotten cave in Portugal, my father had brought forth an aberration and had grown to love it.

My hands shook as I stuffed whatever papers I could in the soap tin and stacked the journal and letters on top. I folded a few of the better drawings and shoved them quickly in my jacket pocket. The rest would have to remain entombed down here forever, or until some future property owner decided to install a state-of-the-art wine cellar. I switched off the gas lantern and climbed the stairs in the dark, using my shoulder to hoist open the trapdoor.

Kylie would be grateful to have answers about our father, even though so much of him remained a mystery and probably always would. Over the next days and weeks, she and I could comb through these papers and pull from them whatever clues we could to shine a light on our family history. Try to close Pandora's box. But first, we had to leave Lundie Bay. Go to Los Angeles as she'd always wanted, or to some dirt-cheap town in Appalachia where sales from my father's memorabilia could cover rent. Someday, when I was ready, I would share "Sanctuary" with her. But, Jesus, not today. I was terrified to even face those dark truths myself.

Upstairs, the shed was undisturbed except for my footprints in the dust. Clutching the documents to my chest, I left the lantern and eased open the door.

"Kylie?" I called in a loud whisper. "I took as much as I could carry."

The silence that answered cut through my chest like a blade. I hissed her name louder, still to no response. When I turned the corner to the place she'd agreed to wait, I found someone waiting for me, but it wasn't her.

In the darkness, his buzzed hair and lean waist were a contour line drawing against the trees behind him. He ran a hand over his scalp as he spoke calmly, "Haven."

That knife of fear thrust deeper. "Rafe."

Silent alarms trilled in my ears. I hugged the journal and soapbox like a hammered-tin shield, though neither item would save me now. I'd left my bag at the house and felt naked without it.

"Where's Kylie?" I asked slowly.

Rafe emerged from the darkness with a predator's slink, only to draw to a stop at the exact meeting point of shadow and light. "She went back to your house. Said she had to pack."

He's lying. Kylie would never have left without telling me. A quick glance at my house did reveal several more lights had been switched on. So, *someone* was there, but I didn't trust that it was Kylie, or at the least, that she was there alone and of her own free will.

I took a step backward at the same time that Rafe dredged clinking objects from his jeans pocket and held them up to the moonlight: a handful of burnished dog tags.

"You found these in the fire pit, didn't you? That's why you never came back that night. I saw that someone had been sifting through the ashes and finally put it together."

My throat went bone dry, but I refused to let Rafe Kahn intimidate me. I'd ventured to hell and back down in that basement and had come out someone else. Some*thing* else. Not even human. My father had loved me, monster though I was, and a father's love carried weight even beyond the grave.

"Did you kill the dogs those collars belonged to?" I demanded, chin lifted.

He'd been waiting for me to ask him. "No."

"Then who did?"

The light from his deck caught his eyes and made them gleam like a nocturnal animal. "Rafe Kahn did."

My heart pounded for the space of a few breaths while my mind tumbled through questions and answers, debating if I should run, worried that Kylie could be dead in the woods.

"What do you mean?" I asked carefully. "*You're* Rafe Kahn."

He tossed the dog tags in the fire pit and stalked forward again. A lunge, and Rafe grabbed my wrist. My father's things fell out of my grasp and crashed to the ground as I attempted to pull away.

"I know what you read down there," he said evenly. His voice dropped further as he dragged me closer by the wrist. "I've read it all, too. Every journal entry. Every letter. I've seen all the drawings. I know the ending of 'Sanctuary.' You have *quite* a story, Haven."

His dark eyes searched mine. "I have one, too."

He forced my hand under his shirt, splaying my palm against his bare skin. I tried jerking away, but he pressed my hand harder against the plane of his abdomen, where I felt unnaturally puckered skin, and finally put it together—a scar.

His lips hovered an inch from my ear. "Now do you know?"

I tried again to pull away, but he held me with remarkable strength.

The night had turned bitter cold. The wind howled at my ears and tossed my hair around my face, blinding me and stroking my skin in equal parts.

"Let me go!" I shouted.

To my surprise, he did, but fire sprang into his eyes.

I stumbled backward, not expecting the sudden freedom, and tripped on the journal. I crashed to the ground, hip smacking the patio flagstones with a bolt of pain. Rafe towered over me. A strange sensation that I was watching one of Rob's films overcame me; I was shouting at the protagonist—at myself—to get up. Run. *TSTL!*

But I had to know.

Breathing hard, I asked, "If you aren't Rafe Kahn, where is he?"

His back was to the porch light now, obscuring his face. "Dead. But don't mourn him. He was a psychopath. When I found him, he was digging a pit over there in the forest behind the cypresses for a pair of dogs he'd killed and dismembered. There are an alarming number of burial sites in the woods back there, and I don't think they were all made for dogs. In my experience, a person who can dismember a dog can easily kill a person. And probably has." He cracked his knuckles, then moved his shoulder in a grim twitch. "Anyway, it worked out. I buried him in the grave he'd dug for the dogs."

The first night I'd come to Lundie Bay, I'd seen a man burning something in the neighbor's fire pit at three in the morning. That hadn't been the person in front of me, I realized. It had been the *real* Rafe Kahn, my father's actual neighbor. The man standing over me had crashed into my life a few days later—or I'd crashed into his, literally—and because I'd had no idea what the real Rafe Kahn looked like, I had no reason to doubt that he was who he said he was.

"I needed his house, Haven," he explained. "I needed to be close."

My palm still tingled from the warm press of contact when I'd touched his torso. Only one person in *Bedtime Stories for Monsters* had a scar on that place on his abdomen, where he had pulled out his own spleen. My eyes scoured every inch of Rafe, searching for any indication that what was happening wasn't truly happening. My father hadn't provided much of a description of the Harbinger other than a silver-haired man dressed in black. Most of the Harbinger's appearance in my illustration had come from my own mind while I'd been drunk and in that strange trancelike state. I'd transformed my father's meager description into a lean, darkly handsome man who was the opposite of my ex-husband. I'd captured the Harbinger's mysterious edge by having his long hair curtain his face, obscuring his facial features, which meant that there was no way I could have recognized him on that foggy side of the road weeks ago, standing by his mailbox. . . .

"You cut your hair. You dyed it so I wouldn't recognize you."

"Can you blame me?" His voice gave an unexpected crack. "I was written to be a liar."

Had he staged the car accident? Shown up with popcorn and the movie as part of a plan? He'd been trying to get close to me, to get me alone. No wonder he hadn't been afraid of Pinchy—Pinchy was his goddamn pet!

A hot wave of terror burned through me.

I had done this. I'd drawn the man of my dreams—there was no world in which I wouldn't have fallen for him. I wanted the Harbinger to be a mystery, to be the kind of man to keep me on my toes, and that's exactly what I had gotten.

Out of the corner of my eye, I scanned the length of the driveway. *Run, you idiot.*

Watching me with those mercurial eyes, Rafe continued, "A few weeks ago, I woke up with dirt in my mouth. I panicked when I realized I was underground. I managed to dig my way out and found myself in a forest. Imagine my shock when I hiked to the tree line and saw an entirely different town than the one I'd left. And then discovering it was actually a different *world*?" Pinching the bridge of his nose, he drew in a long breath and let it out all at once. The trickster edge returned to his gaze. "What can I say? I catch on fast. It didn't take long to figure out how things work here."

"Did you kill Kylie?"

A moment of confusion crossed his face. "No. She's back at your house like I said. I just asked Uncle Arnold to *suggest* that she return and start packing. You've read his tale. Uncle Arnold's voice is extremely *persuasive*." He practically bit off that last word, and the unspoken thrum of danger made me shudder.

Instinct pulled my gaze to the woods, searching for any flicker of movement. "Uncle Arnold is here?"

"You drew him, didn't you?" Rafe's smirk twisted his face but didn't reach his eyes.

He was hiding something.

In the manuscript, the Harbinger's and Uncle Arnold's paths never crossed. The Harbinger's quest to find the Salem Dreamer led him to everything from trading his spleen to the Witch of Went to letting the Decaylings drag him to the bottom of Fathom Lake, but something about Uncle Arnold was so terrifying that the Harbinger intentionally avoided him. So, why would Rafe be asking him for favors now?

Goose bumps bloomed like a rash over my arms as I wondered who was lingering just out of sight in the woods, watching, ready to step in at the Harbinger's signal. It suddenly occurred to me that Rafe, a liar, might not have killed Pinchy at all.

I tilted my face up at him sharply. "Are you going to kill me?"

"*Kill* you?" He looked genuinely puzzled. "What do you think I've been doing all this time if not protecting you?"

"Protecting?" I almost laughed, but no humor showed on his face, and the sound died in my throat. I swallowed it down. "*You* unlocked the bank vault, didn't you?"

"And returned your gun to you. And saved you from Pinchy. And forbade the Witch of Went from cutting you apart. Darling, I even avenged your father. How's that for protection?"

It took me a minute to connect the dots. "You mean *you* killed Dahlia?"

He cut a dismissive hand in the air. "Pinchy did the actual

dispatching, but it was at my request. I was fond of the old man. Your father, my creator. We spent many years aware of each other despite having our feet in different worlds. It was the least I could do."

I almost laughed with the horror of it all, but nothing was funny, absolutely nothing.

He shook a slow finger at me. "You have a way of attracting danger, Haven. It's exhausting to keep an eye on you. Always running off to cavort with the police or your father's literary salon members— as if *they* aren't the ones you should be worried about."

My eyes flickered to the driveway again. My hip ached. My ankle was still weak. Rafe was in peak physical shape thanks to the perfect muscle tone muscles my pencil had given him. I wouldn't make it five feet before he overtook me. And besides, no way was I leaving all my father's documents. All those answers, so hard-won. I'd earned them through torment and tragedy, and Kylie deserved them, too.

So how could I trick a trickster?

There had to be something Rafe cared about. He already had the freedom to kill wantonly, so I doubted anything I could offer would sway him. Nonetheless, my eyes fell on the fire pit where I had burned the illustrations, and I realized that as far as he knew, I *did* possess one thing he valued.

I pushed to my feet shakily and shoved a hand in my jacket pocket, taking out one of my father's drawings. It was folded in half, somewhat crumpled. The paper was thin enough to clearly see that it was an illustration.

I held the paper over my head, backtracking from Rafe. "You know what this is?"

He took stock of me, running a hand over his chin, not answering.

"It's *you*," I hissed. "It's your illustration. The only one of you that I didn't rip up and throw away. *This* is what brought you into this world, and if you don't leave me alone, it'll take you out of this world, too." My hand shook with false bravado. The night I'd burned the illustrations, Rafe had been asleep, so he didn't know that the illustrations were nothing but ash in that very same fire pit we stood beside. He certainly didn't know that burning the illustrations hadn't destroyed the monsters at all.

His eyes narrowed.

I grabbed the edge of the paper, prepared to tear it in two. "So back the fuck off."

His steadfast face was impossible to read—after all, I'd drawn it that way, tantalized by his enigmatic nature. Now I cursed myself for not making him as easy to read as a book.

His hand continued to calmly glide over his chin as his eyes bored through me.

"You think I won't rip it up?" I pressed. "Why, because we made out a few times? I don't care about that. About *you*." My heart fisted, calling me a liar.

"So then do it," he challenged me quietly.

My heart locked for a second. He'd called my bluff. If I really did have the ability to destroy him by simply shredding a piece of paper, why wouldn't I?

Lifting my chin, I showed no emotion as I began to tear the paper with painfully slow speed, calling his bluff on my bluff. RISD had given me an education, but Rob's horror movies had been a masterclass in survival: The heroine only ever won when she stood up to the villain.

Rafe's hand fell away from his chin as his mouth pinched. *"Stop."*

My hands stilled. A surge of triumph rose in me. Then, vindictive, I gave the paper an extra inch-long tear just to torture him. He bolted toward me, hand outstretched to swipe at the paper, but I shoved it into my pocket as I backstepped.

"Truce, okay?" I said. "Your illustration remains intact for another day. But I'm serious, if you fuck with me, I'll take a match to it."

He held up his hands in mocking surrender as his lips curled in a smirk. "Clever, Haven."

Keeping an eye on him, I stooped to gather my fallen items,

clutching them with one arm against my chest. Once I had everything settled, and my thighs bunched, ready to sprint down the driveway, he shot out a hand and grabbed my bicep.

I thrust my free hand in my pocket to threaten him with the illustration again, but he shook his head and murmured in a purr, "Don't bother."

I expected him to fight me, but he didn't glance at my pocket. Instead, he tilted his head to anchor his gaze to mine. His voice entered my head like a wriggling worm. "I know you already burned the illustrations. I watched you do it from the bedroom window."

Blood rushed in my ears. "Then why did you—"

"I like to watch you scheme." He smiled with dark satisfaction. "You aren't half bad at it. Though to get through all of this, you're going to have to get *really* good."

Unexpectedly, he released my arm. Hands raised in real surrender this time, he took a few slow retreating steps.

"Go," he whispered.

I didn't move, my instincts urging me not to trust him.

He tipped his chin in the direction of my house and snapped, "Go on. Learn the hard way. At some point in our lives, we all have to."

Keeping my front to him, I took a few careful steps backward, anticipating that at any moment he'd laugh and pounce like a cat. *More tricks.*

But he didn't, and once I had retreated to the edge of his patio, I turned and booked it down the driveway as fast as my ankle would carry me, glancing back only once.

He'd lowered his hands, his eyes simmering in dark amusement.

CHAPTER THIRTY-TWO

Anita's boyfriend was waiting for her when she arrived home. He was frantic, plying her with questions: Where had she been? Why hadn't she called? Anita calmly explained that she'd had sex with a kind man in suspenders who had taken her to his home and then put her on the next bus once it was over.

Danny Grape stared at his girlfriend in disbelief. Gentle, sweet Anita, who never had so much as flirted with another man since their first date.

Anger overcame him, and he loosened his belt, unable to stop himself. He brought it down on her as she begged him to stop, to explain to her what she'd done wrong, that she'd only done what the kind man had asked—until a small puddle of fluid broke from between her legs, and they both stared at the slick mess.

"It's time," she whispered through her tears, one hand on her belly.

—From "Everyone's Favorite Uncle" in
Bedtime Stories for Monsters

THE TREES WERE a blur. The night was vast. Malice House rose beyond the gate like the last vestige of civilization in the wilderness, and I saw it all at once as it had been throughout time: the old fisherman's cottage; Alice Halliday's spinster house gaining additions, multiplying like the children she never had; my father's simultaneous fortress and tomb, thwarting my charcoal pencils' attempts to capture it.

I entered the gate code with shaking fingers, just cognizant enough to make sure it locked behind me. I limped up the driveway as swiftly as I could manage. Kylie must have seen me approach on the laptop because she flung open the door, waving me in as though jackals snapped at my heels. But it was only the night. The endless, bewitched night.

I barreled through the front door. She slammed it behind me and locked it. Then, after a few heaving breaths, our eyes locked. I threw my arms around her, digging my fingers into her ribs, pressing my palms against her shoulders, needing to reassure myself she was flesh and blood, not a ghost.

"You left," I gasped. "I thought you were *dead*."

She flinched at the word like it was a rotten piece of meat I'd dropped on the counter. "You did? I just came back to the house to pack. We agreed to pack everything valuable so we'd have cash to move somewhere else, remember?"

There was an unfocused look in her eye like she'd had too much to drink, but I didn't smell alcohol on her breath. Her face was dressed with a mask of almost childlike serenity that I had seen before in documentaries about brainwashed cult members.

I dug my fingers into the meat of her shoulders. "Did an old-fashioned-looking man in suspenders tell you that? Big gut?"

Her foggy gaze drifted up and to the right as though struggling to tease a remembered dream out of oblivion. "Yeah, that's right. He told me that you were fine and it was okay for me to leave. Wait—how do you know that?"

The creepily serene mask slipped a little, and a twinge of fear crept into her face as the Kylie beneath the bewitchment fought to surface.

"Hold up, who was that man, anyway?" Her unfocused eyes whipped back and forth, scanning her own memories as panic built.

According to what I'd gleaned from "Everyone's Favorite Uncle," Uncle Arnold's verbal spell wore off after enough time or distance. For highly suggestive people, his brainwashing could last a day. For others, an hour. For the pregnant girl in the story that he'd raped, it only wore off when labor kicked in with its ungodly squeeze of pain.

I snapped my fingers in front of Kylie's face, but it didn't seem to break the spell, so I smacked her on the cheek, wincing as I did it, not wanting to hurt her.

She withdrew with a rush of coiled surprise, ready to strike back, but then stopped. Her eyes cut to me sharp as a knife. "Haven . . . *fuck*. Who *was* that man?" Now that she realized someone had intruded in her mind, she swiped her hands rapidly over her shoulders and arms like she could rid herself of him as easy as brushing off cobwebs.

I leaned back against the front door as my chest rose in ragged breaths. "His name is Uncle Arnold. He came out of Malice. He manipulated you. He can make anyone act unlike themselves just with the power of his voice."

Act unlike themselves. I'd heard that before somewhere—Detective Rice had used that phrase about Eddie Chase's alleged murder-suicide. Had Uncle Arnold had been at the scenic overlook, knocking on that car window with a yellow-tooth smile, knowing Eddie was connected to me?

A wave of sickness pushed up my throat. "Look, I don't think we should wait until morning. We need to pack and get out of town *tonight*."

"You really think that man is so dangerous? What does he want?"

In his tale, Uncle Arnold had been a dissatisfied traveling salesman stuck at the bottom rung of an encyclopedia company until he'd been attacked by a pack of rowdy teenagers on a train platform and left with a damaged windpipe—which gave him his unique *voice*. He became addicted to the power of controlling anyone who crossed his path.

"It's not just him. I think all the monsters are near. The Harbinger is here, too."

I flashed back to Rafe towering over me in his driveway as he explained that he wasn't the peanut butter mogul who lived next door. Why hadn't I seen it before? Even though in my drawing his hair obscured his facial features, I should have recognized his body. Every piece of him had come from my own imagination, my own hand, my own desires. The illustration was long gone, so it wasn't like I could go back and look for clues in the charcoal set of his shoulders or the watercolor wash of shadows on his chest. But still, I should have known.

He's a trickster, I reminded myself. *He knows how to fool people. To misdirect their thoughts. My mind was only ever putty for him to knead and shape.*

"Haven?" Kylie pressed, snapping her fingers like I was the hypnotized one now. "You saw the Harbinger?"

"Yes. You've seen him, too." As though recounting something I'd seen in a movie, I told her about Rafe's deception and watched the shock play out on her face. "He claims that he's been protecting me from the Ink Drinkers and the police, but he's a liar. That's literally his role in the book. He must have some ulterior motive."

Kylie considered this and then used her Converse sneaker to toe my canvas bag on the entryway floor, making the brushes inside clatter together. "Maybe he needs you."

I fixed my gaze on the tip of a brush sticking out of the bag. "What? What for?"

She crouched down to pick up the brush, running the bristles over her palm in figure eights. "Rafe knows you can bring characters off the page, right? What if he wants you to bring over more of his friends?" She angled the brush at me pointedly.

I shifted from one foot to the other uncomfortably. "I've already brought over all the characters from Malice. I did it before I knew what I was doing, when . . ."

. . . when Rafe was encouraging me, admiring my portfolio, assuring me of how proud my father would be of my efforts.

God, what a fool I was. Falling for compliments like a first-year art student.

Angry at myself, I started pacing a tight circular track around the hallway. "If that's what he wants, it doesn't matter. I destroyed the manuscript, so I can't bring any more characters over. I'd have to rewrite the entire book from memory."

Kylie tilted her face up at me. "So why don't you?"

"Are you crazy?"

She stood up, still clutching the brush. "I'm not suggesting you rewrite it word-for-word, but a revised version." She toyed with the brush until she held it like a pencil. A light sprang to her eyes. "*I* could do it. I'm a Marbury. I could write a new version of *Bedtime Stories for Monsters* where the characters don't have their abilities and are essentially harmless—"

Before she even finished the thought, my head began shaking as though my subconscious intuited the danger in tinkering with worlds. I jabbed a stiff finger in the air. "Horror Movie Rule one: Don't mess with the curse. The curse always wins."

But coals burned in the pits of her eyes. "It's worth a try. We could change everything about the story, Haven. I'll rewrite all the chapters, and you'll re-illustrate them—" She actually held out the brush to me, urging me to accept it.

"No!"

Kylie stopped short, rendered silent by the intensity of my reaction.

I didn't like the fever-dream look that had taken ahold of her; it was as though she wasn't entirely in control of her own body. Uncle Arnold hadn't hypnotized her this time, but something else almost had. Something even more insidious.

"It's occult magic," I explained in a voice I fought to keep steady. "Curses work through people, take control of them. For all we know, we could end up duplicating monsters by writing the book again. Setting multiple versions of them loose—it would only make things worse."

"Sequels," she muttered, giving a reluctant nod as the feverish gleam in her eyes dulled. "Harbinger part one, Harbinger part two. Yeah, I get it."

I bobbed my head, relieved she didn't press it. "We need to find someone who knows more about this than we do before we go poking around in the occult." I had a few ideas. Consulting online spiritualists? Asking Rob for a connection? One of the letters I'd found in the basement had a return address in Portugal; even thirty years old, that could be a start. But it was nothing we could do tonight.

The corners of her eyes dipped down as she asked, "Does Rafe know that I'm also a Marbury?"

I hesitated before lifting an uncertain shoulder. "He was the one who freed us in the bookstore, so he might have overheard us telling the Ink Drinkers. And he's read more of Dad's journal than I have, so . . . I don't know. I just know that right now, we should get out of Lundie Bay."

She waved an anxious hand in the direction of the postal bins she'd filled with our father's books and valuables. "These items will finance us for a few weeks. I'm guessing it's more than will fit in your car. My Subaru has more room, and we should probably ditch your car anyway as soon as we can in case people come looking for us. We can stop at my apartment on the way out of town to get my car, and so I can grab a few things. How much more do you need to pack?"

"Not a lot. Laptop. My sketchbook—I have a lifetime of work in there. Art supplies." I dragged my eyes over the objects and furniture that had never been mine to begin with. Once we were temporarily settled, I'd figure out how to sell everything and what to do with the house. My artwork was the only thing that meant anything to me. I could pick up a new VHS player in any pawn shop to keep up my work for Rob. But years of effort and a good portion of my soul had gone into my drawings. When I'd fled New York, I'd had just enough time to grab my sketchbook and art supplies. I'd left everything else, and now I was preparing to do it all again.

"I can be ready in half an hour," I said.

Kylie cased the library one last time for valuables as she nodded. "I'll finish up here."

I grabbed my canvas bag from the entryway and stuffed in the renegade brushes. Weak moonlight shone through the windows as I limped up the steps to the second floor and turned on the primary bedroom's light. The bed skirt ruffled at my entrance, making me go still. But for once, it had truly just been the wind. No Pinchy there this time.

Most of my supplies were still in the cardboard box in the corner. I began shoveling handfuls of art supplies into my bag. In went the graphite pencils. The mug full of my watercolor brushes, some still damp. Tubes of watercolor paints. My sketchbook and any loose drawings. My hands shook uncontrollably as I worked. I had done all this before. It was a headier feeling than déjà vu because it *had* already happened. History repeating itself.

Catherine's blue BOOKMARKS ARE FOR QUITTERS mug paper-weighted a stack of drawings. I picked it up hesitantly. A month ago, that mug had been the first thing I'd seen when Baker had shaken me awake on the sofa while the end credits played for one of Rob's movies—a truly vile one that my husband would never approve of me watching. He was holding up a print-out of my email to my divorce lawyer friend as hot fury simmered in his eyes. *"What's this, babe?"*

A sharp series of thuds from downstairs rattled me back into the present. The mug fell out of my hands onto the rug, but this time, didn't break. The sound came again.

Hammering? Slinging my now-heavy bag over my shoulder, I limped my way back downstairs as I called out, "Kylie? Everything okay?"

I didn't know what I had expected. Maybe to find her using a hammer to pry valuable artwork off the walls. But as I reached the bottom stair, I became aware that the thud sound was coming from the front door. Kylie emerged from the living room with a stack of paperbacks in hand, following the sound just like me.

If Kylie isn't hammering, who is?

The sound began again after a pause. Both our heads snapped magnetically toward the repeated thuds at the front door. Through the beveled glass panes, we made out a familiar face.

CHAPTER THIRTY-THREE

The library sat atop a rocky outcropping, built of the same crumbling limestone and in the same monolithic shape as the hill itself, so if one didn't know it was there, one might simply walk past. But the Hellhound stopped and raised her massive head. It wasn't long before a lantern shone in one of the windows. The Harbinger extinguished his torch and bade the Witch of Went do the same.

"We're here."

—From "Beasts of Sun" in
Bedtime Stories for Monsters

FUCKING JONATHAN TYBEE.

It would have been impossible for Jonathan not to see us through the glass, but he didn't acknowledge our presence in the slightest. He raised the hammer and started pounding again at the upper portion of the door frame as though repairing a loose piece of siding.

I moved toward the door with the disorienting sensation of an out-of-body experience, shifting my angle to peer through the decorative glass that fractured Jonathan Tybee's face into a Picasso. Individual fragments caught his thumb, the hammer's end, his oatmeal-brown Fair Isle sweater.

My hand fell on the doorknob. I twisted viciously.

Locked.

I turned the dead bolt and tugged again, but the door wouldn't give. Peering into the narrow gap between the door and the door frame, I could see that the various locks weren't engaged, but no matter how hard as I pulled, the door only jiggled.

I slammed my hand against the side of the door.

"Jonathan!" I yelled loudly, knowing the wood and glass would muffle my voice. "What the hell are you hammering?"

He lowered the hammer, dug something out of a workman's tool belt hugging his waist, and returned to his task; I could have fooled myself into thinking he hadn't heard me except for a single quick instant when his gaze cut to me, the angled glass multiplying his two eyes into dozens.

Kylie pressed her palms flat on the door as though to stop it from shaking with each thud of his hammer. Her whole body vibrated with every impact. Even her voice pulsated as she said, "He's nailing it shut."

I moved back, needing space, only to instantly realize that she was right. The hairs on the back of my neck prickled. The Ink Drinkers had given us until the following day to leave town, but Jonathan's presence meant plans must have changed. I whirled on Kylie, only to find her already vocalizing the thought forming in my head.

"I'll check the back door." Her shoes squealed as she peeled off toward the dining room.

The front door thumped again in staccato beats as Jonathan drove in another nail. "Are you trying to trap us here?" I shouted. He ignored me. "It won't work, the windows lock and unlock from the inside."

The beveled glass showed his mouth firm into a grimly satisfied line. A terrible premonition overcame me. I made my way through the archway to the library, where I reached for the closest window.

But my hand stilled. Long nails bolted the window frame shut. *All* the windows.

They already sealed the windows—they've already been inside the house.

Mind reeling, I hobbled back to the hallway and smacked my hand against the door. "What do you think you're doing?"

"What we have to," Jonathan answered at last, stepping back from the door to inspect his work. His voice was muffled as though coming from underwater.

"You wanted us gone from the house, not locked inside!"

His watery blue eyes found mine and filled with condescension.

I missed something, I realized. As though it had been electrified, I jerked away from the front door just as Kylie reemerged from the dining room, breathless and pale.

"Nailed shut," she reported in a rush. "The back door and all the downstairs windows."

"They never planned on letting us leave town. . . ." I muttered.

The weight of my bag full of art supplies threatened to drag me down, so I shrugged it off onto the entryway table before turning to her. "They must have come inside the house while we were in the vault. Rice has the gate code. They used my house keys to let themselves in and nail shut every exit except the front door, so that when we came home, we'd be walking straight into a trap. Once they were sure we were both inside, all they had to do was seal the front door."

Jonathan gave me a darkly satisfied look as he slid the hammer into the tool belt around his waist, then dusted off his hands. He angled toward the side of the house and called something I couldn't make out to someone. *He isn't alone.* But no matter how I pressed my face against the door pane, I couldn't see who it was.

I could see, however, that the gate was now open, though there was no sign of his car. He must have parked down at the overlook and walked up. Didn't want any evidence tying him here.

Kylie started shouting expletives through the door, rattling at the knob. Then lighter footsteps clattered on the porch. I moved to the nearest library window to see, not surprised to glimpse an expensive gray puffy coat and salt-and-pepper hair swept into a bun.

"Catherine." My palms left ghostly marks against the cold glass of the upper windowpane. "You don't realize what you're doing. Let us out!"

Without one of her elegant silk scarves or lipstick, she appeared considerably aged. She strode up to her ex-husband with an impatient glance toward me. "It's sealed? And the back door? The windows?"

"Everything," he said, still rubbing the grime from his hands.

She set down a paper grocery bag I recognized as coming from Lundie Bay's natural food mart. Reaching inside, she withdrew a plastic gas can.

"Oh fuck," Kylie muttered beside me.

It echoed in my head with every beat of my heart.

Fuck. Fuck.

My eyes raked the room until I spotted the nearest smoke detector, then stilled. It had been disabled. The battery dangled on a cord, ripped out. I crossed to the bookshelf where Dad had kept his fire extinguisher behind a stack of thesauri—gone.

Liquid splashed against the window, an unmistakable sound. Followed by the unmistakable smell of gasoline.

"They got rid of all the fire extinguishers," I told Kylie.

Her eyes pulled into narrow slits. "The shotgun. . . ."

I nodded quickly for her to get it. As she darted off toward the living room, my fingers pushed uselessly on the closest window frame. There was no point in breaking more glass—the decorative iron designed to keep intruders out now kept *us* in.

For the second time I realized: *Rafe wasn't lying.* He'd warned me about the Ink Drinkers. I should have listened.

As Catherine splashed the windows with more gasoline, I sputtered through the window, "Why didn't you just kill us in the bookstore?"

"Easier to dispose of bodies in a house fire and blame it on faulty wiring," she explained with a shrug as though describing how to rid the kitchen of ants. "It was Letitia's idea. She's already been in touch with the fire chief. He knows the truth about the 'bear attacks' from last year, so he's agreed to be a little slow in answering calls that come in reporting a house fire at the old Marbury place on Cliffside Drive."

My fingernails curled into the fleshy part of my palms. "You're cowards. You don't have the courage to kill someone outright."

Catherine had stooped down on creaky knees to pull a box of extra-long matches out of the health store bag but stopped when I said this. She threw me a wounded look as she straightened. "Cowards? Haven, we tried everything to avoid getting to this point. Trying to convince you to move and sell the house. Staging break-ins to try to scare you away. That mug . . . Letitia got ahold of a report from her New York colleagues, something about a violent incident with your ex-husband, that mug and blood all over the carpet. We thought you'd *certainly* run if you thought your past was catching up to you. But you still didn't. Stubborn as your father."

The mug? There was no way Baker would have called the police after the incident, so a neighbor or friend of his must have reported it on his behalf.

I stepped close enough to the window that my breath fogged the glass. "You *are* cowards. You convinced Dahlia to kill my father because you couldn't do it."

"If only that were true," she said in an exasperated voice. "Dahlia had access to Amory's food; it made the most sense for it to be her. You wouldn't call us cowards if you knew everything we've done. What Jonathan *had* to do."

As the hairs lifted higher on the back of my neck, I gripped the iron bars on the broken pane, ignoring the remnants of sharp glass pressing against my skin. "What are you talking about?"

"That literary agent!" Catherine shouted with surprising

vehemence. "That man from Los Angeles and his girlfriend. They were innocent. They should still be alive. But *you* got them involved!"

My mind scrambled to make sense of her words. "Wait——"

"It was an accident." She was shaking slightly, the box of matches forgotten in her hand. If it hadn't been for the shattered pane, I don't think I could have made out her hushed words. "A junior agent at SunBurst bragged to Jonathan's former assistant that their president was coming to meet with you. Jonathan only wanted to talk to Mr. Chase to convince him to leave town without meeting with you, that the project was a dud. Obviously, we couldn't let that manuscript get out in the world. He had a gun but only to threaten them. The confrontation . . . got out of hand."

My hand tightened on impulse, cutting into the broken glass. I hissed as I pulled back my arm. A line of blood beaded across my palm, and yet *Catherine* was the one who started crying. Her face contorted as she tried to hold off the tears, but they came out anyway. Jonathan adjusted his tool belt and strode over to wrap his arms around her. I watched in disgust as they comforted each other over Eddie Chase's murder.

Jonathan killed Eddie Chase and Francesca Myers. Not any of the Malice monsters. Once I finally found my voice through shock and anger, I sputtered, "You can't pretend it's an accident this time. This isn't a confrontation gone wrong. This is *murder*."

Jonathan fixed me with a cool look over Catherine's trembling shoulder as he consoled his wife. "No," he agreed. "No accidents anymore."

I heard the squeak of Kylie's shoes a second before she returned to the entry hall with the shotgun under one arm. Catherine hiccupped and then clutched her ex-husband's sweater sleeve when she saw.

"Jonathan, they have the shotgun. I thought you took it!"

Confusion blustered over his face. "I put it in the back of the Prius!"

Kylie squared her stance and rooted the shotgun butt against her shoulder. She looked to me for confirmation, which I was only too happy to give.

I bobbed my head anxiously. "Do it."

She took aim at the front door's knob, shuffled her feet to get the best stance.

Then my sister squeezed the trigger.

CHAPTER THIRTY-FOUR

Kestrel taught himself to walk on clumsy, fleshy legs. He could mimic a few garbled words from his red lips. But he would not wear clothes. Clothes trapped and squeezed and hindered. Clothes were for humans, and even when Kestrel was in his human form, he was still always—always—a bird. The hunger of a raptor, the mind of a hunter, the heart of an unbound thing.

—From "Sundown Coming" in
Bedtime Stories for Monsters

THE SHOTGUN RECOIL was enough to send Kylie skidding back a foot. A shower of pellets slammed into the front door, which in turn radiated a cloud of sawdust and splinters. I lifted my arm over my face for protection as soon as the blast reverberated. On the other side of the wall, Catherine let out a scream that outlasted the blast.

I felt a surge of hope—until I lowered my arm.

I'd expected the door to be blown off its hinges like I'd seen in movies but instead, it stood, largely undamaged except for a rash of pearl-sized holes embedded in the thick wood.

Kylie stared at the door in dull shock as she muttered, "It must be birdshot." She looked at the shotgun like she'd never seen one before. "For small game. I thought the gauge meant it was buckshot."

I knew nothing about shotgun ammunition. Birdshot, buckshot, it all sounded deadly to me. I grabbed the doorknob anyway and tugged—still sealed.

No, no, no.

Once Catherine and Jonathan realized that the shotgun hadn't taken down the door, they released their terrified hold on one another. Jonathan ran an unsteady hand over his freshly trimmed beard as Catherine pressed her palm into the soft rounds of her chest.

I saw her lips move in a silent prayer. "Oh thank god."

Devastation pained me even more than the cut on my hand. Reeling, I backtracked into the library and sank on the sofa armrest, feeling suddenly weak-kneed.

"So that's it?" My throat was dry. "The gun is useless?"

"No," Kylie muttered as she fumbled with the shells in her pocket, squinting at the inscriptions stamped on each. "Maybe it can't take down a door, but even birdshot can separate meat from the bone at close enough range." She stuffed all but one shell back in her pocket. She reloaded the gun, then swiveled her face toward the library windows and narrowed her eyes. "It can sure as hell pass through glass."

With long strides, she approached the windows and swung the barrel at them, preparing to fire again. Jonathan's and Catherine's faces drained. Just as Kylie let loose another spray of pellets, they scrambled to get out of the way, hurrying to the safety of the far end of the porch. Glass from the remaining panes shattered into a waterfall on both sides of the windows, booby-trapping the porch and the library floor. I ducked behind the side of the sofa, sheltering my head with my hands.

The glass seemed to fall forever. Once the final pieces settled, I dared to raise my head.

Kylie's scowl told me all I needed to know. "It didn't work. They can move out of the way, and we're caged in by these fucking bars."

She sank onto the sofa, setting the shotgun on the coffee table, and buried her face in her hands.

But I had no intention of giving up.

Facing the bars, I called to Jonathan and Catherine who were keeping their distance now, "Does Ronan know about this?"

He'd told us in the bookstore that he wasn't a killer, and I believed him. He must not have known the truth about how Eddie Chase and Francesca Myers died, because I couldn't imagine him living with that knowledge. Had he known that this was a setup when he came to the bookstore to let us out of the vault, or had Jonathan and Catherine lied to him, too, afraid he would warn us?

"Ronan is a concerned citizen, like us," Catherine called. "Even if he's a bit soft-hearted."

So Ronan doesn't know.

"Concerned citizens?" Kylie spat out the words, twisting around to face her. "You think *you're* the hero here?"

Catherine lifted her pudgy chin.

It struck me with grim certainty as I pressed around the oozing cut on my palm that by most definitions, the Ink Drinkers *were* concerned citizens. They were risking their lives to stop a credible threat to town: *me.*

"None of us are guiltless," I muttered more to myself than anyone else. The Ink Drinkers thought I was the enemy but only because of their perspective. *Look through dirty glasses, see a dirty world.* I twisted to the Tybees and said louder, "*You* trapped us here to kill us, so don't go calling *me* a villain."

Catherine jabbed her box of matches in my direction accusingly. "Are you going to play innocent, Haven? Orion is *dead.* You're just like your father. Oh, the arrogance of that man. He *liked* the power of it; I swear he did. All dementia does is peel away the veneer to reveal a person's true self. Your father lost any shred of morality in the end. Only his angry inner child remained, and he wanted to show off for us, to prove he could do the impossible. He knew exactly what he was doing when he manifested a demon last summer. I think you knew what you were doing, too. Beneath your own veneer, you're just as desperate for adoration."

Her words took me aback. Had I known what I was doing? *No. I hadn't.* I would never have illustrated the manuscript if I'd known what darkness it would unleash.

Catherine stepped closer to the iron bars, emboldened by our failed attempts with the gun, confident she could move away in time if we shot again. She slid open the matchbox and took her time selecting a six-inch match. She waved it, unlit, in my direction. "So, prove you aren't evil. Call off those monsters you manifested. End this."

An unbidden laugh bubbled out of my mouth. "I can't!"

She scowled in disbelief. "You created them, so you must have some control over them."

I pushed up from the sofa to mirror her behind the iron bars. "They're real now. Off the page. You think they'll listen to me? Not all of them are mindless beasts like the thing last summer. Some of them are human. Highly intelligent. Individuals with free will. *I* don't even know what they're capable of."

Jonathan leaned down next to his ex-wife, speaking low into her ear. They hung back from the windows, ready to make a quick retreat if Kylie reached for the gun again. Catherine listened with a grim fold of her lips, then gave a curt nod. She turned back to us, striking the match on the side of the box with a theatricality that made my stomach lurch.

"I'm sorry it has to be this way, Haven," she announced. "In a way, it isn't your fault, but you're like a rabid animal. You must be put down before you destroy others. Kylie, I feel the worst for you. You're as innocent in all this as that literary agent was."

Was. Meaning Kylie's innocence wouldn't spare her, just as it hadn't Eddie Chase or Francesca Myers.

"What a saint you are, Catherine," Kylie hissed. "*So* concerned."

At Catherine's signal, Jonathan reached into the grocery bag and took out a thick rubber-band-bound ream of pamphlets stamped with Lundie Bay Books' logo. He doused it with gasoline.

"Better get back!" Catherine called to us in a mockery of concern as she lit the doused stack of pamphlets.

Kylie immediately raised the shotgun and looked down the sight, but Jonathan hurled the pamphlets through the broken window and scrambled backward, just out of range as she squeezed the trigger.

The pellet spray bit into the wall and remaining glass—but not the Tybees.

Kylie lowered the gun. "Shit."

Shit was right.

Instinct urged me to grab the lit pamphlets and throw them back out the window, but the entire stack was already on fire. I rushed forward, stomping on them with my shoe, only to have the rubber band pop and send loose pamphlets scattering, spreading the fire faster. Flames jumped from the burning papers to the gasoline-soaked rug.

"The curtains!" I yelled to Kylie, but she couldn't get to them in time. Catherine had doused them with gasoline, and flames roared up them faster than I could track them with my finger. I grabbed Kylie's bicep, pulling her back from the fire.

On the other side of the windows, Jonathan and Catherine retreated as orange flames shot out of the house.

Then, improbably, a Honda Civic turned off Cliffside Drive and barreled up the driveway through the open gate. The bobbing headlights blinded my eyes, and I had to shield my face with my arm. At the far end of the porch, Jonathan and Catherine turned in dull surprise. Whoever was behind the wheel pounded on the horn. *Beep! Beep!* The car skidded to a stop, and a second later, the driver-side door slammed closed.

I could only make out the driver once he'd moved in front of the still-burning headlights. Ronan Young came huffing into the front yard, mouth forming a perfect O shape as he took in the rising smoke.

"*What* do you think you're doing?" he shouted at the Tybees. "You said you were just going to talk to her!"

Catherine's face revealed a modicum of guilt like a mother whose son had caught her with another man. But Jonathan only looked irritated by the librarian's appearance. They stomped down the steps to join him in the front yard. I couldn't make out most of their words, but the nature of their argument was clear from Ronan's indignant gesticulating and the Tybees' placating arm waves.

Ronan took out his phone, but Jonathan grabbed it from him. Ronan faced the house and shouted up to me, "I'll get you out of there!"

Jesus. He really believed that.

As the three of them continued to argue, Kylie grabbed my father's Booker Prize from one of the postal bins and started breaking the remaining windowpanes with the brass statue. But it wasn't enough to mitigate the black billows of smoke, which forced me to press my shirt collar over my mouth and nose. My eyes began to sting. The library bookcases on the rear wall—a buffet of dry, crisp kindling—caught rapidly. Flames ate gluttonously through book covers, licking bindings, taking charred-edge bites out of the shelves themselves. Without the fire department, or even a fire extinguisher, everything would go up in a matter of minutes. I considered running to the kitchen to fill bowls with water, but flames were throwing off such intense heat that my skin sizzled even from ten feet away. A few buckets of water wouldn't stop this.

As Ronan jabbed accusatory fingers at the Tybees, Catherine took a few steps to the left, trying to peer through the smoke into the house. Firelight reflected on her face, deepening her wrinkles. Smoke and the dark night made it hard to see, but I suddenly latched onto the shape of a figure standing in the front yard about fifty feet behind Ronan and the Tybees—a person I didn't recognize staring up at the smoke pouring out of the house.

Fresh dread and a little fascination pooled in my belly. *Rafe?*

Then, a shadow of something passing overhead rippled over the dark front lawn. The largest bird I'd ever seen. I could have fooled myself into believing it was a small airplane. I shivered involuntarily despite the intense heat. Whoever was standing on the front lawn remained motionless though in plain sight behind the Ink Drinkers, not glancing up at the alarmingly huge flying object. A small red star burned a hole in the night; the person was smoking a cigar.

Rafe didn't smoke a cigar—but someone else did. Uncle Arnold.

"Haven?" The way Kylie said my name was unnaturally high. "Who's that in the woods?"

Fear began to seize my muscles, but I felt strangely intrigued, too. A psychopath stood twenty feet away from the Ink Drinkers, and they only stood there, arguing amongst themselves.

"You mean the front yard?" I said, keeping my eyes on the figure.

"No." She spoke emphatically. "I mean the woods."

Confused, I whirled to see that Kylie was looking out the hallway window, which faced the strip of trees separating Rafe's property from mine. Something was moving between the trees on my side of the security fence. The longer I looked, the more I knew it wasn't human. The thing was the size of a small bear but moved with a doglike trot.

My heart recognized that creature's outline. I'd drawn the monstrous dog in the woods. The overweight man in the front yard, too.

They're coming.

A shiver shuddered through me. I wanted a father-daughter collaboration; *here it was.*

He came walking up the driveway at last, dressed in the real Rafe Kahn's flannel shirt and black jeans, looking so perfectly ordinary that it was almost painful to know what he truly was. His boots must have crunched loudly on the gravel driveway, but he made no attempt to hide his presence.

Ronan turned at the sound, took one look at Rafe's smug smile, then with a jolt finally noticed Uncle Arnold standing in the front yard. Ronan scrambled into the azaleas, fighting through the branches toward his car. Catherine and Jonathan were slower on the uptake, turning to watch Rafe approach like he was simply a lost tourist.

Ronan reached his car, but then froze before he could grab the door handle. Something behind his car, hidden from my view, growled low. It didn't matter that I couldn't see it. *Ronan* could. The look on his face told me all I needed to know.

In the firelight, the Hellhound lunged. Ronan screamed and darted back into the azaleas, scrambling through the bushes toward the side of the house. Jonathan and Catherine scuttled around the yard for a second before running across the grass toward the gate. But the enormous shadow from something overhead swung back around, eclipsing them. From my higher position, I was able to track the shadow's movements, but they were ground-level and blinded by panic; they didn't see it coming. A monstrous winged creature descended on them with superhuman speed, knocking them both into the gravel. Stretching out into what had to be a ten-foot wingspan, it beat its wings once with a powerful thrust that sent all its feathers fluttering loose in a mushroom-brown cloud, revealing a man's naked body underneath. Prostrate on her back, Catherine screamed before finding the sense to logroll away.

Jonathan tried to push to his knees, but Kestrel grabbed him by the hair in a talon-like grasp, placed his other hand around his jaw, and gave a sharp twist.

I watched, stunned, as Jonathan's head spun one hundred eighty degrees. Only a minute ago, he'd been lecturing me about the difficult choices they'd had to make to protect the citizens of Lundie Bay, and now he was gone. I might not have heard the crack when his neck broke, but I could feel it in my own vertebrae.

Kestrel let Jonathan's body slump to the driveway, standing over it with arms still spread wide like he might sprout feathers again and take flight. But then he let his arms relax to his sides, and after a moment of perfect stillness, his head swiveled toward the house.

CHAPTER THIRTY-FIVE

They were surrounded.

Cloaked figures emerged from every doorway—worker drones in this hive of literary storage. The Harbinger, the witch, and the monstrous dog had reached the heavy wooden inner library doors only to be trapped, with the answer to the Salem Dreamer's location somewhere on the other side.

The Hellhound bared fangs at the encroaching Robber Saints. The Witch of Went drew her dagger. "Are you glad we joined you now, trickster? Or do you still believe you can accomplish anything in this world on your own?"

—From "Beasts of Sun" in
Bedtime Stories for Monsters

I STEPPED BACK from the iron bars that caged us into Malice House's library. Smoke swirled before me like murky swamp water, swallowing me, urging me deeper into the house.

"What the hell was that?" Kylie asked with a tremble in her voice.

"*That* was Kestrel. If we don't want to meet him, we need to get out of this place."

Outside, Catherine had stopped screaming. She'd managed to roll halfway across the yard and was now pushing shakily to her feet, sprinting toward the trees. But even if she managed to get past the fence, I doubted she would get much farther. The forest was where the Malice creatures had come from, dragging themselves out of the ground into a world they had adapted to with alacrity. No one would find safety amid those trees.

With my sleeve pressed to my mouth and nose, I took quick stock of the library. Flames had spread to the rug and the ceiling, gnawing off the wallpaper on the northern wall like peeling river birch bark. My father's neutral beige paint flaked and bubbled away, melting into a gluey puddle against the baseboard. Beneath the paint, the striped floral wallpaper that the room had when he'd bought it was peeling, whole sections curling in on itself to reveal a dark green paisley wallpaper underneath, something hideous from the seventies. Parts of that wallpaper were burning away, too, to reveal a yellow canary print underneath, the canaries repeating over and over, frozen in time. There were even more layers of wallpaper—endless previous iterations from former owners. I could almost hear the eras of the house fall away with each layer of wallpaper; a victrola gramophone, a record player, a silver boom box. . . . The fire was dissecting the house beam by beam and year by year, erasing not only my father's legacy but all the other histories he had wallpapered over in his march into the modern era—into literary greatness.

I kept expecting to hear sirens, foolishly thinking someone must be coming to our rescue, until I remembered that we were entirely alone.

Kylie grabbed the shotgun off the coffee table just as the built-in shelves popped and buckled. There was a terrifying moment when the shelves separated from the wall and fell in slow motion as the final screws and nails gave way one by one. The entire wall of shelves, books, and awards burst into sparks as it smashed to the library floor, sending out a wave of sparks like the ocean crashing against breakers.

Kylie and I scrambled back as the wave of heat forced us into the hallway.

"They might have missed a window upstairs." My words were a tumbling rush. "There's a chance we could get out onto the roof."

"Jonathan was an editor for thirty years, you think he'd miss a detail like that?" She hefted the gun her stance firmly planted. "We can't get out the front, so we have to try the back. The kitchen door's probably made of a cheaper material than the front one. I might be able to shoot it out."

The blast would give away our location to Rafe and his friends outside, but then our location was hardly a secret. We were mice in a trap, skittering uselessly for an exit.

I gave a tight nod.

Clammy sweat beaded on my chest and temples as we made our way through the downstairs rooms that were rapidly filling with smoke. Shotgun shells jangled in Kylie's pockets. A woman's shriek coming from somewhere outside started and cut off abruptly, the sound dead almost as soon as it began.

"That's Catherine," Kylie said darkly.

I tried not to imagine Catherine's head turned the wrong way on her body as we pressed on into the kitchen. Thin wisps of smoke congregated at the ceiling, but the fire hadn't spread this deep. We were lucky it was an old house, built with high ceilings and constructed out of plaster and thick beams that would take longer to burn than that cheap particleboard found in even expensive new houses. The box of dry cereal that had been our breakfast for the past few days sat on the kitchen counter like a relic from another life.

"Let's try this again," Kylie muttered as she raised the shotgun to take aim at the back door. It was a newer door, probably replaced within the last decade. It looked like fiberglass. In any case, not solid oak like the front one.

My heartbeat cranked in my chest as I braced for the blast, but just as she moved her finger to the trigger, the doorknob slowly moved on its own in strange jerking motions. *Click-click-click.*

Kylie lowered the barrel in stunned confusion. *A ghost*, I thought in a flash, until realizing that it was someone attempting to get in from the other side but couldn't get a grip on the handle.

Something heavy suddenly slammed into the panel above the knob, making me jump. The door cracked. A goat-like smell seeping through the crack turned my stomach, reeking of moldy straw and manure and maybe even something long dead.

A massive paw thrust through the crack in the door, knocking chunks of fiberglass to the kitchen floor. I stared in horror, transfixed. The paw didn't belong to any earthly animal I'd ever seen. No dog. No bear. It was covered in bristled fur like hedgehog spikes with seven sharp claws instead of five, each as big as a shark's tooth.

"Shoot it!" I yelled.

Kylie didn't need to be told twice. She steadied her aim and squeezed the trigger. The recoil threw her into me with more force than either of us was expecting. I used the counter to steady myself.

The door was a wreck, though still mostly intact. The shotgun blast had peppered birdshot through the upper portion of the door, leaving a dozen quarter-sized holes above the shattered crack as well as a larger crater in the bottom half that was almost big enough for a person to crawl through.

As Kylie dug frantically in her pocket for another shell, flecks of paint and sawdust coating her hair, she asked in a rush, "Think I killed it?"

My hands curled around the counter edge as my certainty faltered. It was the Hellhound out there, I was sure of it. I'd read "Sweet Cream" enough times to know that we weren't dealing with a cheap B-movie monster that would explode into slime with a single gunshot.

Proving my fears correct, the temporary silence beyond the door was broken in the next instant by a vicious snarl.

We hadn't killed her. We'd only made her mad.

"Get away from the door!" I grabbed Kylie's shirt, pulling her around the island and out of the kitchen as another sharp-clawed paw swept through the hole in the door. The smoke was thicker now in the dining room, churning like angry stormclouds overhead, forcing us to stoop. Watering eyes made the world swim, but when I staggered into the hallway, I saw one thing clearly enough.

Someone was on the other side of the front door, mostly obscured now by smoke and soot clouding the beveled panes.

"Who the fuck is it?" Kylie asked.

"Hell if I know."

I debated what to do. There was a chance it was a townsperson who'd seen the smoke and come to our aid. Or maybe Ronan making good on his promise. But whoever was out there didn't knock or shout to ask if anyone was inside. Instead, the door gave a strange rattle, followed by a soft clink of metal. Daring to step closer to the clouded-over panes, I could make out the vague suggestion of a woman's shape. She was clutching a book, drumming on it in a strange tapping manner with her index finger. The door rattled again, followed by another metallic clatter. Her head suddenly jerked in my direction, as through she could see straight through the foggy glass with crystal clarity.

She reached her index finger toward the door, drumming softly against the glass.

A muffled singsong voice called, *"Haven . . ."*

Kylie and I both rushed to put space between us and the door, when, without warning, every light in the house went off.

Darkness consumed us.

It's the fire, I realized. The flames must have burned the wiring inside the walls and shorted out the breakers. Cut off the electricity. The lights, the landlines, the Wi-Fi, everything would be dead.

I lurched backward, straight into Kylie. Without the overhead lights, the world was bathed in orange and fire red. Twisting, I pushed her toward the stairs. "Go!"

"Go *where?*"

"The attic!"

It was the last place to go. Higher ground. Monsters and the spreading fire had taken over the downstairs level; our only chance now was to make it to the attic and try to squeeze out the small window and onto the roof. Even if Jonathan had nailed the frame shut, it was the only unbarred window in the house, so we could break the glass. I'd seen branches scrape against the window, so there was a chance we could reach a tree and climb down to safety.

Smoke forced us to drop to hands and knees as we crawled up the dark stairs. Visibility shrank to only a few feet on either side of us; we were birds in a storm cloud, flying off instinct alone. Behind me, Kylie was a hair slower as she struggled with the unwieldy shape of the shotgun. Her lungs made an awful wheezing sound from smoke inhalation.

The climb felt interminable. Smoke. Stairs. Smoke. Stairs. My throat burned as if I'd swallowed live coals. My muscles ached from oxygen deprivation, rendering them depleted and shaky. Even my thoughts veered in odd ways, shorting out like a radio on the fritz. Because of the cloudy-brain effect, it took me far too long to realize what should have been obvious.

I stopped so abruptly that Kylie's head collided with my hip.

How many steps did a standard staircase have? Twelve? Maybe fifteen in an old house with high ceilings? We'd climbed at least twice that many.

"The Witch of Went is inside," I said softly, like I was afraid invoking her name would bring her nearer.

It had been her at the front door, using witchcraft to pull the nails free, and now she was under the roof, fracturing reality once more.

"The stairs," I coughed out. "They're on a loop."

Kylie climbed to the same step as me and sank down, massaging her temples like her head ached and not just from smoke. I heard a vicious cough rattle in her throat. "How do we get out of it?"

My thoughts were sluggish. I shook my head, wishing I knew.

Think. Was the Witch of Went actually bending reality or only altering our perception of it? If it were the latter, then the staircase would take us where we wanted to go as long as we pushed past her interference in our consciousness.

"Close your eyes," I told her. "If we can't see what she wants us to see, the effect might break its hold."

Kylie looked doubtful but did as I suggested. Closing my own eyes, I led the way up the staircase, feeling my way by touch. After another five or six stairs, I lost my nerve and cracked open an eye.

I shouldn't have done that.

The faint glow from the fire now revealed that the staircase had fractured into dozens of angled staircases leading off in every direction, a labyrinth worthy of Escher. Each was identical down to the same stair tread, the same billows of smoke rising to the ceiling.

"Haven. Why did you stop?"

I saw that Kylie's eyes were still closed, and I swallowed past the dry coals in my throat. "Nothing. Everything's fine."

I closed my eyes again, shaking.

Over the sound of the roaring fire, I thought I heard a voice. Whispering? Instantly, I thought of my father and his assertions that the house was haunted. So naive in retrospect—the truth was so much worse. I strained to listen but with the echoes in the labyrinthine staircase, I couldn't tell if the whispers were coming from above or below us until Kylie screamed.

Her free hand shot out as she reached for me. I twisted around, eyes flying open. Her eyes were open, too, hollowed out with fear. Multiple sets of hands emerged from the smoke behind her, clutching onto her ankles and calves. In the darkness, the figures looked like ghostly apparitions. Men and women wearing monastic brown cassocks with the hood pulled over their heads, obscuring their eyes. A chant came from somewhere, though their mouths weren't moving.

"Give us your stories
and your stories will live forever . . .

Give us your stories,

And your stories will live forever."

The words reached into my hazy memory straight to the pages of "Late Fees."

"Let her go!" I screamed. Kylie clutched onto the gun with one hand and my leg with the other, using her legs to kick, while I tried to pull her back up the stairs.

But it wasn't enough. There were only two of us and so many of them.

I threw all my strength into pulling her up the stairs, leveraging my body against the wall. It was a grisly game of tug-of-war with Kylie as the rope. I felt myself gaining a few inches, dragging her higher up the stairs, only for the Saints to reclaim those inches and more. They dragged her a few steps down, and I was pulled along with her until I could shove my foot against the baseboard and wedge myself in.

The chanting grew in volume.

More Saints are coming.

Kylie's eyes met mine. Her fingers twisted into the folds of my pants leg, holding on with an iron grip, as she whispered urgently, "Take the gun."

Before I could stop her, she thrust the weapon in my direction at the same time that her left hand released my jeans. Now that she wasn't holding on to anything, the Robber Saints made swift work of dragging her down the stairs as she bucked and kicked and scratched like a wild animal backed into a corner.

Then she was gone.

It had happened in the blink of an eye. *I couldn't stop it.*

For a second, I only stared at the swirling smoke where she'd vanished. My breath was uneven. Too short. Too fast. Every shallow rise of my chest punctuated the same terrifying thought.

Kylie's gone.

CHAPTER THIRTY-SIX

The Witch of Went cleaned her blade on a dead Robber Saint's cloak as she cautioned, "You're too soft-hearted, Harbinger. You hesitate when you should strike."

"Can't you love a weak man?"

She scoffed. "I didn't say you were weak. Nor did I say I loved you."

"Oh?"

She rested a hand on his silver hair, stroking the strands with tender malice. "At least you've never ended up on my table. Yet."

He smirked before turning serious. "More Saints will soon come. We don't have long."

—From "Beasts of Sun" in
Bedtime Stories for Monsters

THEY WON'T KILL HER, a frenzied voice inside my head insisted. *They need her alive.*

Heartbeat speeding up, I turned to find that the staircase now ended just a few steps from where I stood. A fearful moan slid from my lips—no matter how often I'd seen reality shift, it went against the mind to accept it. Water trickled down from somewhere on the second floor, waterfalling its way down the stairs and soaking the treads of my sneakers. A pipe must have burst from the fire.

Shaking, I stomped through the falling water to ascend the final steps.

Everything on the second floor looked different in the dark. My hand went for the light switch on instinct, but, it only flipped with a dead thud. The shotgun was heavier than I'd remembered. How had Kylie checked the rounds? I ran my hand over the various components, but they meant nothing to me. All I could do was hope that she'd left it loaded and the safety off.

I splashed through water flowing down the dark upstairs hallway as though in a dream. The floor in the guest bedroom had fallen away into the living room below. Flames roared up through the hole, but water dripped down as though in some cavernous grotto, keeping the worst of the fire at bay. Still, the walls felt unnaturally warm. Some of the floorboards were already buckled. Every step felt like it might send me crashing down through the floor.

As I passed the primary bedroom, flashing lights outside caught my eye. Following the illumination, I rested my fingers against the bedroom window as blue and red lights coated the yard in a steady rhythm, bathing the property in harsh colors. Candy-apple red. Soho azure. Like a poster for a horror movie, all high-contrast colors. A single squad car rolled to a stop behind Ronan's Honda Civic. They hadn't turned on the siren, only the lights.

Detective Rice climbed out the passenger side, clutching her cell phone. Probably trying to call Catherine or Jonathan. *Good fucking luck.*

Had she come to see if their plan had succeeded, or maybe she'd gotten spooked when the Ink Drinkers hadn't answered her calls? Regardless, if the police were here, the fire department couldn't be far behind. They couldn't pretend for much longer that they hadn't received a flood of reports about the smoke. I took a step away from the window, feet splashing into the rapidly rising water. It was ankle-height now, frigid as a January tide. A miniature lake had formed in the bedroom like nature was taking over the house, reclaiming it.

I turned to the hallway door only to find it blocked.

Rafe smiled grimly. "Found you."

His voice was playfully cruel and set my insides trembling. Except for a single smear of soot on his forehead, he looked so shockingly ordinary as he filled the doorway that time seemed to telescope; it was suddenly weeks ago, and he was on my porch with a VHS cassette and a bag of microwave popcorn and eyelashes that snared me like fishhooks.

Light from the windows threw a peculiar pattern of shadows over his face and for a second, he looked just like the illustration of the Harbinger I'd drawn during those first few nights in Malice House when I'd dreamed of publication deals, of artistic legacies.

A creature of wind, I had thought of him that night. *Slight and quick, his presence almost a feeling of déjà vu.*

My instincts kicked in. I dug the shotgun butt into my shoulder as I'd seen Kylie do, centering the barrel on his chest. I was done trusting Rafe Kahn. If he thought I wouldn't turn violent, it was only because he didn't know that the night I left New York, it was *Baker's* blood in the carpet, not mine. Catherine was right; I wasn't innocent.

"I'll shoot," I warned.

He met my eyes with a challenge of his own. "Put that down, damn it. I can get you out of here."

Jesus. Even with everything I knew, a traitorous part of me still wanted to trust him. He was just so *good* at deception. He wasn't a monster, his wide brown eyes seemed to convey. Sure, he killed the neighbor, but that was only because the neighbor was a dog-murdering psychopath. Who didn't root for a vigilante who destroyed those who deserved it? Even in his chapters, the Harbinger didn't kill or even hurt anyone—though he kept company with those who did.

"Yeah, I don't think so." My finger hovered over the trigger.

He threw a quick hand up before I fired. "Don't you want to get Kylie back?"

A single squeeze of the trigger is all it would take. But he knew he had me. I eased my grip on the trigger.

"I can get her back—I know where they will have taken her, and it isn't far—but we must hurry. Sometimes when they extract stories, they get sloppy. Scramble a few brains." He tapped a menacing finger against the side of his head.

I flinched to hear him speak so callously about brain damage. "You'd help me get her back?"

His hand dropped from his temple as his eyes caught the reflection of the police lights outside turning red and blue, red and blue, like a deranged carnival. "Well, darling, nothing's free."

I shifted my weight in the rising water. It flowed steadily from a corner of the bedroom toward the hall like we were ankle-deep in a creek. Odd—it didn't seem likely that there would be pipes in that particular wall, seeing as it wasn't near the bathroom. The water had risen above my shoes now, numbing my toes through my soaked socks, and was starting to feel like too much water for a burst pipe, anyway. In his thick black boots, Rafe didn't seem to care much himself.

I caught a whiff of rotting leaves and dead things. The smell triggered an olfactory memory—*this has happened before*—at the same time that something rose out of the water and skimmed against the bare skin of my ankle.

Even in the faint light, I could clearly make out the elongated shape of *fingers*. Skin clammy and wrinkled from prolonged submersion. Long, jagged nails. There were only a few inches of water—not enough to submerge a person—but of course, logic had long since abandoned this world. The fingers brushed against my shoelaces, curious, and then suddenly closed around my ankle.

Kicking hard, I tore away from the Decayling and scrambled onto the safety of the bed, letting out terrified sounds that didn't sound human. My phone slipped out of my pocket and fell in the water. For a brief instant, its light was magnified across the room. For a terrifying split second, I saw everything. The greenish-skinned women pulling themselves out of the lake that had supplanted the bedroom floor. Their hair was black strings of algae; their teeth as rotten and jagged as their fingernails.

Rafe knelt to calmly drag his fingers through the water. "Fathom Lake," he said simply. "It goes wherever they go. You should be grateful, really. It's the only thing keeping the fire from spreading."

Hugging my knees in tight as I cowered on the bed, I managed to calm my breath enough to ask, "Did you summon them? Is that why they're here, to save the house?"

His shoulder jerked in a careless shrug. "There's no summoning with some of them, only suggestions. I let them know there would be plenty of warm bodies. They came on their own."

"Warm bodies like mine?"

I still had the shotgun, and it was the only thing keeping him on the other side of the lake forming between us.

"I wouldn't let them take you, Haven. You should know that by now. Trust me at least that much." Leaning in the doorjamb, he pointed into the dark water at the murky shapes of women pulling themselves across the waterlogged rug. "The Decaylings are simple-minded creatures. They only want a snack. Most of the creatures in Malice are like that: Pinchy, the Hellhound, Kestrel when he's in his true form. Don't get me started on the Robber Saints—they look like individuals but really, they're one single organism. Think of the *worst* bee colony. Hard to negotiate with them, but not impossible. In any case, stay out of the creatures' way when they're hungry, and you'll be fine." He ran his broad hand over the stubble on his chin, his eyes on the shotgun clutched in my hands. "The rest of us from Malice are different."

"What, you want more than a meal?"

He smiled coldly. "You've read our stories. You think that with his talent, Uncle Arnold's ambitions don't go beyond selling encyclopedias? And the Witch of Went, well, she was never in control of her desires. Revenge is her puppet master. I simply want what your father wrote me to want. The Salem Dreamer. Someone able to bring order to Malice."

"You aren't in Malice anymore."

His eyes flashed dangerously. "Yes, exactly. So maybe instead of order there, I want to bring a little chaos here."

Trickster. Mischief-maker. Harbinger of evil. All words my father had used to describe him.

My finger moved back toward the trigger, though I knew I couldn't kill him as long as I wanted Kylie back. While I struggled to devise a plan, the bathroom door flung open.

Ronan Young came charging out with my father's golf club raised over his head.

"Ahhhhh!" His red-splotched face twisted as he screamed and splashed through the moldering lake. Before Rafe could react, he brought the golf club down on his head.

The force of the impact made Rafe crash backward into the river that had overwhelmed the upstairs hall.

"Jesus Christ, Ronan!" I yelled. For a meek librarian, he had wielded that golf club like a beast.

Ankle-deep in the water, he lifted the club again, ready to slam it down on Rafe's head . . . until a hand rose from the water and clamped onto his foot. Face slack with surprise, Ronan faltered. His terror-filled eyes latched onto the serpentine shapes moving just beneath the water's surface.

I fumbled with the shotgun, but it was too late.

The Decaylings rushed him, fingernails tearing into his clothes, shredding the fabric and flesh beneath, spilling dark stains of blood. Ronan collapsed into the water with a splash as he struggled.

The Decaylings moved over his body like eels in a feeding frenzy. Bones snapped audibly. Blood swirled in the water like an oil slick.

The red and blue flashing lights coming from the windows created a strobe-like effect, turning Ronan's struggle into a flipbook of thrusting knees, bared teeth.

I raised the shotgun into a position to fire, but there were so many of them. I wasn't sure where to aim. I heard more splashing and felt Rafe's presence next to the bed. Hit by a golf club and still standing—he barely even looked winded.

He clutched my bicep. "Time to go," he said tightly. "While they're distracted."

"They're going to kill Ronan!" I threw my elbow out to hold Rafe off. Ronan had entered a burning building to try to save me. I couldn't leave him to end up a meal for the Decaylings. I scrambled backward to put the bed between me and Rafe and again positioned the shotgun against my shoulder.

I'd seen how ineffective birdshot had been against the Hellhound. Birdshot wouldn't stop the Decaylings, either; there were too many of them. So my only option wasn't to bring *them* down—but the house.

I aimed the barrel upward at a place directly over the horrific feeding frenzy. The ceiling was intact for now, but the paint was already bubbling. Flames from downstairs must have spread up through the wide gaps between walls. Birdshot might not bring down a typical ceiling, but this one was beadboard, already structurally compromised.

I let loose a blast.

The recoil threw me back against the dresser. Pellets sprayed into the ceiling, splintering the plaster and embedding into the support beams. Dust rained down, immediately followed by massive chunks of plaster that splashed into the water.

For a moment, the water went still, as though the Decaylings had dived down deep. My heart thumped triumphantly. I thought it had worked—I'd bought Ronan time to escape. He let out a moan and lifted his head. *Still alive.*

The main beam extending from the hallway gave a sudden sharp, splintering crack. More plaster rained down. As though happening in slow motion, the beam folded in two, collapsing in a spectacular crash, bringing half the ceiling with it.

Boxes from the attic dropped down like boulders, smashing into the bedroom furniture and sending up waves from the pooled water. A box grazed Rafe's head, knocking him to the floor. I lost sight of him in the darkness. Cardboard boxes ripped open, bleeding out their contents. Big, opaque plastic bins slammed into the walls, the lids bursting open. Tchotchkes rained down. Loose papers fluttered in the air like snowflakes. The crash rocked the house hard enough to crack the floorboards beneath it, and a portion of the floor fell away to the library below. Water rushed into the crevice like a whirlpool, draining the miniature lake rapidly, presumably taking with it the Decaylings . . . *but also Ronan.* His arms flailed in the water, trying to swim against the current, but he was pulled into the fiery wreckage below.

Fingers twisting in the bedspread, I screamed after him. "Ronan!"

A box from above slammed into my shoulder, knocking me down into the remaining few inches of water. I fell hard but felt nothing, numbed by shock, and scrambled away from the crater in the floor before I was sucked down, too. The bedroom was wholly obscured by the smoke, fallen debris, and steam rising from Fathom Lake hitting the inferno below. Coughing, I felt blindly along the wreckage for the shotgun, but it was gone—likely fallen into the library below. There was no sign of Rafe. Maybe he'd fallen through as well.

I crawled on hands and knees into the wet hallway, where dampened paperwork littered the floor. Contracts, I assumed, until I saw rainbow-colored crayon marks. In a daze, I grabbed one of the papers fluttering in the air. A child's drawing of a dragon. *My* drawing.

Haven, age 6 was documented in the corner in my father's handwriting.

I snatched another of the falling papers. This was a considerably more advanced sketch of a stag being shot through the heart by an arrow. *Haven, first place, tenth grade art contest.* Now I snatched at every paper I could as they wafted on smoke billows.

A spelling test I'd made a perfect score on.

A ninth-grade poem about the Donner Party.

A black-and-white newspaper clipping of the school drama club's performance of *Macbeth* with me as Hecate.

There were photographs, too—faded and old enough to have the date printed in the corner: me with my awkward middle school haircut, Dad and me on the steps of the Lincoln Memorial, five-year-old me on a rocking chair.

They're all of me.

Dazed, I carefully crossed the remaining sections of floor until I could pull myself onto the temporary safety of the attic stairs. I took a moment to hug my knees, shaking uncontrollably.

Ronan was dead. I'd tried to help him only to send him plunging to his death.

I turned to peer over my shoulder at the stairs stretching into darkness. Panic and smoke blinded me, but a fierce part of my unconscious, the drive to survive, moved my hands and feet for me.

The attic. The only place left to go.

Slowly, I climbed.

CHAPTER THIRTY-SEVEN

*Sundown was nigh. When the first moonlit rays cooled the earth,
Kestrel would return to his nocturnal form. One hour left in his flesh
body. One hour in the state that the milkman's daughter preferred.
She was waiting for him in the barn as she had promised, reclined
in the straw, as naked as he was, legs already spread. She spoke soft
words in his ear as he mounted her in that strangely pleasurable way,
but human words meant nothing to him. He was a bird with simple
cravings: eat, sleep, mate.*

*A minute before sundown, when he and the milkman's daughter
had finished, he'd tried to leave only to find the barn doors locked. He
smelled smoke. The girl tugged on the door, too, screaming, as flames
rose around the barn. Through a crack in the door, Kestrel spied the
milkman and his wife and neighbors holding torches.*

*The girl threw her arms around him, but he shrugged her off.
Sundown came, and he transformed and flew out through the hayloft,
leaving her. Humans could not fly—only birds.*

—From "Sundown Coming" in
Bedtime Stories for Monsters

●

MALICE HOUSE'S ATTIC had always harbored secrets. I'd
assumed that the boxes my father hoarded away in every crevice up

there contained homages to his ego—newspaper clippings about his award nominations, editors' letters extolling his virtues, book swag that he hadn't been able to bring himself to throw out—and though there was plenty of that, I couldn't wrap my mind around the fact that he had also kept my grade school report cards and kindergarten artwork, newspaper clippings and class photographs.

As hard as it was for me to believe, *I* had been as worthy of preservation to him as the awards.

As I continued to climb, smoke clinging to my clothes and hair, tears came in ugly, wailing fits. Part of it came from exhaustion, part sheer terror, part from the awful knowledge that I'd only discovered these tender truths after my father's death. He'd always kept himself at a distance—granted, so had I—and I'd thought the worst of him for it. I'd assumed I was a footnote in his weighty tome when that wasn't the case; I was the glue that bound his story.

The end of the chain hanging from the single attic bulb grazed my cheek, and I batted it away, flailing like a moth had flown into my face. With the electricity out, the only light came from the window, shaded by heavy pine boughs, and the flickering light of flames.

I reached the top of the stairs and shakily dusted off my hands. A wide portion of the floor had fallen into the wreckage below, stretching two full stories down to the foundation, making way for weak orange light to cast shadows over the remaining boxes. Thin smoke danced in the air.

"Oh, hello, dear."

My heart battered around in my chest as a disembodied voice emerged from the darkness. It belonged to a woman and was familiar; elegant and gravely.

I was breathing hard; it took my eyes a moment to adjust before finding a figure sitting on a cardboard box dangerously close to the crater in the floor.

Catherine Tybee. She wasn't dead. The way she sat alone and perfectly still in the darkness matched the unsettling calm of her voice.

I immediately fumbled around the boxes for something to use as a weapon; anything. But all I found were paperback books. Thin paper, flimsy cardboard. It was the story between the covers that held power, not the book itself. I couldn't assault anyone with a mass market paperback.

"Catherine." I pressed a hand to my ravaged throat. My eyes scoured the recesses of the attic, still desperate to escape the burning house. The window was closed and nailed around the perimeter, but it didn't matter—I could break the glass. "You ran *into* a burning building?"

"Oh, you know, better than the alternative," she said with bizarre pleasantry.

Something's wrong. In addition to the fact that the house was threatening to collapse at any moment and monsters stalked the hallways, something was *really* wrong with Catherine.

My fingers finally grazed something metal in one of the boxes. It was fist-sized, a lumpy shape I didn't immediately recognize. I slipped the heavy object behind my back as I asked, "What's wrong with you?"

The last I'd seen, she'd run, well, *rolled*, toward the woods after watching Kestrel break her husband's neck. Kylie and I had heard her silenced half-scream. Something must have caught her and brought her inside the house.

She sat straighter, adjusting her coat. "Goodness, there's nothing wrong with me. Rather rude of you to suggest otherwise." I heard a familiar sound that I placed as a page in a book turning. For some unfathomable reason, in the lightless attic, Catherine was *reading*. Or at least acting like she was reading.

"Catherine," I said slowly, "Jonathan is dead. Ronan, too. We need to get out of this house right now. It could collapse."

"You go ahead, dear. I'm fine here."

I didn't know what to make of the situation. We were in a burning house. Smoke was filling the rafters. The Decaylings' lake hadn't extinguished the flames yet, and the fire department still hadn't arrived. Why was she so repulsively calm?

I shifted my hold on the hard metal object. Now I realized what it was. One of the copper paperweights that a publisher had commissioned for *Feast of Flowers'* tenth-anniversary printing, meant to look like an oversized tulip bulb. I'd been in high school when they'd arrived in the mail, and I'd laughed uncontrollably when my father had opened the package to reveal what looked like giant copper turds.

"Catherine—"

Rustling came from the shadows behind her. She let out a strangely girlish chuckle, then placed a finger to her lips and said to me, "Shh. I'm reading."

I couldn't see her face, only the outline of her hair pulled back in its clip, but she appeared perfectly at ease, slightly bored with the book in her lap, as though waiting for an author's speaking event to begin.

Prickles needled at me, warning me to get away from her. I took another step toward the window, hefting the paperweight behind my back.

Something rustled behind Catherine again, followed by a whisper. Who was she whispering *to*? Then the branches at the window shifted and let in a ray of gray light that struck the outline of a second person hunched behind Catherine, one hand on her shoulder, face pressed close to her ear.

I stumbled backward toward the sloped ceiling, clutching the copper paperweight like a shot put in front of me, ready to chuck it at whoever might rush me. My brain was both sluggish from smoke and jumpy from adrenaline, my muscles so oxygen depleted that I could barely stay vertical.

The other person's voice came more clearly as he whispered into Catherine's ear, "Doesn't that hole look nice, Catherine? Don't you want to jump through it like you were a child again? Splashing in puddles?"

Catherine stood automatically and gently set down the book she'd been holding on top of the box. I watched in horror, transfixed. After tucking in the loose strands of hair around her face, Catherine took a step toward the looming crater.

"Don't!" I yelled.

I threw my hands over my ears, which unfortunately meant having to let go of the paperweight. But I didn't dare allow myself to listen to Uncle Arnold's whispers. I'd seen how completely he had hypnotized Kylie, and now I was seeing it happen all over again. Catherine hadn't tried to hide in a burning building—Uncle Arnold had *commanded* her to. Just as effortlessly as he was ordering her to jump to her death. The idea of what his voice could do chilled me even more than watching the Decaylings' black fingernails rip into Ronan's flesh.

"Catherine, don't! You'll die!"

Catherine adjusted her coat collar and said something with the trace of a smile on her lips, though I couldn't hear it with my hands against my ears. I don't think anything I said could have broken the spell on her, anyway. She peered calmly down at the wreckage below, the fire lighting up her face in a burst of vermilion, revealing a dazed smile.

She took a small jump like a child splashing into a puddle. Except she plunged through the hole in the floor, crashing down three stories into the burning wreckage.

I pressed my hands flush against my ears as I cringed at the terrible sight. Uncle Arnold didn't move out of the shadows, but I knew exactly what he looked like, down to the swollen strain of his belly. I didn't need to see the bags under his eyes or the shiny buckles of his suspenders. I had drawn them. I'd *made* him.

I could faintly make out the movement of his lips in the darkness, but I shook my head fiercely from side to side, pressing my hands harder against my ears.

"I'm not listening!" I shouted.

He finally stepped out of the shadows. Diffused moonlight fell on his pockmarked face. His lips had stopped moving and were now curled in a self-satisfied smile that was somehow even worse. He slowly placed a finger to his lips and then pointed to himself as though promising to keep quiet. *Like I'd believe him.* Drawing a felt-tip pen out of his shirt pocket, he continued to close the distance between us, forcing me farther back into the sloped rafters. With boxes stacked high on either side of me, I was cornered.

Uncle Arnold held out his open palms to indicate he was no threat, then started writing on one of them. I cringed, whimpering slightly, but I'd lost the shotgun and he had a hundred pounds on me—it would be like trying to push over an elephant. He absently gnawed on a fat lip while he wrote, then extended his palm out with another one of his smiles.

I WON'T CHARM YOU.

God, I felt like crawling out of my skin. Smoke billowed up the attic stairs and the crater in the floor, catching in the sloped ceiling, filling it fast. The house shook as another beam downstairs collapsed, sending up a spray of sparks. At last, I heard the wail of a fire engine somewhere close by. Relief shook my body. The fire department wasn't my ally, but I'd been conditioned to trust the sound of their trucks. At the least, they might prove a distraction so I could get out.

Uncle Arnold looked toward the window sharply, annoyed. He whipped out a handkerchief and wiped his brow, then started writing faster on his other palm, spooked by the sirens.

Brandishing a quick grin, he flashed me his hand again.

I'LL JUST MURDER YOU.

Suddenly, it didn't matter that he was nearly twice my size—so much adrenaline flooded me once I saw those words that I prepared myself to hurl every nasty thing I had in me at him. *Claw his eyes. Knee him in the balls.* As the foul man watched my face twist with a feral survival instinct, his smile spanned cheek to cheek.

I threw myself at him, fingernails aimed for his eyes.

But the second my hands were away from my ears, he breathed out words.

It happened so fast. It was too late to turn back time, fix my mistake, see the trick.

"You don't want to hurt me." His lips moved in fast-forward, tongue flicking between his teeth. "You adore me. You want me safe."

I knew what he was doing. Of course I did. But he'd been waiting for his chance, knowing exactly what to say, words well-practiced on countless other victims. I felt myself shifting into two different people. One of me was completely aware of everything that was happening and that I was being manipulated; the other was utterly enraptured by his voice. The latter was far stronger, no matter how the former internally screamed and fought.

The boar of a man watched me apprehensively, as though he wasn't sure his voice would work on his creator. When he saw my hands settle slack at my sides, he beamed in triumph, gluttonous gaze raking over my petrified body.

He took his time now, speaking his words with drawn-out relish, though he spared one annoyed look out the window at the sirens. "Doll, I've been waiting a long time to meet you."

As the wail of fire trucks grew louder—they must be in the driveway now—I felt an unsteady tremor like the beginning of an earthquake. The floorboards at the end of the attic buckled. Nails popped, shooting outward. The floor had already partially collapsed, and now the rest was on the verge of going, too.

Our eyes met, both of us aware and terrified of what was happening.

A joist cracked loudly.

The attic floor broke in two, spreading from the crater into the shadows. Boards splintered. More boxes fell into the wreckage below. The portion of the attic between Uncle Arnold and me broke into a chasm, separating us by several feet. Too far for me to jump across, and, given his general condition, even more impossible for him to cross. Flames licked up between us.

Wide-eyed, he shouted a command to me, but I couldn't hear it over the crashing wreckage. The part of me that was bound to him felt stupefied, which gave way for the cognizant part of me to take control.

He only commanded me not to hurt him—not to stay in the house.

Our eyes met, and I saw the same realization reflected in his eyes. The sirens howled relentlessly outside. He tried yelling again, but his voice was lost. His spell wouldn't work if I couldn't hear him. Scowling deeply, Uncle Arnold attempted to pick his way over boxes and unstable portions of the floor, trying to find a way across.

I dropped to my knees, hunting the floor until I found the tulip bulb paperweight. Then, pushing to my feet, one hand pressing my shirt collar over my nose against the smoke, I smashed the paperweight against the attic window with all my remaining strength.

It shattered, glass falling outward. I hit the glass again and again until I had cleared out as many shards as I could. Smoke was as primed to escape the window as I was. It billowed around me as I thrust my hands and arms through, trying to avoid jagged edges. Glancing back once, I saw Uncle Arnold attempting to drag a bookshelf to use as a bridge, but not making much progress.

The window frame was barely wide enough to wriggle through, even when I contorted my shoulders. Rain fell steadily outside. No longer light mist but proper, drenching rain. The pine branches swayed their boughs, offering me a lifeline. I wriggled until I was halfway through the window and reached out to the closest branch. Stretching my fingers in the rain, I managed to graze the needles. *So close.* I tried again, getting a better hold this time. Behind me, another joist cracked. The entire house shook as one more section of the attic floor crashed down.

As I shimmied farther through the window, wincing when a piece of glass cut my side, a bare foot slammed down over my wrist, pinning my arm to the roof shingles.

I cried out weakly, too spent to scream. A naked man peered down at me with entirely black eyes—the whole orbs dark pools of ink. I blinked up in petrified fear through the rain. *Kestrel.* His nudity was the least alarming thing about him. He was exactly as I'd drawn him. Wiry-strong, those black eyes, small red welts covering his skin like bug bites or a rash everywhere his feathers had been before his transformation.

I tried to wrench my wrist out from under Kestrel's foot. My back half was still in the attic, feet kicking helplessly, nothing to use as leverage. But he crouched with superhuman speed, moving in strange jerking motions like a bird.

This is when he twists my neck. I curled in on myself, burying my face in my arm, shaking from fear. But at the sound of a *whoosh*, I looked up. Feathers sprang from his skin like switchblades, rippling out of his pores with the same sound as falling domino lines, and in a second there was no longer a man before me but a person-sized raptor with the same black orbs for eyes.

With a hop, he landed on my shoulders, his weight pushing the air from my lungs. I screamed as his talons curled into my upper arms, digging painfully into the flesh. Hopping again, pulling me with him this time like a dangling rabbit, he dragged me roughly to the edge of the roof.

"No, no, no . . ."

He fell off the end of the roof—or rather, flew. There was a terrifying second when I was weightless, nothing beneath me, the roof shingles falling away beneath my body. The forest spanned around us all the way to the sea, rain blurring the treetops into swaying phthalo triangles. This was the point in a horror movie where things couldn't possibly get worse, until of course, they do.

Kestrel released his hold on my arms.

Screaming, I fell, with the terrible sensation that the forest was more rising upward than I was plunging downward. Pine boughs whipped my body. Branches tenderized my flesh. The forest was violent and vindictive, tauntingly stoic as it beat me bloody with every falling foot. An ugly cry rose in me as I kicked and thrashed back at the rising trees. But the forest was cruel. A bough the size of my thigh caught me, springy like a trampoline, only to throw me bodily into the unforgiving solidity of a nearby trunk. My head cracked against wood. My vision starburst. Flashes of light came followed by an intense surge of pain, then nothing but a dizzying blur.

CHAPTER THIRTY-EIGHT

It took the weight of all three of them—man, woman, beast—to heave open the wooden door into the Robber Saints' library. Shelves rose twenty feet high. Rows stretched into eternity. Thousands of brown glass bottles lined the shelves, each carefully labeled. The Hellhound put her nose to the stone floor and led them through the stacks to a single leather folio open on a table.

The Harbinger opened the cover, and they beheld the slip of paper inside. His voice rang with reverence as he read the location written in small, precise letters on the map, circling the shape of a bay with his fingertip.

—From "Beasts of Sun" in
Bedtime Stories for Monsters

PINE NEEDLES.

A wet patch of moss.

Dripping rain.

Trees had battered every part of my body. Wet clothes leached away body heat, leaving me a shivering husk. My throat burned from smoke inhalation. I don't know how long I lay on the forest floor in a comatose-like state, stranded somewhere between the house and the cliffs, consciousness and oblivion.

Eventually, my dazed thoughts came together, and I cracked open my eyes, blinking into the rain to find myself tented by a pine-bough dome.

My skull throbbed with the worst pain I'd ever experienced.

I slowly sat up, wincing at a million aches and pains, and tilted my head toward the night sky. Previous events came crashing back, intertwined with memories of smoke, twisted necks, brackish water, Kylie on the stairs, Ronan's screams, that lusciously insidious *voice*. I shuddered to think of what might have happened if I hadn't made it out the attic window. Pain was one way to break Uncle Arnold's hypnotism, and the trees had succeeded in beating the spell out of me.

After wiping my eyes of the lingering film of smoke, an orange blaze beyond the trees slowly came into focus, and I was able to get my bearings. I was in the woods behind my father's property, maybe a hundred feet beyond the fence. The crash of nearby waves was stronger here, so I had to be close to Cliffside Drive. Artificial red lights from fire engines ricocheted through the trees in steady pulses. I could make out the distant shouting of firefighters.

I closed my eyes as a fresh wave of pain gripped me. *Everything, gone.* Even if they saved most of the house's structure, every last morsel of my father's legacy inside would be ruined by fire, smoke, water.

Distant headlights flashed through the trees as a car must have passed along Cliffside Drive. Jonathan's car was parked at the overlook, though, without a key, I was out of luck. I didn't dare go back for my own car and get pounced on by the police. I briefly considered waving down a car, putting as much distance as possible between myself and Lundie Bay. *Except that I can't.*

The Robber Saints still had Kylie.

I pushed to my feet as in a dream, stumbling over the uneven ground toward the blaze like a moth to flame. My only hope was to find Rafe and strike a bargain to get her back, or look for her myself.

I was out of ideas, and energy. Rafe said they were taking her somewhere close—I hadn't believed him before, which had been a mistake. Pain throbbed in every movement, but it felt distant. Adrenaline was dulling my senses, and I was grateful for it. The only thing that felt real—too real—was the trees. Fat raindrops fell on me like shrapnel, making me wince. My shaking fingers pushed against the rough trunks, steadying myself as I made my wobbly way forward.

A howl cut through the night, stilling my steps.

It was too guttural for a dog or a coyote, and wolves hadn't roamed these woods for a long time. Throwing a glance behind me, I saw low branches swaying about fifty feet away in a pattern that was too consistent to be caused by the wind. Something large was moving on the ground toward my direction, and all I could think of was that howl—*the Hellhound?*

I hobbled faster. Pain shot through my nerves with every step. My ribs ached in a way that told me if they weren't broken, they were at least bruised. Whiplike cuts crisscrossed the exposed skin on my forearms, and I ventured a guess that bruises in the same pattern would soon bloom beneath my clothes. *The mark of the trees.* They might as well have branded me.

Limping, I pushed through brambles that snagged my jeans and jacket, catching bits of skin underneath. The howl came again, and I twisted my head around to scan the forest.

Not looking where I was going, my next step didn't land on pine needles. Before my thoughts caught up with me, I was suddenly off-balance. Plunging downward. *Falling.*

It wasn't a terrifying plunge this time. Instead, I immediately slammed into freshly churned dirt that smashed my cheek and worked its way into my mouth. Spitting, I sat up, disoriented, wiping my face to find dirt walls surrounding me.

I'd fallen into a hole.

It was probably six feet deep and not quite as wide; the size of a small closet. My fractured brain moved sluggishly; still oxygen-deprived from smoke, it couldn't fathom why a man-made hole would be in the wilderness. I was too far from Rafe Kahn's property to have hit one of his mass graves . . . right?

Feeling the dirt walls with my hands, I noticed no indication of shovel marks. Instead, odd vertical lines cut into the earth on either side. As I ran my hand along to search for handholds to pull myself out, an object stuck in the soil came away in my fingers.

Though it was too dark to see any detail, I knew the unmistakable feel of a feather. Particularly *this* feather, which was easily over a foot long with a strange tacky substance at the end. I sniffed it and recoiled.

I'd smelled that same scent on Kestrel only moments ago.

My heart walloped. My feet took me backward only to find another dirt wall immediately at my back. My imagination played out like one of Rob's horror movies: I could see a monstrous figure waking here in the earth, stirring, then the clap of panic as dirt filled their eyes and mouth, the frenetic fight to claw to freedom, to air.

A beam of light cut into the darkness, blinding me. I shielded my eyes with my forearm. *A flashlight.* Whoever was holding it shone it steadily on me as they carefully skirted the edge of the hole.

"Haven? Haven!"

Squinting into the radiant light, I made out the outline of Detective Rice's short hair and dangling police badge.

My body unwound with the sheer relief of a human being finding me instead of something otherworldly, though I knew that this woman was just as dangerous. I tilted my face upward, still shielding my eyes against the flashlight. "You've got to get out of these woods, Rice. It isn't safe. Jonathan, Catherine, Ronan—everyone's dead!"

The steady beam of light continued to blind me. Did she already know? She'd probably found Jonathan's body in the front yard; the firefighters would only discover Ronan's and Catherine's corpses when they started picking through the smoldering wreckage.

She crouched at the hole's rim and said in the calm certainty that only a professional law enforcement officer could manage, "No, not everyone. There's an entire town out there, and beyond."

My hands shook as I shoved my hair off my face with dirty fingers. "I'm *in a hole*! What else can I do? I burned the manuscript. I shot at them. They're monsters, they can't be reasoned with. I can't *control* them."

Detective Rice finally moved the flashlight beam out of my face. Once my vision adjusted, I noted the determined cut of her jaw. It chilled me, that look. Even Catherine had taken some degree of pity on me and admitted that I hadn't entirely been at fault. But not Rice. She wasn't going to spare me an ounce of sympathy.

"I don't read a lot of books," she said, "but I know self-sacrifice is a powerful fucking plot twist."

My hands fell away from my face like deadweights. "What are you saying?"

"What's done is done, but I can't let you create more of them, Haven. Either you end it or I will." She rooted around in her pants pockets and then tossed something into the hole. I crouched to find it in the dirt, coming away with a pocketknife.

"*End* it?" I was at a rare loss for words. This wasn't fiction. This wasn't one of Rob's titillating movies. In serial killer thrillers, there was always some noble bystander who sacrificed themselves to save the cheerleader or a mother who held off a zombie horde to buy time for her children to escape. But I wasn't noble. I wasn't loving. I was barely even a person at all—I was just two words written beneath a drawing.

There was a certain power in that, though, being disconnected from what people expected.

Stalemate hung in the air between us, neither willing to voice the terrible choice she'd given me. The silence was only broken when someone called her name. Frowning, her spine straightened, and she twisted in the direction of the house.

Straining on my tiptoes, jumping for height, I could barely make out a uniformed officer picking his way through the woods toward us. Rice glanced down at me with fire in her eyes. As she faced the man, a mask of professionalism slipped over her features.

"Everything's fine here, Cooper."

As soon as she squared her body to the approaching officer, he drew his pistol and fired a bullet directly between her eyes. *Bam.* I stopped trying to jump. He then turned his pistol on himself. *Bam.*

The sound of twin gunshots reverberated in the trees. My knees gave out and I crumpled to the hole's floor, hugging my hands over my head as my mind grasped at straws. From the corner of my eye, I saw Detective Rice sink to her knees at the edge of the hole, blood pouring down her face. Her body wavered in unreliable balance for a half second before tipping precariously in my direction.

"Oh, fuck . . ." I scrambled back as she pitched headfirst into the hole, slamming into the dirt floor. The other officer's body was a few seconds delayed in falling, slumping first to the ground by the edge of the hole. I watched in dread as soil crumbled away and his body, too, slid inch by inch over the side, falling like a deadweight beside Detective Rice.

A set of glassy eyes stared at me, but not for long. Blood pouring from Detective Rice's head wound soon filled the hollows of her eyes, spilling over her temples like she was wearing a blindfold. The other officer was facedown, blood pooling in the dirt beneath the place where his mouth should have been.

I pushed myself as far back as I could, pressing into the crumbling dirt as it rained down on either side of me. My fingers clawed against the walls, leaving fresh vertical scores atop Kestrel's weeks-old ones.

Alone. In the woods. Two dead police officers.

My mind was a brick wall refusing to budge. It wasn't until I heard the crunch of leaves aboveground and saw a shadowed form bend down to pick up the dropped flashlight that it even occurred to me to wonder why a fellow officer would so flagrantly shoot Detective Rice and then kill himself.

People acting unlike themselves.

Uncle Arnold's head appeared over the edge of the hole. He shone the light on me like a spotlight—I the actor, he giving direction.

"There you are, doll. Now, where were we?"

CHAPTER THIRTY-NINE

The moon's soft glow was such a beautiful gift to the night that Pinchy felt compelled to honor it. Though none of his species had ever sung, he raised his small mouth to the sky and summoned a rasping warble. It wasn't lovely or on key, but he knew in his heart that the moon had heard and accepted his song.

—From "Extremities" in
Bedtime Stories for Monsters

"*I* BROUGHT YOU here, you know," Uncle Arnold said proudly as he adjusted himself into a seated position at the top of the hole, feet dangling down like a little boy on a fishing dock who was settling in for a day of lazy pleasure. "To Lundie Bay, I mean."

He cocked his head sharply as though an idea just struck him. "Are you listening? *Listen.* No hands over your ears this time, naughty girl."

I had already started to raise my hands, but now they sank back down. He grinned in satisfaction, wiggling to get more comfortable before he continued.

"The Harbinger came up with the idea to use my voice on your father—this was, oh, way back in that dark time when we were rattling around that house as mere apparitions." He wiggled his stumpy fingers in mockery of a ghost, the gesture all the more horrific because of its truth. "I couldn't compel him without a physical form, but I could *whisper*. I made the old man think he was hearing things, losing his mind faster than he actually was. I used to hiss at three a.m., make him wake in a cold sweat. Pretend to be his own father, back from the dead, whenever he ventured into the woods. The Harbinger thought it would lull Amory into a weaker state where his urge to draw would take over and bring us into this world sooner." He turned his hands palm-up in a helpless gesture. "But that housekeeper killed him before we could get there. Ah, well. Didn't matter. His death brought us *you*."

I listened in rapture, basking in the melody of his voice.

No. Fight it. Don't listen.

But he wants me to listen. I can't not listen.

Uncle Arnold dug in his pocket and came out with a set of keys that he dangled in the air. He pressed his chin in the direction of Cliffside Drive. "The Tybees left their car on the other side of these trees, and Catherine was kind enough to give me the keys when I asked. You and me, doll, we're going to rewrite this world. The two of us have unique talents that set us apart from all those dim-witted muttonheads out there. We can go far if we work together. And we *will* work together. I won't have to sell a single encyclopedia in this world. Far from it. We'll write a whole fucking encyclopedia in the bodies of anyone who looks down on us."

He stuffed his keys in his pocket and snapped his fingers like he was scolding a puppy. "Now, get yourself out of there. Can't do much stuck in a hole."

I was overcome with the consuming urge to escape the pit but, practically, I didn't know how.

When I started desperately patting the wall, he sighed in exasperation. "Use your imagination."

A shudder ran through me as I realized that there *was* one way out.

Cringing with disgust, I stuffed the knife in my pocket, then moved to the anonymous police officer's body. I had no idea who he was; I'd never seen him before tonight. But now I found myself dropping to my knees, thrusting my shoulder against his cadaver and rolling him to a seated position at the base of the hole. There was no way to avoid seeing his face, or, rather, lack of face. He'd shot himself through the mouth, blowing off the back of his skull but taking a good portion of the front with it. Averting my eyes, I dragged Rice's body by the legs and positioned her to sit next to him. I rolled her over so that her torso was on top of his head, the grisliest ladder.

Uncle Arnold didn't offer a hand down to help. He dug a cigar and matchbox out of his pocket and watched as I attempted to climb up the pile of cadavers and desecrated them with my muddy boots, digging my hands into their hair for grip. With one foot on Rice's head, I was able to shove off and grab for the edge of the hole, hearing her neck snap with a sickening crack, then I wriggled onto my belly. From there, I dragged myself the rest of the way out of the hole until I could roll over on my back, staring unfocused at the swaying trees overhead.

Uncle Arnold took a puff of his cigar and chuckled, "Good girl. And remember, you don't want to hurt me."

There was no avoiding his compulsion. This man had driven my father to unnaturally early madness; what would he do with me?

His eyes shifted to something in the trees behind us, and his face soured.

I felt another presence nearby and spun onto my stomach, too weak to sit.

Rafe stood in the woods a half dozen paces away, backdropped by the still-raging inferno in the distance. For someone who had received a severe head wound and fallen through the floor into burning wreckage, he looked shockingly well. *Superhumanly well.*

His eyes fixed on Uncle Arnold, not me. "You weren't supposed to mess with her. That was part of the deal."

Irritation was clearly written on his face, but Uncle Arnold merely took a puff of his cigar, feigning indifference, and gave a tight shrug.

"Deals, Harbinger. Everything is *deals* with you. How much better it would all be if I could compel *you*. But there's barely a you in there, is there? If there was, maybe I'd have you jump off a bridge. No, too uninspired. I can come up with something better than that. Wait—give me a minute. . . ."

"She's mine," Rafe said evenly.

Uncle Arnold chuckled as he tapped the ash off his cigar. "Hey, doll, you don't belong to this blockhead, do you?"

I shook my head, though internally I was screaming.

Uncle Arnold shrugged again, though this time there was cold stiffness to his movement. "You heard the lady. Now, screw off."

But if anyone was a match for feigned indifference, it was Rafe. "No, I don't think I will."

He flicked his fingers, a gesture so fast and casual that I almost missed it. I had managed to push to a seated position, but only barely. Out of the corner of my eye, I detected a shadowy form sliding behind Rafe. From where he sat, Uncle Arnold hadn't yet taken notice of our company. The shape of this new addition was oddly round, not like a person, with two lines rising from the head area like antennae. As though I was watching a scene from one of Rob's movies play out on a television screen, a pale crustacean slowly appeared amid the pine boughs. I was taken aback to see Pinchy not only alive but *here*, in the woods as Malice House burned to ash in the distance. The creature's eight fleshy legs were both nimble and clumsy at the same time. His two claws lifted silently in the air, stretching open, black eyes gleaming, mouth agape.

I watched in sick fascination as Pinchy sidled up behind the encyclopedia salesman. He lunged at his prey before Uncle Arnold had time to register the crawling monstrosity. Uncle Arnold pivoted with a weak cry and, jumping to his feet and grabbing the dead officer's nearby gun, made an impressive attempt to shoot the beast.

Pinchy reared back, dodging the bullet, emitting a strange trilling sound that didn't belong in this world. Then he thrust a claw toward

Uncle Arnold low and fast, impressively agile. He snipped the large man's tendon cleanly through his sock. I saw flesh separate from bone. A gap between leg and foot where there shouldn't have been space.

The salesman gave a garbled scream, then wheeled on me, red-faced.

"Defend me!"

It was like electricity shot through my body. Unable to control my own actions, I reached into my rear pocket and pulled out Detective Rice's pocketknife. Flicking it open, I found myself pushing to my feet and limping over the uneven ground toward Pinchy.

The saltwater beast reared back, poised to strike Uncle Arnold again. The salesman clutched at his halfway-severed foot, wailing like a toddler. Though my muscles were entirely spent, I hurled myself against Pinchy's clammy shell, stabbing the knife blade at his carapace. At first, it only glanced off his exterior, but then I aimed for the more flexible whiteish area around his mandible, and this time it sank in.

Pinchy let out a terrible, wounded cry.

I faltered; the sane part of me felt a flicker of sympathy for the beast even though *I'd* once been the piece of flesh between his claws. But the hypnotized part of me was ruthlessly fixated on protecting Uncle Arnold, and I bunched my muscles, preparing to strike again.

"Goddamn it, snap out of it! Think for yourself!" Rafe dragged me away by the waist.

His strength was undeniable, but I had *that voice* on my side, empowering me to use every ounce of strength left in reserve. Rafe cursed and wrestled against my frenetic lashing out. Knife in my right hand, with my left, I managed to get ahold of one of Pinchy's thin crab-like limbs and held on with fierce determination. Uncle Arnold used the opportunity to stagger back upright, keeping his weight on his good foot. The other was still attached but barely; blood bathed his torn pant leg and boot. He took one dazed look at me clutching the beast, Rafe clutching me, and he grabbed a stick from amid the leaves.

Using it as a crutch, he limped off in a weak half-run toward Cliffside Drive. The increasing distance between us did nothing to lessen the compulsion; the same thought continued to assault my brain: *Defend him. Defend him.*

But fighting against Rafe was useless. It didn't take him long to loosen my grip on Pinchy's leg, pry my fingers away one at a time, and wrestle me to the ground, where he pinned my wrists overhead against the pine needles, his dark eyes boring into me.

In the distance, a car engine cranked to life.

"Leave it. It's no use, he got away. We have more urgent problems." Rafe's command was sharp, but it wasn't aimed at me. The crustacean had looked ready to chase after Uncle Arnold but now gave an uncertain snap of his claw, swiveling his monstrous head at Rafe before letting his abdomen slump and skittering off into the woods.

"Let me go, let me go, let me go."

I was a skipping record player struggling under Rafe's hold. His expression wrinkled in disgust until he glanced to the side, eyes snagging on something out of my line of vision.

"Know any way to snap her out of this? I'd rather not hurt her if I don't have to."

As though pulled by a wire, my head twisted toward the person he'd addressed, my back arched for a better view. The light was poor, but her face was clear enough as she picked her way across the underbrush, dressed in her gauzy black skirt with an oversized menswear shirt tucked into the band. She was middle-aged, dark locks falling nearly to her waist, no makeup. Though she wasn't pretty, her features dared you to find fault with them.

Unlike most other Malice characters, there was nothing monstrous-looking about the Witch of Went, though I knew from "Kaleidoscope" how vicious she could be with the men who dishonored her. I had no illusions that she would spare me because I was a woman.

She hitched up her skirt so she could squat next to me, tilting her head this way and then that as though appraising vegetables for a stew. I tried to look away, but Rafe grabbed my face by the jaw and pressed my cheek against the cold ground.

"Wake up, little *doll*," the witch said in a menacing whisper as she dug the pad of her index finger into my third eye.

Like being doused with a bucket of water, I snapped back to myself. My body was my own again—or it would be if Rafe didn't have me pinned. My hand slackened, letting the pocketknife fall. My whole body started shaking uncontrollably. Without meaning to, I burst into tears from the terrible violation of my mind. Rafe released his grip on my wrists, and I curled into a ball on the ground, sobbing in cathartic bursts, my body's means of purging Uncle Arnold's sticky malice.

The witch spared me no sympathetic glances, but Rafe rested a soothing hand on my back. In the distance, I heard a loud crack followed by several shouts—another one of the house's support beams breaking.

I didn't have to look up from the forest floor to know that Malice House was gone.

CHAPTER FORTY

There are some people who argue the world needs monsters to make heroes of humankind, but they don't argue that for long. Not once a tentacle eases itself around their throat.

—From the Introduction to
Bedtime Stories for Monsters

WHEN THE WAVE of catharsis abated and my mind was once more fully my own, my first act of free will was to smack Rafe's hand away from my back. "Don't touch me."

His eyes again flashed with a nocturnal-animal sheen. "That's a hell of a way to say thank you. Honestly, Haven, you have a hard time realizing who your friends are."

Despite his harsh tone, he pushed to his feet, granting me the requested space, and paced tightly while scanning the bruise-black forest with intensity. The witch climbed down into the hole to poke at the officers' bodies.

I rustled to my knees in the damp fallen leaves and regarded Rafe through eyelashes clumped with Rice's blood. "Looking for your pet? You told me he was dead."

He shrugged the accusation away. "I just told him to stay in the woods, out of trouble. And it's a damn good thing I did, isn't it?"

When after several moments there was still no sign of Pinchy, he made a *tsk* sound that pursed his mouth. "I think you hurt his feelings."

Delirious laughter threatened to rise up my gullet, but the urge soon died. "What about Uncle Arnold?"

"What about him?"

"He's a psychopath who could make a nun commit murder. And he's out there, completely free to manipulate whoever he wants."

And who he wants to manipulate most is me.

The rain now fell in drenching sheets again, though the tree cover gave us some protection. Combined with my already-soaked clothes and the chill barreling in from the ocean, I was ice to the bone.

Rafe paced a few feet away from where I sat, still giving me some space as he pulled up his flannel collar against the rain. The water formed rivers down his cheekbones and neck, disappearing into his shirt. "He and I had a deal, but it appears he decided to renege. Those who break a bargain with the Harbinger seal their own fate. He'll pay—just not today."

As bold as his words were, something less certain wavered in his eyes. He was bluffing. Worn down by the violence of the night, he couldn't hide his true face behind its usual mask of indifference. *Uncle Arnold scares him*, I realized. He had even said so aloud in "Beasts of Sun." And this was a man who kept monsters like household pets.

Rafe extended a hand down and said gruffly, "Now, come with me. We didn't enter a burning house to save you out of altruism."

The witch climbed the makeshift ramp of cadavers back out of the hole with nonchalance, brushing blood and brain matter off her hands like kitchen scraps. Bile rose in my stomach, burning my throat even more than the smoke. The Witch of Went had struck me as perfectly cogent in *Bedtime Stories*, but now I detected an unhinged glimmer resting dormant beneath the firm set of her mouth, prompting me to take an instinctive step away. Rafe started moving through the underbrush, and I had no choice but to follow with a bruised-body limp, the witch's presence at my heels sending tremors up my back. We skirted the wilderness side of the property fence in the direction of Rafe's house. The old metal birdfeeder materialized out of the darkness like a vestige of a nightmare, throwing me back into the past in sharp relief; I could see myself there in my mind's eye, dressed in my father's oversized rainboots, unearthing ghosts.

The fence's gaps allowed for staccato glimpses of my backyard, where the fire engine's lights painted the remnants of the house red, then red again, then red again. The firefighters were around the front of the house, but we could hear their shouts and the deafening roar of hoses. It felt like it must be someone else's house; it couldn't possibly be mine. Not *my* entire life going up in flames.

At the fence corner, Rafe continued straight into the narrow strip of woods that separated our properties. This time, the trees obeyed logic, remaining firmly planted. The lights in his windows didn't disappear only to reappear at my rear. My feet crunched predictably over the path I intended, though my head was still swimming, rendered punch-drunk by smoke inhalation and trauma. I wouldn't have been surprised if with the next step I was back in Lundie Bay Books, or my Chelsea apartment, or my childhood bedroom in Maine. We left behind the corybantic strobe lights and at last reached the sentinel line of Leyland cypresses bordering Rafe's backyard, a tidy division between wilderness and his manicured back patio.

Rafe pressed on toward his back door, but the witch stopped at the cypresses as abruptly as though an invisible string held her back. She said simply, "Harbinger."

Rafe made a turnabout, his forehead a map of wrinkles. Her stance indicated she had no intention of continuing.

The woman curled her fingers around a strap that crossed her chest and said in flat, emotionless words, "I go no farther. We came together to find a way out of our world and into this one; you led that effort, and in return, I helped you save this woman. Our bargain is fulfilled."

Rafe squared his shoulders to her, considering her long and hard, and I recalled their complicated history; their first meeting in the forest outside Went, finding each other again at the Night Market, the erstwhile romance, then her decision to join his quest. My father's manuscript painted Malice as a harsh land, but these two had found something as akin to friendship as possible there. Judging by the haze that filled his eyes, I thought there was a moment where Rafe was going to ask her to stay, but then he shifted his stance, shoulders rolling back, perhaps reading both the independence and touch of madness in her eyes, and simply asked, "Where will you go?"

"Wherever I want. This is a vast world, and no pencil commands my steps now." She again adjusted the strap across her chest, as though it held a heavy weight, but whatever it was remained unseen behind her. "You have a new name here. So shall I claim one. I've decided to go by Dahlia, after the old housekeeper. *She* doesn't need it anymore."

Dahlia. Did it have to be that name, of all names? The witch's eyes snapped to me as though I'd grumbled the thought aloud, and for a second, I feared I had. I bowed under the ferocity of her gaze and my body hardened, prepared to face her witchcraft, but she only tugged the strap across her chest and over her head, adjusted her oversized shirt back around her waist, and then extended a bag in my direction.

My bag. It was my canvas bag with my art supplies and sketchbook, which I had assumed was destroyed in the house fire like everything else. My spine went straight to see it. As though drawn by my own invisible string, I limped to where she stood at the edge of the woods, palms itching to caress the rough fabric.

She dangled the bag over my waiting hands, letting it hover like an offering.

"Your paints," she said as her mariner-gray-blue eyes seared into me. "Your paintbrushes. Your sketchbook. I saved them from the fire because wherever you go from here, you'll need them." Finally, she lowered the bag into my waiting hands but did not yet release the strap. "Take care with your talent, Haven. Women like us must be vigilant. Don't make the same mistakes your father did." Her eyes danced over to Rafe with a touch of mystery. "He gave the Harbinger the worst thing any writer can give a man."

"What's that?" My words were barely audible through my cracked lips.

"Desire."

She relinquished my bag, letting it sag into my waiting arms, and I found myself hugging it to my chest like a mother clutching a newborn. The fabric reeked of smoke but was undamaged. My brushes and tubes of paint rattled against one another inside. It was heavier than I'd expected, and I felt the shape of my laptop inside as well. The corner of the sketchbook dug into my chest just beneath my ribs, as though it was trying to find a way to crawl back inside my body, be one with me again.

The Witch of Went left without any further words of goodbye, simply striding into the forest until we could no longer hear her footsteps or smell the earthy crush of mushrooms.

Behind me, Rafe stroked his chin, making a small grunt in his throat. "I pity the men who cross her."

I faced him, still hugging my bag tightly. "Don't they deserve what she does to them?"

My father had written her to be nearly uncontrollably bent on violence, and so she was. Frankly, it was what I had loved most about "Kaleidoscope." Her unabashed, unapologetic feminine rage. It made her a sympathetic character, so long as *I* wasn't the one tied down to her table.

Rafe gave a more ambivalent wag of his head. "Her initial victims, yes. But after a while, her rage engulfed her, made her see almost everyone as a perpetrator. There's a point where the victim becomes the victimizer—and that's the added tragedy."

I thought of Orion, who certainly hadn't struck me as an evildoer—his worst sin maybe being an uninspired taste in fiction. His only crime had been finding himself in the wrong place at the wrong time, an easy mark for the witch's ungovernable wrath.

I spared one more look at the inferno still blazing through the trees, and when I wrenched myself away from the sight found Rafe holding open his back door.

It was only once we were inside, door firmly closed against nature, surrounded by the reassuring symmetrical lines and crisp angles of his home, that my muddled thoughts began to clear, giving way for my broken body to surrender to the tremors that could only come with a moment of safety—safety however illusory whenever the Harbinger was involved.

"Sit." Rafe jerked his index finger at one of the barstools while he took a bottle of water out of the fridge, which he slid to me across the kitchen island. I set my canvas bag on the counter, a few brushes and pencils rolling out, which I corralled with my arms.

After a long drink of water that felt heavenly on my raw throat, I wiped my mouth. My eyes shifted to the back hallway, then the windows. Rafe had said that the Robber Saints would keep Kylie close; it would make sense if it was somewhere on his property.

I craned my head to him. "So, where is she?"

He propped an arm against the counter and leaned his weight on it casually, as though we had all the time in the world. "I could tell you, and I could even get her back. The Robber Saints owe me for bringing them to this world filled with more stories than they ever imagined. But that isn't how any of this works. If you want her, I want something in return." He picked up a thick angled brush, running the soft bristles against his thumb. "I wasn't lying when I said you were talented, Haven."

He extended the brush in my direction, and I snatched it only to throw it to the floor, where it clattered and rolled beneath the island. "I'm not drawing anything for you, if that's what you're thinking. No more monsters. No more of your friends or pets. I'll go the rest of my life without picking up a paintbrush if I have to."

Rafe didn't seem troubled by my determined little speech. "Are you so certain you can control yourself?"

I swallowed, already aware of the preternatural itch blooming on my palms to pick up a pencil and start drawing. My father had believed he'd found a way to avoid the curse, using what he called "averted writing" to satisfy the urge without manifesting precisely what the curse wanted—but *still* the curse had won in the end. It looked for opportunities—altered states of mind like exhaustion, mental confusion, intoxication—to force an artist's hand. How was I going to traverse my entire life clear-headed? *Impossible.* There would be inevitable moments of weakness. The curse knew it. So did Rafe.

He rested his forearms on the counter, inclining his body toward me. "You and I see the force that brought us here differently. To you, it's a curse. To me, a blessing. The truth is, Haven, even though you're no more human than I am, you've had the good fortune to spend your entire life in the real world. You've never experienced what it feels like to exist between planes, bookmarked in your own story, caught somewhere between a fictional world and a real one, barely able to push over a picture frame or snack on toast from our side. Always waiting for someone to *pick you up* and read your tale. The world Amory created, Malice, isn't any place to make a life. There are edges to our world like the sharp precipice at the end of a piece of paper. Imagine if your entire existence was confined to one book. You never met anyone but those characters, never traveled anywhere but within the borders of the map printed in the front matter. Even an exceptional writer like Amory can only build a pale reproduction of the real world. That's all fiction is: an imitation."

"And?" I challenged. "You aren't there anymore. Congratulations. You made it to the real world—and so did all your cruel companions, at liberty to terrorize regular people, if not outright slaughter them."

His eyes simmered enticingly to hear the cold sarcasm in my voice; I think he relished my anger. As he straightened, a smirk teased back the corners of his mouth. "Tell me this, if 'regular people' are so innocent, then why do they pay so dearly for your recaps? Why are 'regular people' unable to stomach horror movies but are still desperate to know what happens in them? It's because *everyone* needs that darkness, Haven. Even the ones who can't bear to face it still crave it; maybe them most of all. Everyone has a beast inside them that needs to be fed."

I thought of the Ink Drinkers, so certain they were concerned citizens risking their lives to save Lundie Bay, yet to me they'd been murderers. It was like my father said: *Feed the beast a few bites here and there and it won't demand a feast.*

"It's human nature," Rafe continued. "If 'regular people' don't have monsters, then *they'll* become monstrous. People need a rallying point, and nothing brings them together more than facing off against a common enemy. What's more of a common enemy than a monster? A real, true monster? So, am I crazy to think it's better to have an oversized lobster who pinches off a few feet than nuclear war? A corpse or two instead of global pestilence?"

As much as I wanted to dismiss Rafe's argument—and there were ample counterpoints, like that monsters didn't preclude those other things—the core of his message lodged in my mind, not only because my father had made a similar point, but because Rob had as well.

He'd found me on a message board about seven years ago. I'd picked up a burned DVD from a give-away box outside a used bookstore. It had contained the most gruesome slasher film I'd ever seen, but as vile as it was, it didn't affect me. I ended up down an internet rabbit hole on a message board talking about how the movie wasn't scary, and Rob saw my post and asked if I'd want to write recaps of niche films for his dark-web site. He claimed there was a small but rabid underground market for it. Frankly, I thought it sounded asinine.

I asked why anyone would pay for that. He wrote back a whole thesis about how horror movie recapping was a public good and that it's only through brushing against the dark world that we truly feel safe.

"I won't make monsters for you," I said.

Rafe dragged his head back and forth. "That isn't what I want. That's never been what I want. I didn't pull out my own spleen, let the Decaylings nearly drown me in Fathom Lake, risk my life to break into the Saints' library because I wanted *more monsters.*"

My eyes darted briefly to him in confusion. *Those were all hurdles on his quest to find the Salem Dreamer.*

Slowly, the jagged-edge pieces of this invisible puzzle began to snap together, forming a final picture that didn't match the image on the box.

His eyes bored into me. "I want *you,* Haven."

CHAPTER FORTY-ONE

This world no longer cares about the fears of an old man. Loss of bodily functions, loss of memory. Physical pain. Exploitative relatives and abusive caregivers. Attractive women who once called gray hair distinguished and now treat me like someone's dopey grandfather.

But I'm humoring myself to think the world ever cared about an old man's fears. The truth is, it never gave a damn about anyone's.

—From the Introduction to
Bedtime Stories for Monsters

THE SALEM DREAMER never appeared on the pages of *Bedtime Stories*. It was always only offhand mentions of what the Harbinger sought on his journey across Malice. For that reason, I had never attempted to draw him, had never spared him much thought at all. I'd spent all my energy giving form to the gruesome characters who made up the eight short stories within the manuscript instead. Now, every mention of the Dreamer in the manuscript came rushing back to me, circling like sharks around the same clue: *The one who can bring order to the chaos.*

Not him, I realized. *The Salem Dreamer was never a* him.

Blood rushed in my ears as I understood the gravity of my over-sight. A terrible chill numbed me from the tips of my wet shoes up over my clammy calves and dipping into my inner thighs as Rafe stalked slowly around the kitchen counter, shadows from the pendant lamps cloaking his eyes.

"I wanted out of Malice," he explained. "As much as any of us had free will there, that's what I most desired. But we were never truly in control of ourselves so long as we were bound to those pages. Your father wrote me to seek the Salem Dreamer, and so I did. I sought the Dreamer through countless hardships all the way to the Robber Saints' library, where their maps finally told me where I could find her."

The final pages of his story returned to me. He'd found the map and circled the location with his finger. *A bay. It had been a bay.*

His eyes gripped mine in their unforgiving fist.

It had been *this* bay.

Pressing my hands flat on the counter to root myself to some-thing solid, I said slowly, "When my father wrote that manuscript, he couldn't have known that I would draw your portrait. He couldn't have meant the Dreamer was *me*."

"It doesn't matter. The story took on a mind of its own, found its own conclusion. I sought someone to bring order to chaos, and don't you see? That's exactly what you did. You took us out of that hell where our lives weren't our own and brought us here—where reality doesn't shift or change, where not everyone is fighting tooth and nail for themselves, where we can determine our own fates. What is that if not order?"

I knew my origin made me something other than human, but what Rafe was saying made me something else entirely: a creature tied to Malice. Truly one of them in every sense.

"I've sought nothing but you," he said, still moving around the counter with a predator's keen step. "And now that I found you, did you really think I'd let you go?"

My body and mind wanted to surrender to all the pain I'd put it through, shut down and give in. I picked up a pencil and pressed the sharp point against my jeans beneath the counter to force myself to stay present.

"Finding the Salem Dreamer was a plotline," I said in a hollow voice. "And you did it. You found me—you and Uncle Arnold and the Witch of Went—and brought everyone here. So your quest is finished. In turn, if what you're saying is true, and I needed to fill the role of the Salem Dreamer, then I did it, too. I brought you all out of the whims of Malice into a stable reality. We've enacted the roles the curse forced us to fulfill. So, you don't need me anymore. We can go our separate ways."

His pitying look made me realize that even after everything, I was still naive when it came to the ways of monsters.

Quietly, he said, "Darling, maybe *I* want you, too." He leaned on the counter, capturing my gaze. "Not the Harbinger, but whatever I am now."

I swallowed, reeling slightly, the pencil going slack in my fist.

He was still at the far end of the counter, too far away to stab him, not that I was under any illusion that a sharpened pencil would do damage where a golf club hadn't. He reached out to toy with the strap of my canvas bag. "I think it's what you want, too," he added quietly, not meeting my gaze. "You may hate me, but you also love me. You can't help it."

I designed him to be my ideal man, I thought. *Someone I couldn't help but love.*

That included having him be the type of man to love me in return. It was an awful twist of fate, but as much as my distrust of Rafe went to my soul's core, I also saw qualities in him that weren't so easy to walk away from. *His sarcasm. His secrets. The knife's edge touch of danger.*

"Don't you want answers?" he asked in a voice bordering on a whisper. "Don't you want to understand the forces that created the both of us? You can't hide your true self from me, Haven. You're a seeker, a wanderer, just like I am. For all either of us know, there might be others who can do what you can, and who's to say what aberrations *their* pencils have brought forth. Our brethren could be just in the next town over. . . ."

My eyes fell closed, head shaking involuntarily. But as much as I wanted to deny it, I *had* been curious about the Acosta family, especially Martim and Della. If "Sanctuary" was to be believed, they could cursework just like my father and me. But I'd been so distracted by the discovery in the basement and the attack on the house that I hadn't yet considered the possibility that there could be other monsters out there, summoned by other artists and writers.

I brought my hands up to cover my face as a barrier between myself and the world.

Rafe moved closer as he said, "No one wants to be alone, Haven. Everyone seeks out like-minded individuals. Those who share a similar past. It's all part of understanding the curse. We both have different pieces of the puzzle. You've uncovered clues in your research. I, too, have gathered information from watching the old man work. If we bring our knowledge together, we have a chance of understanding this."

My fingers slid down my face, stopping just below my eyes. I muttered into the bowl of my hands, "But I want to end the curse, and knowing you, you want to use it." I let my hands fall back into my lap. "Manipulate it to work your little deals."

He waved off my concern as insignificant. "Our ends don't matter in the here and now, that's why they're called *ends*. We're at the *beginning* of all of this." His cheek tugged in a brief smirk as he lifted a hand in the direction of my property. "Besides, if it isn't obvious already, you have nothing. Your home is burning along with everything you own. You have no money, no resources. *I* can help you. The former Rafe Kahn was considerate enough to leave a notebook full of his passwords next to his computer. Bank accounts and credit cards are immensely useful; I assure you his funds are substantial. And nothing buys answers like money. We can go to Portugal to find your relatives, to specialty libraries around the world. Anything you want."

My gaze shifted to his small kitchen window, where, beyond, the night was unnaturally orange, the flames from my house an artificial sunrise. Somewhere, Kylie was out there, and I doubted she cared much about our moral debate.

Rafe straightened, tapping an impatient finger on the counter. "Let me also remind you that Uncle Arnold is out there and *will* come looking for you. He wants to use you in far more heinous ways than I do. And there are other dangers. Try as you might to avoid the curse, one day you'll slip up. You'll drink too much wine or be sleep-deprived, and before you know it, you'll find a pencil in your hand and a finished sketch and story on your desk. You'll want me close, then."

Rafe Kahn was a spiderweb I'd unknowingly stepped into head-first and now I couldn't fully separate myself from. And if I was being honest, maybe a part of me liked to be tangled up.

I squeezed my hands together beneath the counter, ignoring the insidious itch spreading over my skin to pick up one of the pencils that had spilled out of my bag.

Slowly, testingly, I let my hand fall over the closest pencil. Pleasure rippled through my hand, up my arm, to the base of my skull like the relief of a warm bath after a long day.

A writer is compelled to shape stories, my father had written. *An artist compelled to build images. The curse knows this.*

I shook my head. "You aren't giving me a choice. If I say no, you'll tie me up, stuff me in the pantry with the peanut butter."

"I wouldn't." His eyes traced over my face as his hand fell on the counter an inch from my own. A silent invitation. All I'd have to do was extend a finger to accept.

"I've never tried to stop you from doing what you want."

But he was dangling Kylie's life over me, which was almost as devious as restraining me. He wielded deals to get what he wanted, controlling me as certainly as if I'd been in handcuffs.

Baker had tried to shackle me, too.

We stared at each other across the single barstool that separated us. His cavernous house had shrunk to just him and me, the only two souls left in the world, and it might have remained that way if I hadn't ticked a glance at the clock on his microwave. Every minute, Kylie was in more danger.

I inched my hand in a spider's walk away from his. "No."

He was offering me a choice in the same way Detective Rice had when she'd thrown down a pocketknife and commanded me to *end it*.

Rafe's eyes simmered. I half expected him to go against his word immediately and throw me over his shoulder, but he merely snatched up a pencil and started tapping it with menacing patience against the counter, *bu-bum, bu-bum,* like a heartbeat.

I placed my hand over his, silencing the sound, and he went dangerously still at the sudden contact. I said in a hushed voice, "No more deals, Rafe. No more bargains. And no more lies, either. You say that you've grown beyond the Harbinger, so prove it. For once in your life, take an action with no strings attached. You don't have to trap me into doing what you want by leveraging Kylie."

A muscle jumped in his jaw. He looked confused, as though without a bargain, he was as lost as an artist without a brush. He stared moodily at my hand over his on the counter, seeming to war with himself for some time. For as effortless as he'd made adapting to this world seem, it had to have been painful to find himself stranded in a new reality. And I wanted to wring even more out of him.

"You ask too much, Haven," he said softly. "We can't change."

My fingers tightened over the ridges of his knuckles. "Yes, we can. I know because *I* changed."

My thoughts turned back like a clock to the last night in New

York, and in painstaking detail, I explained to him precisely what had happened.

That night, Baker had come home to find me asleep on the sofa, passed out from a long day at the kitchen table working on a painting of Red Riding Hood, while one of Rob's horror movies played in the background.

He'd shaken me awake, hard. Initially, groggily, I'd thought he was mad about the movie—

Until he held up an email printout of my conversation with my divorce lawyer acquaintance.

"What's this, babe? Divorce?"

Still half-asleep, I'd reached for the remote to turn off the TV. He grabbed it out of my hand harder than necessary. I fought back for it, both of us rising to our feet, and he shoved me into the wall with enough force to paint a bruised mural on my skin.

He'd hit me before. The first time, I'd accepted his assurance that it would never happen again. The second time, I'd called the police. But Baker had managed to twist things. He called me the initiator and said he'd only been defending himself, trying to ward me off. I'd actually laughed to hear his wild claim—until they believed him. I'd been drinking, not him, though it was only a single glass of wine. He pointed to claw marks on his arm from my self-defense. It was only when I was in handcuffs in the back of a police car that I finally understood: Powerful men always win.

So, when he slammed me into the wall this time, I knew police weren't an option. He came at me again, and I grabbed the first thing I could—my BOOKMARKS ARE FOR QUITTERS *mug—and slammed it into his face. Blood spurted out of his nose onto the carpet.*

"Damn it, Haven! I'm calling the police!"

While he was cradling his nose, searching for his phone, I saw my paint scraper on the kitchen table. I wanted to hurt Baker. To kill him. All I had to do was slit his throat.

But I didn't.

"Don't come after me," I said to him, holding out the shaking knife. "I'll ruin your life. I can do it." After I'd discovered our marriage was a sham, I'd reached

out to Rob, whose shady connections had dug into Baker's grandfather. Leverage against Baker was the only way to get away from him, and his grandfather's fame—and trust funds—meant everything to him.

I continued, "A friend of mine hacked into old banking records and found out your grandfather wasn't the outstanding public figure everyone thinks he was. Turns out Claude Gauthier got awful touchy with the schoolchildren who toured his research vessel. My friend has copies of the receipts to the families he paid off. If anything happens to me or if you come anywhere near me again, my friend emails everything he has to a long list of journalists."

Baker had stared at me in disbelief as blood gushed between his fingers.

"I didn't kill him," I emphasized quietly after finishing the story. "I had the chance, but I didn't take it. I just made sure he'd never bother me again and ran."

That night, something inside me had stayed my hand. I couldn't call that regulating voice my humanity because I *wasn't* human; but maybe that was what gave me courage now. That I, a character brought forth from a curse with only the most basic story line, could resist the impulse to do evil. If I could redirect my dark impulses, then maybe the others could, too.

"Tell me where Kylie is, Rafe," I asked, squeezing his hand. "That's all I need to know, her location. I'll do the rest."

He scowled, though he let his hand linger in the shelter of mine. "*You'll* bargain with the Robber Saints?"

A moment of stark uncertainty passed through me like a ghost, but then I dipped my head. "Yes."

His scowl hardened into an even crueler glower, though I knew him well enough now to see the mask for what it was—his sneer was toothless. "You'll change your mind. You'll seek me out again once things start coming for you, in those long nights when you yearn for someone who understands you. For the person you *designed* to fulfill your desires." His words rang with menace, but it was the undercurrent of hurt in them that echoed the loudest.

"Maybe," I agreed. Fortune-telling wasn't one of my talents.

Maybe there would be a time weeks, months, years from now when I decided that Rafe Kahn was exactly what I craved; but first, I needed my own life. Just like the Witch of Went, it was my turn to find my place in this world. And I couldn't do that with yet another manipulative man at my side. There was only one person I wanted to navigate this new life with, and it wasn't him.

I asked again. "Take me to Kylie, Rafe."

He grimaced and pulled his hand violently away from mine as he paced the length of the kitchen, looking for all the world like he was about to rage and rant, but then he finally stopped, braced himself on the kitchen counter, and sighed.

"She's in your father's basement."

CHAPTER FORTY-TWO

The story extractor was a tool, but it was also a weapon. Silver, long and narrow, coming to an acute point that could easily puncture an ear drum if not held by a steady hand; if necessary, pressure applied at the extractor's base would cause a needle to spring forth, piercing not just the ear but some length into the brain, where a practiced hand could bring death with a single quick rotation of the wrist, the same motion as turning a book's page.

—From "Late Fees" in
Bedtime Stories for Monsters

OUTSIDE, THE WEATHER had turned. Rain gave way to a drippy mist that padded the air as though we were underwater. Firefighters' shouts carried across the distance from my property to Rafe's, and a low-lying cloud of smoke now wafted knee-height, thick enough to blanket the ground in thin cottony wisps. Through a broken wall of branches, I watched as flames continued to ravage Malice House. They had scaled from ground level all the way to the attic, just as I had. The apex. The last place to go. Neither rain nor Fathom Lake nor fire hoses had managed to extinguish them. It was almost as if the house *wanted* to burn, determined to end its Frankenstein existence.

At the fire pit, Rafe's steps scuffed to a halt. He lifted a long finger toward the shed that crouched at the edge of his patio like a hunched fiend, perfectly still for now but coiled to strike in a second's time.

"The Robber Saints sniff out stories like bees to honey," he explained. "The first Rafe Kahn wasn't a reader, so there aren't many books in my house. And with the books in yours destroyed, the nearest stash of stories is the basement. Pictures can tell a story, too, you know."

Oh, I knew. Still, something about his words made me shiver in the cool mist. As an illustrator, it was my job to tell a story through images, but most of the drawings that filled my sketchbook brought *someone else's* words to life. Wolves from fairy tales, illustrated scenes from the classics, fan art from my favorite television shows. There were illustrators who wrote their own accompanying prose, or who told narrative through images alone, but it was never an avenue I'd considered.

My hand felt for the canvas bag slung over my shoulder, comforted by the familiar pokes and prods of sketchbook corners and pencil tips. Now, I pressed my palm over the flat plane of the laptop inside.

"You should leave Lundie Bay tonight, too," I told Rafe, turning to him so fast that the mist ebbed and flowed in a dance around us. "Sooner or later, the police will come knocking on your door asking about the fire. They'll look into you, and when they do, they'll realize you aren't the elderly businessman you say you are. Paperwork catches up with everyone eventually. If you're gone, they won't care as much."

Rafe's eyes sought out the red sportscar in the garage, but fleetingly. His expression was flat, uninterested—until he fixed his gaze on me instead and turned dangerously curious. He took a few slow steps in my direction, towering a head over me. Earlier in the night I would have given ground, intimidated, but not now.

"I hope you're right," he whispered. "That we can change. But don't hold your breath, Haven. Keep looking under the bed. Shine a light into the darkness. And on those nights when you lie awake, terrified of the calamity warring inside yourself, afraid you're less human than others—because you *are*—remember, you aren't alone."

He ducked his head to press a kiss to my soot-stained cheek, and for the briefest moment between heartbeats, I wanted him to linger, his tenderness a promise I could fall into. But he pulled away, taking with him the smell of woodsmoke and something metallic, like the scent right before lightning, leaving a vacuum between us.

"Good luck," he murmured, this time without a trace of sarcasm, as he went back toward the fire pit.

I hugged my arms for warmth as I forced my attention away from Rafe and onto the shed. Had I really been here mere hours ago, Kylie by my side with her shotgun, as I prepared to descend and discover my father's secrets?

The events of the night were a blur as certainly as if they were a movie alternating between fast-forward and rewind. The Haven from yesterday felt like an entirely different person, one still tied to the rambling old house, to her ex-husband. I'd traversed fire and been remade just like in fairy tales, though, I realized, instead of being a reborn bird with sun-tipped wings, I was still ensnared in the in-between, on the verge of emergence but not yet broken through. There was still so much to learn, a curse to unravel.

When I'd visited the shed earlier in the night, it hadn't seemed as though a soul had entered it in years. I knew now that Rafe had gone to the basement, but he was able to move like a breeze over a lake, leaving nothing but the slightest ripple. Now, as I moved steadily closer, I noticed fresh signs of life—fingerprints on the dusty window that weren't mine, muddy prints several sizes larger than my own leading to the entrance.

I used my flip phone screen as a light as I eased open the door. Inside, the old terra-cotta pots were now broken, the rug kicked back roughly into a corner. Heavy scuffling sounds came from beneath the floorboards along with a thinner patter of whispered voices. I lowered to a crouch and, after adjusting the strap of my bag over my chest like a badge of courage, knocked on the trapdoor.

The scuffling sounds stopped and in the eerie borderline silence, my heart picked up speed.

Kylie. Had they already pulled her ideas from her like they had in "Late Fees," stabbing a silver straw in her ear canal?

The wooden stairs beneath the trapdoor groaned.

Slowly, the wood plane eased upward with a sigh of tired hinges. I moved back from the yawning maw splitting open the floor and squeezed the strap of my canvas bag tighter.

The apricot glow of lantern light bled up from the basement as a woman climbed the final steps, closing the trapdoor tidily behind her. A gray-brown cloak hugged her shoulders, held in place by the pewter book-shaped clasp. Her auburn hair was loose down to her clavicles, cut blunt and unadorned. Though she appeared in every way human, there was an unsettling silence to her, a wax dummy come to life. She shifted her stance, resting a graceful hand on her hip, flashing the long metal straw fastened to her belt—the extractor. Like a bee's stinger. *A tool and a weapon.*

I felt myself sink into her strange stillness. "I'm—"

"You are known," she answered flatly, and the resonance of her voice shook me—I'd half expected her to speak in the chanting chorus of all their voices at once, not a single woman's tenor.

In their chapter, the Robber Saints initially appeared as devoted story collectors, librarians not entirely unlike Ronan Young—granted, with cloaks and torches in place of bobblehead figurines and bow ties. Now, however, I knew that the extractor at her side held a needle that could sink six inches into my skull, bringing instant death, and that, near the end of *Bedtime Stories*, these hive-minded beings had fought viciously to defend their library. I was under no illusions that this woman nor her companions downstairs were anything but ruthless.

"You have someone down there who I care about greatly," I said.

Her face didn't register even moderate interest. "She's ours. We collected her, and as soon as one of our senior archivists arrives, we'll harvest her stories. You may have whatever is left over."

Unlike Rafe, there was no cruel taunt to her words, but her directness chilled me; I'd almost rather deal with Rafe's whims and caprices.

I slid a hand down my bag to cup the rounded corner of my laptop. "I can offer you a trade. Something much more valuable than a novice writer's musings."

The woman's head tipped sideways in an appraising manner.

My hand traced the laptop's hard edge through the canvas. There were only so many things I could offer the Robber Saints. The problem was, in our world stories sprouted like weeds; they practically infested bookstores, libraries, online forums, bouncing around in daydreamers' skulls, flashing on millions of phone and TV and movie screens. The Saints didn't need *me*. All they needed was to open their arms and let tales fall into them like autumn leaves after a storm—*except* not every work of fiction in this world was freely available, ready to be plucked off the vine and juiced as easily as wild raspberries. No, not the most interesting ones.

I planned to tell the Robber Saints about Rob's archives. His online recaps of underground films were incredibly rare. The Saints could scour the world and never, ever find those accounts. And I'd spent enough time around discerning book people to know that what really piqued their interest was the rare titles. Rob's website was hidden behind encryption servers, security walls, and authentication forms, but he'd granted me access. I had the location, the passwords.

The Robber Saint gave a small tip of her chin. "Show me what you have."

I dipped my arm into my bag to fetch the laptop, but something stayed my hand. *You're betraying Rob.*

It was true that we'd never met, that I knew no details about his life, and that "Rob" probably wasn't even his real name. Regardless, we'd built a rapport over the years, even a friendship. He'd gotten me through the darkest days of my marriage, given me a means to independence, even helped me blackmail Baker.

He'd committed crimes for me.

"Hold on." I slid the laptop back, suddenly feeling lost. I might have been a soulless creation brough to life by accident, but I couldn't do that to Rob. My hand took on a mind of its own, riffling through my brushes and pencils. For a brief moment my fingers closed around a foreign object, and I wondered if the witch had slipped me something when returning my bag—women of Malice sticking together—but I soon realized it was only a twig that must have fallen in sometime during the night.

Shit.

When my fingers grazed the bottom of the bag, my hopes ended there, too. Then I ran a curious fingernail along the edge of my sketchbook. Adrenaline shot through me, warning me, trying to stop me with numb fingers and tingling extremities.

Hesitantly, I pulled out the sketchbook, knuckles whitening where I held it. "Yeah, this. I have this."

Stuffed to the gills with years of artwork, the sketchbook was even thicker than the laptop. The illustrations beneath the cover ranged from lazy doodles to half-finished portraits to ready-to-submit pieces. Between the creamy sheets bound by silver binder rings, I'd stuffed in loose-leaf artwork in roughly chronological order. Some pieces dated back to kindergarten, scribbles that I'd gotten in the habit of tucking away in my bedroom desk drawer after watching my father pull down that dragon drawing from the fridge. I'd acquired the expensive sketchbook—the kind where you could add in extra sheets of paper—in high school after earning cash from playing assistant at my dad's writing courses. I'd filed my best childhood artwork between the pages, as well as assignments for art class, doodles on the backs of pop quizzes, shading and line studies. After a lifetime, the sketchbook was bursting to the point of straining its silver rings.

Faced with the prospect of handing over the sketchbook, it struck me that this collection of paper was the closest thing I had to a soul. Nearly thirty years' worth of dreams and toil. The quality of the pieces inside tracked my growth from child to girl to woman. It was the first thing I'd thought to take with me when I'd fled New York, the only thing of any real value. Brushes and paints could be replaced. This was the sole possession that would pain me to lose; I might as well have been offering her my right hand.

Focusing on my sister, I banished the pain and handed it over.

The cloaked figure flipped through the sketchbook with a discerning eye, taking her time tracking the progress of my drawings from childhood scribbles to professionally trained illustrations, and then closed it. "We can't use this. We are the keepers of words, not images."

Her hand went to her hip with the slightest hint of menace, her middle finger toying with the tip of the extractor.

She tapped the heel of her boot on the trapdoor, a signal.

"That's just it," I pressed in a rush, keeping my eyes on that deadly silver straw, as Rafe's voice rumbled through my head. "Pictures can tell a story, too. It's true. You've dedicated your life to harvesting and cataloging prose because that's as far as the definition of a *story* goes in Malice. But not here. This is a vast world; artists and writers have changed the old ways of thinking about fiction."

More footsteps came on the stairs beneath our feet. The trapdoor eased open again, and my heart leapt to my throat.

"You're robbers, and robbers are clever." I began speaking faster, glancing around the shed for a shovel or shears in case I'd need to fight. "Innovative. Always hungry for the next big thing. You're also librarians, which means you're committed to acquiring a complete collection. Put those two things together, and I'm offering you exactly what you need. Something new, something revolutionary."

Another Robber Saint emerged from the basement in eerie

silence, a black-haired man with a scar slicing across his chin. Without even glancing at the woman, he moved to stand between me and the main door. He folded his arms, his own silver extractor catching the moonlight.

The woman opened my sketchbook back up to one of the wolves I'd done in New York. She gave it probing consideration, head cocked as her eyes danced with the lines and shading, and I continued to scan my surroundings.

No shovels. Not even a damn trowel. Through the open trapdoor, more shadows moved toward the stairs. A boot creaked as another Saint began to climb upward toward us.

The woman slowly shook her head, dragging my attention back to her. "Perhaps, but we can get images anywhere, too. As you said, this world is vast."

"Sure," I acknowledged quickly. "There are images everywhere, but these are rare, and that makes them valuable." My eyes darted to a heavyset woman rising up through the trapdoor, not just an extractor at her side but a sword the length of my arm. My feet moved backward on their own, but there was nowhere to go. My back pressed against a table filled with old seed packets.

I insisted, "You'd be hard pressed to find drawings as meaningful to a creator as these. Besides, I'm not just trading you my sketchbook. I'm trading you an idea. To change your definition of what a story *is*. If anyone understands what ideas are worth, it's you."

As the third Saint joined the man by the door, blocking any form of exit, the first woman closed the sketchbook with an unreadable expression, though she didn't immediately decline my offer. *Come on, come on.* I thought she might consult with the others, but she didn't so much as glance at them, or at the fourth Saint coming up the stairs, a blond-haired boy, barely more than a teenager, with ferocious faint blue eyes. Rafe had described the Saints as drones in a bee colony, sharing some kind of unspoken means of communication. The younger

Saint sank back into the shed's shadows, while at the same time a fifth hooded figure emerged from the trapdoor, silently crossing to stand by the broken pots.

They're forming a circle.

I didn't know how many more remained below in the basement with Kylie.

The heavyset Saint drew back her cloak to lay bare her sword in stark threat. My muscles constricted deep in my belly as I hardened myself to what might come next. A malevolent brine seemed to saturate the shed's already stale air. My skin felt clammy beneath their gazes, but it wasn't actually *me* they regarded. Their attention sliced straight through me to the stories buried within.

Slowly, their leader tore a page from my sketchbook and handed it to the statuesque woman. I pressed a hand to my breastbone like she'd ripped something from my own body. Next, she turned to the man with the scar on his chin and ripped out another page. My legs felt suddenly bloodless at the same time that a swell of anger inflated my chest: *How dare she destroy my life's work.*

She ripped out other pages for the rest of the Robber Saints. Everything about her movements was calculated in that eerie calm way of theirs. Surrounding me in that infernal pentagram, they each held a page that contained one of my illustrations. Their leader had ripped them out haphazardly, so some were recent, others were childish things from grade school.

"Evaluation," she commanded.

Their five heads inclined over my pages in identical movements. My heart rattled around in my chest as I took in this sinister ritual that, I could only assume, would determine my future. In a flash, I was back in the Lundie Bay Books vault with the eyes of the Ink Drinkers on me as Catherine muttered the worst words any artist could hear: *Haven, I don't want to discourage you . . .*

Past and present melded, and, reeling, I could already feel the Saints' rejection coming like the cold blast of air before rain. Sweat dampened my skin as the air grew more and more stale until I was no longer certain it *was* air and not waterlogged cotton that clogged my lungs and stole the last of my strength.

The five Robber Saints looked up simultaneously. Something in the air shifted. I understood: Without a word, they had reached their decision.

"We accept your deal," the leader said and rapped her heel again on the floor.

Relief climbed out my throat in the form of a ragged cry. I pressed a hand to my mouth, overstuffed with emotion. The bag's weight around my shoulder felt too light without the sketchbook. It was *wrong*. Something was missing, because of course it was. The closest thing I had to a soul was now in the possession of the Robber Saints, already torn apart, now to be liquified and bottled in their library, cataloged, never to be seen again.

But in the next instant, Kylie came, slowly climbing the stairs, using her hands to pull herself up, looking like a shell of a person; but, like a shell, I saw the toughness in her, nearly unbreakable, able to withstand wave after wave of hardship and still arrive at the shore intact.

Though her eyes darted between the hooded Saints, they settled at last on me, and she let out a cry. I wasn't sure what happened next; it was a blur again like that skipping movie. Only that she was on her feet, and we had our arms around each other, sobbing into each other's shoulders, fists coiling into clothes, holding each other to the point of breathlessness.

I'd lost a soul but gained a sister.

✦

Nights in Malice lasted sixty long hours, but the night that Malice House burned felt interminable.

The firefighters had been at work all night, and no one had yet come knocking on Rafe's door asking questions about dead bodies in the front yard and amid the wreckage.

Jonathan. Ronan. Catherine. Detective Rice. Officer Cooper.

The fire chief had been in league with the Ink Drinkers and must have decided to keep things quiet to prevent a panic while they made up a lie about faulty wiring.

By the time Kylie and I staggered back into Rafe's house, there was no sign of him. We found the kitchen cabinets open, bedroom drawers rifled through and left pulled out, his car gone. We each grabbed a jar of peanut butter and went back outside to sink into the Adirondack chairs circling his fire pit, an audience to the most disturbing horror movie I'd ever seen: the destruction of my home.

By the time sunrise bled Easter colors into the world, the firefighters had finally extinguished the flames. Once the last of the trucks left, Kylie and I picked our way over to the house, standing in the gravel driveway, facing the smoldering husk. What wreckage remained was charred and charcoal, burned-out beams emerging from soot like fossils. I'd have to decide if I wanted to rebuild the house or let its carcass slowly rot back into the forest. Even now, the tree line on the far side of the house seemed closer than it had ever been. Maybe it was just the altered perspective from not having the house there, but I'd swear the evergreen boughs *were* nearer.

Kylie slipped an arm around my waist. I hugged her close by the shoulders, and together with my sister, we turned away from the wreckage, facing the ocean instead. Listened to the repeating crash of the waves. Exhaustion tried to lull me into a trancelike state, and my artist's eye was already deconstructing the mercurial aquamarine colors, mentally mixing paints to capture the exact hues. My hand itched to snake into my bag, pull out a brush, and start painting on anything at hand; a rock, a flagstone, my own skin.

But Kylie closed my hand in her own, and the itch ebbed.

We'd soon leave Lundie Bay, taking the long cliffside road down the coast, few possessions between us, a flaccid handful of cash to fuel both us and the car until we could find more solid ground. From there, it would be moving with fate's tides, the push of hiding from Uncle Arnold paired with the pull of trying to understand the family curse.

And we *were* a family. We'd found each other beneath the gabled roof, though it wasn't the house that had brought us together. A legacy had, and legacy transcended four walls, fireplaces and attic windows, staircases and bookshelves. Legacy stretched into a world filled with monsters under the bed, mysterious relatives, and truths yet to be discovered in the bewildering night hours.

Hand in hand, we left Malice House to smolder.

EPILOGUE

*

SAFEHAVEN: Rob, are you there?

SLASHERDASHER: Always here, H.

SAFEHAVEN: I've run into some trouble. I need your help. Those people who make the movies you send me . . . can you put me in touch? The ones about curses, summoned demons. I don't care if they seem crazy and think their movies are fact instead of fiction. All the better if they do.

SLASHERDASHER: Poltergeists still after you?

SAFEHAVEN: You have no idea.

SLASHERDASHER: You might be surprised. I'm a very open minded individual. Look, how soon can you be on a plane to Los Angeles?

ACKNOWLEDGMENTS

Years ago, while writing one of my previous books, I experienced a strange sensation as though the story were being channeled into my head from something somewhere, and I was merely transcribing it. I think most authors have wondered if we're tapping into other realms when we put their stories on the page, and what—if any—control they have over our stories once they're in the world. The idea for *Malice House* came from mulling over how stories are born and the responsibilities of creators in relation to their works. Though I hope my characters aren't crawling off the page to murder anyone, I do wonder about the dangerous power of words and how they are actively reshaping our world.

So many people contributed to making this book into what it is. My gratitude goes to my stellar literary agent, Barbara Poelle, and to everyone at Hyperion Avenue, including the incredible Adam Wilson, Amy King for her stunning cover design, Jen Levesque for her leadership, and Ann Day, Daneen Goodwin, Kaitlyn Leary, Dina Sherman, and Andrew Sansone for their efforts to put this book on shelves so it can hopefully keep readers wide-awake at night. To Megan Miranda, Gwenda Bond, Carrie Ryan, Beth Revis, and the Bat Cavers—your minds are frighteningly brilliant, and I love it.

Thanks as well to Andrew Shook, Zac Bass, John Snyder, and Edwin Arnaudin for sharing their valuable knowledge about things I know nothing about: police detective procedures, the mechanics of house fires, all things firearms, and moviedom. I'm also grateful to my parents, who are lifelong book people and not the inspiration for the nefarious booksellers in these pages. A special thanks to my husband, Jesse, for helping me navigate my career during a pandemic and allowing me to run away to a cottage to write when I needed to escape into fiction.